BLOOD DEBT

BLOOD DEBT

THE DIVINE VAMPIRE HEIRS, BOOK THREE

by

GINNA MORAN

ISBN 978-1-942073-80-2 (soft cover)

This is a work of fiction. All of the characters, organizations, and events portrayed in this novel are either products of the author's imagination or are used fictitiously.

Cover design by Silver Starlight Designs
Cover images copyright Depositphotos

For Inquiries Contact:
Sunny Palms Press
9663 Santa Monica Blvd Suite 1158
Beverly Hills, CA 90210, USA
www.sunnypalmspress.com
www.GinnaMoran.com

To the ladies of Write Bitches,
You are amazing rock stars, and I'm so happy to call
you my friends. ♥

THE VAMPIRE LIFESTYLE

I STAND FROZEN, GAPING AT the dead guy sprawled across the gleaming marble floor. Under the scruff of his cheeks, he looks no older than me...I think. I'm sure if he shaved, he'd look more boyish than man like Austin, who I clutch onto from behind for dear life.

From my position, it's hard to see the complete view of the guy I desperately try not to react to. It takes everything in me to stop from freaking the eff out, though my wild heartbeats surely give me away.

I mean, what the actual hell? Who invites the Divine Heirs to a supposed gathering and leaves a body right in the foyer? The all-female Vaduva Coven, that's who. The last thing I expected entering the grand mansion of Viorica Vaduva, a prominent board member of Donor Life Corp, was to discover a dead naked guy with a raging boner I thought would have died with him. The information wasn't exactly something I wanted to learn. I wish I could get my eyes to avert to look at something else.

Blood drips onto the tiles from the multiple puncture wounds on his arm. Another fresh bite mark sends rivulets of blood down the guy's ribcage to soak into what might be a ripped shirt. If Kingston hadn't enjoyed ripping clothes off and leaving them piled on the floor, I wouldn't have known, but I can't tell for sure.

"Shit," I whisper, wobbling on my legs.

Diego hooks his arm around my waist in silence, and I step on his foot to give myself another inch while I dig my fingers into Austin's shoulder to stand on my tiptoes again without falling over. Stupid flats. If I were wearing heels, I could glimpse what my guys are inconspicuously trying to hide me from.

"Looks like someone had an awesome time," Kingston whispers from his spot behind me.

Heavy footsteps thump across the tile, drawing my attention to the arched entryway to a lavish living room in stark whites and silvers. A crystal chandelier casts dots of rainbow lights across the sleek furniture that looks like it's never been used.

"Cover your eyes, beautiful," Diego says, pulling me closer. "Stop looking."

"It's already branded into my mind."

Kingston makes a weird sound in his throat. "Guess one of us will have to help you forget."

Austin stands taller, moving to try to block me. "We know you're curious, but it's considered rude."

Rude? Like leaving this guy on the floor isn't? I'll never get used to vampire customs. Not even sure if I want to.

Another naked man stumbles from the living area, a wide smile across his face. His deep laughter echoes through the vaulted ceiling room, and I release a groan and shift to press my face into Diego's chest.

"Jonathon, get back here!" a light, sultry voice calls. "We have guests."

The man glances over his shoulder and laughs again. Turning to us, he wags his brows and holds out both his arms, showing off his wrists, scarred by old bite marks. "Where are my manners? Would you like a taste?"

One second the man stumbles toward us, and in the next, he vanishes, his laughter haunting the air as someone removes him from the room far too fast for me to catch sight of. I sink closer to Diego, hugging my arms around him, practically burying myself in his tuxedo jacket.

"Merrick! Come clean up this mess. I told you the Divines were visiting." The loud screech of Viorica's voice startles me as she appears in the foyer next to the dead guy.

Crossing her arms, she glares at him like he's the one in the wrong for daring to die right where the world can see whatever her coven's been up to. Viorica sighs and looks in our direction, her eyes meeting mine for a moment without saying anything. It's not the first time she's ignored me, but she's obviously ignoring my guys as well.

Diego must sense my unease because he rubs his hand up and down my side in a smooth motion and whispers, "She'll greet us when she's ready. We're guests in her home and in her territory. It's customary not to go over and beyond to make us welcome, because really, we're not. It's business."

"Oh," I whisper, knowing that Viorica can hear us. The only reason Diego doesn't whisper in a pitch only I can hear is because Viorica is too aware of my presence. She might be staring at the guy, but I can feel her attention smothering me.

"You'll get used to it, babe. Just don't take offense," Kingston says.

"You forgot to inform her not to focus on my staff," Viorica says, bringing her gaze to mine.

Placing her hands on her hips, she smiles at me, which I'm pretty sure might be the first one I've ever seen on her direct at me. The last few times I've met the regal, mostly unfriendly vampire, she had been cold and seemingly annoyed by my mere existence. I thought she hated my guts for no other reason than I was a donor and beneath her, but according to my guys, it's the opposite. I don't know how true that is, but the fact that she's smirking at me right now might confirm it. If only she didn't look so terrifying.

I flick my eyes away from the naked dead guy and to the

glass ceiling acting as a mirror with the bright lighting of the decorative sconces along the walls. Friggin' hell. I can't escape the view no matter what, and the view of the guy reflecting on the ceiling is worse than what I can see over Austin's shoulder because now I can see his entire body.

Kingston chuckles from behind me, and I catch his gaze on the ceiling, watching my reaction. "My apologies, Viorica," he says. "You must understand Jewel's curiosity. We keep our staff clothed in our household."

"That's usually the case here," Viorica says with a sigh. Jerking her neck to peer at a hall behind her, she yells, "Merrick! Get in here now!"

Viorica nudges the body with the toe of her stiletto to roll him onto his side. The guy gasps and flops upright, directing his attention to the four of us in front of him. Scratching his neck, he blinks a few times, his brows furrowing over his brown eyes.

I release a breath. "Thank God."

Kingston chuckles yet again. Dude just can't keep himself composed around me. "Did you seriously think he was dead, babe? I thought you got my joke about someone having an awesome time..."

I swivel and glare at him, my eyes stopping him from finishing his thought. What else was I supposed to think? The guy was sprawled out and bleeding right in the foyer. "I thought you meant someone else."

"Oh, I had a fantastic time as well, Ms. Divine," a feminine voice responds, interrupting our conversation. "If only my Sebastian could keep up."

"He looks rather up to me," I mutter, making Kingston tip his head back and laugh.

I shift my attention away from Kingston and jump at the closeness of the beautiful vampire all up in Austin's space. He stands firm without reacting to the fact that half her body presses against his as she peers at me.

"Maybe you could give him some pointers, Ms. Divine. My mother told me of your matching arrangement, and I have to say, you don't look as exhausted as I expected being in Divine care. And if I know Kingston and Diego like I think I do...hmmm, I don't think they could resist you, so you must surely favor Austin more. He is quite handsome."

Opening and closing my mouth, I try to say something, but my mind and mouth don't agree with how to respond. My first instinct is to defend my guys and then myself. But my mouth wants nothing more than to tell her to back the hell away from Austin. While he remains expressionless, I know he doesn't appreciate the fact that she practically hangs onto him.

"Isn't that right, Austin? Your desires are far different than your brothers. Ms. Divine must be well rested with you," she says to him, inching her face close enough that she could kiss him if she tried, and there'd be no chance for him to back up quickly with me right behind him. "I know you and Samantha always had that in common. Which is a pity. We could've had a lot of fun together. Still can. I doubt Jewel can sati—"

A growl sounds through the air, and the vampire flashes her fangs at me in a smile without finishing her sentence. I realize the strangled, guttural sound came from me, and it makes Austin stiffen, Diego hold me tighter, and Kingston laugh again.

"Merrick!" Viorica yells, clearly not amused. "Leave the Divines alone and clean up this mess. Now. You have five minutes to dress appropriately and join us on the terrace."

The beautiful vampire's brown eyes flash silver, and she reaches up and pats Austin's cheek before spinning to strut the few feet back to the naked guy now just sitting on the floor, covering himself up with the ripped shirt.

"Come on, baby. Let me walk you back to your room," Merrick tells the guy, holding out her hand to help him to his feet. "You're excused for the night."

I stand in shock, watching as she snuggles against him while strolling with him down the hall to an elevator. She kisses him so deeply that I avert my gaze, catching sight of Viorica staring at me, gauging my reaction.

"Please excuse my daughter," Viorica says. "She's quite enamored with the new member of my staff."

"Uh, yeah. Sure," I manage to say.

From my knowledge, the human staff isn't required to donate blood unless they procreate, which is why some households try for a greater female-to-male ratio to encourage such a thing. It's a workaround way to add to personal donations without the exorbitant fees of a Blood Match if they find gen. pop. blood substandard. But I thought the blood donations went to a shared stash between the whole coven, and that guy's bites looked personal to her. Possessive.

In the Divine household, only Mitchell drinks from the Divine's personal stash. If my guys drink blood on an occasion where they have to maintain their appearances as to not reveal that my blood alone can sustain them, they always choose gen. pop.

I don't know if it's because of me or because they don't like to treat the staff at the Divinity Estate as a blood source, but either way, seeing Merrick and her human, clearly her lover, swirls a dozen questions through my head. Vampire life is confusing as all get-out. Every coven seems so different though they follow the same Donor Life Corp laws—mostly.

"We treat our staff with kindness and respect, and sometimes, they show us gratitude in...unconventional ways you will not see in most vampire households," Viorica continues, answering my silent questions before I can badger Austin. Clicking her heels on the tile, she crosses the room to finally greet us personally. "You know, if more households would follow my practices, it'd be less likely that the staff would turn against their employer. Money can't buy loyalty."

Damn. None of my guys react to the obvious slap-in-the-face comment. As a board member, Viorica would know that my guys had to replace half of the staff at the Divinity Estate after Katherine paid and promised them who knows what to get them to risk their lives. But Viorica has something wrong, because she doesn't know the whole truth about the situation. Katherine proved that money could buy loyalty—some humans will be loyal to whoever pays more.

"Despite what you think, we are kind and respectful to our staff," Austin says, straightening his shoulders. "Most importantly, we're professional."

"And traitors can't always be helped, so don't give us this bullshit about how a little extra care will prevent such occurrences," Kingston says, coming up behind me.

Diego shifts on his feet. "Or do we have to remind you of the incident with Layla."

Oh, man. I bounce on my feet as curiosity has me stepping closer to Austin. I'll never admit it, but I can't help but devour all the vampire gossip my guys are willing to share with me, and now I can't wait to spring on Austin later to ask him about it. He's my go-to for information. Diego second. Kingston is a master secret keeper and always talks circles around subjects. He'd never admit it, but I know he freaks out about what I'll think being a human and all. Vampire life gets weird sometimes. Freaky too.

Silver flashes in Viorica's eyes, but she doesn't scowl like I expect at Diego's comment about the mysterious Layla. Instead, she proffers her hand to each of my guys. "Which is why I've called you here tonight. I'm returning the favor I owe you."

Favor?

"So follow me," she says before I can ask. Viorica speeds away, requiring Diego to lift me off my feet or else there'd be no way I could keep up. I barely manage to keep pace with his long legs even at a human speed.

"Jewel, I hope you don't mind, but I've arranged a dinner date for you with my daughter Samantha. Until you transition into a true Divine, I must keep my business affairs separate from you."

"Dinner date?" I ask. Merrick mentioned someone named Samantha having a lot in common with Austin, which I'm pretty sure she was insinuating was due to his lack of experience, something Austin chose to withhold himself from. At least, that's what he told me. From Merrick's flirting, I can tell it wasn't like the option wasn't there.

I silently tuck away the question to add to the dozens of other ones I want to ask my guys later.

"I hope you don't expect us to entrust Jewel's care in Samantha's hands," Austin says. "She lacks restraint when she's excited, and I know how much she wanted us to introduce her to our match."

What? I don't know why I'm surprised my guys have talked about me to others. It stirs all sorts of stuff inside me. Mostly good. It really makes me feel like an important part of their life, something hard for me to grasp some days.

I glance at Austin in hopes he'll look at me, but he keeps his eyes ahead and gives nothing away.

Viorica lifts an eyebrow. "I assure you Jewel will be safe. Unless that's not your concern. Are you afraid she might enjoy her time here too much, boys? I wouldn't blame you. All of my girls are rather happy."

Kingston huffs. "Yeah, that's the least of our concerns, Vi. Samantha's forty-three percent match doesn't threaten me."

Viorica releases what sounds like a cross between a purr and a growl, the deep, velvety sound confusing me. I can't tell if she's amused or annoyed by this info bomb. I knew Viorica and Mitchell were rivals, and four of Viorica's daughters applied to match with me and didn't pass the questionnaire portion, but hearing by exactly how much intrigues me. "So then you don't mind."

"I'll escort her," Diego says, speaking up. "If that's okay with Jewel."

Silence falls between my guys and Viorica, and it takes me a second to realize they've stopped in the middle of a hallway with a view of Midnight Valley from their hillside mansion. I blink through my confusion, trying to orient myself to the lack of motion. I hate moving quickly in an unfamiliar area, because I'm pretty sure I could never find my way out of here if I were to get separated—though I know none of my guys would let that happen. My sapphire bracelet has a tracking device hidden inside it to help assure it.

"Um—"

"My staff's chef prepared an exquisite menu tonight."

My stomach growls at the mention of food, and I peer

down and glare at it for betraying me when I was about to tell Viorica I wasn't hungry. The idea of whatever happens on a dinner date with a vampire that isn't one of my matches freaks me the eff out. It's uncomfortable as all get-out, but especially if this Samantha vampire is anything like Merrick.

"And as a woman in a household of all men, I think you deserve the chance to connect with another female, Jewel. My Samantha could be good for you after your Blood Vow. I know you grew up surrounded by sisterly bonds. Don't you miss that?"

Son of a twatwaffle did she just strike one of my fragile nerves. I've managed to learn how to keep my shit together for the last two months since Orlando was granted guardianship over Ramona to assure his future blood source remains in good shape. I know I should be grateful that Donor Life Corp denied him the opportunity to take me. But sometimes it's impossible. And Viorica destroyed the wall I built around my thoughts of Ramona, and even the mention of our life growing up sets me off like a bomb and destroys my steely resolve.

"I—I am rather hungry," I say instead of answering her question.

Viorica smiles, keeping her hands twined together though she looks like she'd hug me if she could make it through the solid barricade of muscle my guys create between us. "Superb. Samantha awaits your arrival in the study." Turning to Diego, she says, "Do you remember where that is?"

He nods and turns to his brothers. "Keep me updated."

Austin turns and hugs me first. "Take a breath, Jewel. We won't be long."

Sliding his hands around my waist, sandwiching me between him and Austin, Kingston says, "Don't have too much fun with Samantha...or Diego for that matter."

I roll my eyes, though he can't see me. "Just be quick."

Viorica, Kingston, and Austin disappear, and I spin to face Diego. He offers me one of his brilliant smiles that lights up his sparkling gray eyes, and I can't help myself from closing the space to sink back into his arms.

"Before we go, can you at least give me a hint as to what kind of favor Viorica owed you?" I ask him.

Bringing his lips to my ear, he whispers, "One of Viorica's daughters fell in love with one of the staff here, and he nearly killed her. I don't know all the details, but he managed to leave the city and made it to Dark Terrace Ranch. We caught the guy, and instead of issuing the automatic death sentence tied to treason, we offered to let Viorica handle him."

I grimace. "Oh."

His phone chimes from his pocket, and he pulls it out. "Now she's extended us the same courtesy."

"She found one of our staff?"

He clears his throat and peers around the empty hall. "And it seems he's a Blood Rebel."

TRAITOR

I HUG MYSELF, FOLLOWING ALONGSIDE Diego to a sturdy set of double doors at the end of a long hallway. "Are we going to kill the man? Who exactly is it?"

Draping his arm over my shoulder, leaning down to do so, Diego pulls me closer to him. "It's not our decision."

"So he is a dead man," I murmur, knowing exactly what Diego means when he says it's not our decision. Mitchell would never show someone who committed treason, especially because of the man's Blood Rebel status, any sort of mercy.

"I'm sorry, Jewel."

Before I have time to process his words, one of the doors swings open and a vampire with golden tresses, round green eyes, and sharp ass fangs appears in the doorway. I gape in her direction, stunned by her familiarity, though I've never met the girl before. She looks to have transitioned at an age younger than me. Maybe sixteen or seventeen. Her cheeks more round than mine...actually she kind of reminds me of Austin.

"Diego!" she squeals, rushing to my personality match. Throwing her arms around him, she hugs him for a moment and kisses both his cheeks, making him laugh. "I thought you'd be with my mother."

He raises an eyebrow. "You know what the Blood Match contract entails."

The vampire steps back, rubbing her hands together without looking at me. It's strange. Usually, I'm the first person they look at no matter where my guys take me. Even the staff at home looks at me first. I'd think I was invisible if Diego wasn't holding my hand.

"See, that's what I told Mother when she suggested such a thing," she whispers, lowering her voice to a pitch I shouldn't be able to hear.

"She did try to test us."

"Always. I did think it would be Austin to escort Jewel, though. How is he? What about Kingston? All my sisters are taking bets about who will kill who first. I could not imagine what you three must be going through with—"

"Jewel, this is Samantha," Diego says, cutting her off, knowing well enough that I'm hanging on every single one of her words, especially because they pertain to my guys.

I'm used to being ignored and treated like I don't exist in

front of strangers, but I sometimes wish I could react. My guys would never kill each other like she says her sisters think will happen. I hate that I can't shout to everyone who dares question us that we make it work.

Her eyes finally shift from Diego to look at me. "Can I greet her, Diego?"

"Of course you can greet me. Diego's not my master or whatever." I hold out my hand to her without waiting for Diego to respond. "And it's nice to meet you, Samantha."

My offer for a handshake turns into a surprise hug that makes me scream. All I can think about is how close her mouth is to my neck and how easy it would be for her to bite me. As quickly as she embraces me, she lets me go, shuffling a few feet back.

"Oh, Jewel. I didn't realize you were afraid of me. I'm sorry," she says, hugging her arms around her chest. "I wasn't going to bite you no matter how adorable you are. I love your dress by the way and your neckl—what! A Blood...*three* Blood Vows?"

"Viorica didn't tell you," Diego says like he's surprised.

She steps closer, hovering her fingers over the three roses pieced together to create the bouquet pendant without touching it. "Probably because Jewel hasn't made her decision." Looking up, she meets my gaze. "Any idea who you like best?"

I frown without responding.

"May I suggest you pick Austin?"

Diego groans. "No, you may not, Samantha."

"What he said," I murmur, tilting my head. "But why Austin?" My mouth speaks before my mind can catch up.

"Beautiful, how about you let Austin fill you in—"

Raising my hand up, I press it to Diego's lips to stop him from talking. I have enough questions to ask Austin already, and I can't stop my curiosity from getting the best of me. Apart from Mitchell and the guests of the Divinity Estate, who keep topics platonic, I've never met someone who was friendly enough with my guys to have some sort of opinion.

"Well, haven't you seen him? Gorgeous. He's sweet, kindhearted..."

"Was once related," Diego says, twisting his mouth.

My eyes widen, and I gasp. "I thought you looked simi-lar...and that's weird. Siblings? Austin never talked about his human family."

"Cousins," Samantha says. "Distant cousins."

"By generations," Diego adds.

"Whatever, I can still vouch for him. He's been waitin—"

"All right, Samantha, that's enough." Diego scoops me up and starts racing us away, but we don't get far. Samantha blocks our way, clocking Diego in the shoulder. She somehow manages to shove him into the wall without touching me, her hands pressed to his chest and holding him in place.

My hands lace around her wrists and all three of us stare at my brave limbs that react without me thinking. Samantha could rip my arms off, yet here I am trying to pry her hands away from Diego.

"I didn't give you permission to touch him," I tell her, feeling all sorts of awkward. Shit balls. I'm ridiculous. For one, the words come out squeaking. And two, I might be a little jealous sometimes, but this isn't one of those moments. I think Samantha might be the first vampire that doesn't intimidate me. Sure, her hug scared the shit out of me, but she's bubbly and cute and called me adorable without mentioning making me part of her diet like others have.

Diego releases a loud laugh, thudding his head into the wall with the motion. Samantha grimaces and drops her hands to her sides in confusion. By the look on her face, I'm certain no human has commanded anything from her ever.

"Jeez, and I thought Kingston was possessive. I couldn't figure out how in the universe she matched with him over me, but now I sort of get it," Samantha whispers to Diego, her mouth unmoving.

Diego kisses me, silencing any response that might accidentally escape my lips. If Kingston's possessive, he hides it well from me. Yeah, he's vocal about being jealous, but he's mostly playing around.

"Jewel, I'm sorry for crossing whatever boundary you built around the Divine brothers, but it wasn't my intent. I only wanted to stop Diego from killing our friendship before it could even start," Samantha says.

Whoa. A vampire who isn't one of my matches apologizing to me? That's weird and a little unsettling. "Friends?" I manage to spit out.

"Yeah, friends. Especially if you pick to officially match with Austin and accept his promise," she says, eyeing Diego. She winks at him. "Okay, maybe Diego too. Not Kingston, though. You're on your own there."

"Wait, what's up with—"

She laughs. "How about we continue this over the supposedly delicious dinner waiting for you?"

I look to Diego for his response, and he shrugs. "It's up to you, beautiful."

My stomach growls, drawing both their attentions. "I am kind of hungry."

Samantha smiles, flashing her fangs. "Good, because I'm starved."

"Would you like a drink, Mr. Divine?" Naked Guy Number Two from earlier, thankfully now wearing some pants, holds up a small crystal chalice filled with what might possibly be his own blood to Diego.

Diego accepts the glass, watching me as I watch him. Neither of us has to whisper to each other to know that he took it to follow whatever vampire social norms go along with a dinner invite, though it was technically for me. He would much rather drink my blood, but we have our own rules to follow. Austin draws blood for meals except in extreme emergencies. When I agree to be bitten, privacy is a must and rarely for a meal so that I don't feel a blood supply.

"Okay, so then what *can* you tell me?" Samantha asks,

downing her glass in one gulp. "Ever since Mother told me you matched with all three of them, I've been obsessed. I've never heard of anyone getting three Blood Vow proposals."

"She's all of our perfect match," Diego says, speaking for me.

"According to the program," she responds. "But you know it's more than science if you've promised a Blood Vow."

He leans into me, dangling his glass from his fingers without drinking it. "Which is why we allowed Jewel to make the final decision."

"You know how many people would kill to be you, Jewel?" Samantha says.

I shrug. "Not as many as you think."

"I guess from a human perspective, you're right." She takes my empty bowl and scoops another glob of chocolate pudding into it, topping it with whipped cream. I can't shake how eerily similar she is to Austin. If Diego didn't take the bowl from her and hold up another bite to my lips, I'm pretty sure she would have. "At least, according to the Blood Rebel in the basement, the only one he wants to kill is you."

"That seems to be the consensus," I mutter, taking the bowl of dessert from Diego to feed myself. Nerves get the best of me, and I start shoveling the contents in my mouth, swallowing without really enjoying it. "Kill me or cage me."

"Well, don't worry about—"

The door to the study swings open and three female vampires saunter in at a human's pace. Merrick leads the way, smirking at me in Diego's arms with one perfectly arched brow raised on her forehead. The other two vampires, one redheaded like Viorica and the other with blond hair a few shades darker than Samantha's, both keep their eyes on Diego. I glance at myself, double checking to make sure I didn't disappear.

"What are you doing here?" Samantha asks. "Mother said—"

"Mother is busy." Unlike her sisters, Merrick keeps her eyes locked on me. I always thought Austin had hungry eyes, but Merrick's look famished.

Diego gets to his feet and flips me over his shoulder in one quick motion to block me with his tall frame, using the wall to cover my back. Gasping, I cling to his jacket, trying to orient myself to the sudden movement.

"Holy shit balls," I mutter. "Warn me next time."

"Sorry, beautiful. No time. They're not supposed to be here, which means—"

"Merrick, get out of here!" Samantha yells. "Jewel is Austin's future."

Hell if she doesn't seem super set on me going through with the Blood Vow with Austin. I thought only my guys and me—and annoyingly Mitchell—were the ones invested in my relationships. And I hate how she reminds me that according to the Blood Match Program, in ten months, they'll try to force me to choose one of my guys to fulfill whatever belief they have in their precious infrastructure so the world doesn't know of the flaw.

But I won't allow—and my guys won't allow—them to shove me into the imaginary ideal box I don't fit in. Because I won't choose. Not even pretend. Because even if my guys know I pick them all, I don't want to upset the balance we've created.

"Tell that to Diego," the redhead says, keeping her gaze on my personality match. "Maybe he'll finally accept my offer for a good time again instead of constantly having to wait for his—"

Everything happens so fast that I don't have time to brace myself. Diego's body crushes me into the wall, stealing my breath. And then he's gone. I fall to my knees and cough, my chest heaving.

Diego roars. And I mean full-on, loud, scary, animalistic roaring like he miraculously shifted into a lion to unleash the sound of his fury on the world. Something crashes next to me, and I scream at the sight of the vampire with dark blond hair pulling herself from the hole her body created in the wall.

She rights herself on her feet, flashing her fangs at me. I scramble away and grab on to a vase, chucking it at her as she saunters closer, stalking me like a predator playing with their prey just because they can. She could've already had me, but she obviously enjoys seeing my attempt to fight her.

"Diego!" I yell, grabbing onto the desk rolling chair to push at the vampire.

"Layla, knock it off," Samantha says.

Samantha rushes at her sister with her fangs flashing, but the dark blonde, Layla, charges me incredibly fast. I fall back and hit my ass on the floor. The rug stops me from sliding away, so I crab walk toward the desk. Layla snatches the desk chair I try to shield myself with and swings it at Samantha. It collides into her, knocking her clear across the room and into the wooden doors, splintering one under the force.

Something shatters, sending glass cascading through the room. Diego fights against Merrick and the redhead, looking hella scary with his scowl. And he keeps roaring with every hit they manage to get on him.

Someone grabs me from behind, dragging me away. I scream and thrash, freaking the eff out that my life will end at any second. A dozen thoughts explode in my mind. If I die, Ramona will forever be in Orlando's debt. Dana and Fallon will be alone in this world. And my guys? They'd be devastated. They'd do something that could jeopardize their own lives. From the moment I met them, they put me before them. It was the first time someone had done that. Even my dad didn't do that, not if he was who people claim him to be.

"Jewel, I'm not going to hurt you," Samantha says. "Please, stop fighting."

"Just let me go," I cry.

Two familiar growls hum through the air, and a table collides into the wall over my head. If Samantha didn't spin me and shield me with her body, the piece of furniture would have crushed me.

"Sammy, throw her to me." Austin's voice draws my attention from my impending demise, and I catch sight of him standing across the room. Diego and Kingston's forms blur with the other vampires as they destroy the place, the Vaduvas playing a game of keep away.

"Don't you fucking do it, Samantha," Merrick snaps. "Mother will think your loyalty lies with a Divine. You'll be cast to the shadows, and I couldn't stand to lose you, baby girl."

"Sammy, please," Austin begs.

Samantha doesn't get the chance to decide because Merrick flies at us and away from her brawl with Kingston. Another female vampire materializes in front of him, her long, black hair swaying at her bare waistline, her stomach and back exposed from her crop top.

And then she kisses him.

The surprise kiss shocks him so much that he freezes and darts back, his wild eyes meeting mine. He tries to rush to me, but the black-haired vampire stops him and shoves him against the wall, pinning him in place by grabbing his—

"Everyone stop!" I scream.

My voice reverberates through the room, and surprisingly, I can now see the vampires as they pause, probably shocked that I managed to yell out. This is friggin' nuts. My guys use the sudden distraction to their advantage and close the space to me, but Merrick's faster. Spinning me in her arms, she props me against the wall, forcing me to sit on the edge of a shelf while standing between my legs to get right in my face as vampires love to do when they're about to break into someone's mind.

"Stop it, Merrick," Samantha says. "You think you're stronger than the Divines, but they will kill you if you do that to Jewel. You're messing everything up for Austin."

Merrick runs her finger along my cheek. "Stop being such a bleeding heart, Samantha."

Samantha steps closer. "He loves her. They all do."

"Love is dead. Jewel should know what kind of life she can have. There is nothing stronger and more powerful than a sisterly bond. She should've matched with us. She was perfect. We had everything in common."

"We have nothing in common," I mutter. "And this sisterly bond you're talking about. That's dead. My sister betrayed me. She tried to destroy everything I did to give her a better life. She took me for granted."

"She was also a donor," Merrick says. "But you, Jewel. You're more. Break your contract to the Divines and let us arrange a new one. Out of the Blood Match Program. We will bring your family here, and you can see exactly what life should be like."

Diego, Austin, and Kingston all growl simultaneously at her words. A few more things break, but they're outnumbered, and I know they wouldn't kill any of the Vaduvas unless they try to hurt me because Viorica is one of the few, sort-of allies we have, even if my guys claim they're rivals.

"I'm happy with the Divines," I say.

"Because of the romance," Merrick says. "You're just like Samantha. I still don't understand how Kingston or Diego could've matched better with you than she did. We thought our only worry was Austin."

"Feels like someone rigged the whole thing," the black-haired vampire says from in front of Kingston. She runs her finger over his jaw, making him tense even more. "Was it you, lover?"

Lover? Shit balls. I knew both Kingston and Diego were most definitely experienced in the whole sex department, but I had never expected to come face-to-face with someone from one of their pasts—maybe even a couple someones with the way Layla eyes Diego—and I don't know how I feel. What I'm supposed to feel.

"He would never!" I shout, struggling in Merrick's hold.

She glares at me. "How are you so sure?"

"I just know," I say.

"Well, I'm going to find out," she says.

"I'm giving you five seconds to release Jewel back to us or you're going to—"

Merrick locks me in a stare, ignoring Kingston's fury. She flashes her fangs, the long incisors peeking through her plump red lips, which I'm not so sure are stained with makeup. A million reactions try to explode from me at once, but my mind takes control, and I fall into the act my guys have ingrained into me on how to deal with asshole vampires.

"Don't take your eyes away from me," Merrick says to me.

"Stop her, Samantha!" Austin yells. "She's purposely trying to break our contracts."

"I'm not going to hurt her," Merrick says, smiling at me. "I just want her as much as Mother. I want her to be our sister."

I try my best not to react to her words, keeping my body relaxed.

Merrick cups my face. "Tell me you want to be my sister."

"I..."

"Jewel, tell me."

"No."

KEEPING UP WITH THE VADUVAS

I'M PRETTY SURE THE LAST thing Merrick Vaduva ever expected from me—probably from life in general—was that she would be bested at her weird possession game she's trying to play. Swinging out my hand, I smack her right across the face so hard that her head jerks sideways. The force stops her from reacting quick enough that she leaves herself open, and I shove her so hard that she loses her balance and trips over the broken rolling chair.

"Don't you ever try to manipulate my mind again," I say, hopping down from the shelf.

The black-haired vampire abandons Kingston to catch her sister before she falls. Kingston flies to me, throws me on his shoulder, and rushes toward Diego and Austin, now free from the holds of Layla and the redhead.

"You little rebel," Merrick says to me, smirking from her sister's arms. "You're stronger than you look. Diego must be working you out, or up, pretty well. I know how he likes it."

Diego turns a color I haven't seen on him in a long time. "Shut up, Merrick."

She licks her lips. "Why? Sisters don't keep secrets. Jewel should—"

"I'm not your sister," I snap. "And I don't ever want to be a Vaduva."

"But with us, you don't have to choose, and you'll never be controlled. I know how much Kingston needs to get his way. I'm rather surprised he'd let you consume blood and give up his control."

"And Kingston's favorite thing is to play with people's emotions, right Gabriella?" the redhead says to the black-haired vampire.

"Shut up, Heidi," Kingston says, his voice deepening with his rage. He brushes his lips to my ear. "Don't listen to them, babe. They're trying to get into your head since they can't manipulate you how they want."

Merrick glides closer, swaying her hips, her movements giving her a graceful yet seductive air I'll never master. "They must really like you, since they don't give their blood to anyone, no matter how much fun it could've been with us."

I grimace at their words. I knew that there was intimacy involved in vampire blood drinking, but I never gave much thought about it or how vampires would do that kind of thing with each other. They can't provide the same nutrients to survive, so it's mostly about the biting or whatever. I never really asked.

"What's so great to you about Jewel, boys. A donor like her can't keep up," Merrick says, smiling at me from her spot across the room.

"It's not all about that," Austin says.

Layla rolls her eyes, reminding me of Ramona. "Obviously for you. But with Diego? Yeah, right that it's not."

"Most definitely it is with Kingston," Heidi says.

I could've lived the rest of my life without knowing all the details Merrick's purposely telling to get under my skin. Unlike with Samantha, who was spilling things about Austin to make him look better, Merrick wants all of my guys to look worse.

And I hate myself a little that it is getting to me. But not because I think less of Kingston and Diego. I could never. It's about me and my crappy problems. The Vaduva sisters are gorgeous and powerful. Just seeing them stand up for each other, even Samantha trying to protect Merrick by trying to discourage her from attempting to get in my head, makes me realize what I lost with Ramona. With Dana and Fallon. With Brayla.

I love Austin, Diego, and Kingston, and I would never trade my life with them or my chance at forever, but our relationship doesn't replace the ones I consider as close as sisters.

"Okay, this is enough," Samantha says. "If you think teasing the Divines will make Jewel suddenly like you, you're wrong. Look at her."

Ah, hell. Please don't look at me. Way too many gazes settle on me, including all three of my guys, and my burning eyes betray me by not blinking fast enough to stop the tears from escaping.

"Now there's no way Jewel will ever want to be my friend. I wanted to bridge the divide between our families, and you burned it before I even set the foundation," Samantha says.

Merrick's features scrunch. "Samantha—"

She shakes her head and turns to Austin. "Please accept my apology on behalf of my sisters. Mother would never find this behavior acceptable. My dinner date with your Blood Match was intended only as that."

Kingston and Diego glare at Samantha, and despite how sincere she sounds, I don't think either of them believes her. Austin's eyes remain soft toward her, and something about how their green eyes match makes me believe her words.

"Thank you, Sammy," Austin replies.

"Yes, thank you, Samantha." Viorica's voice booms through the room, drawing everyone's attention to her. "Your suggestion has led to quite an enlightening night."

Materializing in front of me, Viorica faces the four of us. Her eyes flash silver as she takes me in, studying me so intently that I feel naked under her gaze. Kingston sets me on my feet, nudging me behind him where Austin covers my back, and Diego takes my side just like how we entered the Vaduva mansion.

"How so?" I ask. I snap my mouth closed, regretting the question immediately. I'm so used to speaking freely with my guys that I forgot that I need to keep my mouth shut.

Viorica rubs her lips together in thought, probably deciding whether or not she'll respond to me. "It seems Merrick's poor behavior might have confirmed something the Blood Rebel said to me, Mr. Divines."

Ugh. She whispers the words, not relenting to answer my question to me, clearly showing where she thinks my place belongs. So much for the sisterly bonding bullshit Merrick was spouting. I wasn't considering it at all, but now I know she was really messing with my head.

"What are you implying, Viorica?" Kingston asks, taking on a formal, business demeanor I don't really like on him. It reminds me of the first time we met and what a jerk he was. "You cannot put any weight on the words of a man who cannot have his mind broken. You are aware of the problems the Divine Region faces, and I will not allow you to try to take advantage of the situation."

"Then you wouldn't mind staying until Mr. Cera's mind turns malleable so that I can interrogate him myself," she says, crossing her arms.

Kingston turns to look at the three of us. He shares a silent conversation with Diego and Austin, worry lining all of their faces.

Flipping around, Kingston faces Viorica again. "You must provide us a room in another location and call us to supervise the interrogation."

"Why? We have plenty of guestrooms right here," she says.

"Must I remind you who you're talking to, Viorica. Because it looks to me like you had your daughters set us up in an attempt to steal Jewel from us. I would hate to have to get my father involved. The rest of the board might even consider this an act against our alliance."

Viorica flares her nostrils, and a few of her daughters release growls, but nothing as scary to compete with the threat in Kingston's voice. "Very well. I will accommodate you in one of my towers. You will be escorted by security, Mr. Divine."

Kingston nods his head.

"And so you know," she continues. "If there is any truth in Mr. Cera's words, it would be you who would have committed an act against our alliance."

My stupid eyes won't stop crying no matter how tightly Diego holds me in the backseat of our car. His large hand kneads into my back, working through the tense muscles bunching under my skin.

"Please, don't cry, beautiful," Diego whispers. "Everything is going to be fine."

"She thinks you manipulated the outcome of our matches," I say, sniffling. "It's bad enough that Orlando tried to take me from you, but now I have to worry about them. This blows. You'd think they'd know that if Kingston was going to manipulate the results, he'd have matched me solely to him."

"Damn straight, babe," Kingston says from the front seat. "I'm dying to have you to myself, so I can show you how much none of the Vaduvas mea—"

Diego swats Kingston in the back of the head. "Shut up."

I groan. "Yeah, I don't need the reminder that you had sex with probably all of them."

"Ouch, babe," Kingston says. "I'd never sleep with S—"

Austin elbows him this time. "Kingston, you're not helping."

Sighing, I finally manage to stop crying. Diego snuggles me close, using his sleeve to dry the hot tears burning pink streaks down my cheeks. A dozen thoughts go to war inside my head, begging for my attention.

"Obviously, I did help, because our girl isn't crying anymore," Kingston says.

"Because she's now panicking." Diego cups my face and peers into my watery eyes. "Jewel, take a breath."

The edges of my vision blur. "I can't."

He smiles, rubbing soft circles on my wrist. "You just did."

I swallow the burning in my throat. "Doesn't feel like it. It was—this was a lot."

Tonight was not how I imagined it would be when an invitation to join the Vaduva's for the evening showed up on the guys' calendar. It was Mitchell who insisted as a way to help ease me into my role as a future heir, but I think it was because he didn't want to attend to the matter himself.

"I know, beautiful. And I'm sorry you got dragged into that shit show. None of us wanted to bring you here, but we couldn't turn down the invite." Stupid vampire customs. Damn Mitchell. It would have been one thing to send one of my guys, but forcing all three, which forced me, was shitty.

"You should've told me about your history with them," I murmur, shifting my gaze to meet both Kingston and Austin as they stare at me. "I felt blindsided."

Kingston scrunches his nose, looking super cute, thankfully ruining the unbidden annoyance rising in me the more I think about tonight. "Babe, you knew Diego and I were experienced."

"I know—"

He reaches out and takes my hand. "And you know we love you. You're our perfect match."

"Unless someone else tampered with our results like Viorica said." Holy shit balls. Dumb rebel mouth. I can't believe those words just fell out. And I regret saying them immediately. Diego snaps back in the seat like I slapped him. Kingston blinks, his serious face turning so pouty like my suggestion pains him, and Austin sits behind the wheel, holding his lips firm but his glassy green eyes show that my mere suggestion crushed him.

I groan and cover my face. "I'm sorry. I didn't mean to let them get to me. But why would one of the traitor staff suggest such a thing? What do they get out of it?"

"Some sort of twisted satisfaction," Austin says, speaking up. "He's a Blood Rebel, Jewel. He probably has ties to Hayden, who no doubt wants to see our contract broken so that you would take Ramona's place."

His words, though disturbing, reassure what my heart knows. What my blood, body, and mind knows. Austin, Kingston, and Diego match to me perfectly on every level, and no friggin' vendetta against us can change that.

"He's right, beautiful." Diego leans forward and kisses me, pulling me into his lap to stroke his fingers across my bare leg. "Viorica won't get anything real from him. We just need to wait it out."

I sink into him. "I wish we could do it at home."

"At least we don't have to do it under the same roof as the Widows," Kingston says, referring to the nickname they gave Viorica's coven of all female vampires. "I nearly stood back and watched Austin tear all of them apart. And that's saying something because of Samantha."

"What's up with her anyway?" I ask. "You can totally take offense, Austin, but she was weird."

"Why?" he asks, turning the engine off when the security detail escorting us pulls next to the curb outside of a half-demolished tower. I used to think Dark Terrace Ranch was shitty, but it doesn't compare to Midnight Valley. The hillside where the Vaduva mansion sat was nice, though the city itself is ugly and dirty and falling apart.

"She was kind of friendly," I say. "Super invested in our matching and tried to convince me to pick you. She also asked Diego's permission to greet me. It was weird. "

"Not weird," Austin says. "She was being respectful. Anyone who does something without permission does so to test power. You belong to us."

I raise an eyebrow.

"To the world that is. You know we belong to you," he adds.

Nice save.

"You two might, but I'm pretty okay with owning our girl." Swiveling in his seat, Kingston meets my gaze. "You're mine...later."

Austin elbows him again, and they glower at each other. Diego shakes his head, shifting me away. He plants his lips to mine, so I turn my focus away from his brothers to pay attention solely to him. The car falls silent as Diego kisses me deeper, sliding his tongue into my mouth. Humming under my breath, I press my hands to his chest to inch some space between us.

"Diego," I whisper. "Now's probably not a good time."

"Just one more kiss, beautiful. I need you to know how much I love you and that you're okay even after what you found out tonight. I didn't mean to keep it a secret."

I give in to another kiss. "I'm more than okay, and I get

it."

"I'd like to make sure you're okay too, babe," Kingston mutters, annoyance deepening his voice.

"The best way to do that is to go scope out the area and make sure our room is secure, bro." Diego blocks me from the world, absorbing my body heat while pressing my back into the seat.

"We should stick together," Kingston argues. "Look what happened the last time you were left alone with Jewel."

I grip Diego around his neck, stopping him from breaking away from me. "Kingston, that's unfair," I say with a sigh. "It wouldn't have mattered who escorted me tonight."

"Well, he and Austin wouldn't let me kill them."

"Because we have enough enemies," Austin says.

Kingston groans. "I hate when you're right. And...I'm sorry, Diego. We'll check the room out, but you better get ready to move."

The car doors slam, and Kingston and Austin leave me alone with Diego. He peers out the windows for a moment, taking note of half of Viorica's security remaining here and the other half following my guys.

I touch Diego's chin to get him to look back to me. "I really am okay," I say. "You don't have to worry. I get it. You actually had lives before me. Long ones." Nothing like my life living in a tiny box, only leaving between sunrise and returning home well before sundown.

He tips his head, narrowing his eyes on me. "We still

have lives, Jewel. And you know what?"

"If you say they're better with me in it, I'll—"

"Kiss me?"

I nod and brush my lips to his. "That works."

He chuckles. "Good, because I want at least a dozen more to show you that you have nothing to be jealous of."

I purse my lips. "I'm not jealous."

Smirking, he hums his fake agreement.

"Okay, I was totally and infuriatingly jealous. They're just so friggin' gorgeous, and you guys have this history. I suddenly feel like I have a lot of catching up to do."

"Decades," he teases.

I groan.

"So you know, the history isn't that great. And I'm going to be honest with you, beautiful. Yeah, I had sex with Layla and Merrick, but it only happened because..." His words trail off as he considers what exactly to say to me. "This is going to make me sound bad, but it happened because I can't hold a conversation with either of them. Shit gets boring as hell."

"I must keep you too entertained then," I murmur.

He laughs. "But I love it."

"Me too." I pull him closer, taking his shirt out from his dress pants to rub my fingers across his skin. "But maybe on our next night I can bore you instead."

The smile that lights his face sends my heart fluttering. "I never thought I'd like the sound of that. Technically, there's still plenty of night left."

I sit up and meet his gaze before catching sight of Austin and Kingston heading our way. Diego ignores their tap on the window, and I laugh and squeal as he buries his face in the crook of my neck, purposely sending tingles through me.

"Nice try, Diego," Kingston says. "But we gotta go. All is clear inside."

Austin opens my door and helps me out. I smile at my guys, feeling a lot better after my conversation with Diego. They close in around me like a sexy, protective wall no one would dare try to break through.

"Unfortunately for us, one room," Kingston adds.

"That doesn't sound so bad," I murmur.

Kingston spins to walk backward, facing me. "It sounds awful."

"Three times the cuddles."

Squeezing my hand, Diego pulls me closer. "Whatever you want."

"No," Kingston says.

Austin pushes Kingston. "After tonight, anything she wants."

I laugh, tipping my head back. "Lucky friggin' me."

ONE PERCENT

"I CALL DIBS ON THE bed," Kingston says, plopping down on the edge of a bed half, maybe even a quarter, the size of the super king beds I've grown used to. Smiling at me, he pats the spot beside him. "Don't worry, babe. I'll make lots of room for you."

I narrow my eyes and place my hands on my hips. "Then you better make room for Diego, dude. It's still my night with him."

Diego slides his hands around my waist and rests his head on my shoulder. "And Austin's day with Jewel, or did you conveniently forget?"

Turning to Austin, I smile at him. "I don't mind being the meat to this friggin' delicious sandwich if you wanna get cozy early."

Diego and Austin laugh at my joke, but Kingston only flares his nostrils, glaring at his brothers. Kicking the toe of his shoe, I draw his attention to me, and the bastard narrows his eyes even more. And then he sticks his tongue out.

"Kingston, really?"

He flops back without responding, refusing to give up his initial claim on the bed barely big enough for two of us. He smirks at his brothers, daring them even to try to get him off the bed. Diego steps forward first. I tense in Austin's arms, nudging him back so I don't find myself in the middle of a brotherly fight that might make one of them destroy the bed. But Diego surprises me by slumping next to Kingston with his long legs partially off the mattress.

"Come here, beautiful," Diego says, motioning me forward. "There's still room."

I raise my eyebrows at the two of them getting settled instead of throwing punches at each other. They still never fail to surprise me. But now looking at the two of them and then to Austin, I know there's no way the four of us will fit on that probably purposefully small bed in this shitty room Viorica arranged. It might've been worth the wrath of the Satan Sisters to have enough space for us all. "Um, if there's room for one more, then Austin can have it. I'll take the floor and cuddle with myself," I say, spinning in Austin's arms to meet his vibrant green gaze. "Unless any of you want to join me. The carpet looks ten times thicker than what we used to have in

The Boxes."

Austin smirks and presses into me, nudging me toward the bed. He spins me so quickly with him that the world blurs. I shriek and laugh, disoriented by the sudden movement. Kingston and Diego both heave a breath. I jostle, realizing I'm now lying flat on top of Austin, who jumped right onto his brothers.

"We're not sleeping on the floor," he says to me. "We promised you cuddles, so you're going to get them."

Kingston huffs. "I didn't promise anything."

I hum under my breath. "Maybe you should re-read our contract. It's mandatory."

He tries not to laugh, attempting to play hard to get. "Only on my night."

"Fine. Your loss, dude."

He chuckles and then coughs, clearing his throat.

Diego slides his hand up onto my stomach. "Scoot closer. I'll take his share."

Shifting to the edge of the bed, Diego turns on his side to give me a sliver of space to try to squeeze into. I reach out and dig my hand into Kingston's ribs, seeing how far he'll let me push him. He grumbles something I can't understand and then sighs, suddenly flipping onto his side but away from me. I knew he'd relent and give us space.

Austin and I sink between his brothers in a weirdly satisfying—at least for me—double the meat vampire sandwich I'm pretty happy to have found myself in. Seriously, how we've all managed to fit blows my mind. And surprisingly, Austin's sculpted muscles are more comfortable than probably even the lumpy bed.

I roll over to face Austin, meeting his smile. Diego wags his eyebrows at me, just as amused. "See, Kingston? This isn't so bad." Actually, it's really friggin' amazing. I don't care that we're piled on a double bed in a crappy, probably plague-infected room, because just being this close to all my guys does something good to my insides. I've been tense and on edge all night, getting led into strange territories and messed with that this moment feels like I'm breathing for the first time and all three of my guys' colognes blend perfectly together in a scent that smells like love and comfort—like home.

Spreading my arms out, I hook one around Diego and the other around Kingston while scooting up to snuggle my face next to Austin's. I giggle, and I mean full-on, high-pitched, uncontrollable giggle that they're letting me do this. We've had plenty of group hugs and moments where they all care for me, but this is different. There's no real reason except that I can. Who knew it would be such an emotional release.

Austin laughs into my hair as I wiggle, moving my arms and legs to make an invisible snow angel like I've seen in the old Christmas movies when humans got to celebrate. Except nothing my hands touch on my guys' bodies is anything like snow. They're all sorts of hard in different spots, and most definitely not cold as I warm them up, especially the more I move.

I brush my lips to Austin, feeling his body react to my continuous shifting as I get comfortable. Diego laces his fingers through mine, bringing my hand up to rest with both of his under his chin.

Kingston rejects my hand, clutching his together instead. "You're enjoying this way too much, babe," he mutters, stiffening at the touch of my fingers tracing lower down his chest. "You should try to sleep."

I smirk without looking at him. "It's not even light out. And you know, I'd enjoy it more if you'd stop denying me your affection and just hold my hand."

"Too bad," he says, turning to block my arm from stretching down as far as my hand can go. "You're going to have to wait for my night when I can properly accommodate your needs."

"Fine, then I'll just hold your—"

Kingston crashes to the floor, and I fall between Diego and Austin. Flying to his feet, Kingston crosses his arms and glowers at the fact that Austin shoved him off the bed. And just when things were starting to settle. Sheesh. The incidents of tonight have them on edge despite how well they've been keeping it together for me. Their fighting is obvious.

"I think we all need to take a breath and relax." Because if my guys don't, this might turn into a longer night than it has already been.

Austin shifts and curls against me, turning his back on Kingston. "I'm trying to, Jewel."

"I was about to be plenty relaxed," Kingston mutters.

Austin shoots upright. "You know what, Kingston? Jewel told you what she needed from you, and it wasn't for you to play games with her. I know what you're doing, and this isn't your time."

Ah, hell.

"*My* games? You know the rules. If Jewel initiates—"

Austin growls and throws a pillow hard enough to knock him back. "You were purposely—"

Kingston attempts to grab Austin by the front of the shirt, but he doesn't even pinch the fabric before he crashes into the wall, leaving a body-sized crater.

Holy shit balls. What in the actual fuck? I'd expect this from Kingston and Diego but not from Austin. He's usually calmer than this, chiding Kingston for his actions and lack of filter but never really lashing out.

Scrambling to my feet, I hop from the bed and rush between Austin and Kingston. I brace myself for what I know was a reckless decision on my part—I mean, even a brave human knows better than to get between two angry vampires—and hold my hands up to each of their faces in an effort to get them to look away from each other.

They stiffen, glaring at each other from over my head.

Diego darts to my side and slides his arm around my back, pulling me against him. I might be willing to risk a limb to make sure my guys don't tear one from each other, but Diego won't. He won't let me jeopardize myself as his brothers fight over me with the chance that they could easily tear me apart, though I know they'd never.

Kingston reaches out and grabs my free hand. "Babe, you have to let us work it out. I can handle Aust—"

"Not happening." I tug my hand away from him. "Kingston, out."

"But, babe." Before he continues to argue, Diego grabs Kingston by his shirt and drags him to the door. The both of them exit, and I listen to Kingston complain that he did nothing wrong because I was teasing him first.

"Thanks for the blame, Kingston," I mumble under my breath, knowing they all can hear me.

"Now you made her feel bad," Diego says. "I don't know why you just couldn't—"

I groan. "I can hear you."

The two of them fall silent, their footsteps thudding down the hallway as they give me more space, so it doesn't feel like we're in the same room to my sensitive hearing. They always pick the worst times to fight. It's not like at home where someone can blast music in the hallway surround sound...if they remember.

I press my ear to the door to judge how quietly I need to keep my voice. While privacy is rare and mostly pretend, I'm getting better at recognizing when I have to at least try. Turning to Austin, I stare at him for a moment, trying to collect my thoughts, especially after overhearing Kingston basically blame me, though it's totally his fault too.

Austin sits quietly on the bed, scrubbing his face with his hands. Having him react as he did toward Kingston was the last thing I expected from our night. He's usually stoic and put-together, but especially when it comes to Kingston's bullshit behavior—something that doesn't feel so amusing in this moment as I meet Austin's eyes.

I fiddle with the vial of blood attached to the vow pendant on my neck, which is a reminder of the promises each of them made to me. "Austin," I manage to say, now feeling extra bad that my joking went too far. "I'm sorry. I wasn't actually going to...you know, with Kingston. Especially not with you and Diego next to me. You've made your boundaries pretty clear, and I respect that. I was just—I don't know what I was attempting."

He twists the vow ring with the drop of my blood on his finger. "It's not that, Jewel. You did nothing wrong asking for comfort and affection from all of us. The boundaries are for us, not you. Sure, it might be awkward as hell for those of us uninvolved if you decide to take things further, but we'll manage. It's what we agreed on. We understand you have different wants and needs from each of us."

Heat blooms across my face at such a thought. So not going there...I think. "Okay, so before my face bursts into flames, what's up? If it's not about me, what is it then? Kingston doesn't usually piss you off that much."

Sighing, he says, "The Vaduvas got to all of us tonight, fighting dirty and playing on our insecurities. I hate that they made you question us, but they also made me question myself and the chance I have with you. Kingston doesn't make it easy either. I don't appreciate the games Kingston likes to play, especially on nights that aren't his. I know you two have connected on a different level, and that's fine. But he purposely baits you to get you to do exactly what he wants, taking advantage of your desire to make sure we all feel wanted. And it's not the first time, either."

Plopping down next to Austin, I slide my arms around him, snuggling against him at his concerns. I know Kingston well enough to know that he loves his games. He's been playing them since the moment I met him. His intention tonight wasn't lost to me, because I was playing my own game with him too, but I guess Austin—and Diego—wouldn't recognize it since I don't tease them as often as I do Kingston.

"Oh, Austin. Thank you for looking out for me, but you should've said something."

"I'm sorry. I didn't want you to feel bad about it. You're not doing anything wrong. You can be with any of us whenever you want."

"Maybe so, but I care about your feelings," I murmur, brushing my lips to his. Austin relaxes under my touch, devouring every light kiss I offer. "And I never want you to feel bad either. Because what we have together is so amazing to me. Please don't think otherwise or compare it to what I have with Kingston."

He nods. "I'm sorry, Jewel. I love what we have too. He

just sometimes gets under my skin, especially with his posses-siveness over your body match, always rubbing it in without even having to say it. I love him and would risk my life for him, but damn it do I want to punch him in the nuts."

Yeah, I can see that going over well. "I know the feeling with my sister—except the nut punching—maybe a boob punch? Is that a thing?"

He chuckles.

"At least he didn't try to stake you, trade you in a blood debt, or try to force you to call off our Blood Vows," I say, leaning into him. "I think it's the sibling curse."

"I'll accept his annoying habits any day, especially if they lead to moments like this."

"I do love these moments." I close the space between our mouths and caress my lips to his, determined to obliterate his adorable pout with a dozen kisses. "It's exactly what I need."

His lips stretch into a smile through my kisses. "Me too, Jewel."

"You know what else?"

"Hmmm?" he murmurs, giving into my sudden need to show him the attention I know he craves from me but keeps under control, especially around his brothers.

"A ninety-nine percent body match is damn near perfect. Let me show you."

I don't know what comes over me, but I push Austin back on the bed to kiss him harder, sucking his lip between mine before sliding my tongue over it and into his mouth. I kiss Austin all the time, but not often like this. He keeps constant control over his actions and words and doesn't initiate things between us. I'm not so good at it either, so we mostly just enjoy each other's company, cuddling and talking instead of doing things that'll both steal my breath and return it.

There's something about this moment, about being open with each other with our guards down that ignites a part of me that wants to further explore my relationship with Austin. He's always so considerate and receptive to my needs, and I want to do the same for him.

Austin reacts to my fervent kisses, digging his fingers into my hips to align my body to his, so I can feel exactly how aroused I make him. He rubs his body against me through our clothes, building good pressure between my legs that has me squirming like crazy.

I grind against him in an attempt to find release to everything he builds inside me, causing his fangs to extend. My tongue grazes one of them, but I don't let Austin pull away from me when I taste a hint of my blood. I sink more into him, feeling the length of his excitement bulging through the light material of his dress pants.

Trying so hard not to make any noise, I hold my breath. The last thing I want is to reveal to any random vamp close enough to hear how much I enjoy being with my perfect match for nutrients. I uncontrollably gasp and exhale a pleading whimper anyway. It's just as embarrassing as my loud ass moans, but apparently Austin loves it because he pulls away long enough to smile before abandoning my mouth to kiss the sensitive skin below my ear.

His fingers roam up to tease the side skin of my boobs threatening to spill out from my halter top dress as it twists from my movement. "Is this okay?" he whispers, sucking my earlobe into his mouth.

I respond by rushing to untie the strings to give him permission to continue. Goosebumps prickle over my skin at the cool air from the AC whispering over my body. Austin's eyes rove over me, hunger darkening the vibrant green color. I capture his stare, wetting my lips, ready to feed into his desire.

He lets go of his restraint and hesitation and bends up to kiss every inch of my exposed skin, running his tongue along the curves of my breasts, sucking and kissing me in a way that makes me reach down to mess with the button of his pants. The Jewel-proof thing refuses to open, and Austin chuckles, doing it himself before I start dropping F-bombs that'll surely have his brothers teasing us about the universe trying to intervene.

I push thoughts of Kingston and Diego away to focus solely on Austin and the friggin' amazing sensations his tongue creates over my skin. Pressing my lips into his shirt, I muffle my rebel mouth trying to alert the world that Austin uses his knowledge of the human body to figure out what I like and what I'm pretty sure I could never live without again.

And damn it do I feel inexperienced as I try to work my hands over Austin. He brings his mouth back up to meet my lips, smiling through his kisses. Sliding his fingers over mine, he guides my inexperienced ass through the motions but not in a way that embarrasses me. He loves every second of silently teaching me what he wants, giving me the confidence I totally needed. It makes me even more excited because he lies back to let me take care of him for once.

I never realized how much I wanted to do more than tease Austin until I shimmy lower, hooking my fingers to the waist of his pants. He lets me tug them down, his cheeks flushing with color as I drink in the sight of his body.

He doesn't move an inch, his heartbeat speeding in thrums in an attempt to race mine. I inhale a few deep breaths, letting the anticipation build between us as I work up my nerve to do something I've never tried, taking our relationship to a level of intimacy we both want.

Adjusting my body slightly off of him, I kiss his abs, working my way lower down his stomach. His muscles tighten and loosen under my tongue, his skin tasting more sweet than salty. Nerves and excitement course through me the more desperate Austin's hands become, tangling in my hair but never pulling.

"Jewel," Austin murmurs. "You don't have to—"

A moan cuts off his words, and I take my time discovering what Austin likes with my mouth. He whispers he loves me a dozen times, his voice deepening, breathless. I love the way my name sounds on his lips, reminding me of the time he told me how beautiful he thought my name was when I asked him why he never called me anything else.

He runs his fingers through my hair only to sit up to massage the length of my back over and over again like he can't resist touching me. A hint of warm sweetness coats my tongue, and Austin suddenly digs his hands into my sides in a warning I ignore. He gasps and moans my name again as he releases, surprising me with a taste sweeter than his blood. I peer up at him to watch the pleasure scrunch his face until he opens his eyes. I wipe my lips with my fingers and smile like an idiot. I can't help it. I can already feel the good change in our relationship. It leaves me buzzing all over.

Running his finger across my cheekbone, he stares at me with a dozen emotions lighting the dark hunger in his vibrant eyes. I almost ask him what's up, but he pulls me higher and hugs me, snuggling his face into the crook of my neck. He gently rolls me over with him, flipping me onto my back. Lust and hunger still radiate in his expression along with something else I can't decipher.

"Can I taste you?" he asks, his voice deep and raspy with a thirst I'm certain he thinks only I can quench. His Adam's apple pops up in his throat as he swallows, waiting for me to respond.

I suck my bottom lip between my teeth and nod, combing my hair away from my neck. But he doesn't bend down to my throat. He smiles and shimmies lower between my legs. It's then that I realize what he meant. I was expecting him to bite me—maybe because of the hunger in his eyes or his desperate touch mapping my skin—but he doesn't. His question had nothing to do with drinking my blood at all, though I know how much he enjoys it.

Retracting his fangs, he grins again, listening to my heart pick up speed. He tugs me to the edge of the bed in one swift motion, keeping his eyes locked on mine. My breathing escapes in light pants, my heart ricocheting in my ribcage as his hands slowly spread my legs to stop me from rubbing them together.

"Austin," I whisper, clutching his shoulders. "I've never let—"

He silences my words with a kiss before I tell him I haven't done this. Kingston tried twice, but his overzealous excitement had made me hesitate. Nothing more nerve-wracking than a vampire who can't control extending his fangs.

But Austin's calm and very much in control of himself, his fangs staying in check, his heartbeat even, his fingers gentle. I want to do this with him. "Just tell me if you don't like it or want me to stop."

His head disappears under my dress, and I grip the blankets, nerves rushing over me as Austin takes me to the edge of something I'm pretty friggin' sure I never want to return from. My whole body shudders, and I arch up and hide my face in the pillow to muffle all loud ass noises that escape me.

Blush warms my skin, my body humming on the rush elicited from Austin. His hands hold mine the entire time, and he shifts with all my movements and releases what sounds like a purr in his throat when I accidentally shut my legs on his head, electricity seemingly exploding through me. Another dozen breathless whimpering noises escape me as my body clenches and relaxes until he slows down and lets me catch my breath.

He pulls himself on top of me and rests his body between my legs, his usually cool skin warm against mine, dragging more desire from me. I'm so ready to continue wherever he wants to take me, but he stops, framing my face with his arms.

"I want this so much, but I don't think I'll be able to stop, Jewel," he says, running his fingers along my jaw.

"I don't want you to stop. I love when you let me be this close to you. You starve me, you know," I say, teasing him before I kiss him. "Of your affection."

He grins, resting his face next to mine, breathing into the pillow. "I don't mean to. If we were at home—"

"Oh, um. Shit." I close my eyes and listen for embarrassing commentary to trickle through the door. "Whoa."

"What?"

"I think the side effect of Katherine's venom wore off or something. I can't hear anyone."

He chuckles. "Because no one is there. But I heard the elevator, and the last thing I want is to deal with—" Snapping his mouth shut, he shakes his head. "They're back now."

Pursing my lips, I study him. Obviously, Austin pays more attention to what's around us than I do. And now I know why he let his guard down for me. I'm sure he wouldn't have been comfortable taking things as far as we did if his brothers were near. He's ten times more reserved than them.

"From where? Viorica's? Does that mean?" I was so consumed with Austin that I didn't hear Kingston and Diego leave.

"By the pretty quiet return, I'm going to assume it went okay."

I nod. "You're right. They'd have broken down the door if it hadn't. But why didn't we all go? I thought—"

His intense gaze captures mine, silencing my questions. Leaning close, he exhales a soft breath in my ear to whisper, "You happened to kick them out at the right time, so I let them handle it. I hope that was okay. I didn't think you wanted to go back."

I rub my lips together and grin. "Definitely not. Staying here was a million times better. A billion. It was a sign from the universe."

"And the universe loves us as much as I love you." The words come out so quietly that there would be no way for anyone except for me to have heard the whispered breath that sends more tingles through me.

"And as much as I love you," I tell him back.

He smiles and tucks my hair behind my ear.

Kingston groans and taps on the door. "Are you guys finished hugging it out or whatever? As adorable as you sound gushing your love to Austin to make him feel better, I really want you to invite us back in, babe," Kingston says through the door. "We still have time to get to Dark Terrace Ranch before dawn if we hurry. Please don't make me share the fucking bed when I have to keep my hands to myself."

"Seriously, Kingston?" I ask.

"Yeah, seriously." The door flies open as if my voice gives him permission to enter the room. And I really wish he would've asked instead of assuming. Kingston freezes in surprise, his dark eyes wide. I'm pretty sure finding me and Austin like this was the last thing he expected—hell, I wasn't exactly planning it.

"Kingston!" I yell.

Still, he doesn't move, narrowing his eyes on us.

A man yells from behind him, drawing my attention away from the sudden wildness in Kingston's dark eyes. Diego strolls in, restraining the man in his arms, more focused on him than the position I'm currently in with Austin. The man thrashes so violently that I almost think he might have a chance to get away, but Diego shoves him into the wall.

"Fuck, Austin," Kingston says, his voice low. "And you think I'm the one playing gam—"

Austin flies off me so fast I don't have time to react as he thrusts Kingston out of the room and into the hallway, slamming the door on him. He fixes his pants, a dozen emotions crossing his face.

Diego twists and looks at me from over his shoulder, his eyes darting to my state of undress and he quickly shifts the man in his arms away from me. I rush to fix my dress, the

Blood Rebel still fighting Diego, snapping his teeth through a whole bunch of swears aimed directly at me. My cheeks burn because he totally got a show, but I try my best not to react to his slew of words. It's nothing I haven't heard before, coming from someone against my Blood Matching, but it sure pisses my guys off.

Diego slaps his hand over the man's mouth. "Beautiful, I'm sorry."

"Damn it, Diego," Austin says.

"Give the asshole to me. I'll shut him up," Kingston says, smashing through the door, sending it off the hinges. If Austin wasn't there to stop it, the door would've flown across the room and into me. Dozens of wood pieces cascade over the bed, and one pelts me right in the middle of the forehead.

"Ouch! Shit!" I screech.

Pain bursts in my head, shadowing my vision. Something warm trickles between my eyebrows and down my nose. I don't even have the chance to reach up to assess the wound before Austin's in front of me, cupping my cheeks with his hands.

"Fuck, babe. I'm so sorry," Kingston says, rushing to me.

Austin growls at him to stay back. Diego drops the man to his knees and comes over next, gripping Kingston's arm to stop him from attempting to get close to me again. All of our nerves are on edge, especially because we're in unfamiliar territory and responsible for bringing this man back to Mitchell where I know he'll meet a terrible fate.

I blink as pain burns through me, blurring my eyes with tears. Damn unexpected hazards of having hot, extremely strong vampire boyfriends. Kingston's lucky I love him and will intervene between him and his brothers. Austin and Diego look ready to shoot splinters at him right in his heart. "I'm okay. I'm okay," I repeat, fanning my face. "But how bad is it?"

Austin turns my head from side to side without responding. I swear I'm gushing blood at this point, and all three of my guys stare at my forehead with indecipherable expressions. Diego hands Austin his medical bag that always stays nearby, and the second Austin takes his hands from my face to reach inside, I automatically touch the giant ass splinter. It drops to my lap, and both Diego and Kingston suck in deep breaths.

"It looks worse than it is. Head wounds tend to bleed a lot," Austin says, pulling out supplies from his medical kit.

I press my hand over my forehead. "Well, stop it already. You're wasting my blood."

"I can help with that," Kingston says, poking my nose, getting blood on his finger. He sticks it in his mouth and licks his lips.

Diego swings at him and misses. "You're skipping because of that."

Kingston closes in on me again, pouting while trying to help me put pressure on my forehead.

"Get back, Kingston!" Austin yells. "Don't touch her."

It doesn't help that Kingston keeps sucking his damn fingers.

Leaning forward, I touch my fingers to Austin's cheek even though my hand is covered in my blood. Austin inhales a deep breath, his nostrils flaring. Both his brothers stare at us as I try to calm Austin down.

"I really am okay," I whisper. "It only hurts a little. It was an accident."

"Die, you son of a bitch," a gruff voice says from behind my guys.

Austin's eyes widen, his mouth forming an O. Everyone was so focused on me that they weren't paying attention to the Blood Rebel. The last thing I expected was for the man to hang around instead of fleeing.

Kingston yanks a silver stake from Austin's back, and Austin falls into me. Diego and Kingston both fly at the man, each taking one of his arms. He yells out, fury distorting his already ugly features, and Austin pulls away from me, his green eyes flashing silver, his fangs extended.

I reach to grab onto his bloody shirt, but I'm not fast enough.

All I have time to do is take a breath and brace myself.

And then the man screams.

"Austin, please." My voice catches in my throat, fear rushing over me. Not for the man, but for Austin. I don't know what shifted in him, but I'm freaked out that he'll do something he'll regret. If he bites this man, it'll definitely be a kill bite, and when he cools off, he'll regret it no matter how awful this man's been tonight.

Austin freezes a foot away from the man, his body rigid as he fights with himself. Diego and Kingston don't look like they're in better control, their eyes shifting silver, their fangs flashing. My good senses beg me to stay where I am on the bed, but my heart drags me across the room to my guys.

"Please," I whisper again. "I'm fine. Don't do this, especially on my behalf."

The man's chest heaves, his body shuddering. He focuses his attention on me from over Austin's shoulder because Kingston and Diego hold him off his feet. His ferocity and bravery remind me of the Blood Rebels I met in Haven Springs, and it gets under my skin at how willing he is to die.

"He's a traitor to the Divinity Estate," Kingston says first.

"Doesn't mean you have to kill him," I argue, bringing my hands up to press against my splitting headache.

"I don't need your help, you blood slut," the man says.

All three of my guys growl.

I ignore him and slide my arms around Austin, tugging him away before he can act without thinking. Turning him around, I cup his face, so he has to hold my stare. His jaw twitches, his nostrils flaring with the anger he now tries to suppress. "Will you please bandage my wound? It hurts." I glance at Diego. "Can't you mind manipulate him to shut up?"

"Viorica gave him her blood so we couldn't find out what she asked him before we got there," Kingston says, releasing a deep growl in his throat.

I groan. "So tie him up or something. You could've at least disarmed him, and then Austin wouldn't have been hurt."

Running my hands under Austin's shirt, I touch my fingers to the bleeding spot on his back. Austin remains quiet but relaxes under my touch. If Viorica wasn't the scary ass ruler of this region—or a vampire—I'd most definitely give her a screaming piece of my mind.

"We were just trying to get back to you as quickly as we could," Diego says. "We're sorry. We didn't expect you to be hooking up with Austin."

"Yeah, babe. You need—"

One glare from me stops Kingston from finishing his sentence, and he sighs and releases the Blood Rebel, sending him to the floor. He spins around, lacing his fingers behind his head without looking back at me and Austin. Diego restrains the man with his belt and hangs him over his shoulder despite his flailing.

"Your next words better be that I need to take it easy and let you guys take me home, Kingston," I say. "And you also better not say anything about me feeding Austin on the way either."

Kingston's jaw tightens. "What about—"

I shake my head.

Exhaling the most dramatic breath I've ever heard in my life, Kingston composes himself and steps closer. "Babe, please take it easy and let Austin take care of you. I want nothing more than to get you home so you can rest."

I smirk. "Thanks, Kingston. That sounds like the best friggin' idea ever."

"You're lucky you're hot as hell when you boss me around, babe," he says, keeping his arms crossed.

"She should do it more often," Diego murmurs, smiling at me.

I roll my eyes. "All right then. Go get the car, Kingston. You're driving with that guy in the front seat."

He groans. "Seriously?"

I nod. "You obviously don't want to cuddle me with your brothers, so yeah. I'll be in back with Diego and Austin."

"Fucking A," he mutters.

Crossing the room to him, I stand on my tiptoes and brush my lips to his. "And Kingston?" I whisper into his mouth too quietly for anyone to here.

He purrs deep in his throat, keeping his hands at his sides. "Yeah, babe."

"Save the games for your night. I do enjoy them."

Nodding, he kisses me back. "Whatever you want, babe."

"Good. That's exactly what I want to hear."

HOW TO TEASE A VAMPIRE

"I HATE YOU!"

Ramona screams, rushing at me. She swipes a silver stake from inside her jacket and jabs it at me. I flounder back out of the way. Warm arms envelop me from behind and lift me off my feet to spin me away from my sister.

"Ramona-babona," Dad says, raising his hand at her. "Stop it this instant. Jewel is family."

"She's a traitor to humankind. Look at her, Dad." Ramona waves the silver stake in a circular motion at me.

My dad swivels to peer at me with his blue eyes a shade lighter than mine. His jaw twitches from under his scruffy face, and he gives me a long once-over, starting from my eyes to trail down to my feet. Reaching out, he takes my hand and tugs up my arm, rolling the sleeve up to display fresh bite marks still bleeding.

"Oh, Jewel-babewel," Dad whispers, his eyes narrowing as he inspects my wounds. "What did I tell you about the shadows?"

"To stay out of them," I murmur. "But Dad, it's not what you think."

He drops my arm. "I didn't raise you this way. You have no idea what you're doing."

"I did this for Ramona," I say. "You left us."

Crossing his arms, he glares. "I told you to wait."

I glower right back at him. "We were going to get kicked out of the apartment."

"Better to fight than submit. You would've had a better chance that way, honey." Dad turns away from me and strolls across the space to Ramona. He grabs the silver stake from her hand and slaps it against his palm. "Now you're wasting everything I sacrificed for our family. Everything your grandfather and great-grandfather sacrificed."

Tears burn my eyes. "I'm sorry."

"She's not!" Ramona yells. "She cares about no one but herself."

"Are you kidding me?" I ask, fury rising inside me. "I did this for you."

"You did this to me."

One second Ramona stands next to Dad, and in the next he falls to the ground, pouring blood everywhere. Brayla materializes next to Ramona and combs her fingers through my sister's hair, pushing it away from her neck.

The sun slinks across the sky faster than I have ever seen it, shifting behind a building to cast a shadow over me.

"My precious Jewel." Orlando's cool hands wrap around my waist, spinning me away from Brayla and Ramona. I stand frozen, peering into Orlando's eyes. He reaches up and glides his fingers across my cheek. "How I've missed you."

Biting his lip, he sends blood splashing down his chin to stain the light fabric of his shirt. He leans in, closing the space even more, and I can't stop peering at the blood streaming from his mouth.

An uncontrollable, breathless moan escapes my lips, making Orlando smile. He hovers so close that I think I can smell the spiciness of his blood so much so I can almost imagine it dripping across my tongue.

"You want it, don't you?" he whispers, locking me in his gaze.

"Yes," my mouth says without my permission.

"You need it."

I nod. "Please."

"When you belong to me. But now...Ramona?" Orlando turns to face my sister, and I gasp as Brayla holds her lifeless body.

Fear rushes through me, and I scream.

"Oh, lover. You didn't," Orlando says.

Ramona's body thuds to the ground.

"I just want Jewel," she murmurs. "You promised."
"Very well."

A scream rips through the air, and I thrash, fighting against the sudden restraints tying me in place. Hands grab my wrists, dragging me, and I flail, trying my best to break free before Brayla and Orlando can tear into me.

"Jewel, hey. Hey, open your eyes. It's me. You're twisted."

The second Austin's soft voice tickles my ear along with his breath, I relax and sink deeper into the soft mattress of the bed. Opening my eyes, I meet his serious gaze. He unwinds the sheets from me, starting at my arms and working his way over my body until I'm free. I thrashed so much in my sleep that I basically restrained myself.

A towel hangs around Austin's hips, his hair damp from his shower, and I drink him in as my racing heart settles. "That was a bad one, huh?" he asks, nudging me onto my side so he can slide onto the bed behind me to spoon me against him. "I knew I should've woken you up when we got back to give you more blood."

I hug his arms to my chest, twining our fingers together. "It was about Ramona. Brayla killed her." I refrain from sharing the parts about Orlando or how my stomach aches horribly at the mention of vampire blood. I want nothing more than to forget it and push it to the back of my mind.

Austin murmurs his sadness for me under his breath. "Try not to worry too much. Part of the agreement to let Orlando take her early was a guarantee that she'd maintain her good health."

"Good health doesn't mean much when he could be mentally torturing her or keeping her locked in a cage," I murmur, squeezing my eyes shut only to snap them back open again because the dream flashes through my mind.

"The board assures she's not," he says.

"I don't trust the board."

"Do you trust me?"

I shift in his arms and turn to face him. "Of course I do."

"If you're worried, I could always respond to one of the messages—"

My eyes widen, and I shake my head. "No, don't. Please. I just—I can't."

Austin puffs out his bottom lip before brushing it to mine. In the last two months, Brayla has sent over two hundred messages and called half as much in an attempt to reach out to me. But even the thought of talking to her sends fear stealing my breath away. I can't get the image of her flashing her fangs and biting my dad from my mind.

My guys have been the ones communicating, but only for the sole purpose of getting updates on the board's behalf. Because if Orlando breaks the contract that allowed Ramona's early arrival into his care, he could face enough penalties to send him to the shadows. But the last thing I want is to hope for poor treatment of my sister no matter what. The thought kills me.

Austin subtly nods his head and rests his forehead to mine. "I understand. Just take a breath and let me get dressed so I can feed you."

I sit up and curl my knees to my chest, watching Austin enter the wardrobe. It's only the second time I've stayed here with him. We barely made it to Dark Terrace Ranch before sunrise, and Austin and I slept in his top floor suite at the Blood Match Center. But it was better than the room in Midnight Valley. Thank God we didn't have to spend the day there.

Austin appears again a few moments later to answer a light tap on the door. The Donor Life Corp staff member, dressed in black, hands Austin a tray and disappears as quickly. Like at the Divinity Estate, all staff members aren't allowed in our suites.

Austin's phone chimes from the sleek night table similar to the décor of our room at home, and I beat him to it, recognizing the familiar ring he set up for my cousins. I groan and rub my eyes, shifting my sleep-twisted shirt before I finally set the device on my knee and accept the call without setting off the projection.

"Jewel! We've missed you!" Dana and Fallon smile at me from the tiny video screen of Austin's phone. I had no idea how much I needed to hear their voices after my nightmare until this second. "You were supposed to call us this morning."

I yawn, covering my mouth with my hand. "I'm sorry,

you two. We got in late."

Austin sets down the tray of breakfast foods the Donor Life Corp human chef cooked up for me. "Yeah, Jewel didn't even want to wake up to leave the car."

"Hey, Austin!" my cousins call at the sound of his voice. "When are you bringing Jewel to visit us?"

Austin and I share a look, knowing well enough that it might not be any time soon. With the sudden shift in power in Haven Springs, Donor Life Corp continues to evaluate the human-only community. Their choice of new leadership must settle the unrest created by the Blood Rebels, who infiltrated and tried to take over the place all of the Blood Matches' heirs go to when a donor successfully enters the program.

"Hopefully soon," Austin says, finally answering them.

"Maybe you and your brothers could come," Dana says. "It would be nice to see you again as well."

My heart melts at my cousin's suggestion. Because they see what I see in my matches. Unlike Ramona, they trust that I'm safe and happy under my three perfect vampires' care despite what most humans think.

If only my guys could really go with me, it'd be a lot easier. But vampires still aren't allowed. I don't want to risk it because my guys would make it happen if I asked. Four people—three humans and one vampire—from the Divinity Estate died the last time I went, not to mention a few humans, like Laurel, who died by my sister's hands.

Fallon presses her lips together. "Did you know Dougie

says your name, Austin? Well, it kind of sounds like tin-tin."

I raise my eyebrows at Austin. "Looks like someone made quite the impression."

Austin shrugs and smiles, putting a plate of food together to bring to me in bed. Dana and Fallon gossip about a few of their new friends while Austin hand-feeds me pieces of a lemon poppy seed muffin. I usually only let him feed me the first bite because he loves seeing my reaction, especially if it's something new like this. But tonight, I give in to his continued affection.

Talking to my little cousins in Austin's arms like this stirs both happiness and sorrow inside me. Joy, because this is how I imagined things to be after realizing how perfect my life would be matched to my guys. Sadness, because Ramona should be with Dana and Fallon. She should be the one there for them because I'm not. Even though Ramona severed our sisterly bond, I still can't help the love and grief I hold for her now. I feel so helpless that I can't do anything as she remains in Orlando's care. I just have to trust that he respects the law and leaves her alone for the next eight months until her eighteenth birthday.

I never thought I'd think this, but I hope he keeps Brayla away from her too.

A knock sounds on the door to Austin's suite, drawing my attention away from my cousins. Kingston and Diego talk to each other outside the door, but neither of them barges in. I think they learned their lesson after walking in on me and

Austin in Midnight Valley.

"Hey, girls? Can I call you two back in a few hours?" I ask, realizing they're both staring at me in silence. I feel bad for not talking much. I just love listening to the two of them chatter. Feels almost like they're here instead of on the phone. "I need to get ready to head back to the Divinity Estate soon."

Both my cousins nod and pout, tears rimming their blue eyes, a few shades darker than mine. I hope that one of these days they won't cry when I have to hang up. It took over a week after they had to return to Haven Springs without me and Ramona to even get them off the line for more than the few hours they were asleep.

Last night was the first moment since Ramona was given to Orlando that I didn't virtually let them tag along on my dates with my guys. Even Kingston's been a good body match about it, though it stops any and all of his seduction. He only complained a little that we haven't been enjoying our match as much as we should. If he had it his way, we'd never leave our room.

"I love you both. Forever and infinity," I say to my cousins.

"Always and beyond," they both respond.

I click off first, knowing they won't do it on their own. Shifting between Austin's legs, I rest sideways with my head on his chest and listen to his heartbeat as I try to get myself together. I still can't shake everything that happened last night between the Vaduva sisters and the Blood Rebel. How Viorica accused my guys of manipulating their matching to me.

Another knock sounds on the door, but I can't find my voice. Tears burn my throat, and I consider calling Fallon and Dana right back just to hear their voices one more time. Austin rubs his hand in smooth circles between my shoulder blades in an attempt to push the grief out of me before I really lose my shit.

"I'm sorry," I murmur. "I'm trying to stop. I know the risk of attracting attention, especially here."

"You guys can come in, but only if you're prepared to snuggle the hell out of Jewel," Austin says instead of responding to me.

I release a breathless laugh at his words.

A second later, my guys smother me in a cocoon of their muscular goodness. Sometimes, they argue and don't always agree with each other, and I don't always make things easy, but when it comes down to it, they're always here for me when I truly need it without complaint.

"Twelve hours," Kingston whispers into my hair.

"What happens in twelve hours, dude?" I ask against Austin's chest, my nose and mouth pressed into his shirt.

"That's when I get to properly cuddle you the way you want me to."

I giggle and snort, cringing at the sound. "I don't know. I'm pretty sure this is the only proper way for me to be cuddled from now on."

He play-growls at me, and I wiggle in Austin's lap to free

my head enough to turn my face to brush my lips to Kingston's cheek. Breaking my arm free next, I tug Diego's head closer and turn the other way to kiss him. They finally release me when they're certain I won't start sobbing again, and Austin pulls up the hem of his shirt to wipe my damp cheeks.

"Thanks," I say to each of them, scooting off Austin to plop back on the bed. He drapes his arm around my shoulders and offers me another bite of the lemon muffin, picking up exactly where he left off.

"Anything for you, beautiful," Diego says, squeezing my hand. "I know it's been a rough few weeks."

I shrug. "You guys always manage to make things better."

"Damn straight," Kingston says.

My guys sit around with me, each taking turns feeding me while making me laugh. Anytime we're outside of the Divinity Estate, we tend to stick with each other. I love my individual time with them, but I also love what we share together. I've always admired their loyalty and protection as brothers, and it never ceases to amaze me that they share their bond with me.

"Okay, babe, as much as I love feeding you..." Kingston's words trail off with a glare from both Diego and Austin.

I laugh and hold out my wrists right under Austin's and Diego's mouths. "Don't get mad at Kingston. It's okay to tell me you're starved. I know it's been a while since you've eaten."

Bumping their chins with my arms, I purposely taunt

their deep-seated nature. A familiar clicking sound cuts through their soft breathing, and I spot both their fangs extending to peek from under their lips. I drop my hands to my lap and grin at their reaction, seeing the desire and hunger darken their eyes.

"Haven't you heard it's dangerous to tease a vampire like that, babe?" Kingston says, clearing his throat, his own voice deepening. "My brothers don't have my restraint."

"You have restraint?" I tease, bringing my arm up to his mouth next. "Prove it. Just try to resist. You know I like feeding you."

His fangs extend, his nostrils flaring. "Babe."

"You know you can't resist," I say. "Especially if I ask you to...bite me."

Poking my finger to his fang, I prick myself, drawing a drop of blood. All three of my guys inhale a breath. Goosebumps prickle over my skin at the way each of them long for me. Kingston licks his lips, staring at my finger. My heart picks up speed with anticipation. I fully expect him to react with the silver flashing in his eyes. He could easily snatch my hand and bring my finger to his mouth before I could blink, but he just continues to stare.

I realize his gaze flicks to Austin's. Kingston won't do it after Austin's annoyance last night, but I'm pretty sure Austin's no longer bothered by Kingston. At least not now.

I shift in Austin's lap, feeling the hardness of his desire against me, but neither of us reacts. All I do is lean back enough to brush my lips to his earlobe to whisper, "Kingston's going to regret all the games he plays."

Austin chuckles.

Kingston narrows his eyes even more.

Slowly, I bring my hand to Kingston's lips but stop short, trying so hard not to laugh. Austin slides his hand across my stomach, leaning forward, daring his brother even to move. The blood drop clings to my finger, and I hover it so close to Kingston's mouth that he could easily dart his tongue out for a taste.

I yank my hand away with a laugh and suck on my own finger. "Whoops. That was wasteful, wasn't it?"

"Babe, you're lucky you're in Austin's arms because you're straddling a dangerous line," he says, burning daggers at me.

"Dangerous line, huh?" I ask, sweeping my hair over my shoulder. "The only danger I risk with you is that you'll cuddle me to death."

Austin laughs and hugs me tighter, kissing my bare shoulder that I exposed to him. "You know our girl is fearless."

"Yeah, she slapped Merrick," Diego says. It so wasn't funny at the time, but now that he says it, his chest puffing with pride, I can't stop from giggling.

"It's only because I had you there," I say. "You all make me brave."

Diego brushes his fingers over my knee. "You don't even

want to know what you make me."

"You're right. We don't want to know," Kingston says.

I smile, giving Diego a once...twice, okay, third time over, meeting his grin with my own as I try to magically summon X-ray vision. "He was only going to say hungry, right Diego? Should I test your restraint too?"

"No, babe. No more games. You made your point."

I pop out my bottom lip. "But I was having fun."

Kingston reaches out and runs his finger along my pouty mouth. "And Diego has no restraint."

"Oh, I have plenty of restraint. But unlike Kingston, I don't play games. If you ask me to bite you like that, I'm warning you now that I will," Diego says, sliding his fingers higher up my leg to dig into the sensitive skin of my thigh. "I'm not denying you what you want from me."

Tingles rush through me. "Shit."

I totally walked into that because Diego knows exactly what to say to me to shift my mind from joking to serious in a good way. My teasing backfired on me. Diego smiles his irresistible smile, daring me to give into my own need as his match. Now I can't stop thinking about everything that comes along with Diego's bite, and it's a whole bunch of stuff I like.

He licks his lips, totally friggin' tempting me. But it's not a game. It's not to rile me up to get a reaction like Kingston does.

I release a small breath. "Okay, I'm done. If I don't stop, I might let all three of you bite me at once, especially with how hungry you look. And that would be weird...right?"

OhmyeffingG. They all look at each other in consideration, and I gape, just the thought making me nervous as hell. I was kidding. I'm not sure I could survive such an encounter with my three matches.

"Fuck. Me," I whisper under my panting breath. This has gone from what's supposed to be breakfast to something more in line with a little special dessert.

"What, babe? You didn't think we'd consider it?" Kingston asks, flashing his fangs at me.

"Yeah, I'm not opposed, beautiful."

Austin kisses my neck. "If you want to try, I think we could do so safely."

I wriggle away from them and get to my feet, putting an unusually huge amount of space between us. Their gazes bore into me, heating every inch of my body, the weight of their desire smothering away any bad emotions that were arising in me. Now, all I can think about is how wanted I feel in this moment, and not just for my blood.

But...holy shit balls.

Diego tips his head back and roars a laugh, elbowing Kingston hard enough in the ribs to send him off the bed. Kingston peeks his head up from the floor, grinning at me, and Austin gives me the cutest smirk.

I clutch my chest, my body still buzzing.

All three of them close in on me, engulfing me in a hug.

Austin meets his lips to mine. "I'm sorry, Jewel. That was

too good to resist."

Kingston takes me in his arms next and nuzzles his nose to mine. "And damn you, babe. The next eleven hours, three minutes, and fifteen seconds will be excruciating. I warned you it was dangerous to tease hungry vampires."

Big hands slide around my waist, spinning me around. "And who knows, maybe we'll get to that point together sometime, but not when we're hungr—"

"You mean starved," Kingston quips.

"Or here for that matter," Austin says.

Austin pulls me back from Diego, rubbing his hands up and down the length of my back until my heart stops racing. I glare at the three of them the whole time Austin draws my blood to fill up their glasses. My guys each add their own blood to another glass for me, letting me watch them. With each passing week, we've all become more comfortable with the situation, and they no longer feel the need to hide the act like they used to when they first started giving me their blood.

"To...bitch slaps and bravery," I say, holding my glass up to theirs.

They all chuckle and gulp down my blood, watching me sip theirs much slower than usual. I lick my lips and stick out my tongue, my stomach still doing all sorts of fluttering under their attention. Just when I sink lower in my chair to escape their smirks, the familiar ding of the elevator draws our attention from each other and to the door.

The world suddenly spins, and I find myself in the bathroom, the shower running and the music on. Austin stands between my legs as I perch on the counter. Blood sloshes in my glass, jostled by the movement.

Austin takes the cup from me before I spill it. He holds it to my lips. "Drink quickly."

I stare into the glass with wide eyes. "What's going on?"

He doesn't respond until I start guzzling, my throat making all sorts of dumb noises in the process. I expect my stomach to react badly after the strange feeling caused by the dream, but the sweet blend sends tingles over my tongue, settling my oncoming nerves if anything. "Mitchell's here."

There goes my resolve. Who knew all it would take was a single name to steal the warmth my guys filled me with. Austin frowns at my reaction, swiping the glass from my hand to rinse it off in the sink and set it down. He envelops me in his arms, breathing into my hair without a word, the music and shower spray drowning out whatever conversation takes place on the other side of the door. It's the only way to create a sense of privacy, and Mitchell won't question it.

"Clothes on or off," Austin whispers into my ear. I might have exceptional hearing, but I can't hear the same things Austin does. He and his brothers have trained themselves to listen past things. It gives them an advantage like with the shock noise alarms set up at the estate that disorients unexpected vampires.

I tilt my head back and look at him, caught off guard by his question considering Mitchell is outside the door.

He smirks at me and leans in. "We're supposed to be in the shower."

My mouth forms an O. "Only off if you do."

Warm water cascades over my head, surprising me, and I laugh out so loud that I'm sure all of Dark Terrace Ranch heard me. Austin crashes his mouth to mine, stealing my breath with the most amazing kiss to get me to shut the hell up.

"Whoa," I say, my hands slipping down his naked chest. Holy shit balls. I've never been undressed so quickly. "This was the last thing I expected."

He grins. "If only I didn't have to leave you. Stay here while we handle Mitchell, okay?"

Setting me on my feet, Austin exits the shower, pulling a towel around his waist. He walks backwards, devouring me with his eyes, restoring the warmth Mitchell's sudden arrival stole from me. I twitch my fingers in a wave.

"Maybe hurry back," I mouth to him.

His smile widens even more before he disappears and closes the door behind him. Lasting only a second under the steamy stream of water—because there's no friggin' way I'm going to remain naked and alone in the shower—I pop the opaque glass door open and step out.

I wrap myself in a towel and tiptoe across the gleaming tiles. Squeezing my eyes shut, I focus on pushing the music away in an attempt to hear what they're discussing. I wouldn't put it past my guys not to tell me everything Mitchell says to them as a way to protect me.

"Donor Life Corp...Viorica...the board." Mitchell's deep voice hums in and out of my hearing. "Show them...perfect."

"No," Kingston, Austin, and Diego say in unison, their annoyance raising their voices to a pitch I can hear.

"Nothing...worry. Jewel...Divine," Mitchell continues.

I sigh and walk to the shower to turn off the water so I can hear better. Mitchell doesn't know that I can hear him, but my guys do. I just hope they don't try to change the subject from whatever Mitchell discusses with them.

"The board has never once questioned the results," Kingston says, his voice hot and sharp with anger. "Even when we know that certain clients use the loopholes to match."

"There were no errors. This is retaliation," Diego says.

Austin groans. "What do they even get out of this?"

"You knew the position you were putting yourselves in asking for an extension to continue this game."

"It's not a game. She's our future," Kingston snaps.

"You can't share her forever. Two of you will have to give her up."

I release a ragged breath.

Mitchell continues, saying, "The Vaduva Coven holds great interest in Jewel and won't let this go lightly. You know if a decision isn't made, Viorica will use her power to influence a new outcome. We cannot risk jeopardizing our alliance. I won't risk our status to start a war for your obsession with one donor, Blood Vow or not."

"Shit balls," I whisper under my breath.

"Do you understand?" Mitchell asks.

None of my guys verbally respond, their silence so sharp it cuts through me.

"Now, please. Prepare the estate. Do what you must to assure Jewel acts properly for the occasion. She is still your blood source and must act accordingly if you want the board to remain on your side."

I grimace.

"But you know that could put her at risk," Austin says.

"Figure it out," Mitchell snaps.

Kingston groans. "She won't like this."

Something crashes. "Then make her," Mitchell says. "Also, no gen. pop. blood for the occasion. I want the board to have the best."

A door slams upon Mitchell's exit, and I don't get a chance to move before the bathroom door knocks me back. Austin catches me, securing my towel before it falls off me, and just hugs me against him for a minute.

"We're screwed, aren't we?" I ask him. "Viorica's not going to let this go."

"We're going to be fine," he assures, combing my messy hair from my face.

"Yeah, babe. There's only one type of screwing in our future," Kingston says from the door. "In ten hours, thirty-seven minutes, and ten seconds. But who's counting?"

Diego shoves him. "Not if Jewel's not prepared."

I groan. "Prepared for what exactly. I couldn't hear everything."

"A test," Kingston says.

"What?" I ask, my stomach twisting at the thought.

He sighs. "We have to prove how awesome we are together. Whatever Viorica extracted from the Blood Rebel annoyed her enough that she and the board have now requested to see us all together in a...somewhat normal setting. You know, show them that we are great matches."

"But don't freak out," Diego says.

I squeeze my eyes shut, trying to suppress the panic rising in me. "Of course I'm freaking out. How can they continue to do this? We matched. We're perfect together."

Austin cups my face. "Look at me, Jewel."

Opening my eyes, I get captured in Austin's stare.

"This isn't a test. We don't have to prove anything, because what we have together is real. No one can deny it no matter how much they want to. I promise you I will not allow anything to jeopardize our forever." The certainty in his voice slows my out-of-control heart.

I blink away my tears and nod.

"None of us will," Diego says.

Kingston flashes his fangs. "I'd like to see them even try."

FEAR TRIGGERS

"HIT HIM AS HARD AS you can, babe," Kingston says from the other side of the blue mat that takes up a huge portion of the gym. "With your fist this time, not your mouth."

I flip him off and turn my attention back to Diego, circling me at a human speed. "Maybe if he'd defend himself, I wouldn't feel the need," I say to Kingston, trying not to smile at Diego.

"He doesn't for a reason, babe. You know he likes that shit."

Diego laughs. "Yeah, beautiful. Nothing you can do will hurt me much."

Stopping in my tracks, I place my hands on my hips. "Then what's the point if vampires are a bunch of masochists?"

"Generalize much, babe?" Kingston quips.

I roll my eyes. "Whatever."

"He's right, Jewel," Austin says, strolling into the gym. "You know Kingston's terrified you'll try to bite him."

Kingston shoves Austin, making him laugh. The two of them throw punches at each other, blurring through the room. I jerk my head around in an attempt to keep sight of them. Diego drapes his arm over my shoulder.

"There's no friggin' way. I don't see why you even bother teaching me," I murmur.

"Because I know you have it in you, beautiful," Diego responds. "There's more to fighting than how fast or how hard you can hit. Now don't try to follow them with your eyes. Make strategic guesses of where they're going to land next."

I tap my finger to my chin and study Austin and Kingston's blurry forms. Kingston hits the wall opposite of us, sending plaster across the mat. Austin's laughter rings through the air, and he turns to glance in our direction.

"Show off," Diego mutters. "Careful Austin, you know how our girl acts toward the loser."

Kingston takes the opportunity to jump on Austin. They both skid across the floor in our direction. Diego spins me out of the way only to bring my legs back around to kick them both into the wall.

"Fuck, Diego. You can't use our girl as a weapon," King-ston says.

"You okay, Jewel?" Austin stops in front of me. He'd roll up my pants to check out my legs if I let him.

I nudge him away with my foot. "Don't even think about it."

"Try and stop me," he teases, grabbing for my pant leg.

Scrambling away, I nearly eat shit on the mat because I was too slow to pull my leg out of his reach. Kingston catches me before Austin does. I wriggle to my feet and dart around him, knowing that there's no way Kingston can resist playing keep away with me from his brother.

Austin evades Kingston enough to reach for my sleeve, and I screech and laugh, pulling toward Kingston's other side, dragging Austin closer. Neither of them hit each other, extra aware of my closeness, and Kingston hugs Austin to keep him in place.

"All right, babe. I got him. Show him what you got," Kingston says. "Austin can take it."

Austin elbows Kingston in the stomach, making him heave a breath. Spinning around in Kingston's arms, Austin playfully snaps his teeth at me over his brother's shoulder. The two of them push at each other, holding their grounds. Austin manages to grab my wrist again, pulling me into Kingston's back.

Kingston risks a punch and clocks Austin in the shoulder and knocks him away. Even not at vampire speed, Austin's incredibly fast and strong. Kingston admitted his brothers were better fighters than him, but Kingston knows strategy, and he can predict Austin's moves pretty accurately.

I twist on my feet and dash away. I expect them to fight each other some more, but Austin breaks away from Kingston and chases after me.

"Shit balls!" I scream.

He doesn't stop, but he doesn't fly at me either. My heart races, adrenaline coursing through me along with a cold wave of sudden fear and confusion. I mean, what the actual hell? Austin doesn't usually scare me, but I feel like I'm racing the sunset in Dark Terrace Ranch.

"Don't let him catch you, beautiful," Diego calls from across the room.

I screech again. "Come on, Kingston. You heard him. Don't let him catch me."

Kingston releases a low growl. "Don't worry, babe. I'm going to catch you first." The way his voice deepens, his dark eyes flashing silver, sends another burst of panic through me.

"Ah hell," I whisper. "Guys, um—"

Austin rushes closer, and I shriek and run toward Diego. Kingston shoves past Austin to stalk me, but my body wants nothing to do with it. My mind knows they're joking around. The only thing I'm at risk for is their delicious affection, but damn it. I can't stop the fear from squeezing my chest.

I trip over a crack between mats and land on my stomach. Crawling forward, I race to get to my feet. Strong fingers latch on my ankle, tugging me back, and I release a loud ass scream that could probably be heard for miles. I'm sure the whole estate heard me, but I couldn't help myself.

"Stop!" I jerk my foot away and curl in on myself, my stomach twisting, my chest tightening from my panic. "Just stop!"

Silence falls over the gym, my guys probably thinking I'm having some sort of nervous breakdown.

A cool hand touches my shoulder. "Beau—"

I reflexively swing my fist up to fight without thinking, my body still reacting to my frayed nerves.

My hand collides into something soft and most definitely not the hard muscles I'm used to, and a thud sounds out beside me a second before Diego releases the strangest noise I've ever heard.

"Fuck," Kingston says.

I snap my eyes open and catch sight of Diego on his side, clutching his groin, his face redder than I thought possible.

"What happened?" I ask, pushing up to crawl to him, my fear turning into confusion. "Why'd you let me hit you like that?"

"Pretty sure Diego didn't just let you punch him in the nuts," Kingston says. "But nice aim. That's one way to take down one of us."

"Take down?" I hover my hands over Diego still trying to catch his breath. "I wasn't trying. I was—I was scared as hell."

"Scared of what exactly?" Kingston asks, coming up beside me.

"I..." I don't want to say it. My guys will feel terrible if I admit that what was supposed to be a fun game of chase turned into me freaking out and junk punching Diego.

"Us," Austin says quietly, squatting down next to me to touch my back. "I'm sorry, Jewel. I missed the signs."

"The signs?"

"Your fear cues. It's in your human nature to be scared of us, especially if you feel like we're hunting you. It's just that it's been weeks since you showed them toward me. I mistook them for something else."

"But I'm not afraid of you," I say.

"You sometimes can't help your instincts, beautiful." Diego groans, sitting up. "Which, while shit that hurt, is probably a good thing. I know you can fight if it comes down to it."

Shifting on my knees, I hug him. "I'm sorry. Is there anything I can do for you?" I frown the second the words leave my mouth.

Kingston growls deep in his throat. "You better not say what I think you're going to say, bro."

Jetting out his leg, Diego kicks Kingston's feet out from under him. Austin remains silent beside me, and I reach up and hold his hand, knowing that even though my reaction wasn't actually directed at him, he still feels guilty about it.

"Only you would suggest something like that, asshole," Diego says.

"Well, I *am* her perfect body match."

"By one percent," Diego and I say in unison.

Diego howls a laugh and raises his hand up to me to high

five. I automatically slap my hand to his like we always do af-ter a practice fight, and as always, he laces his fingers around mine and pulls me on top of him. I plant my hands on each side of his face to peer into his steel gray eyes.

"Are you sure you're okay?" I ask, pursing my lips.

"I don't know. Let me see." He leans up and hovers his mouth an inch away from mine, and I smirk and kiss him, knowing it's what he's waiting for.

Pulling away slightly, I raise an eyebrow in question. "Well?"

"Hmm," he murmurs. "Pretty sure I'm good."

"Let me double check." I swivel on Diego's lap, feeling the extent of him through his workout pants. I try to keep my face expressionless as he watches me, but I'm positive my flaming cheeks give me away. Licking my lips, I ease away from him. "You're most definitely good."

Kingston groans obnoxiously loud, spinning on his heels and covering his ears like he can't handle anything else that doesn't involve him. I'm pretty sure he sputters more than his usual swear words, but I don't understand what they exactly mean.

"I know Kingston's good," I say to Diego. "Doesn't look like he needs a single cuddle."

Diego catapults to his feet, taking me with him. He sets me down and nudges me toward Austin, who quietly stares at the mat.

I offer my hand out to him, studying his unreadable expression, and he lets me pretend I'm strong enough to pull him to his feet. Wrapping my arms around him, I snuggle against him for a moment, breathing in the fresh scent of his T-shirt, listening to the sound of his heart.

"What about you, Austin?" I ask, pressing my fingers into his cheek. "Are you okay?"

"Only if you are, Jewel," he says, offering me a whisper of a smile.

I kiss him. "Of course I'm okay. Haven't I ever told you that your hugs make everything better?"

He lifts me up so I can wrap my legs around him too. "I can think of a dozen more things that'll make you feel better."

"I think Jewel's fine," Kingston says. "We're trying to toughen her up, not coddle her."

I ignore his remark and kiss Austin again. "What did you have in mind?"

Austin starts walking away. "Dinner, a swim, some time away from Kingston? Maybe something sweet like you?"

"I'd like that."

Diego clears his throat. "And you can have all that, beautiful, but first, you and Austin have to get through me."

I frown. "What?"

Kingston crosses his arms. "Me too, babe. You obviously need a better incentive to get you to fight."

"Austin," I say.

"Don't you give in, bro. You know she needs this," Kingston says.

Austin sets me on my feet, glaring at his brothers. "We can do this."

"Are you kidding me? There are two of them and one of you. Unfair advantage."

Taking my hand, Austin smiles at me. "Actually no. I have the upper hand. I have you."

Kingston growls. "Not for long."

Diego smiles and rubs his hands together. "Brace yourself, beautiful."

"Oh, jeez. Guys, I can't do this," I say, stepping behind Austin.

"Try for me," Austin says. "I really want the rest of my night with only you."

I swallow, fear igniting inside me. "But I'm scared."

"Use it like before," Diego says. "And remember what I said about strategy."

Kingston grumbles, positioning himself to try to grab me. "Don't help them. You're on my team, Diego. And I don't know about you, but after the visual those two burned in my brain in Midnight Valley—"

"I don't remember a thing. I have too many of my own good memories," Diego says, smirking at me.

Squeezing my hand, Austin draws my attention to him. "Don't let him get in your head. We're getting the rest of our night. Now, get ready, Jewel. On the count of three, we'll start."

Diego cracks his neck and rolls his shoulders, holding his

hands up just waiting for the chance to stop me from leaving with Austin. "One."

Kingston inches closer next. "Two."

Austin gives me a little push. "Three."

I clench my hands. "Fuck. Me."

THE DIVINE FUTURE

I RUB THE TOWEL THROUGH my damp hair, strolling from the bathroom in one of Kingston's shirts. To my surprise, Kingston didn't insist on keeping me company in the tub after Austin dropped me off because he had a few things to take care of for the dumb party in a few hours.

"Jewel!"

I freeze at the sound of my little cousins' voices echoing through the room. Swiveling, I turn and face the projection of them lighting up the wall. Sunshine halos Dana and Fallon in golden light from the window behind them, and Kingston sits cross-legged on the rug.

"Kingston told us all about your night. I can't believe you took Diego down in one punch. He's ginormous," Dana says, bouncing in her seat. From the smirk on Kingston's face, I'm pretty sure he left out the fact that I only did so by accident.

"Did Kingston mention I knocked him off his feet too?" I ask, sticking my tongue out at my body match. Granted, Austin might have shoved him first, but I guessed right where he would land and stuck my leg out while he was too busy dodging his brother. Still, it assured that Austin and I got the rest of our night alone.

"Oh, my gosh! Really?" Their eyes widen, and Fallon claps in excitement at my revelation. My cousins grew up only hearing horror stories and how impossible it was to try to fight a vampire. That makes me extra badass in their eyes, though we all know my guys would be the last to ever hurt me on purpose.

Kingston motions me to come to him, and I nestle myself in his lap, leaning against his chest. "Only because I let her," he says, kissing my cheek.

"Yeah, sure," Dana says. "That's what Ms. Patty said all the boys say when they're bested by girls."

Kingston chuckles. "Damn, you caught me. But she used my love for her against me."

I pat his cheek. "All's fair, dude."

"I'm sure she'll never let me forget," he says.

Dana and Fallon laugh, looking happier than when I last saw them. According to the timer in the corner of the projection screen, Kingston's been talking to them for over forty minutes. Just knowing that he passed on a bath with me for work only to have put his work off to entertain my cousins makes my stomach all sorts of fluttery. He could've ignored their call and didn't.

"You know you could've told them I'd call them back," I whisper to Kingston too softly for my cousins to hear as they catch me up on their day.

"I know, but they're having a hard time adjusting, and I do want them to like me," he murmurs.

I smile and meet his dark eyes. "They do."

A knock sounds on my cousins' side of the line, and Fallon disappears only to return with Dougie. The little guy curls his fingers in Dana's hair and grins a toothy smile the second his attention draws to the screen.

"Hey, Dougie," I say. "How's your mama?"

"Mama," he repeats, stretching his arms away from the screen.

"I'm doing well, Jewel," Mrs. Diggs says, stepping behind my cousins. "Just stopping by to check on the girls. I hope everything's well for you all."

"It's been interesting. Busy," I say without giving too much detail. "Hey, have you talked to..." I can't even get the words out of my mouth. I might choose not to talk to Brayla, but Mrs. Diggs does, not knowing that she's responsible for this mess.

She has no idea that Brayla accepted Orlando's Blood Vow or that she was the one who killed my dad. I let Diego make sure my cousins didn't remember the incident that was brought to the board's attention when Orlando came to collect the Jordan blood debt. It's up to Brayla to announce her Blood Vow to her family, and she hasn't. I wish I knew why. I wish I didn't have to pretend.

"Ramona's fine, dear. Brayla promised me she would watch out for her," Mrs. Diggs says, knowing what was on my mind. Even though I know Orlando must declare her health status and prove he has not been accepting her blood too soon, I don't trust the board to assure it. I like my information to come from someone who actually talks to Brayla.

Kingston's tablet beeps from the floor next to us, and he scoops it up to click on the screen. "Wish we could talk longer, but Jewel and I have a last minute party to arrange. Can we call you all later?"

Dana and Fallon pout, but Mrs. Diggs wraps an arm over each of their shoulders. "Oh, how interesting. Brayla mentioned Orlando taking her to a party. Do you think...?"

Kingston and I look at each other. The whole situation leaves me on edge. Why would either of them come to a Divine party? Orlando isn't on the board. I don't even think he's from this area.

"I'm not sure. I've been so busy that I haven't had time to talk to her lately." Or at all. On purpose. But Mrs. Diggs doesn't know that. She won't mention it in front of my guys either. All she truly knows is what Brayla tells her, which is probably that my guys don't allow it. No human would call out a vampire like that though.

"It was arranged by Mitchell. I'll let you know if she shows up," I add, forcing myself to smile.

Shit balls, I seriously hope not. Even though I miss Brayla. Terribly. I miss her as a human. I still can't process everything that happened and having her show up would only make things worse. I'm supposed to somehow prove my compatibility to my guys. It should be easy, but I'm nervous as all get-out.

No matter how much anyone says that we'll be okay, I know if it came down to jeopardizing alliances or saving me, Mitchell might not see the worth of allowing my guys to protect me. The practice fighting doesn't help my fears. I'm afraid they're trying to prepare me in case I'm thrown to the shadows. I am a human after all.

"It would be so nice for you to see each other again. I know she misses you," Mrs. Diggs says, drawing me from the storm of panic brewing inside me.

Kingston hugs me tighter, in tune to my body trying to betray me to Mrs. Diggs. "Jewel misses her too," he says for me. "Vampire politics just makes things...difficult." That's one way to excuse why I'm ignoring Brayla.

She nods, buying it. "I'm sure."

Silence draws between us, and I gnaw my lip, running it back and forth between my teeth. Dana and Fallon study me, knowing me as good as Ramona always did, but neither of them says anything. They wouldn't even know what to say. A shadow of the feeling about everything that happened with

Ramona lingers inside them, even if they don't know why the thought of her would make them nervous.

"Well, I'll let you two go. Tell your brothers I said hello," Mrs. Diggs says to Kingston. "And Jewel, you take care of yourself. We love you. Maybe you can visit soon."

"Maybe," I say weakly.

The second the line disconnects, Kingston flips me onto his shoulder and hops up and spins us, making me screech. "I swear, babe. Don't you even think about it. No tears. It is my sole mission to make sure you don't stop smiling. I will not let you kill my boner today."

I laugh. "Such a romantic."

"You know it," he says, turning his head to offer me his best, cockiest smile.

He's lucky his quick distraction worked. Because he was totally right. I could feel the tears starting to burn the backs of my eyes.

"And thanks for the whole entertaining my cousins thing. It really does mean a lot to me. I know they weren't exactly part of the deal but—"

"They're family."

I grin and practically attack the side of his face and neck with my lips, showering him with so many kisses that he laughs. He cranes his head in an attempt to meet my mouth, but I purposely kiss everywhere else I can instead. Releasing a playful growl, he spins me again. Dizziness throws off my aim, and he sneaks a kiss to my mouth, and I laugh into his lips.

Kingston sets me on my feet only to engulf me in his arms. His deliciously sweet yet spicy scent stirs something inside me, reminding me of how his blood tastes apart from his brothers. It's a strange thing to think about, because we've never even had an intimate blood sharing moment, but I can't stop the weird ass fantasy from consuming me.

Luckily for Kingston, his tablet chimes, stopping me from asking to bite him. I'll tease him about it forever after what Austin said.

"Babe," Kingston says, groaning. "Come play lapsies with me for a bit. I have one more thing I need to take care of for tonight."

Reaching down, I graze my hand along the waistband of his pajama pants. "You sure you will get anything done?"

He smirks. "Probably not, but who cares? It's only finalizing and approving the guest list for security clearance. I don't care if the guards let anyone in or not."

"Wait, you have the guest list? That means you could—"

"Orlando would have to own property in one of the neighboring territories. He doesn't. He has no known address."

"Are you sure? Mrs. Diggs said—"

"I'll prove it." Kingston guides me to his office and sits down to mess with his computer. "I know it doesn't seem like it to you because we've kind of isolated ourselves the last few weeks, but vampires love to party."

"You mean sit around and drink blood, pretending that

you all like each other?" I ask, resting my hands on his shoulders. "The Boxes had better parties than that."

"Might be better if we did pretend. Just because we're allies doesn't mean we like each other."

"Like with the Vaduvas?" I ask. "Though you had to like them a little to—"

"Fuck," Kingston says, leaning on his elbow.

"You knew I'd ask about it, Kingston."

Kingston reaches up and rests his hand on mine. "I know, babe, but that's not why I'm swearing. Look." He points to the screen.

"You're shitting me," I say, looking over Kingston's shoulder at the guest list on his computer.

The name Orlando Ortega lights up from the list under Kingston's finger. My knees shake, wondering how he ended up on the guest list. This had to be Mitchell's doing. Or Viorica's. The Donor Life Corp board knows that my family has a blood debt to Orlando and the shit he pulled with trying to declare a breach of my contract to encourage the board to release Ramona early to him.

"But you said...oh, fuck. Kingston, this can't be happening. Uninvite him. Deny him access. Set a damn trap. Tear him apart. Something. I won't survive otherwise."

"I want to kill this guy almost more than anything, but we don't know exactly who we're dealing with. And we won't know unless we let him play his little games. That's how we strategize against someone of his obvious power."

"I don't like this," I say. "I know you guys think Orlando's a Blood Rebel and that he's targeting you, but it sure as hell feels like he's targeting me. I just wish I knew why."

"Because you're fucking amazing, babe. The best. Have I mentioned delicious?"

I can't stop my mouth from smiling.

"And now I just want to toss this computer and devour you."

"After you finish your work." I slide one of my hands into his shirt and hold him in place. "Now, tell me how Orlando managed to get an invite here," I say, twirling my finger to get him to look around. "Was it Mitchell? Viorica?"

Kingston swivels back and forth in the chair. "Always with the questions. You know they can wait or I can have Diego and Austin handle this."

I release him and place my hands on my hips. "Kingston."

Sighing, he relents and taps the screen a few times, bringing up a map. "So, it wasn't an invite extended by the board, which is good news for us. They'll be on edge about his arrival as well. Less scrutiny on you."

"So then how?"

He grumbles, tapping the screen some more. "It looks like he inherited part of the Duchanne Region."

"You mean stole it." Of-friggin'-course. Katherine Duchanne was Orlando's lover, or whatever, after all until she betrayed him by coming after me.

"No, it was definitely a gift. The Duchannes could never even give the Ombre Noire country community away, and I'm nearly certain Roger Caruthers was the only one left there."

I shiver at Master Caruthers' name. "What's wrong with the place?"

"It remains at the bottom of a canyon, shaded next to a cliff for the majority of the day," Kingston says, tipping his head up to look at me.

I try to remain expressionless, though just talking about all of these vampires reminds me of their unwarranted vendettas against me, and it ruins my mood even more. "Sounds like vampire heaven."

Kingston frowns, his muscles flexing on his arm. He continues to mess with the computer at a speed I can't really follow. I know he's rushing to finish his work so that he can give me his attention. "That's what everyone first thought until the human population was decimated and the local blood source tapped out. Was a bad investment considering those who lived there had to import gen. pop. blood from other regions."

Now my grimace matches his. My guys make it easy to forget that other vampires consider me a food source regardless of my Blood Match—of our Blood Vows, even. "No wonder Roger was determined to match me out from you."

Kingston clicks off his tablet. "Yeah, the only way he could even get a human staff was to include a no-bite clause."

"So why do you have one here?" I ask.

He snaps his teeth at me, trying to lighten the mood. "Who says we do?"

I roll my eyes, knowing he's joking. They have a no-bite policy to keep the guests from attacking the staff. The same goes for those who work for Donor Life Corp.

"The fact that I overheard you arranging something that sounded a lot like a catering service for blood donors—which, I must say, so not cool, dude—proves it."

Hopping up from his chair, he spins me off my feet and plops me on his desk, knocking over a few trinkets in the process. He leans in and hugs me, resting his head on my shoulder. "I think I'm just going to run away with you. Please, let me."

I pull back to meet his eyes. "Kingston."

His dark eyes hold mine, all hints of his usual playfulness gone. "I'll convince Diego and Austin. I just—I'm afraid."

"About what? I am your perfect match. Diego and Austin's too."

"Not that. That's the one thing I'm certain of. What I worry about is that if you have to go through with this party, you'll change your mind."

Confusion furrows my brows. Worrying about my safety is one thing, but why would he worry about me changing my mind? "Change my mind? If you think for one second I'd ever consider Viorica's offer—"

"I meant about us. About our vows. I can protect that hot little body of yours tonight, but I can't protect your fragile heart from our way of life. And if Orlando shows up, Brayla will too, Jewel. How can I save you from that if we don't run away?"

I study Kingston's dark eyes, now more serious than I've seen them in a long time. I tug him between my legs to hug him, not allowing any space between us, and then I respond to his question with a kiss.

He reacts, combing his fingers through my hair, sliding his tongue over mine in a way that sends my whole body yearning for him. The last few weeks have been all over the place between us as I process and deal with the sudden changes that keep happening in my life, and it's starving us both of the deep-seated need that comes with our body match. With our vows. With the progression of our relationship together.

"I've fucking missed you, babe," he whispers, picking me up so that I wrap my legs around him. "I mean it. I ache without you in my arms all the time, and these last few weeks have been brutal. I thought everything that happened might have ruined it between us...especially the Vaduvas."

I rest my head on his shoulder, letting him carry me across the room to the bed. "Ruined it?"

Snuggling his face in the crook of my neck, he whispers, "Your desire to be with me. I know I sometimes play games with you, and I'm sorry. I just fucking love your attention."

"Kingston," I say, leaning back to meet his gaze again.

He doesn't stop talking and says, "My brothers were obviously right about the one percent not really making a difference. And now that you and Austin have—"

Slapping my hand over his mouth, I silence his words. "Dude."

He licks my palm, getting me to jerk my hand away.

"Yeah, I'm jealous as hell, and I know I can't ask you about it—not that I want to. The visual was enough—but—"

"I haven't slept with Austin yet, but you have to be okay if I ever do. Diego too. I love all of you in my own way."

Reaching up, he brushes the loose strands of hair behind my ear. "Jewel, it's fine. I know—"

This time I kiss him to shut him the hell up because I know there is no friggin' way he'll try to talk with my mouth against his. "No more talking," I murmur through breaths, nearly gasping. "I don't...want to think...about Austin right now...or the Vaduvas and Orlando."

His fingers hook to the hem of my shirt, and he pulls it off. Breaking away from my mouth, he works his lips over my throat. "Mmmhmm."

"I don't even want...to think about the party later." My words extend with a loud ass moan, my whole body awakening to the desire Kingston elicits from me.

He chuckles against my skin, working his fingers down my stomach to tease along my waist without going any further. "Mmm."

"All I want is to be with you right now. Because I've missed you."

Kingston brings his mouth back to mine, and I suck in

his lip, grazing my teeth over it. My hands blindly map down his chest as he doesn't let me pull back to see what I'm doing, insisting on kissing me so long that I huff for breath. I finally manage to grab the hem of his shirt and pull it off him.

He grinds his pelvis between my legs through our clothes, and I link my fingers around his neck and my legs tighter around him. Flush warms my body, and I rock harder, my excitement building, my body arching and begging with another breath to move past the clothes already.

"Jewel, can I continue?" he asks softly, my name so sexy on his lips.

Reaching down, I answer him by sliding my hand into his pants between us. He moans, the click of his fangs extending sounding in my ear. He grazes them against my shoulder through kisses, enjoying every second of the attention I show him.

I rush to finish undressing him, my whole body humming with energy and lust like I've consumed his blood even though I haven't. It's just our closeness and how hot and excited he makes me that ignites everything unexplainable and new inside me. Anticipation cascades over me as Kingston whispers my name again, our hearts crashing together through our ribcages in an attempt to be together.

He takes his time undressing me completely, running his fingers over my breasts, appreciating the view of my body as I wait beneath him. Bending down, he locks his lips with mine again, caressing his tongue over mine while lying on top of me to feel my warm skin against his.

Taking initiative, I draw my hands lower, wrapping my fingers around him to adjust his body to mine. His fingers join mine and rub between my legs as I explore his body, desperate to satisfy the burning need lighting his eyes.

He smiles at me, studying my face as I squirm, shifting under the sensations he creates with not only his hand. I release a breathless moan and reach up to slide my hands around his back to dig my fingers into his taut muscles.

And then he gives in to my body begging to feel him completely, both our desires hot and desperate, exceeding our constant flirting and teasing. Kingston sinks into me, bringing his hand around to cup my butt to pull me close.

Gasping, I grip onto his shoulders and lose myself to the good pressure and electrifying sensations that explode through me in wave after delicious wave. Our breaths mingle through kisses, Kingston's love for me a constant whisper against my lips. Blush heats my body to warm him in a way that leaves him panting.

He hugs me close, careful and gentle, grazing his teeth along my neck without biting. I cling onto him and let him enjoy my body like I enjoy his—our match and connection undeniable. We move in perfect sync, my hands running down to explore Kingston's muscles. He meets my gaze, watching me with an intensity that I want to drown myself in. My whole body tingles under his touch and his soft kisses as he brings me to the point of release before him, knowing exactly what I like because my mouth can't hold anything back.

Kingston stifles his own moan by molding his lips to mine until we both slow down and lay together, just soaking in the love we share. The love that reminds me how perfect he is for me. How perfect our bodies and souls are for each other.

"Pack your bag, babe," he says, pressing into me, not even caring about the sweat glistening over my skin.

"We're not running away," I say, cupping his face to kiss him again, my heart still ramming into his as it tries to remain as close as possible.

Propping up on his elbow, he shifts his weight off me to look into my eyes. "I'm nearly certain Diego and Austin will be on board when they find out about Orlando."

"Kingston," I say, twisting my lips.

He groans.

I cover his mouth. "Less talking."

"Less talking," he repeats.

I hide my face in his neck. "More cuddling."

"Definitely more cuddling."

"And no more worrying," I say against his skin. "Because we're together. And you are strong as hell. Powerful."

"You forgot sexy."

I laugh. "Damn straight. I can't keep my hands off of you."

"I never want you to."

"My perfect body match," I say, trailing my hands down to squeeze his butt.

He moans again, devouring my mouth with another hot kiss. "We'll show them."

I tip my head back and scrunch my nose. "Not like this."

He chuckles. "Definitely not like this. But there will be no denying it. You're the Divine future, my future, Jewel."

"And you're mine."

HONEST

"PLEASE, HOLD STILL, MS. DIVINE." A woman, who introduced herself as Blair, aims a shiny metal contraption at my eyeball. "I don't want to pinch you."

I lean away, hitting my back on my vanity table. "Pretty sure that's what that torture device does."

Sighing, she sets it down and grabs a silver tube of mascara. "Will you at least let me apply mascara?"

I shrug. "You won't poke my eye, right?"

"If you hold still."

Except that seems physically impossible at the moment. My feet won't stop bouncing, and any time I'm not twisting my robe between my hands, my fingers tremble. Nerves flutter my stomach so much that I couldn't even take more than the one bite of the cherry-topped crepes Austin brought for me.

"Skip the makeup, Blair," Kingston says from the bed.

I twist and glare at him. "No, I want the makeup."

"Why?"

"You won't understand."

Pulling the blankets with him, Kingston crosses the room, giving both me and Blair a view of his chiseled abs. Blair trains her eyes on her makeup kit, keeping her head bowed. Neither Kingston nor I had expected the woman to knock on the door just after sunset, but Diego arranged for her arrival to give me some extra pampering for the party.

"Try me," Kingston says, pulling up his office chair to sit beside me.

I sigh. I'm not exactly in the mood to explain to Kingston that being in a room full of friggin' attractive vampires hits hard on my self-esteem. I know it shouldn't, but it does. Knowing that both Kingston and Diego slept with the Vaduva sisters doesn't help in the matter.

"Really, Kingston. It's nothing. I just want to look nice," I finally say, straightening my shoulders. I motion to Blair to continue, and she silently swipes mascara over my eyelashes.

"You're fucking stunning. There's no way you'd never not look nice, babe," Kingston says. "You don't have to do anything more to yourself for me. I'd bone you no matter what."

"Kingston," I hiss, swatting his leg.

"What?"

A knock sounds on the door, and I hear both Austin and Diego in the hall.

"Go away," Kingston says before I even have a chance to respond. "We're naked."

I playfully smack his leg again. "Stop it. And don't you dare drop the blanket in front of Blair. You're for my eyes only. Got it?"

He chuckles. "And they say I'm possessive."

"I'm trying to save Blair from being scarred." I meet the woman's eyes, and she darts her gaze back to her makeup kit. "And you guys can come in. Hopefully with news that the party was canceled."

The door swings open and Diego strolls in first, wearing a gray tuxedo that matches his eyes. The slim fit accentuates all his delicious muscles, sending my heart racing at the sight of him.

"Really, babe? I'm sitting here, giving you the best view of my body as I possibly can, and you're drooling over fully dressed Diego?" Kingston asks.

"One percent, bro," Diego says.

I bite my lip between my teeth and ignore both their quips. "You look friggin' hot."

Austin comes in behind Diego, carrying a dress bag in his hands. He lays it across the unmade bed and smiles at me. I give him a slow once-over with a grin stretching across my face. He combed and styled his usually messy hair back, his eyes popping in color with the emerald green of his tie. God, he looks sexy as hell too.

Kingston runs his finger over my bottom lip, pretending to wipe drool from the corner of my mouth. "This is worse than when you sleep. They're not even naked."

I stick my tongue out at him.

"Maybe you desensitized Jewel to your body already," Austin says, smirking at me.

Kingston groans. "After last—"

I whack him again, making him chuckle.

"Let's just say, I highly doubt it." Leaning over, he waits for Blair to apply my lipstick and then kisses me, immediately smearing the bold plum color. He glances at the woman. "No lipstick."

"Kingston."

Blair sets down her makeup brush.

"Look in the mirror, babe. Lipstick won't stop any of us from kissing you," he says, grinning, the plum color smudged on his lips.

I wipe the back of my hand across my mouth. "Fine. No lipstick."

He slides his hand up my bare leg and under my robe to squeeze my thigh. "Still think you should forgo anything else. You're ravishing. I'm already concerned you'll be too...delectable. Right, guys? Tell her that she doesn't need to do this for us." Kingston looks to his brothers for their agreement.

Diego shifts his eyes to me. "She isn't doing it for us.

Right, beautiful?"

I tighten my jaw at Kingston's dramatic reaction of wide eyes and flared nostrils, fake horror crossing his face and only nod my confirmation to Diego.

"You are not seriously trying to make yourself even more attractive for people who would love nothing more than to eat you, and not in the good way that I want to." Kingston runs his fingers between my legs, smiling as I trap his hand before he can attempt to do anything. He flashes his fangs at my reaction. "Which I think you might like if you ever let me try again."

I catch sight of Austin's reflection in the mirror, and we lock gazes. Rose-colored blush blooms up my neck at our memory together, brought on by Kingston's remark. Austin picks now out of any other damn moment to break his usually stoic expression to smirk at me.

And Kingston notices the look I share with Austin. Diego does too. They look at each other and then to me and Austin, and I sink lower into my chair under all the intensity and various expressions crossing all three of their faces.

"Damn," Diego murmurs. "Lucky bastard."

"Fucking A," Kingston says, brushing his hand through his hair. "You let him but not me?"

"Kingston," Diego and Austin say in unison.

He releases a low growl. "I'm not going to ask her for details."

I groan and turn to Blair, sitting quietly with her hands in her lap. "You're excused, Blair."

The four of us watch her gather her makeup kit and shuffle across the room with her head bowed. Austin opens the door for her and then closes it. He and Diego meander closer despite the fact that Kingston glowers at them.

"This is my night, and I want to have a private conversation with our girl. Out," he tells them.

"No, stay," I say, pressing my lips together. "You should really get ready, Kingston. This can wait."

He leans back and crosses his arms. "I'll be distracted all night."

I release a long breath of air, blowing strands of loose hair out of my face. "Fine, but they stay. Obviously pretending to have privacy makes things more intense between the three of you, and I want to be honest. It's better than having you all hold things in to just burst out at random. Especially you, Kingston."

"Babe."

I reach out and take his hand. "Kingston, dude. I love you. I do."

"But?"

"But nothing. I just wanted you to hear it. Now, for your question."

"Why him and not me?" Kingston repeats. "I know he's your nutrients match and all—"

Diego punches Kingston so hard that the chair flips out from under him, sending him crashing to the floor. He's up in a flash, charging Diego to shove him into the closest wall. It takes Austin stepping between them to get them to stop.

"This is why we agreed to the rules in the first place," Austin says, holding his hands up.

"I'm aware of that, Austin," Diego says. "But I'm not going to stand back and listen to him make remarks like that to her. He's embarrassing her. He should know better by now."

"It was a simple question," Kingston mutters. "Kill me for wanting to know if I'm doing something wrong. It's called an open and honest relationship."

Austin balls his hands into fists. "You mean one where you're so insecure that you play games for our girl's attention. If you were confident in your supposed hundred percent body match, you wouldn't need to ask her about what we do in private or why. It's our business."

Holy shit balls. Sweat beads on my forehead at the unexpected direction this conversation took. "Guys, please."

Kingston growls, not hearing my plea. "Supposed? What are you implying?"

"Stop it," I say louder.

"I don't know. Should I be implying that maybe—"

"Enough!" I scream, jumping to my feet. "You guys promised me that my relationship with each of you wouldn't get between you."

"Babe, he—"

"No, Kingston. You guys are going to stop talking and start listening to me. Now get some clothes on," I say. I turn to Diego and Austin. "And you two come sit down with me."

The three of them shut up and listen to my instructions to my relief, moving to get comfortable on the bed with me. It's the only place in Kingston's room where I can be close enough to all of them.

I sit in silence, twisting my fingers together to figure out exactly what to say. Because I don't like this fighting. It's one thing to tease each other and get mad or jealous but to start questioning my Blood Match or relationship? I'll never survive this party if we're not all on the same page again.

Austin quietly hands me a glass of water from the night table, and I take a sip, clearing my throat. I wait a few minutes until their anger melts into worry, clearly displayed across each of their faces.

"Kingston," I start, turning my attention to him first. His dark eyes meet mine, all narrow under his pinched brow, clearly upset over the fight with his brothers. "You are my body match. There is no denying our attraction, but I also can't deny the attraction I have for Diego and Austin."

I expect him to make a quip at them, but all he does is nod.

I turn to Diego next. "And Diego, there's no denying that you're my personality match. You went through the trouble of bringing in someone to try to help with my insecurity over not being as pretty as the Vaduvas even though I know you think I am. But you did it for me, and I appreciate it."

"Wait, the makeup shit was about the Vaduvas?" Kingston asks, leaning forward. "They're not even attractive—"

"Nice try. You slept with like all of them, so obviously you think they're attractive. But that's beside the point. The makeup was about me. Not you. Not them. Me." I shift my attention back to Diego. "And you recognized that, Diego. But I also need you to recognize that I can handle Kingston and his lack of filter. I know both you and Austin like to keep him in check, but you both need to know that he is my body match, and I can't have you guys questioning it."

"I'm sorry, Jewel," Diego and Austin say in unison. Diego adds, "You're right. He obviously won't let anyone deny it. I just wish he wouldn't rub it in all the time."

I grab his hand. "You should also know that I think your body is also a great match for mine."

"She's partially right. You can handle her crazy ass zombie bite," Kingston says.

Tensing, I wait for Diego to knock Kingston off his bed, but the two of them laugh. Austin links his fingers through my free hand, knowing I'm inwardly groaning. My guys can go back and forth between fighting and joking like flipping me over their shoulders that my head spins.

Diego surprises me by trying to make my savagery sound appealing to Kingston. I knew my guys sometimes talked about me and gave advice to each other, and they used to do it a lot through the whispers I used not to hear, but this is new level stuff. I mean, I'm sitting right here.

"I'd let you bite me if you wanted to," Austin whispers,

drawing my attention to him.

I blush, the thought exciting me more than it should. "You are friggin' mouth-watering on all sorts of unexpected levels."

His cheeks redden deeper than mine, though he smiles and squeezes my fingers. "Kingston was right about our nutrients match. No denying it. Everything about you is incredibly lickable."

My body hums as I automatically inch closer to him. Smirking at my reaction, he dares to run his fingers across my bare leg in a tease that makes my body freeze in anticipation. I release a strangled, high-pitched, most definitely not-at-all attractive cross between a snort and a giggle and possibly a gasp at his forwardness, his words the last thing I expected him to say to me right now. And I love it. He's getting bolder.

"Shit, Austin," I whisper, my voice breathless.

He smiles again.

"Fuck," both Diego and Kingston say, looking between us. They obviously heard most of our conversation. I hadn't realized they had stopped joking around.

"That's it. Both of you out. I want my private conversation with our girl," Kingston adds. "We still have an hour until people start showing up. Another hour after before we have to make our formal appearances."

"Which means only two hours to make sure Jewel is completely ready," Diego says. "Have you even gone over what she should expect? The feeding arrangements? Who she should acknowledge and who she shouldn't? The floor plan of the ballroom and the hidden exits? Where the sound alarms are? Who's on her protection detail if something happens?"

Kingston sighs. "No. I've already decided I'm not subjecting our girl to the party. If she's under the scrutiny of basically every vampire, they might try to pull the shit Viorica did. And can you blame them? Look at our girl." He flashes his fangs as he drinks me in, making me feel naked just sitting here, though I'm cozy in my fluffiest robe.

They all look at me, and I squirm under the weight of their stares, sweat prickling over my skin, my body still blushing. Diego smiles and combs his fingers through the strands of my hair now hiding my face. Austin brings my hand to his mouth to kiss the back, and Kingston holds open his arms to me, begging for me to give into them. I let him tug me forward into a hug I hadn't realized I needed.

"Comforting to know you're more concerned with the impossible," I say, wrapping my arms around his neck, burying my face in his open dress shirt. "Makes the awkward reunion seem not so bad."

"Awkward reunion?" Austin asks.

Kingston tenses. "Damn it. No wonder you guys didn't come barging in sooner. I must have forgotten to send you the guest list. There was a new addition."

"Orlando." The second his name leaves my mouth, all the warmth in my body washes away, leaving me shivering in Kingston's arms.

Diego growls and balls his fingers into a fist. "How the hell could you forget something like that?"

Austin reaches out and punches Kingston in the shoulder. "The asshole tried to take our girl."

"How much time have you wasted?" Diego asks.

I'm pretty sure if I wasn't in Kingston's arms, Diego and Austin would start a fight. Kingston realizes this, because he locks his hands tighter around me, using me as a shield. And I let him.

"Calm down," I say to both of them. "I'm the one who asked him to distract me."

"You try remembering even your own name with her legs ar—"

Reaching up, I cover his mouth with my hand. "Don't even go there, Kingston."

"Yeah, don't. I get it. But now we need to strategize," Diego says. He turns his attention to me. "I know you're nervous about tonight, and you don't want to think about it, but we need you to focus, beautiful. I have a feeling someone invited Orlando to trip us up."

"No, he's apparently our new neighbor."

Diego and Austin look at Kingston, who replies, "Ombre Noire."

"Before you start getting worked up with all the last minute stuff, just remember he can't ruin this for us," I murmur. "I won't let him ruin anything else. I won't let him get to me."

"No, *we're* not going to let him get to you," Austin says.

I nod, suppressing the rising panic clenching my chest. Orlando targets my family and friends. He plays with my life. I know my guys think he's a Blood Rebel and out for the Divine name or whatever, trying to use me to get to them. Not many vampires would care what happens to a match's heirs, and my guys don't treat me like most vampires do, so how would Orlando know to involve those I care about? I knew my guys had enemies, but Orlando turned things personal against me for a reason I can't figure out.

Kingston rests his chin on my shoulder. "I still think we should run away, babe."

"I have to agree," Diego says.

"And make Viorica think her suspicions were right," Austin says. "No."

"I think we should leave the decision up to our girl." Diego touches my foot, bringing my attention away from my hands, my body refusing to do anything apart from listening to them as they contemplate what to do. "Beautiful? What do you think? If you say the word, we'll go."

As much as I hate the idea of tonight, I know things could be worse off if I did let them act rashly and take me away. Who knows what the board will do or what Mitchell would do. This is more than about our Blood Matches. This is about my family. About our futures.

"I agree with Austin," I say, rubbing my lips together. "We should stay. We have nothing to hide. We'll show them."

"And Orlando?" Kingston says.

"We'll show him too." I shift and look at him. "Maybe we can use this to our advantage. Send him a warning that we can't be messed with."

"And how do we do that?"

"Brayla. She was my friend."

"Who transitioned into a vampire," Kingston says.

"You're a vampire."

Diego purses his lips. "She's changed."

I suck my bottom lip between my teeth. "Then I'll remind her who she was. She can change again. I changed you, didn't I?" I ask all of them.

Kingston hugs me. "I love when you're right, babe. But I'm arming you in case."

I smirk and pat his cheek. "I'm good."

"Really? You can't take her down the same way you did Diego."

"She won't need to," Austin says.

"That's right," I say, motioning for the three of them to close in and hug me. "Not when I have the three of you."

"But a knife might help," Kingston murmurs into my hair.

I laugh. "Whatever you want. I just know you'll keep me safe."

UNWELCOME GUESTS

"A WHITE DRESS? YOU'RE MAKING me attend a vampire party in a white dress? Is this a joke?" I spin around in front of the full-length mirror, watching the shimmery, embroidered fabric sway with my movements.

"It's tradition," Kingston says. "All those Blood Matched wear white at formal affairs."

"Impractical is what it is," I mutter, holding up the hem. "And these shoes? You're guaranteeing I can't run if I have to."

Jerking my leg out, I kick my heel off and accidentally send it flying at Kingston. He catches it midair and chuckles, throwing it onto the pile with the rest of the shoes I've discarded for hurting my feet in the corner of the wardrobe.

"I guess I was right about you hating every pair of shoes I've picked out for you," he teases, reminding me of our first week together when I thought I wasn't allowed to wear shoes because they were hidden behind a mirror in my closet.

"Just go barefoot. No one cares," Diego calls from the bedroom. "We love taking turns carrying you anyway."

"You are *not* carrying me all night," I say, bending down to look at the racks to see if I can find something else.

Austin knocks on the doorframe, dangling a pair of wedged heels from his fingers that at least don't have spikes to balance on. "How about these?"

I sigh and motion him closer. He helps me put them on, letting me hold onto his shoulders while he buckles them for me. Diego appears in the doorway of the wardrobe next, and the three of them drink me in. I twirl again and lift the dress to check out my shoes in the mirror.

"Hot, babe. You can wear those with this later." Kingston holds up a sheer nightie from the lingerie drawer I have only picked something to wear from a handful of times.

Diego swipes it from his brother and wags his eyebrows at me. "Perfect for our day later."

Kingston growls.

I laugh. "We'll see. If it's between that and this dress, I'll pick that...or nothing."

Austin and Kingston swear, making Diego smile wider.

Strolling between Diego and Kingston, I raise both my arms and glide my fingers across their chests as I pass them by.

The gesture stops them from glaring at each other over the nightie that Diego folds and pockets in his tuxedo jacket. Austin smirks at me, rubbing his lips together, and I offer him my hand to pull him along with me. While it's technically Kingston's night, they're all my dates.

Kingston and Diego zip around us to take their spots on the edge of the bed. They take turns filling a glass with their blood before handing it to Austin to complete. The three of them watch me gulp it in silence, the intensity of their stares sending tingles through me. Heat blooms from my lips to travel down my throat in a familiar wave.

I lick my lips and smile. "I guess I'm ready when you are."

"Good. Your bag is all packed," Kingston says, motioning to a suitcase.

I roll my eyes. "Nice try."

"Last chance, beautiful," Diego says.

"It's probably better if I escort you, Jewel." Austin takes the glass from me. "You might never make it to the ballroom with these two."

"Yeah, because I'd stop at least a dozen times on the way to distract her," Kingston quips.

Diego smiles at me. "I do have your favorite movie waiting in our room."

I tap my finger on my chin. "That does sound like a good alternative."

One second I'm holding Austin's hand, and in the next,

I'm curled in Diego's arms as he swings open Kingston's door. Both Austin and Kingston block our way, making me laugh. Diego jerks one direction, attempting to dodge around them. My laughter echoes through the air, my nerves not so bad when they're playing around like this.

"Okay, okay. Put me down." I pat Diego's cheek. Brushing my lips to his, I whisper, "Please."

He groans and deepens our kiss. "Don't want to."

"Don't worry. I promise we can continue this later."

Diego reluctantly sets me on my feet. "We'll leave early."

I poke his bottom lip. "Good. Because I've missed my alone time with you."

Linking my fingers with Diego and Kingston's, I stroll between them with Austin right behind me, sandwiching me within their muscular bodies just the way I like because it makes me feel safest.

Both vampire and human staff rush through the hallway, greeting us with short bows. Voices hum through the air in the hushed tones of vampires that seem to always test my acting skills since I'm not supposed to hear them unless they want me to.

I've never seen the Divinity Estate so alive, the main house open to guests for the first time in weeks. Blurred forms stop along the hallway, and I catch sight of a few unfamiliar vampires taking notice of me between my guys. It takes everything in me not to bow my head and look at the floor. Their curious gazes send my nerves thrashing inside me. If Diego and Kingston didn't tug me along, I might have frozen in fear at the unwanted attention.

"Babe, try to relax. You're sweating more than when—"

I step on Kingston's foot. "You try to relax when you're put under the scrutiny of a bunch of people who want you dead."

Diego tightens his fingers through mine, trying to squeeze the trembles away. "Dead? No one wants you dead, beautiful. To taste you, maybe."

"Diego, Austin. Cover us a moment," Kingston says.

Kingston surprises me by spinning me from Diego to press my back to the cool wall, caging me in with his arms. His midnight dark eyes capture my gaze but not in the intrusive way a vampire does to break in and manipulate a human's mind. Closing the space, he caresses his lips to mine, kissing me softly until my body starts to relax.

"I think we fucked up," Kingston says, half-talking to his brothers while still focusing on me. "She's too nervous."

I swallow, licking my lips. "I'm trying not to be. I just don't want to mess up or give anyone a reason to doubt us."

"You won't, and I don't want you to worry about anyone else anymore. This is supposed to be a party, and your introduction as a future Divine," he says. "Let's try to have fun."

"Fun?" My voice squeaks at the word.

He nods and kisses me again. "Yeah." Looking over his shoulder, he glances at Diego and Austin shielding us from curious onlookers. "You guys agree?"

"Agree," Diego says, meeting my gaze.

"Are you sure you want to show our girl what it's really like to be a Divine?" Austin asks, his voice deepening with the words. "You don't think—"

"Tell him, babe," Kingston says, cutting him off.

He eases away and nudges me toward Austin, who gathers me in his arms. Austin cuddles me close for a moment. "I just worry you might—"

"Change my mind?" I ask.

He nods. "How'd you know?"

"That's what I was afraid of too," Kingston says.

Diego slings his arms around me and Austin, reaching out to motion Kingston to move in. "Our girl would never. That's the one thing I'm certain about."

I smile. "He's right. You, you, and you plus me. Always."

Kingston releases a long breath. "Now if you'd just tell me why him and not—"

Austin shoves him and laughs. "Not a chance."

"Babe."

I pull away from Austin and wag my finger at him. "Come on. Let's get this party over with."

Diego slides his arm around my back, pulling me from his brothers. "Yeah, and then you can tell me later. Or just show me."

I laugh and shake my head. "I guess we'll see."

"Holy shit balls," I whisper under my breath for the hundredth time in the last few minutes. I don't know what I was imagining or expecting, but it definitely wasn't this.

"We told you already. They were all well-paid," Diego murmurs, coming up beside me. "And they signed up for the position. Try not to let it freak you out. Mitchell insisted no gen. pop. blood for the occasion."

Kingston slides up on my other side. "And don't worry, babe. You won't catch us biting any of them."

"Yeah, because you'll be expected to bite me," I whisper. "I *am* your Blood Match."

"I don't care what's expected. You don't have to do any-thing you don't want to, beautiful," Diego says.

Kingston squeezes my hand. "Especially climb on one of those tables...unless you want to. In private. For me."

I groan. "Yeah, no. Those look terribly uncomfortable."

"No one complains," Kingston says.

"Maybe if you were the one to lie on it," I say, snapping my teeth at him.

Diego chuckles. "I'd gladly for you."

Austin rests his chin on my shoulder, drawing my atten-tion away from the beaming smile lighting Diego's handsome face. "They're fine, Jewel. We monitor the situation closely. If it makes you feel better, if something does happen, their heirs get auto-admittance to Haven Springs at the expense of the vampire who fails to safely drink from the source."

"Which has never happened," Kingston says.

I stare at the man in a pair of shorts, lying on top of the

narrow, rectangular table easily accessible from both sides. My stomach rolls at the sight of a woman in a deep purple gown chatting with the man, both of them smiling, and then she brings his arm to her lips and bites him. He closes his eyes for a moment as she drinks from him, acting completely unfazed. She doesn't drink long and slides something into the pocket of his shorts. I watch her disappear into the crowd of mingling vampires, some with humans hovering by their sides.

"See," Diego says. "He's fine."

Kingston waves his hand at the man's shorts. "And pretty happy for the bonus."

I roll my eyes. "Looks like it. You know, I've heard about jobs like this in Dark Terrace Ranch. At one of the restaurants on Red Ridge. But the horror stories revolving around that place kept anyone with good sense from even inquiring," I say, recalling the one and only time I went to the hillside with my dad to assist him with fixing a broken door.

"Because that place is full of blood debtors. Nothing like this," Kingston says. "No one apart from us could afford to properly run an establishment like that in the city. Plus, there's a strict quarantine and positions like this require travel."

"Ugh." Just the mention of someone living a life like that under a blood debt freaks me out. It could've been my life—it still could be my life. Or Ramona's.

I gape at another vampire approaching a different man on another table. The two chat just like the woman and the other human had, acting like this is all sorts of normal. But seeing the casual exchange and then watching the vampire bite him like it's no big deal makes me twist away and hide in Austin's arms since he's closest.

"Jewel," he whispers. "You don't have to worry. They really are okay."

I release a breath against his shoulder, letting him run his hands up and down my back to smooth away my tense muscles. Kingston steps behind him and blocks my view of the feeding table. Diego presses into my back, hugging me, and Austin by default, nuzzling his nose into the crook of my neck.

"I can see why you always deny my calls," a familiar voice says from in front of me. "Your boy toys keep you busy twenty-four seven, don't they?"

Mixed emotions crash through me at the sweet tease of Brayla's voice. My heart practically bursts with excitement, though my mind screams to calm the hell down.

"Don't hold it against the Divines, lover. Can you blame them? Surely they always vie for her attention." Orlando's smooth voice kills all the excitement my heart tried to ignite in me.

"Looks like she handles them well enough."

"The Jordans are tough. Resilient," he responds. "Quite delectable. Am I right, Mr. Divines?"

Three deep, terrifying growls rip from my guys, though they keep their voices low as to not draw more attention to us.

Orlando's comment drags my attention to him, and he smiles, his vivid blue eyes attempting to capture mine from over Austin's shoulder. "Relax. My words hold great compliment for your precious Jewel and her heirs. Though maybe you're offended because you don't understand the exquisite taste of your beauty. I happen to notice not a single bite or scar on her."

"That you can see," I snap. Whoa. Where the hell did that come from?

And I hate that my rebel mouth betrayed me, because Orlando's grin widens, creeping me out.

Neither Austin nor Diego moves, but Kingston swivels in place to greet Orlando and Brayla. My heart pounds like crazy against Austin's chest the longer Orlando gazes at me. Brayla smiles, keeping her fangs in check so I can't see the vampire Orlando made her. If I didn't know she brutally murdered my dad, I'd still think she was the same girl from The Boxes, just better taken care of like me.

Brayla steps partially in front of Orlando in the defensive way my guys do for me. "Behave, lover. I don't think Jewel's boy toys take compliments well. They've always been protective since the second I met them." Inching my way, Brayla risks closing a bit of space to peer at me from around Kingston. She wiggles her fingers. "Right, Jewel?"

I don't respond. The words freeze on my tongue. I knew that seeing her in person like this would be tough, but my mind still can't wrap itself around it all.

And then hot anger explodes through me, and I shove myself against Austin, yelling incoherently because all my words try to escape at once. "You killed him!"

There goes my plan to try to use Brayla against Orlando. I can barely stand to look at her, let alone be within reach of her, as our last video call replays in my mind over and over again. How she bit my dad right in front of me, putting the transfer of his blood debt into motion. How Orlando tried to use it against us. How he did use it against my sister and Donor Life Corp allowed it.

"You have a lot of friggin' nerve showing up here tonight," I continue, my anger now directed at Orlando. "How dare you. I'm gonna—"

Diego locks his hands around my waist, yanking me back as Austin stands strong in front of me, though I still manage to push him a few inches. My sudden burst of strength makes both of them sandwich me in place, Diego begging me to take a breath in one ear while Austin pleads with me to remember that I shouldn't be this strong, doing his best to calm me down. Orlando and Kingston both flash their fangs at each other, and sudden silence falls through the dim room.

"Get her out of here before I have security throw you both out," Kingston says, pointing his finger at Brayla. "I will not allow anyone to ruin Jewel's introduction as a soon-to-be true Divine. Understand?"

"Wait. Please, wait. I just have one thing to tell Jewel. Just let me tell her, and we'll leave. It's the only reason I asked to come." Brayla's soft pleas snuff out the burning anger darkening the edges of my vision.

Kingston flashes his fangs again. "I don't give a flying fuck after the shit you pulled."

I blink my eyes, clearing my vision from the threatening tears. "Wait, Kingston."

He spins and faces me. "Babe, she doesn't deserve a moment more of your time. They're not staying. They've proven hostile with their comments alone."

"Jewel, please," Brayla begs, drawing my attention to her. "I know you can't understand now, and what—what I did was unforgivable. But I wasn't myself yet. Orlando gave me too much credit when I didn't deserve any. I just couldn't control myself. I was so angry with the lack of response from you. We promised to be best friends forever. I thought it was the only way to ever talk to you again."

Her words sink in, her pleas reminding me of the girl I grew up with in The Boxes. She's right. We did promise to be best friends forever. But I also promised always to protect my sister, and obviously I suck at promises. The thought alone worries me, and I absently reach up and fiddle with the vow necklace around my throat.

"Is that all?" Diego asks, digging his fingers into my hips. "A pretty damn lame excuse for mentally torturing our girl? For scarring her? Trying to steal her from the life we promised her?"

"I wasn't thinking," Brayla says.

"Doesn't change what you helped Orlando accomplish," Diego says. "Jewel loved you, and you broke her heart."

"You nearly stole her eternity," Austin adds.

Kingston points at Orlando. "And *you* fucking stole her sister."

"Now leave," all three of them say. "If you try to contact Jewel again, consider it an act against the Divines."

Orlando flares his nostrils, narrowing his eyes at my guys, but he doesn't attempt to fight or anything. All he does is turn his attention to me and smile, which makes matters worse. Diego flies forward, knocking Orlando back. The two of them never touch the ground as Orlando retaliates and shoves Diego into one of the tables with a human on it.

The human man screams out, crashing to the ground. Orlando manages to flip Diego onto his back, flashing his fangs in his face. My asshole stalker reminds me a lot of Mitchell, his strength overpowering Diego, sending my heart racing.

Orlando punches Diego in the face, sending blood spraying from his mouth. My whole body tenses at the sight. I break away from Austin and rush toward Diego. Kingston cuts me off, wrapping his arms around me.

"Let him go!" I scream, fighting against Kingston's death grip.

"Diego's got this, babe," Kingston says.

Another fist to Diego's face makes me unsure.

And then another.

I elbow Kingston, attempting to break away from him. He spins me around and covers my ears at the sound of bones breaking and a yell ripping from Diego.

I scream.

VAMPIRE AFFAIRS

THE SHOCK ALARM BLARES THROUGH the air, louder than my wails, and Kingston accidentally squeezes the breath out of me. Orlando drops to the ground along with nearly the entire room apart from our vampire security staff and my guys. Diego jumps to his feet and kicks Orlando in the stomach, sending him rolling. It only takes a few seconds for him to orient himself to the noise to face Diego again.

Sobs wrack my chest, my fear for Diego's safety turning me into an incoherent mess. Kingston tries to spin me away from the scene, but I manage to gather all my strength and rip free from him. Brayla surprises the shit out of me by stepping between me and Kingston, giving me the split second I need to get to Diego.

I hold my hands up, blocking him like I could actually protect him from the raging lunatic. Orlando freezes inches away from me, his blue eyes attempting to capture my glower. But he can't. Not with my guys' blood in my system. He tilts his head at the realization. Strong hands wrap around my waist to yank me away but not before I jerk my leg up and surprise kick Orlando as hard as I can right in the junk, sending him to his knees.

Kingston howls a laugh so loud that it's the only sound left when the shock alarm leaves the grand room in utter silence. He releases Brayla, not pushing her or anything like I expect, just letting her go, and she rushes to Orlando's side.

"I told you this was a bad idea," he mutters to her. "She'll never see our side of things if they don't allow it."

"She's my best friend. Trust me. Now go. You shouldn't have attacked back," she murmurs, pulling him to his feet.

Diego high fives me. "Beautiful, you are so incredibly hot right now. I can't believe you did that. I love your crazy ass protectiveness."

I don't respond to him, gaping at Orlando as he disappears, leaving Brayla behind. Austin spins me in his arms, kneeling down to inspect my body for injury, and Kingston yells at everyone to mind their own damn business. None of my guys caught the interaction between Brayla and Orlando, and I can't help replaying their words through my mind over and over again.

"Jewel?" Austin asks, drawing my attention to him.

Kingston stands behind him. "Is she okay?"

"Beautiful, answer Austin please."

I turn my attention to Diego and gasp. "Holy shit balls! You're hurt. Oh, God. Here." Pulling my hair back, I expose my shoulder to Diego, knowing my blood can help him out. From the look of his crooked nose, it's definitely broken. One of his eyes swells shut, and his jaw doesn't fare much better, now darkening with an oncoming bruise.

"I'm pretty sure she's okay," Austin says.

Diego stands in front of me, brushing his fingers over my shoulder. "I'm fine too."

I shake my head at his response. "You're obviously not. Drink, Diego."

"Let her take care of you, my son." My blood cools at the sound of Mitchell's voice cutting through the room. He saunters from the arched doorway at a human's pace, taking a moment to drink in the sight of the party he has barely bothered to show up to.

Swallowing, Diego holds my stare, searching my eyes. "Okay, beautiful. But not here."

A few murmurs hum through the air, and I can't—well I guess I can—believe the guests sound mildly disappointed he wants to be with me in private. I twist and peer at the crowd, offering them my best glare. I mean, come-friggin'-on. It's not like anyone else will be given a taste.

"Perhaps you can offer Austin and Kingston a drink as well," Mitchell says, stopping in front of me and Diego. Okay, so maybe just Austin and Kingston will get a taste. I was prepared to be put in this position, but damn him. Mitchell puts me on the spot for everyone to hear.

Austin and Kingston close ranks around me, shutting our circle from the obviously engrossed onlookers.

Mitchell keeps his hands at his sides, and he doesn't attempt to lock me in his manipulative stare either. He shocks me by flicking his eyes past me toward the crowd. I realize without anyone having to tell me that this might be some sort of test.

I twitch my lips into a smile. "Of course I'd be happy to if my health keeper says it's okay for tonight."

"As long as you eat something, Jewel," Austin murmurs. "I can grab my kit and be back."

I want nothing more than to beg him to do so, but I catch sight of Viorica in the crowd a dozen feet behind Mitchell. She dares me to prove that I'm uncomfortable feeding my guys in public, though I shouldn't be as their match, not after so many weeks. I just hope my rebel mouth behaves for once. Because this is going to be awkward if it doesn't. They have gone out of their way to make biting a pleasant experience to me, and I'm not used to feeding them outside of emergencies without having my blood drawn. But that part is only in my personal contracts to them. My contract with Donor Life Corp just says I must sustain them, and tonight's a special occasion, which is a clause that if my health keeper says it's okay, then I can give blood to all of them.

"I'm fine, Austin," I say, sucking my bottom lip between my teeth. I turn my gaze to Diego. "And here is perfectly acceptable." My voice struggles to sound out loud because of nerves.

"Babe," Kingston whispers. "Seriously. We're not asking you to put yourself out there like this no matter how much I enjoy everyone's jealousy."

I smile, ignoring Kingston's quiet comment only to me. "Shall we sit? I'd like to try to enjoy the rest of the party. Hopefully interruption free." As I say the words, I step back from Mitchell to put another foot of space between us. "It'd be lovely for you to join us, Mitchell. Haven't my matches done an exceptional job with the party?" My sweet voice comes out fake as hell, but either Mitchell chooses to ignore it, or he doesn't notice.

He offers me a charming smile and holds out his arm to me. "Sounds exquisite." Turning to my guys, he adds, "Invite Ms. Ortega to join us. I'm rather curious as to why she remained when her creator did not."

Ugh. I keep my eyes trained on the room in front of me, not reacting to his words. He whispers low enough that I wouldn't be able to hear them if I was still a normal human. Austin disappears, leaving Kingston and Diego by my side. The crowd parts away as Mitchell strolls me across the dance floor and toward a large rectangular table with chairs positioned on only one side to give us a view of the room.

For the first time, I notice a small section of round tables filled with a huge selection of food. Three human guys dressed in white tuxedos talk among themselves, and I recognize one of them. I can't remember his name, but he Blood Matched on the same day as me. And from the looks of it, their vampire matches obviously don't have the same fears as my guys because all three humans sit unattended.

"So, are you guys totally just overprotective? They're all alone," I say to Kingston. I'm most definitely kidding, especially after everything we've been through, but no one around knows the extent of it. I'm probably the only Blood Match who doesn't get any true alone time. Not that I mind. I was never alone growing up.

He raises his eyebrow at me. "They're also not as delectable as you, babe."

I smirk. "How would you know?"

Tightening his jaw, Kingston keeps his face indecipherable. "A feeling."

"Yeah, sure. Don't let him fool you. Kingston knows from a finger prick test," Diego says. "He used to always sample applicants before they were matched."

"And I thought I was special," I tease.

Kingston attempts to elbow Diego, but he spins out of the way to walk backwards in front of me.

"You're more than special. You're extraordinary, Jewel," Mitchell says, acting like we were even talking to him. "Divine."

Double ugh. I hate when he butts in with compliments

that sound so damn charming coming from him, yet freak me the eff out because I despise any attention he shows me. I don't think I'll ever forgive him for the massacre with the Blood Rebels. He just...I push the thoughts away. I tremble, recalling how awful that day was and try so hard to forget it to remain cordial in Mitchell's presence.

Kingston squeezes my hand, helping to stop me from reacting to his dumb pun. Diego glances at Mitchell, keeping his expression in check, though I can see how much it bothers him too that Mitchell always admires me in a way that would be mounds better if it came from one of my guys.

"She is, isn't she?" Kingston asks, doing a far better job at disguising his unease.

I know it's hard on my guys considering that Mitchell is their dad, or father-figure in better terms, but he's betrayed them in a way they never thought he would, showing a side of himself they either never expected or denied existed until they met me. Under Mitchell's charisma lies a predator they worry about with me more than anyone considering he broke into my mind and does things against their wishes.

Diego pulls out a chair and sits down before me, motioning for me to sit on his lap. The intensity of the walk across the dance floor was enough to nearly make me forget the whole feeding my guys for a room full of vampires thing.

And now that Diego holds his arms open for me...holy shit balls.

"Everything all right, Jewel?" Mitchell asks, standing by a

chair, waiting for me to sit first.

I clear my throat, shifting on my feet. "Yeah, it's great."

Kingston nudges me forward with his hand, pressing it to the small of my back. I relent to the pressure and let him guide me around the table. I sink down onto Diego, dangling my legs sideways, purposely sitting so I can easily turn my back on Mitchell even with the empty chair between us.

Kingston doesn't waste a moment to pull my legs onto his lap. Soft lips caress my shoulder as Austin sits on our other side. An additional chair slides out, but I don't look to watch Mitchell offer Brayla a seat. I don't even look at her. I'm afraid of all the emotions she drags out of me, and I need to remain calm.

"I picked all your favorites," Austin says, stretching his arm over my shoulder. "Try this. I think you'll like it."

None of my guys allow even a moment of silence to let my nerves get the best of me. I don't know what I was thinking, but I didn't expect to be this comfortable, even under the subtle scrutiny of the board and all their guests.

If a woman in a bikini didn't climb onto the table in front of Mitchell and Brayla, I'd pretend this was another normal dinner where my guys feed me and patiently wait for me to return the favor.

The woman darts her eyes to mine before turning to Mitchell. "Hello, Mr. Divine. I hope your night has been extraordinary. Are you hungry?"

"Ms. Ortega, would you like the first taste?" Mitchell asks

Brayla.

"Yes, thank you, Mr. Divine. And please, call me Brayla."

"You may call me Mitchell," he responds. "No need for formality with your old mortal bond to Jewel. It's not often for two friends to be promised Blood Vows, you know. I assume your transition has been good."

"Indescribable. I feel rather lucky," she responds. "Orlando has provided an exceptional life for me already."

Ah, hell.

As much as I try to resist giving either of them my attention, my curiosity gets the best of me, and I slide my legs off Kingston to turn in their direction. Diego adjusts me on his lap, and Austin offers me another bite of pasta, not giving me a chance to butt in and comment.

"He does offer his apologies for his actions tonight. We did not come to start any trouble. I know Orlando hasn't started off on good terms with the Jordan blood debt, but you must understand that it was me who begged him to attempt to file a breach in Jewel's contract."

"You?" Mitchell questions.

She frowns. "I admit at the time I was selfish. I wanted my best friend in my household no matter what, but I've adjusted the last few weeks and see much more clearly that Jewel is where she is destined to be. An eternity as an ally is far better than enjoying a short life with her."

Diego hugs me closer, resting his chin on my shoulder. I blink the burning tears away, bending forward to mess with the buckle of my shoe, so no one sees how much her words get to me.

My guys said Brayla changed. And she has. She's a vampire. She brutally murdered my dad, but I can't stop thinking about her reason why. Or how she's here now, pleading for my forgiveness. She's remorseful. I can't help feeling that I was right. Brayla might have changed, but I can still change her. Her transition shouldn't be the death of our friendship. Because I love her. She's my family, too. People do crazy things for the ones they care about. I know that. I've seen it and done it.

"All I want is to try to make amends with Jewel, especially with her upcoming Blood Vow to one of your sons." She looks to me when she says it. "The transition was nothing like I expected, and I'd love to be here for her."

"That is very kind of you," Mitchell says. "Right, Jewel?"

Or sneaky. The small voice inside me that wants to suppress the forgiving side of me grows louder and screams for me not to be gullible. Words mean nothing without actions to back them. "I'm sorry, Brayla. It's going to take a lot more than an apology to make up for all the bullshit."

"Jewel." Mitchell glowers at me, making me feel like a kid being chided, but I don't cower away. It helps that Austin straightens in his seat, shielding me with his body.

Brayla touches Mitchell's shoulder. "It's fine, Mitchell. I knew an apology wouldn't cut it, so that's why I wanted to extend an invitation to your family to the Shadow Crest Villa in Ombre Noire."

I blink. "An invitation?"

"You could visit with Ramona," she adds.

I open my mouth to accept when Kingston, Diego, and Austin all say, "No."

"But—"

Austin plops another forkful of pasta in my mouth, stopping me from arguing. I swallow automatically without chewing, feeling the lump slide down my throat. There is no way I'm about to let them make this decision for me. How will I know for sure if I can't see if she's really changed or if this is all a ruse to get into my head without breaking into my mind?

Diego shifts me around and plants a kiss to my mouth, this time assuring I don't open it again. And he keeps kissing me, prodding his tongue to the seam of my pursed lips, begging me to give in until I can't resist his whispered plea.

"Perhaps you boys just need a little time to discuss the matter," Mitchell says, drawing my attention away from Diego. He scoots his chair back and stands. "Brayla, would you care to dance?"

Brayla tips her head, studying me, and then stands up. "I'd love to."

Mitchell leans down to close the space between the four of us. "And maybe you wouldn't be so disagreeable after being properly fed. Might I remind you of tonight's importance?" He pats each of his sons' shoulders and then he winks at me.

Ah shit. Again, I forgot.

We watch in silence as they disappear on the now crowded dance floor. Some vampires continue to keep their eyes glued on the table, but it's not as bad as when I first sat down. Thankfully, I'm not as entertaining as they had obviously hoped.

"Is this your first bite, hon?" I startle at the sound of the woman's voice as she lies on the table in front of us. "I'd be glad to offer a taste to your misters."

"You're excused," Kingston says, waving her away.

I frown, watching her go. "What the hell is wrong with me?"

"You forgot she was there, didn't you?" Diego asks, chuckling.

Hell yeah I did. Heat burns my cheeks, and I sink against him. It doesn't help how quiet the lady was. I didn't watch, and she didn't make a single noise as both Mitchell and Brayla fed on her, the bite marks on her arm now staunched from bleeding. "I'm the worst. Does this mean I'm going to be a total savage? I can't believe I just—I just shut her out."

"Jewel," Austin says, sliding his hand over mine. "It's natural for you to block out something like that. It doesn't mean you'll be a savage."

"I don't know, Austin," Kingston quips, ruffling his fingers through my hair to push the strands away to kiss my shoulder. "She kind of already is."

Diego punches him at the same time I swat his chest. "Not the time to tease her, bro. She's shaking."

"Fucking A." Kingston gives me a once over and brings my hand up to his cheek to feel my annoying trembles against his skin. No wonder Diego keeps shifting me. I'm practically vibrating. "Clear the way. I'm getting her out of here."

I swallow and rest my head on Diego's shoulder, letting both of them attempt to rub the quivers from me, Diego working my back while Kingston sneakily slips his hand up my dress to massage my legs.

"I'm not going anywhere until one of you bites me already," I say, clearing my throat again.

Kingston flashes his fangs. "All right, babe. Come here. Watching you squirm on Diego's lap is making me...hungry. I'm starved."

"You can go first when you defend our girl's honor," Diego says, tightening his hold on me. He puckers his bottom lip at me, dimpling his chin. "I'm injured, and she's the only one who can make me feel better."

"Which means I should go first so neither of you accidentally overdo it," Austin says, tugging me away from Diego, despite his growls. Diego releases me instead of initiating a teasing game of tug.

I laugh, the noise high-pitched and squeaky, totally embarrassing. But I can't help it. What I thought would be all sorts of awkward actually proves to be something familiar I can lose myself in. The playful banter between my guys over who gets to bite me first reminds me of their first game of Rock-Paper-Scissors to see who'd get the first night with me.

"He's probably right," I murmur, cuddling against Austin's comforting body. I nudge Kingston with my shoe. "I mean, you two can barely control your fangs as it is, especially when you're worked up."

Austin chuckles in my ear. "I thought that might've been why."

I close my eyes and laugh. "Austin. You're spending way too much time with your brothers. It's not nice to tease them...even if Kingston totally deserves it."

"Wait, what?" Kingston asks, narrowing his eyes while tilting his head.

Neither Austin nor I respond to Kingston's question.

Kingston and Diego look to each other before bringing their gazes back to me. The intensity of their once-over, Kingston's midnight depths and Diego's stormy grays, sends my heart racing as they drink me in inch by inch. Realization lights their expressions, and I bite my lip as I smile.

"Babe, you think I'm going to—"

I gently tap the toe of my shoe to his chin, getting him to shut up. "We'll talk about it later. But now, I just want to feed you and maybe dance."

"And then get out of here?" Diego asks.

I run my finger across his shoulder. "Definitely that."

Combing my hair with my fingers, I pull it to one side and expose my collar to Austin. The clicking of his fangs extending sounds in my ears, his body tensing under mine in sudden anticipation. He brushes his lips to my skin, kissing me feather soft, waiting for me to relax a bit. I squirm some more, my stupid body totally going to betray the fact that my guys and I don't cross this line often.

I open my mouth to tell Austin that I'm ready for him to bite me, but I meet the gazes of the Vaduvas staring right at me from the place across the room. I stiffen, my body reacting to the sudden fear they stir inside me, and Austin freezes.

A soft growl escapes his lips. "I can't do this to you, Jewel. Not like this. Not in front of them. I can tell you're uncomfortable, and I never want you to be like that with me no matter who causes it."

"Austin, it's okay. I'm okay," I say, shifting to straddle his waist, hiking up my gown in the process. With my eyes focusing on Austin, it doesn't seem so bad. "I'm your Blood Match. This is what we do."

He shakes his head. "You're more to me."

"He's right, beautiful. The board can fuck off if they doubt our matching," Diego says, squeezing my hand.

Kingston stands up and holds open his arms. "Damn straight, babe. Let's get out of here so I can bite you in the comfort of our bed."

I laugh. "Can I have at least one dance? You guys did go through the trouble of putting together this party. Maybe Mitchell will forgive the no biting thing if we show him we can still have an awesome time without it."

Austin licks his lips and releases a breath. "She's right. We can't just leave."

Kingston taps his finger to his chin, peering once over his shoulder. "Fine, but let's make it three dances."

VAMPIRE CUSTOMS

"UGH. I'M SO FRIGGIN' HOT." I rest my palms on the cool marble counter, staring at my sweat-drenched face. "I think I'm melting." I swear my guys have selective vision that looks past my flaws because none of them told me I'm sporting raccoon eyes from my smudged mascara.

Diego slides up behind me to peer over my shoulder. "You're right. About being hot. Sexy hot. Not the melting kind." Knew it. Reaching around me, he flicks on the faucet and runs a towel from the linen cupboard of the guest bathroom under it. "But let me help you."

I turn in his arms to face him, and he lifts me up to set me on the counter. The fabric of my dress clings to me, making it nearly impossible to move in. I shimmy back and forth, failing to tug up the hem of my gown. "I seriously hate this dress. I want out of it."

Diego chuckles. "Don't tease me. Once it comes off..."

"It's going in the garbage," I muse.

"If only we didn't have to stroll through a damn party."

"Just run fast."

Diego tips his head back and laughs before wincing and rubbing his bruised jaw. Austin reset his broken nose for him, and it seems to be healing, but his other injuries are taking a bit longer.

I pout my lip and gently reach out to graze my fingers over his purpling skin. "I'll try not to make you laugh again."

"No way. It's worth the pain." Diego runs the damp towel over my forehead and across my cheeks. "And it's not so bad. I've been through worse."

He continues to pat my face with the cold cloth, cleaning my skin of the runny makeup I regret insisting on. I lift my hair off my neck to cool off, and he hesitates, trailing his eyes over my collarbone. His fangs click and extend uncontrollably at just the sight of the skin I expose to him. Goosebumps prickle over me, and I shiver as he runs the cloth over my throat.

Gliding my finger over his full bottom lip, I playfully tap his fangs, just light enough to quicken his breathing and tense his body in a good way that makes me feel hotter than hell. "You're hungry."

"I'm a lot of things," he says, gently biting my finger but

not enough to draw blood.

I pull away and pat his cheek. "Especially patient. But you don't have to be. We're alone, you know."

Diego hums deep in his throat, studying my face in consideration. Peering over his shoulder, he glances at the door and then back to me. I insisted that only one of my guys follow me into the bathroom to wash my face, so Kingston and Austin remain outside on the dance floor.

My three dances with them quickly doubled, and I'm surprisingly having so much fun that I decided I didn't want to leave. My guys were right about vampires loving to party that even the people hired to feed them have left the tables for a bit of fun, mingling about like they just didn't get fed on. I don't think I've ever seen such a sight. This is nothing like The Boxes after dark. I guess things are different when the risk of death is minimized compared to running for your life in a free-for-all for those who break curfew.

"I could ask Austin to get his kit," he says, brushing his fingers along my shoulder. He licks his lips, already devouring me with his eyes, clearly wanting nothing more than for me to recognize he's only putting the thought out there to hide his desire to bite me, knowing we're still sort of in the public eye.

But I don't give a shit right now. We don't have an audience, and I want nothing more than to share this moment with Diego with our hearts still pounding, the thrill of how much he yearns for me washing over me in delicious waves. How much I want him back.

Sliding my hands down the front of his dress shirt, I unfasten a few buttons and use the fabric to pull him closer against my knees. "Now what's the fun in that?"

Diego leans in to kiss me, the tight fabric of my dress keeping him from fully sinking into me. I kiss him slowly at first, running my fingers into his shirt, grazing the taut muscles of his broad chest and hard nipples, warm from dancing but not nearly as sweaty as I am. I shift on the counter, attempting to get my gown to move. I want nothing more than to let Diego close the space between us as his tongue slides over mine, and he kisses me with a hunger that ignites a hell of a lot of desire inside me.

I moan into his mouth, grazing my teeth over his lip. He sucks mine back, nipping it with his fangs just enough to accidentally draw blood. Yanking back, he brings his finger up to my mouth, running it under my chin to wipe the drop of blood.

"I'm fine, Diego," I murmur, dragging him back to me for another kiss.

He lets go of his caution completely, deepening his kiss, sucking my lip a little harder as his hands travel down to dip into my bodice to glide over my breast while pushing my strap off my shoulder. Breaking away from my lips, he works his mouth over my jaw, licking his way to my throat. I rock back and forth on the counter, struggling with my gown again until Diego bends down and hooks his fingers to the hem to hike it up.

Tingles burst through me, feeling his excitement press against the sheer fabric of my underwear, ensuring a daunting amount of space between his body and mine. I release a breath of a moan, pursing my lips together to try to stay as quiet as possible, though the pulsing music outside the door assures at least a teensy bit of privacy.

"Jewel," Diego whispers, my name sounding just as breathless on his lips. His fangs graze the skin of my shoulder, begging to sink down. "Can I bite you?"

I nod my head, combing my fingers through my hair to pull it completely out of the way. Diego slides his hand up my back, pulling me closer. I inhale a few deep breaths in anticipation. Pressure squeezes my shoulder a second before his fangs pierce my skin. He moans deep in his throat, sucking harder as blood drips down my clavicle in warm rivulets. His tongue follows, and he licks my skin in a way that makes me ache in a good way. He doesn't let a single drop escape, moaning his pleasure of tasting me, allowing me to satiate his hunger.

Running my hands down the front of his body, I rub my fingers over his raging boner through his pants, setting him off even more. His teeth pierce my skin a second time, and he sucks and licks with hungry desire that far exceeds tasting my blood. His hand expertly maps the skin of my leg up to touch me in a way that pulls a loud ass moan from me in the process.

I shimmy off the counter and jump into his arms, unable

to control myself. I just want to feel him against me. My un-expected movement sends him stumbling back a few feet, and he hits the wall mirror behind him, shattering it.

"Oh, sh—" I don't even get the words out before Diego brings his lips back to mine and spins to lay me down on a chaise lounge situated in the corner of the grand bathroom.

I gasp a few deep breaths, my skin tender and buzzing, just craving more of Diego's affection. Diego steals any other embarrassing noises I make with a kiss that ignites my hunger for him into complete starvation, and I bite his lip hard enough to make him bleed.

Something snaps inside me, my desire turning feral at the delicious taste of his blood, blood I haven't had apart from his brothers' blood in weeks. The sweet, syrupy flavor sends heat exploding through me. I rip at his dress shirt and brush my lips to his skin for a second before sucking just enough skin to bite without breaking through.

"Harder," he whispers, encouraging me to do something I know he likes.

Biting down, I sink my teeth into his shoulder until sweet warmth fills my mouth. I slide my tongue over the blood and swallow, my body on the edge of something indescribable. I hurry to unbuckle Diego's belt and slide my hand down to feel exactly what I do to him.

His fingers explore me in a quick and desperate way that builds a crazy amount of pressure. I squirm under his touch, just waiting for my body to implode or explode at the sensations he creates with his fingers.

The second I reach a point of release that sends me jerking up to cling onto him, Diego moans and bites me again on my other shoulder. I sink my teeth into him, pretty set on devouring him in this moment as he shifts on top of me to tease me with the weight and heat of his body.

I lean away from him and trap him in my gaze for once, his gray eyes studying me, asking me his silent question of what I want to happen next. Reaching up, I trail the back of my hand over the already lightening bruises of his jaw and across my blood still staining his lips as he licks it away, just taking a moment to let the love we have for each other sink into me.

Shifting my legs, I open up completely for him, nodding my head in consent. His eyes darken with lust and need. We both pant, our chests heaving, our hearts pounding in a race to out beat each other.

And then he freezes and groans, dropping his weight on me without proceeding.

"Jewel, I'm sorry to bother you." The soft, familiar voice of Brayla hums through the heavy door. Diego must've heard her approach over the music, his hearing still better than mine. I lack the focus he does at narrowing and ignoring sounds. It's how he can tolerate the shock alarms. "But I just wanted to let you know that I'm leaving."

Diego frowns, but he doesn't say anything, automatically shifting off of me, reading the look on my face. I release a shaky breath in an attempt to pull myself together, my desire for Diego still burning hot through me.

"It's probably better this way, beautiful," he whispers, engulfing me in a quick hug. "You deserve more than a quickie inside a bathroom...though I really, really want to."

"Damn straight she deserves better," Kingston calls, banging on the door. "You're lucky I'm trying to control my jealousy tonight and didn't want to embarrass her."

So much for that.

Diego helps me to my feet and embraces me again, kissing me sweetly. "Give us a minute. Jewel wants to say bye to Brayla, and then I think we're going to call it a night as well."

Kingston grumbles words I can't decipher and then something hits the door, and he heaves a breath.

"Sounds good, Diego," Austin says.

I sigh and shake my head, deciding against saying anything to the two of them with Diego begging me to ignore them with his heavy stare.

He gives me a slow, slightly torturous in an achingly good way, once-over. A smile lights his face as he drinks me in. I inch closer to run my fingers over the bleeding bite marks I left on his skin, staining his white dress shirt dark red with his blood. I crinkle my nose, which he promptly kisses until I smile.

"I loved every second of this with you," he whispers. "And don't you dare let Kingston tease you about it."

I blush. "I enjoyed it too. A lot."

Diego beams me his brilliant smile, making it incredibly difficult to peel myself away from him. Taking my hand in his, he tugs me toward the exit without giving me a chance to glance at myself in the mirror over the sink. He picks me up and carries me over the broken glass of the wall mirror we accidentally shattered, and I notice a potted plant knocked on its side, spilling soil across the tile. The room's more wrecked than I thought.

One awkward glance at my dress sends my heart sliding into my stomach because I'm not much better. Stupid white dress. I can feel the stickiness of Diego's blood still on my chin and can already hear Kingston calling me a savage now.

"You look fine," Diego murmurs.

"Yeah, sure." I rub my arm across my chin. "Let me clean up."

He chuckles. "Seriously, you're fine. You're still stunning. You have no idea."

"Diego."

"Please? For me."

I purse my lips in consideration. This is totally a vampire thing, thinking any sort of blood spill is hot. "Okay, I'll let you parade my savage ass around, but just this once."

He smiles. "Sexy not savage."

Opening the door, Diego blocks me to double check that everything is all good in the ballroom. The bass of the music thuds through the air in rhythm with the rainbow lights that illuminate the room in a magical glow now that the party has really started.

Kingston leans over to peer at me from behind Diego. His gaze travels to the bathroom, and he tightens his mouth, raising his brows. "What the—"

Diego punches Kingston in the arm. "If you say a damn word that embarrasses Jewel, you'll regret it."

Sliding around Diego, I step in between him and Kingston before they start fighting. "The mirror was my fault."

"Are you hurt?" Austin asks, clearly not as enthralled by my current state as Kingston, who looks like it's taking everything in him to keep his mouth shut as he gapes at me with a mixture of jealousy and lust flashing his eyes silver.

Stiffening beside me, Diego subtly reacts to Austin's question as it clearly gets to him.

"She doesn't look hurt to me," Brayla says, shifting on her feet behind the wall my guys create around me.

Heat burns my cheeks. "No, I'm great."

Diego releases a small breath, squeezing my hand. "I didn't drink too much."

"Shit, babe. You look—"

"I'm great. It really was an accident," I repeat. "Diego made sure I wasn't cut by the glass."

Kingston combs strands of my hair off my face. "No, you look...fuck I'm hungry."

Brayla releases a giggle, drawing my attention back to her. "Looks like Jewel was too." She has the nerve to wink.

By the sound of a dozen clicks of extending fangs, a

bunch of nearby vampires might be hungry as well. I automatically reach up to touch the bite marks Diego left, realizing my movements caused them to bleed and drip onto the bodice of my white gown. Nerves clench my chest, and I try to suppress the sudden fear arising in me.

"Shit." Kingston looks incredibly pouty that Diego cleans the dripping blood with his finger to lick off. His eyes avert to the crowd, and I realize they're not focusing on me.

Then a strange buzzing noise sounds through the air so softly I might have imagined it.

"Kingston, Austin," Diego says. "Did you hear that?" I guess I didn't.

"My sons, I advise you to prepare Jewel or get her out of here," Mitchell says, his voice a tone too soft for most to hear.

"Dad, you didn't," Austin says, closing the space to me.

"A gift from the Vaduvas," he replies.

I blink a few times, peering past Kingston at the crowd, searching for Mitchell and the reason he mentions that my guys should get me away. I expect to see all the vampire guests to be flashing their fangs at us, but no one moves. Everyone stands utterly still, peering around, smiling in anticipation. A few people blur through the room, and I tense, but it's only those vampires who brought their Blood Matches rushing to stand beside them.

"Sorry, Brayla. No time for heartfelt goodbyes," Kingston whispers to her.

"What's going on?" I ask, my voice quivering. The intense fear grows inside me, reminding me of what it was like to run on Starlight Row after sunset. I can't see any other vampires, but I can sense them. I feel like I'm being watched. Stalked. It feels exactly like when Orlando was sneaking around the estate without my guys' knowledge. But worse.

"Nothing to worry about, beautiful," Diego says, hooking his hand around my waist. "But it's time to go."

"Go? Where?"

He doesn't get the chance to tell me where. The lights snap off, leaving the room in darkness, and then the world around me blurs.

FINDERS KEEPERS

"KINGSTON, TAKE HER."

I screech out at the sudden jolt from Diego's arms to Kingston's. Kingston silences my scream with a kiss I have to gasp away from to breathe. A couple low, creepy noises reverberate through my bones, coming from somewhere behind us, but I can't see anything in the pitch black wherever the hell we are.

"No need to be scared, babe. You should be quiet though," Kingston whispers in my ear. "Because I never thought I'd say this, but I really don't want to kiss you again to shut you up."

I don't respond to him, keeping my head buried in the crook of his neck. The speed in which he races me through the dark unleashes a wave of dizziness through me, and I swallow a few times to try to settle the wooziness threatening my insides.

"At least until you wash your face. You just made me way closer to Diego than I ever wanted to be."

"Kingston…" I let my words trail off. I don't even have a response to his comment, and talking makes it hard to keep myself together.

"But damn, you're making me so hungry," he adds. "How come you never let me bite you like this?"

"Because you don't let her bite back," Diego says from somewhere in front of us.

I groan.

"Shut up, the both of you," Austin says. "And watch out, Kingston. Sounds like Jewel's getting sick."

It's Kingston's turn to groan. "Here, you take her."

Locking my legs tighter around Kingston's waist, I stop him from tossing me through the air again. I squeeze my eyes shut, trying my best to pull myself together. Because Austin's right. My stomach won't stop twisting, and I can't concentrate on anything other than the sound of my racing heart in my ears. Kingston strokes his hand up and down my back, silently smoothing the trembles from my body.

"I'm begging you, babe. Don't puke," Kingston says. "Almost there."

My stomach heaves, and the next thing I know I'm on my knees, my palms pressing into the floor runner. A light blinks on next to me, shadowing the edges of my vision. Kingston holds up his glowing tablet to my face, and Austin squats next to me.

"How much blood did she drink, Diego?" Austin asks.

"Not a lot." Diego kneels beside me. "Right, beautiful?"

I bob my head.

Austin grazes his fingers over my shoulder. "Do any of Diego's bites hurt more than usual?"

"I didn't release my venom if that's what you think," Diego snaps. "I love Jewel, but I know the plan. Don't accuse me of going against you. I have just as much restraint as you both."

"That's not why I asked," Austin says. "Just checking her pain scale."

"Yeah, you bit her a lot, bro." Kingston shoves Diego hard enough that he falls back on his ass. "Maybe you drank too much and made her sick."

I shake my head. "Stop it. All of you." Inhaling a couple of breaths, I finally get the nausea rolling through me to subside. "It's your damn throwing me around like a doll and running through the dark."

"And she's scared," Austin murmurs.

"I told you there was nothing to worry about, beautiful," Diego says.

"Yeah, babe. We're just relocating our little party," Kingston adds.

"Why?"

The second the word escapes my lips, the shock alarms blare through the air. My guys wince but don't react more than usual. Austin covers my ears instead of his own, seeing as the shrieking noise hurts my eardrums enough to send me arching forward to curl in on myself.

The alarm cuts off, leaving my ears ringing, and Kingston lifts me back to my feet. "We gotta hurry."

Bending down, I clutch my knees. "Hurry, why?"

"You carry her, Austin," Diego says without responding to me. "I'll run ahead to make sure it's all clear. Don't need to get into any fights over you-know-what."

I press my hands to Austin's chest before he can pick me up. "Clear? Fights? What are you guys hiding from me?"

A soft murmur sounds from somewhere to the right. "Shit." Kingston turns off the light on his phone.

"What is—"

Austin presses his lips to mine, cutting off my question with a kiss. I swear. I love to be rudely interrupted like this, but I'm annoyed that my guys are ignoring me.

I pull back, squinting my eyes to try to make out his features. "What, no tongue?"

He chuckles in my ear. "No time."

"Sure, that's it," I say, remembering Kingston's remark about Diego's blood on my face. I bet I look gross despite what Diego said.

Another strange murmur sounds out again, stopping Austin from responding. Instead, he slides his hands down the entire length of my body until he reaches the hem of my dress. Kingston sighs at the time Austin spends gathering the fabric to make it easier to pick me up. It's still fast, but not Kingston-fast. He's an expert at hiking up my dresses no matter my position.

Austin hooks his fingers to my waist and lifts me up, letting me wrap my legs around him so he can use his hands if needed. "I'll go slow," he whispers into my ear, his soft voice unintentionally turning me on.

"Shit," I murmur. "I need you not to talk unless you're fully prepared to make out with me."

"Ah hell. Give her back," Kingston says. "Diego left her with lady blue bal—"

Austin spins, making me shriek, and he braves another kiss to my lips. Sliding his hand lower, he pulls me even closer to him. I sigh and rest my head on his shoulder. I need to get myself together.

"What? No tongue?" he asks teasingly, strolling with me in his arms.

"Careful," I whisper. "Kingston might've been right. I'm struggling to focus with your arms around me. And I'm still feeling extra bitey."

I snap my teeth next to his ear, and he laughs, kissing me again while adjusting his grip on me to carry me by my ass. Kingston grumbles from behind Austin, keeping a close enough pace that I can distinguish his silhouette from the rest of the creepy shadows.

"One coming up," Diego calls from somewhere ahead of us.

"One what?" I ask.

"Nothing, ba—"

A whimper breaks through my heavy breathing, and I tense in Austin's arms. I twist to try to get a look at the hallway in front of us, but the only thing I can see is the blinking red light of one of the security cams.

"Is that?"

"It's nothing, babe."

"It was someone. Who's there?"

"Beautiful, listen to—"

Snaking my hand into Austin's tuxedo pocket, I retrieve his phone and tap the screen, sending a soft glow through the unfamiliar hallway. My back hits a cool wall, and Austin sandwiches me to it with his body. Kingston stands right behind him, attempting to snatch the phone from my hand.

"Sneaky, babe. Give it to me," he says, grasping his hand over mine without ripping it away even though he could easily do so.

"Why won't you let me see anything? Why is it dark? Where are we even going?" All the questions tumble from my mouth at once. "How come I've never been in this section of the estate?"

Austin sighs, bowing his head against mine. "We should just tell her."

"No way," Kingston says, tugging at the phone I squeeze

harder so he'd have to put more effort into taking it from me.

"Kingston," I say.

"Fuck, fine. We're in the middle of a little party game, and we don't want to play," Kingston says, breaking first before Austin.

"Party game?"

He closes the space and peers at me from over Austin's shoulder. "That's all you need to know." If I leaned forward, I could kiss him. I consider it for the vague answer he gave me.

I arch back instead and peer at Austin. "What isn't Kingston telling me, Austin?" I ask him.

He groans.

"Don't, Austin."

Ignoring Kingston, I cup Austin's cheek with my free hand, stroking my fingers along it. He tilts his face to deepen the weight of my fingers, totally trying to distract me by kissing my hand. My attempt to use my affection to get what I want backfires more often than not these days. "I know you're looking out for me, but—"

"Viorica arranged a hunt with criminals from Midnight Valley. Finders keepers," Diego says, his words practically tumbling from his mouth.

"Diego," both Austin and Kingston say.

He shrugs. "Our girl is tough. She can handle it."

I groan, my mind trying to wrap around what sounds like a horribly twisted game that I really want no part of. I mean, what the actual hell? I knew that criminals in Dark Terrace

Ranch usually met their final donations, but I had no idea it could be in such a barbaric way.

"Are you kidding me?" I ask, my voice rising. "That was the noise I heard?"

"There are a couple hiding here," Diego admits. "We don't want you to see them, and it's better we keep moving. The guests aren't afraid to fight for what they want."

I press my hands into Austin's chest. "Let me down."

"No."

"Austin."

Austin squeezes me tighter. "They're dangerous, Jewel. Armed. "

"Then disarm them."

"That would guarantee they don't stand a fighting chance in this game."

I scowl. "They already don't."

Austin finally sets me on my feet, and I nudge past him, holding up his phone through the dark room. I catch sight of a figure squatting under a table, something sparkling in their hand. Possibly a knife. It's hard to tell.

"This is sick," I murmur, stepping closer. Diego blocks my way, and Kingston and Austin surround me from behind. Friggin' hot vampire sandwich. If I wasn't so annoyed, I'd appreciate their protectiveness. "Not cool. Like the shadow vamps on Starlight Row."

"I knew it," Kingston mutters. "It's going to ruin it for us. Viorica knew it too."

I spin, bumping my back into Diego to face Kingston. "Then fix it. You said it was a game of finders keepers. Find them and keep them."

His dark eyes flash silver at me. "I don't think you understand the game."

Tightening my jaw, I straighten my shoulders and glare, nostrils flaring and all. Kingston doesn't budge. He presses his lips together, remaining unnervingly expressionless to my reaction.

"Kingston," I say.

"Jewel."

"You know this is effed up, right?" My voice comes out softer, shakier.

"This is why I wanted you to run away with us." He glances around me at his brothers. "You guys should've listened to me."

"I did," Diego says.

Austin sighs. "You know why we couldn't."

"She's going to resent us." Kingston doesn't look at me while he says it, talking only to his brothers, and his serious features shift, his lip pouting.

I realize I might've asked too much of them. Or maybe I've forgotten my place in the world outside of them. I know they're doing everything in their capabilities to see to it that we have the life we want together. I know they're trying their best. But to know that Kingston thinks my love for them could be so easily discarded hurts me.

Neither Diego nor Austin responds to Kingston in a moment they should be quick to knock some sense into him about my feelings. Swiveling on my feet, I wave the light in their faces, catching sight of the same concerned expression that mars Kingston's handsome features. They don't say it, but they agree with him. They're worried about losing my love.

I lick my lips, still tasting the sweetness of Diego's blood, and try my best to keep my voice even. "Kingston..." My words trail off as a thousand responses swirl through my mind. Responses I can't even manage to say because I suddenly feel sick again. So I inhale a deep breath, straighten my shoulders, and slide between Diego and Austin to break their circle.

"Jewel, please don't walk away," Austin says, blocking my way. But he doesn't stop me. He strolls backward, facing me.

He doesn't see the approaching figures behind him. But I do.

Silver eyes flash in the light and the figures materialize closer. Everything happens so fast that my mind can't process what my body does. A vampire, still hidden in darkness, shoves a human right at Austin, and I tug him out of the way, my sudden strength throwing us both off balance.

Austin spins to take the brunt of our fall, leaving my back exposed. Kingston and Diego grab my hands to drag me out of reach, but not before pain explodes through me. The intensity fogs my mind, my eyes shadowing. I can't tell where I was hurt. Only that pain radiates through me.

"Jewel. Jewel, hey. Look at me," Austin says, hovering over me. A light shines in my eyes, burning my vision, making the shadows worse. "I know it hurts, but I need you to sit up and drink."

His cool arm slides around my back, and I jerk at the burning pain swelling through me. I think I black out. When I open my eyes, Diego holds me against him, pressing my mouth into his shoulder. My teeth bite deep into his skin as he restrains me, pouring more blood in my throat. I cough and spit, thrashing against him, bucking my body, my back killing me.

"Almost done, Jewel," Austin says. He presses his cool fingers into my neck, the pressure enough to stop my body from fighting. "You're doing great."

"We gotta move," Diego says.

"What should I do with him?" Kingston asks.

I wriggle in Diego's hold, trying to twist around to see who Kingston's talking about. The movement sends burning electricity zinging through me, and I release a scream Diego stifles with his hand.

"Leave him," Diego says.

"Yes, leave him." The feminine voice whispers through the air, tensing my muscles. "I'd love to take him off your hands."

All three of my guys growl.

Something crashes.

"Finders keepers," a second feminine voice says. It's Brayla. "And he's mine. Is he worth the fight to you, Layla? Or is it Gabriella? There are so many of you man-eaters it's hard to keep you all straight."

The other vampire hisses. More crashing. A thud. Glass shatters.

"Enough! Back the fuck up, Gabriella," Kingston says. "Brayla, know you're not considered a Divine ally. You'll leave me no choice but to intervene."

"Thank you, lover," Gabriella says.

"I said back up," he says again. "I'm not your lover."

I struggle to turn in Diego's arms, but he's friggin' using his death grip on me. The world shifts, and he stands. I yell into his shoulder again at the movement. Austin materializes in my line of sight, flashing a light in my eyes again.

"We have to go, Kingston," Austin says, rubbing his fingers across my forehead. "She's in pain, and I need more synthetic skin."

A yell sounds through the air and another round of thumps and thuds, followed by more glass breaking, erupts through the air.

"I've called finders keepers," Brayla says. "You'll let me take the man. It's what Jewel would want."

Gabriella coos in her throat. "I'm pretty sure Jewel would want him dead, right Kingston? Allow me to send him off in the best way possible."

Brayla huffs. "You obviously don't know Jewel like I do."

Austin touches my cheek. "Kingston, come on. Go clear a

path. Hurry."

Gabriella yells out, and for the first time, I see her. She crashes into the wall in front of me and flashes her fangs. I expect to see Kingston dart in front of her, but Brayla surprises me. She lifts the vampire up by her neck, showing her crazy new strength.

"I think you forgot who created me," Brayla snaps. "I'm an Ortega. Is one guy worth your pain?"

Shit balls.

Sweat drips down my forehead, and Diego shifts me again, turning me so I can no longer watch. Gabriella hisses. The world blurs, stealing my view as Diego charges through the dark. Austin runs behind him, clicking off his light when we enter through a door and into another hall.

"You c-can't leave h-her," I murmur, my tongue heavy in my mouth. "She's my friend."

"She'll be fine, beautiful," Diego whispers. "Don't worry about her."

"He's right, Jewel," Brayla says. "I'm fantastic. You look like shit though."

All of my guys growl.

"Brayla?" I whisper.

The world comes to a halt, and a light flicks on, shadowing my vision. Pain erupts through me, and Diego lays me down on my stomach.

"Get out of here, Brayla," Kingston says.

"No. She might be your match, but she's my friend. And

she's hurt."

"No thanks to you...or him," Austin says.

"It wasn't me," she says.

I roll on my side and groan. Silence falls over the room, and I blink through my hazy vision. "Brayla?" I ask again.

She materializes in front of me. "I'm here, Jewel."

Kingston digs his fingers into her shoulders. "Not for long."

I reach out and clasp her cold hand. "Please, don't go."

She touches my cheek despite the angry noises all three of my guys make. "I won't, Jewel. I'm your best friend forever."

"Always," I automatically whisper like I used to when we lived in The Boxes.

The world turns dark.

BEST FRIENDS FOREVER

SHADOWS DANCE THROUGH THE ROOM, blurring and coiling around me. I shiver at the ice flowing through my veins. My feet move without my consent, dragging me toward the long, narrow table. Dozens of blurry faced vampires applaud my arrival, and my mouth widens in a smile. I climb a short set of steps onto the table and peer at all of the dinner guests with silver eyes flashing and sharp fangs dripping blood. It's all I recognize on the vampires' faces.

"How exquisite," a smooth voice whispers.

"No, she's simply Divine," another voice says, chuckling. "Or should I say simply Vaduva?"

"And what a treat for you to join us, Jewel. Please, come closer. Let my sons take a look at you one last time."

Mitchell's voice draws my attention across the room. Three silhouettes emerge from the arched doorway and cross to stand at the head of the table. Strolling forward, I move without having to think about it. My heart picks up pace, pounding in my ears.

Diego, Austin, and Kingston meet my gaze with serious expressions, blooming fear in my core to travel up and around my lungs, stealing my breath.

"Go on, Jewel. Show them what they couldn't keep forever," another voice says. A figure materializes next to my guys, and Viorica flashes her fangs at me.

Slowly, I pull the side zipper on my dress, letting it drop to the floor. Goosebumps prickle my skin as I stand exposed in my bra and underwear.

"Maybe they'd like one last taste?" Viorica prods.

My head nods, though my soul screams to stop. But I can't. My mind reacts to Viorica's words, and there's nothing I can do but follow her instructions and lie before my guys. Mitchell materializes beside them, and he lifts my hand and touches it to his face. Austin, Kingston, and Diego drink me in with their eyes, remaining utterly still.

"I was afraid you'd break their hearts, Ms. Jordan. I warned you," Mitchell says.

I don't respond. I can't.

"This was Austin's fault," Kingston says, flashing his fangs.

Austin rises to his feet. "My fault? You pushed her away.

You put yourself first.”

“We all ruined it,” Diego says.

“You’ve shamed the Divine name, my sons,” Mitchell says. “Jewel was your future, and now you won’t have one.”

Viorica runs her fingers along my clavicle and rips my vow necklace free. “But she will. So, enjoy your last taste, boys.”

“No,” they say in unison.

“Jewel, say your goodbyes to the Divine Heirs.”

“Goodbye.”

A scream rips through the air, stinging my ears. I thrash, breaking through the fear consuming me from my nightmare. Cool arms engulf me, tightening around me to stop my body from jerking.

“What’s wrong with her?” Brayla’s soft voice cuts through the panic pounding in my ears.

“She’s having a nightmare,” Diego says. “Here, Austin. Give her to me.”

“Just be careful of her back,” he murmurs.

Their soft voices calm my racing heart, and I manage to pull myself together enough to open my eyes. My body aches as Austin hands me over to Diego. I feel like I’ve been dragged down a paved road, though I know I haven’t. Diego situates me on the plush recliner he sits on to face him. He cups my face, searching my eyes for a moment, and then he leans close and sweetly brushes his lips to mine.

Pulling back, he says, “You’re safe. It was just a nightmare. You were injured and blacked out."

I swallow the burning in my throat. "It felt real."

"It wasn't."

Tears blur my eyes. "But it still felt real. And horrible."

"Want to talk about it?" he asks, swiping a tear away before it splashes my face.

I shake my head.

The memory of my nightmare plays over and over again in my mind. How I had no control over my body. How Viorica said they lost our forever. How I had to say goodbye. Closing my eyes, I suppress the dream and focus on listening to everyone's hearts beating. Three I recognize apart from my own. One of the new ones feels familiar, but the last racing heartbeat ignites terror through me all over again.

I jerk in Diego's arms to try to get a better look behind me. The movement sends fire burning down my spine in a hot wave that makes me gasp in pain. Cool hands touch my back, snuffing out the heat with careful fingers. It's then that I realize the zipper is pulled down on my dress, exposing my back, but I'm wearing Kingston's tuxedo jacket backwards.

Austin rests his chin on my shoulder. "Better?"

I roll my shoulders, expecting more pain to burst through me, but only a dull ache remains. "What happened?"

"What is the last thing you remember?" Diego asks.

The freaky ass nightmare. I don't say it, though. Instead, I respond with, "Finders keepers."

Kingston groans from somewhere behind me. It's the first

noise he's made since I woke up. Diego glares at him from over my shoulder. I'd swivel around to peek at him if Austin wasn't so close, still rubbing his cool hand carefully across my back.

"What else?"

I scrub my hand down my face and look at my blood coated fingers. Heat burns up my chest to my neck. "Our time at the party."

Diego smirks as I say it. "That was fun, wasn't it?"

I bob my head. "But I also remember...Kingston?"

The sudden urge to have all my guys close to me overwhelms my thoughts. My nightmare gets to me more than it should, and Kingston's words about the game ruining our life together sneak back into my mind.

"I'm here, Jewel," Kingston says from behind me. "What's up?"

He doesn't come any closer, making me frown. Something about the even tone of his voice digs into me. I never thought I'd hate the way my name sounds on his lips, but it's enough to get my body to cooperate despite the ache to pull away from Diego. Austin realizes I'm on a mission to get to my feet and stands up to give me space. Diego helps me by letting me use his broad shoulders to steady myself. My knees wobble for a moment, and I straighten my back, stretching through the pain until it subsides, and I can turn around to meet Kingston's gaze.

He leans against the wall with his arms crossed, standing

over where Brayla perches on a rolling chair with a man un-conscious by her feet on the floor. She hops up, but Kingston snatches her by the shoulder, and she plops back down.

"Is he...?" I motion toward the man.

"No," everyone says, answering me.

"I saved him." Brayla reaches down and strokes the man's arm. "Your boy toys wanted to leave him to get devoured by one of the man-eaters, and I thought you'd appreciate if I didn't let her."

"We were showing him mercy," Kingston mutters, train-ing his gaze on the floor. "He stabbed Jewel."

"Gabriella would've been more humane than whatever the hell you're planning," Diego says.

"Maybe if he had done it on purpose," Brayla says.

Kingston's eyes flash silver. "He tried to attack Austin."

"No, he didn't." My voice comes out low and raspy, hoarse from all my screaming.

"Uh, she didn't hit her head, did she, Austin?" Kingston asks.

Anger sneaks up on me, and I shuffle closer to him. He meets me halfway, purposely making sure he remains between me and the guy—or more likely Brayla. Standing with only inches of space between us, Kingston reaches up and combs my loose hair from my face, his serious expression morphing into a pout the longer I trap him in place with my eyes.

I lick my lips and swallow. "I didn't hit my head, dude. And I know what I saw. Another vampire had the man and practically threw him at Austin."

Kingston's frown deepens. "And you thought Austin would've killed him or something, so you pushed between them...incredibly fast, I might add."

I shake my head. "No, I wasn't protecting the man."

"You were protecting Austin?" Diego asks from his spot on the recliner.

Austin touches my shoulder, drawing my attention away from Kingston, though Kingston doesn't let go of me. "Jewel, as much as I love that you wanted to protect me—"

"Don't do that ever again," Kingston says, cutting him off. "You could've been killed. Austin? Not so much. That was st—"

Swinging his fist, Austin clocks Kingston in the shoulder, knocking him away from me in the process. "It was brave, Jewel, and I appreciate it," Austin says.

"It was badass," Diego adds.

"It was...not something you should've done." Kingston risks Austin's growl to move closer.

"Jewel, you're probably the only human in the world who would risk your life to save a vampire from a little pain," Brayla says.

Brayla's sweet voice pulls my attention in her direction. She offers me a smile, not the ones I'm used to that brighten her face, but one with a whisper of caution. It's strange. The longer I share breathing room with her, the easier it is to forget the damage she caused my life. I should hate her. I should still be angry. But maybe she was right about the transition into being a vampire taking a toll on her. It wasn't her fault after all. It was Orlando's. He did this. She was caught in the crossfire of whatever it was that my dad started.

"Because I love them." I turn my attention to my guys, hoping they remember that despite the doubt they displayed over the possibility of the game ruining the whole vampire thing for me. "You know, I thought I was pretty clear when I accepted their vows, but it seems they might need a little reminding sometimes."

Brayla presses her lips into a line and stands, reading my mind. We grew up together after all. She knows me as well as anyone. She closes the distance but keeps a few feet away. I'm nearly certain it's because Kingston will intervene if she tries. "A reminder never hurts. If you don't mind watching my new friend, I'll give you a minute. I think I might want to continue to play this game for a bit."

I frown.

"Don't worry, Jewel. I know you well enough to know that if I hurt them, you might never forgive me. So I'm going to find who I can, and I'm going to keep them. Something your boy toys are obviously afraid to do. But not me. I'll do anything for you. You're my best friend."

Brayla saunters toward the door where Diego escorts her out, touching his palm to the lock to open it. She wiggles her fingers at me and winks, disappearing into the dark hallway outside. Strange noises trickle in through the open door until

Diego shuts and locks it again, turning his attention back to me. Now that we're alone—at least almost alone because the man remains knocked out on the floor—I'm suddenly more nervous that I should be.

"Fuck, she's such a manipulator," Kingston says, lacing his fingers behind his head.

I grab him and tug his arm, linking my fingers through his. "I don't think that's what she was trying to do."

"You said you saw a vampire push the guy at Austin. What if it was her?" he asks.

"It wasn't."

"So you saw them? In pitch darkness?" he prods.

I sigh. "I just know she wouldn't have done it."

"Like you knew she wouldn't kill your dad?"

"Kingston," Diego says. "Chill out."

"How can I? Our girl was stabbed right in front of us to-night. What if someone was trying to get us to breach our contract again?"

"Only Jewel or her heirs can file the claim," Austin says.

"What if—"

I turn and cut Kingston off with a kiss that makes him both sigh and groan, but he doesn't pull away from me. He digs his fingers into my hips, closing what little space I left between us. His tense muscles relax under my fingers, and I smile against his mouth, trying to ease myself away. But he doesn't let me. He kisses me deeper, sliding his tongue into my mouth and caresses it over mine, his hunger and desire for me pushing away whatever doubt he carried.

"Better?" I ask him through a kiss.

He shakes his head. "No. Need more. Starved. Antsy. Just keep kissing me. Need affection."

I laugh and tug myself back, patting his cheek. "And I want nothing more than to give it to you, but under one condition."

"A condition?" he asks, raising an eyebrow.

"Don't doubt my love, thinking it can be so easily discarded."

Ah, hell. The friggin' pout he gives me seizes my heart, stealing my breath. You'd think I yelled at him and told him no more kisses forever with the way he reacts, sagging his shoulders, dimpling his chin with the puffing of his lips. For a second, I'm pretty sure his dark eyes glass over, but he blinks, and they return to normal.

I shift and peer at Austin and Diego quietly standing nearby. "That goes for all of you," I add. "Because you thinking a sick party game thrown by someone else could possibly ruin the life we planned together hurt me. It's like you don't trust that I could love you."

"I'm sorry, beautiful," Diego says. "We just—we know it's a lot to take in."

"We also know how awful some of the vampire lifestyle is to you," Austin adds. "I can only imagine how this makes you feel, and we want nothing more than to protect you."

I hug them tighter, squishing them closer. "I don't generalize all vampires anymore, so please remember that I'm not going to hold who you are against you. I'll only hold who you are against me. In the best way possible."

"So what would be your deal breaker?" Kingston asks, surprising me. I think this might be the first time he's ever ignored an innuendo.

"What, no joke?" I ask him.

"I just need to know—and then you bet I'm going to let you hold me against you. Hopefully while you let me suck on your neck. In the bloodiest way possible."

"I—um..." My voice trails off. "I don't know, honestly."

"Obviously not murder," Kingston says. "I mean, you forgave Austin."

Austin groans. "It was self-defense."

Diego hooks his arm around Kingston's neck and rubs his fist into his hair. "You act like you haven't killed anyone."

"Not without good reason...since I've met our girl." Kingston darts his gaze to mine, checking my reaction.

I tighten my jaw, remaining as expressionless as possible. I know that my guys had lives before me—long lives. But I don't exactly want to think about their lives before. I don't want to think about what it would take for me to break my Blood Vow promise either.

"I'm a changed vampire. Mostly. I still want to kill that guy...with good reason," Kingston adds, pointing to the unconscious man.

"Dude," I murmur.

Kingston straightens his shoulders. "If our places were reversed, you'd understand."

Would I? I have no idea. I can only imagine what it's like for the man. I don't know what kind of criminal he was, but if I were put in a position of fighting for my life for shits and giggles among vampires, I might've done what he did. He was literally shoved into it by a vampire. Because I remember he was trying to hide.

Diego nudges Kingston with his shoulder. "I wish they were reversed."

I roll my shoulder, the ache in my back annoying me. "Me too. I feel like shit. How long do we have to stay here, anyway?" Peering around Austin's medical lab, I take in the mess of medical equipment I'm sure is covered in my blood. "I just want to feed you all, curl up in bed, and watch the sunrise together."

"I want all of that," Kingston says, flashing his fangs.

I smirk and move my hair over my shoulder. "Then make it happen. Because I want out of these clothes. Like now."

Kingston purrs in his throat, the soft noise making me smile wider.

Diego slides his hand across my ass to hook his fingers to my hip, pulling me away from Kingston. "Sorry, bro. It's my day with Jewel, so I'll be the one making it happen."

"Lucky for me, sunrise isn't for another three hours."

"Time Jewel needs to spend healing, not overexerting herself," Austin says, speaking up. "And I recommend you stay off your back for a few hours."

"It's a good thing there are plenty of other posi—"

Austin shoves Kingston, shutting him up. "You know we have to stay guarded until sunrise, and I'm not going to hang outside either of your rooms so you can—"

I press my finger to Austin's mouth. "We're going to stay together, and you're right about needing to heal. I'm still achy. But I don't want to stay here."

"It's better if we do," Austin says. "Finders keepers is still going on. We might have to see everyone off as well when it's over."

"Plus, there's that guy," Diego says, motioning to the supposed criminal. "None of us will protect him, and he can't stay here."

"Then one of you better get me something new to wear," I say, placing my hands on my hips. "Because I'm sure I look gross. Feel it too."

"You look hot, babe," Kingston says. "Mouthwatering."

I roll my eyes. "Only you, dude."

"No, you are sexy as hell right now," Diego adds, leaning to kiss one of his bite marks through Kingston's jacket like he memorized exactly where he left them.

Turning to Austin, I raise my brows. "You think so, too?"

He smiles. "Kingston's not the only one you're making feel starved."

"So obviously no mind control without permission," Kingston

says. "Though even if I could, I wouldn't. Not after our first day."

"That's enough, Kingston." I don't look at him or Diego as I step into the shower despite their heavy gazes burning into my back. One look over my shoulder at my ravaged skin nearly made me faint, though Austin used synthetic skin to staunch the bleeding caused by the knife dragged across my back. Better just cut than stabbed, I guess.

I release a soft moan at how amazing the water feels on my skin. Diego and Kingston both chuckle, enjoying this way too much. They can't even see me naked, but I'm sure they're imagining it. I'm actually surprised neither of them offered to join me or that they remain where they are without sneaking glances over the chest high wall of the lab's bathroom.

I don't want to ask them either and start a fight or end up with the three of us squished in here, because I'm not sure I could handle such an adventure. So I stand alone and enjoy the steady stream of hot water as it washes away all the blood—a mixture of mine and Diego's—from my skin, bringing me relief.

"Killing my brothers would probably be on the list," Kingston adds, continuing to make his mental list of deal breakers.

"Is that the only thing stopping you from trying?" Diego asks.

"Sometimes. Mostly when you put Jewel in danger. You can't tell me you haven't wanted to annihilate me either."

"Oh, all the time. And our girl is always safe with me. You're overprotective and underestimate her ability."

"Do not. I just like to treat her as gently and lovingly as she deserves."

"But doesn't always like. I mean, look at this."

"Shit." Kingston sucks in a breath. "That's a big nope for me."

"I guess she'll never crave you like she does—"

"Can you guys stop talking like I'm not here?" I laugh and turn to face them, catching Diego pulling up the collar of his shirt. Tingles rush through me at the look he gives me, and I realize he's tall enough to see me over the wall from his spot.

"I don't know about Diego, but I have to pretend you're not, so no, babe. Accept this as pretend privacy."

"He's right, beautiful. I want nothing more than to slide in there with you."

Kingston strolls closer and bounces on his feet to take his obvious peek at me. "And don't you invite us, either."

"Why?"

Austin materializes in the doorway, holding a dress bag in his fingers. He hangs it up on a hook and steps closer to the shower. Kingston groans and strolls back toward the wall and leans against it next to Diego.

Opening the shower, Austin smirks as he takes me in. "Because they lack the restraint I do, and I was serious about you needing to heal."

Austin surprises me by undressing and stepping into the

shower with me. Both Kingston and Diego mutter to each other by the door, but neither of them leaves the bathroom. I glance away from the two of them staring at the floor and to Austin, who now stands only a foot away.

He lets me drink in every delicious curve of his body that sends goosebumps over my skin. Now that we've done something next level with each other, I can't stop my body from reacting. He's changed in front of me before and after swimming a dozen times, but now something has shifted between us. It's more than doing something day-to-day like changing. Baring ourselves like this turned intimate. And I'm enjoying it way too much.

"You have one job, Austin. Don't lose focus or I'm going to start doubting your restraint," Diego says. "And then we'll test mine instead."

I bite my lip between my teeth. "I don't think you guys took in account my lack of restraint."

"Shit," Kingston says.

I laugh. "I'm kidding."

"She's not," Diego says. "Look at her face. I want her to look at me like that right now."

Kingston smacks his hand on the wall. "Austin. One job. Don't make us come over there, especially because Jewel looks extra bitey."

Austin grins at me and closes the space only to reach around me to grab the bathing sponge hanging next to the dispenser of jasmine-scented soap. I release a small breath at his closeness, practically panting and not because of the steamy air.

"May I?" Austin asks, holding up the soapy sponge. "I'll be quick and careful."

I bob my head and lift my damp hair from my neck.

"I'm so jealous right now," Diego murmurs to Kingston.

Austin smirks, ignoring him. "I'll apply more pain reliever when I'm through."

A rap on the door draws my attention away from Austin. Kingston and Diego rush from the bathroom, leaving us alone. If it weren't for the voices trickling through the air, I'd take advantage of Austin's closeness to distract me a little. But I don't get the chance. Austin quickly helps me clean up and dress, leaving no time for the fun I want to have with him with his brothers in the other room.

"I'll make it up to you later," he whispers in my ear, adjusting the straps of the backless gown he brought me to maintain my appearance. So much for my makeup, though. At least the blood and smeared mascara are gone from my face.

"Seriously?" Kingston shouts from the other room. "Are you crazy?"

"No, I'm just good at the game," Brayla responds.

Austin frowns at me and takes my hand, pulling me with him to the door. I startle at the sight of Brayla in the hallway outside the lab with what appears to be at least a dozen humans piled on the floor behind her. I don't think I'll ever get used to seeing her like this.

"You can't just collect them. The game doesn't work like that. They're criminals. This was supposed to be their final dona..." Kingston's words trail off, and he slumps his shoulders to peer behind him to look at me. "There are rules. Babe, you have to understand."

I grimace. I didn't give him the nickname Rule Breaker without reason, but I guess he only breaks the rules in regards to me. I don't say it, though. He looks like he feels bad enough already.

"I'm sure she will understand," Brayla says. "You made it clear that you don't want to help me save them."

"Save them? You'll—"

"Orlando will be happy to have them on our staff," she says. "I already told him."

I step into the room, tugging Austin along with me. Diego stands next to Kingston, rubbing his hand down his face, looking as unenthused as my body match is over the situation. Brayla turns from her pile of humans and to me, flashing me a smile without fangs.

"I promise you, Jewel. They will be fine," she says. "And your invite is open-ended. You could come over and check in on them anytime."

I glance at Austin for a reaction he doesn't give. Kingston and Diego share a silent, expressionless conversation that I can't decipher. "Why go through all the trouble?"

"Like I said, I want you to forgive me. I don't want to

lose your friendship again," Brayla says. "You're too important to me. I know Orlando has done some unforgivable things to your family, but he gave me a life beyond anything I imagined. He saved me. I want to work through everything and make it right."

I rub my lips together in thought for a moment. "This would be a start."

"Babe, you can't believe her. She's manipulating you."

Turning to Kingston, I shake my head. He groans and laces his fingers through his hair but doesn't argue with me. "By assuring these people don't meet their final donations? I don't care if she is as long as something good comes from it."

Diego closes the space between us to look into my eyes. "Beautiful, I know you think this is the right thing, but—"

"It is," I say, holding strong.

"I just need a way out." Brayla risks entering the room, reminding me how tough she is. My guys might have intimidated her when she was still human, but she braved them then and still braves them now. She might have changed, but deep down, she's still the person I know. "Maybe a small hand to speed things up."

Diego touches my cheek. "We can't be a part of this. We have too much to lose. It's one thing not to play but to purposely show mercy toward those convicted of crimes in Midnight Valley would create a rift in our alliance with the Vaduvas."

"And you know how strategic Viorica is. She'll use whatever she can to benefit herself," Austin adds.

"Then don't be a part of it," I say. "I can show Brayla out and drag at least one of the smaller guys. We don't need your help."

Kingston touches my shoulder. "Babe, please reconsider."

"Reconsider saving lives? No," I say, strolling past him and into the hallway.

"You won't regret this, Jewel," Brayla says, beaming a smile. "I promise."

I lace my fingers around the wrist of the smallest man and test my strength, dragging him a foot. Austin hovers behind me but doesn't help me. Neither do Kingston and Diego. I pull the man a good ten feet before I set him down and straighten my back, doing my best to ignore the ache over my spine.

"You're really not going to help?" I ask my guys, annoyance lining my words. I thought if they saw how much I struggled, they might give in and help me after all.

"Is that a deal breaker?" Kingston asks.

I frown. "No, but—"

"Then no," Diego says. "We're sorry, beautiful. We already told you. We can't help."

"We shouldn't even let you," Austin says.

Kingston steps up beside me. "Don't expect us to intervene if Brayla gets caught either."

Brayla hoists two guys up, one on each of her shoulders. "I won't need your help. I survived Starlight Row all my life as a human."

I can't stop staring at her. She's the same yet different. Better? That's yet to be decided. "She's right."

"And we're going to be fine, Jewel," she says. "You know why?"

I peer at her without responding.

"Because we've always survived this life together."

TOUGH

"I'M IMPRESSED. YOU'RE STRONGER THAN before." Brayla takes the last man from me and sets him against the wall outside of Austin's room.

Fortunately for us, our section of the palace is off-limits to the rest of the party guests. Walt, the new head of security didn't even say anything as Brayla and I strolled past him. The only response he got was from Kingston, and it was him muttering about how hungry he was, but those who are around the four of us know that Kingston will skip a meal if he can't have my blood over sinking his teeth into anyone else. He swears it's only until my Blood Vow, but I can't stop worrying about feeding him sometimes. Like now. I'm pretty sure he's more reactive because of his hunger.

"You kind of have to be strong being a Blood Match to the Divine Heirs," I say, swiping sweat from my forehead.

"I bet." She giggles. Full on, snorty giggles, and follows my line of sight to my three sulking vampires leaning against the wall. They watch us work in silence, still dead-set on not helping. I for sure thought one of them would break, but they're obviously having their own competition between each other on who can resist me the longest.

"I meant because of all their enemies." I smack her arm with the back of my hand and automatically recoil and hug myself.

That gets Austin to take a step closer, though he pauses when he sees that Brayla doesn't react.

"Sure that's it." She wags her eyebrows at me and bumps her shoulder to mine, reminding me of a million times she's done so before. "And it's okay to touch me. I won't bite you, Jewel. Not like that guy." Wiggling her fingers, she waves at Diego.

I blush, heat engulfing my entire face. "We have fun," I whisper, knowing my guys can still clearly hear me. "It's never boring with any of them."

Brayla laughs again. "I can tell."

Turning my back on my guys, I touch my hand to the door and activate the palm pad to unlock it. I grab the closest man to me and drag him into the room I share with Austin. There was no way I was going to drag these men any farther, and Austin's was closest to the elevator.

"The balcony is right—"

"Jewel, watch out!" Brayla's yell cuts through the room, making me nearly jump from my skin.

The world blurs around me, and I land with an oomph on the plush carpet right next to the man. Kingston hovers over me, haloed in the light from the ceiling, and lifts me off my feet. Something crashes to my right, and one of the chairs from my dining table topples across the floor next to me.

"Let her go," Austin says.

Someone grunts and groans. Definitely female and vampire. But it's not Brayla.

I frown, peering over Kingston's shoulder as he runs me across the room toward the bathroom. He sets me on my feet and blocks my way.

"Why the hell is there a man-eater in your room?" Brayla asks, her low voice practically spitting out the words. "I thought you were exclusive to Jewel."

"I am," Austin says. "And you shouldn't be in here." His voice shifts from annoyance to something softer as he obviously talks to someone else.

"I didn't realize you still had access," Kingston says.

I stand on my tiptoes. "What? I thought no one but us had access to our rooms." Fear shakes my voice. I know I'm safe with my guys, but just the thought of someone sneaking into our room when it's supposed to be protected reminds me of Orlando and how he was stalking me. "Who's here?"

Samantha pops up in my line of sight, and I screech and

stumble backward. If Kingston didn't twist and catch me, I'd have landed hard on my ass. But that might've been better, because his arm hooks along my back, sending a wave of pain through me. The edges of my vision shadow, and I black out for a split second.

"Fucking A, Samantha. You should know better than to move like that. Jewel startles easily." Kingston's annoyed voice pulls me right back to the pain igniting through me. I find myself breathing in the sultry scent of his dress shirt with my legs wrapped around his waist, the both of us on the bathroom floor.

"Whoa, what the heck happened to her?" Samantha asks. I can't see her, but I sense her presence behind me. I shiver in Kingston's arms, burying my nose deeper into his shoulder as I try to suppress my panic and pain. "She looks like someone cut down the length of her back."

"Someone did. One of your criminals tried to stab her, but we were quick to pull her away. She'll be all right," Austin says, kneeling beside me. He leans in for a closer look at my face, studying my watery eyes with a pout. Gently gliding his finger across my cheek, he smears a stray tear. "Luckily, the wound is shallow."

"But painful as shit," I say, heaving a breath as he touches his cool fingers over my skin. I never thought I'd be thankful for the backless gown he picked out. I nearly complained about having to get back into a dress until I saw the thought he put into it. I can't imagine anything being comfortable against my skin for another few hours until I heal more.

Kingston adjusts me on his lap and carefully holds my hair up out of the way. "Maybe you'll think before trying to save Austin from injury next time."

Diego squats by my other side. "Good thing our girl is tough."

"Wait. She did what?" Samantha asks, now engrossed in our conversation.

"You can thank one of your sisters for that. If you all were trying to impress Jewel or whatever, you totally failed," Brayla says, interrupting. "She didn't enjoy your stupid game of finders keepers."

Samantha strolls behind Kingston and looks down at me. "Not my idea. Why do you think I'm in here?" She says it to Brayla but keeps her eyes trained on mine as Austin carefully massages something into my back.

"To cause trouble," Brayla says. "Thought you might've seen my collection of party gifts."

"Party gifts?"

"I'm taking the humans I caught home."

"But—"

Brayla releases a creepy ass guttural sound from her throat. "Try and stop me."

Samantha tilts her head, still keeping her eyes glued to mine. I don't look away. I'm a little afraid that if I do, she'll try to mess with me. I know she and Austin had a human familial bond, but it's not the same anymore, diluted by the fact that Samantha's part of the Vaduvas and Austin is a Divine.

"No, it's quite okay," Samantha says. "If the Divines aren't intervening—"

"We're not involved," Diego says.

"And I do what I want," I say, huffing a huge breath of relief at the numbness overtaking my back.

"That's super cute, Austin," Samantha says, looking at him behind me. "Letting her get her way. I bet she likes that considering..." Her voice trails off with her thought. She doesn't have to say it for me to know she was going to mention something about my place in the world and how few humans get their way, which is true. "I hope she realizes you're the best choice for a permanent match."

"Sammy," Austin warns, his words stopping me from responding.

"How do you even know it was Austin letting her get her way?" Kingston asks.

"Because he carries the same compassion as Jewel. I highly doubt you'd allow it from the goodness of your heart, Kingston. I imagine you're only complying to assure she doesn't turn on you."

"Damn," Brayla says.

"You know Jewel, correct?" Samantha asks Brayla in a whisper I'm not supposed to hear. "Don't you think Austin's better suited for her?"

"Uh, I don't know. All I know is she's in love with them all," Brayla responds just as quietly.

"Yeah, right," Samantha says. "Look at her. She's clearly uncomfortable in Kingston's arms. And I'm pretty sure she regrets letting Diego bite her. She keeps rolling her shoulder."

OhmyeffingG. I want so badly to yell at her to shut up, but I can't even react. Kingston stiffens at her words, and Diego grumbles under his breath. Austin squeezes my shoulder, trying to keep me calm.

"One more thing, Jewel," Austin says, applying ointment to the bite marks Samantha so annoyingly pointed out.

She taps her foot, continuing her conversation with Brayla. "I'm just saying. Now that I've met Jewel and after talking more with my mother, I still don't understand how Kingston and Diego matched better than me. We'd be great friends."

"Sammy, really?" Austin says. "Can you stop?"

"Maybe so, Samantha, but not because of what you think," Brayla says, ignoring Austin and surprising me. "It's clear to me that your lack of understanding Jewel is why you didn't. If you don't see how perfect the Divines are for her, then it's obvious to me how they matched better than you."

"Damn straight," Kingston mutters. I think for the first time tonight, Brayla might have said something that could possibly win him over.

"Whatever," Samantha says. "She's still going to have to choose."

I dig my fingers into Kingston's shoulders at her words. I can't remain quiet any longer. Sucking in a deep breath, I compose myself and press my palm into the cold tile floor to push up without asking Kingston for help. He does so any-way, lifting me to my feet with him.

"Samantha, it was nice to see you and all, but I'm going to have to ask you to leave. I need to help Brayla since no one else will."

"Oh," Samantha says.

Kingston relaxes, probably thankful I didn't blow up and reveal I could hear every detail of Samantha's conversation. "Not going to work, babe," he says, running his hands over my frame without touching me to make sure I'm okay.

I sigh.

Samantha steps up to meet me straight on. "What if I help you?"

"Really? Why?" I ask, eyeing my guys glaring at Saman-tha. "Isn't that against the rules?"

She shrugs and smirks at them. "Mother would appreciate the effort I'm putting in to show you how things could be."

At least she's honest. "Well, okay then. Just don't get your hopes up. I'm pretty set on being a Divine."

That makes Kingston, Austin, and Diego all smile.

Samantha holds her hand out to me. "You never know. Things could change."

"Not this," I say.

Tugging me forward, she leans in and whispers, "I guess we'll have to wait and see."

Except I never want to find out.

PERFECT MATCHES

"IF YOU WANT DOWN, YOU'RE going to have to jump by yourself," Kingston says, leaning on the railing to peer at Brayla and Samantha below.

Diego taps a few buttons on his tablet. "Because both of them have been denied access to re-enter our living quarters."

"Seriously?" I ask.

Kingston swings his leg over the banister and moves in front of me. Bringing his mouth to mine, he kisses me sweetly, cupping my face in his hands without holding on, just balancing on the ledge. "Super serious," he whispers, brushing his lips to mine a few more times. He pulls away and smiles at me. "But don't worry. I'll catch you."

Launching backward, he drops from the balcony and

lands in a crouch just like I've seen people do in movies. I'm pretty sure he only did so to show off, which it totally worked, because I can't stop myself from returning his brilliant smile. If it wouldn't be so ridiculous for me to do so, I'd clap, because damn, that was awesome.

He holds open his arms and motions for me to jump. "Come on, babe."

I stick my tongue out at him and turn to Diego. "You're not going to make me jump on my own, are you?" I ask him, closing the space between us.

He lifts me off my feet and sets me on the railing to kiss me. "We could just stay here."

I groan. "Diego."

"The more you pout, the more I'll just continue to kiss you," he says against my lips.

"Don't let him distract you, Jewel," Brayla calls from below. "He's wasting time and doesn't want you to see me off. And as much as I'd like to wait, I can't."

I slide off the railing and push Diego back so I can twist around and look at the drop to the ground again. Diego jumps, not giving me the chance to plead with him, and lands next to Kingston. They both smile at me.

"You can do it, beautiful," Diego says. "Don't be scared."

But I am scared. The last time I jumped off a building I thought my stomach was going to crash through my head. And that was in Austin's arms. It's different having to do this myself.

"What if you don't catch me?" I ask.

"One of them will catch you," Austin says, coming up next to me.

I grab his hand. "Jump with me?"

He tightens his jaw.

"Pretty please," I add. "I'll love you forever."

He chuckles. "That's a given."

I scrunch my nose. "We can make a deal."

"No using your affection against Austin," Kingston calls. "That's unfair."

"All is fair, dude," I say, flipping Kingston off. "You should know that."

"I knew he should've jumped first," Diego says. "Restraint, my ass."

I ignore them and turn back to Austin, sliding my arms around his neck. He smiles at me, his emerald eyes shining in the soft lighting trickling from his open balcony door. He doesn't say anything as he waits for me to make my move.

I kiss him deep enough that he closes the space completely to press his body to mine. "Please don't make me jump alone."

"Of course I won't. I'm not making you jump at all."

I sigh.

He chuckles.

"Austin."

"About that deal."

"Really?" I ask, pressing my hands to his chest.

Kingston growls from below. "I swear, Austin."

"I can't think of anything," Austin's quick to say.

"Ask her to pick you!" Samantha yells.

"Good thinking," Austin says, pulling away to peer at his cousin.

I glare at him, making his smile widen. "You know I already do," I whisper too quietly for anyone else to hear.

He kisses me again. "Then I guess there's nothing else. You're on your own to jump. Or we can just stay here."

Headlights beam on from down the driveway, drawing my attention away from Austin to below.

"Hurry, Jewel," Brayla calls.

Sucking in a deep breath, I summon my nerves and head to the railing. Austin stands nearby and at least lets me use his arm to hold onto while I swing my leg over. I wobble on the tiny ledge. If Austin didn't grab me by my sides to balance me, I'd have fallen backwards. Diego and Kingston made it look so easy.

My heart picks up speed. "Someone better catch me."

Austin smiles at me. "Don't worry. I will."

The weight of Austin's fingers releases as he disappears from in front of me. He moves so quickly over the railing that I don't have time to brace myself at the sudden shift in my weight. My feet slip on the ledge. I dangle from the balcony, my body automatically reacting to the fear that wants me to hold on for dear life. Except I can't. I drop down, screaming as my stomach rises in my throat to steal the noise from me.

Strong arms encircle me, breaking my fall, and Austin grins at me and nuzzles his nose to mine. "Told you I'd catch you."

I gasp a few deep breaths, my eyes still watering from the wind of falling. "Shit."

"You should practice your jumping," Diego says. "Maybe that's what we'll do tomorrow night."

"But I was hoping you'd give me the honor of your company." Orlando's smooth voice cuts through the air, tightening my muscles.

I peer away from Austin to see the silent van parked a few feet away with the door wide open to the cargo space in back. The only time I recall ever seeing a vehicle like this was when I was little when Dark Terrace Ranch wasn't quarantined and allowed humans to be taken in and out of the city.

"Since it seems you've managed to make amends with Brayla," he adds, smiling at her.

"Not completely, lover," Brayla answers for me. "But I hope this is a start. I still have to prove to Jewel that I can follow through with my promise to her."

"It's not about you, Brayla," I say, shifting in Austin's arms until he reluctantly sets me on my feet. "I just—I can't. Not with him." I point at Orlando.

"Perhaps if you see how well I care for your sister, you might change your mind," he muses.

I glower. "The fact that you have her in the first place—"

"Please, Orlando. Jewel is my friend, and you have to behave. You know it's a touchy subject, and I hope we can work through it." Brayla steps between us and risks the growls of my guys to put her hands on my shoulders. I motion for them to stay back and meet Brayla's eyes. She offers me a closed lip smile and then hugs me to her. "I don't want to lose you, Jewel."

I don't know how to respond. "Brayla, you have to understand. This life? It's not The Boxes. What Orlando did, well—"

"Precious Jewel, I do hope you can forgive me," he says from over Brayla's shoulder. "You know, without me, you might have never even matched. I hope you realize that and take it into consideration. We don't have to be enemies."

"You tried to stop me from matching," I say, glaring at him.

"Quite the contrary. If I wanted to stop you, I would've. But I was kind enough to let you go. You can thank your father for that." He peers at Kingston. "And you should thank me, Mr. Divine. If Jewel wasn't late, you might have never applied. Then again, this could have been easier. One less to choose from."

Kingston flies at Orlando, but he spins out of the way, and Brayla steps between the two of them. Samantha grabs onto the backs of both Diego's and Austin's jackets and keeps them from starting a fight. I stroll over to the unconscious pile of humans, drawing everyone's attention to me.

"It's time for you to go, Mr. Ortega. I don't want to have

to call security and tell them that you're attempting to take home criminals from the game," I say, my voice betraying me by going soft instead of hard and threatening like I intended. "That would assure Brayla breaks her promise to me."

Everyone knows I'm flat out lying, but Orlando only nods and hoists a man into the van. Brayla helps him, and they load up their vehicle faster than I could move to even get one guy inside, though Kingston slides up beside me and holds my hand, keeping me from trying. I'm pretty sure I'm the only reason he doesn't try to attack Orlando again too.

"Jewel," Brayla says, closing the space to me. "I had a lovely night with you."

I raise an eyebrow. "If you say so."

She laughs. "I do hope the next will be better. Please, keep in touch. Call me if you want to visit or if it's even just to talk. I'll let you see Ramona too, okay?"

Hugging me once, she turns away and slides into the passenger's seat of the van, letting Orlando shut her door. He watches me the entire time he strolls around the hood, his blue eyes flashing silver once before he gets behind the wheel.

"I'll see you around, precious Jewel," he says, smiling at me. "Thanks for showing my lover a good time."

And like that, they're gone.

My whole body trembles as the night catches up to me. A mixture of emotions rolls through me, bringing tears to my eyes as Brayla disappears from my life again. I should be used to being without her by now, but something about seeing her tonight got under my skin.

I didn't know how badly I missed her until she left this moment. The fact that I feel this way, knowing she killed my dad, makes things worse. Kingston was right. Apparently murder isn't a deal breaker to me. Or maybe the anger I carry for my dad still burns too hotly. I wouldn't have been put in this position had he not disappeared. Then again, I wouldn't have met my matches. It's a double-edged sword stabbing through me.

"I'm sorry you miss your friend," Samantha says quietly from the other side of Austin. "I know how much friendship means. I couldn't imagine not getting to hang out with my sisters all the time. There's something special about that kind of bond. Right, Austin? I know you couldn't just abandon your brothers."

He only nods.

Kingston hugs me tighter. "I'm sorry, too," he whispers. "Why don't we head back inside and do what you planned on doing?"

I lick my lips. "Are you just saying that because you're starved?" I keep my voice light, teasing. I'd much rather joke around than think more about Brayla or the disaster of a party. All I want to think about is my guys.

Kingston flashes his fangs at me. "I'd be lying if I said I wasn't."

Bringing my hand up, I prick my finger on his fang, sending blood splashing on his lip. He closes his mouth around my finger faster than I can pull away and sucks it, making me laugh.

"Don't tease a hungry vampire," he mumbles.

I pull my hair from my neck. "If you really can't wait—"

Kingston tugs me closer to him, making me screech at the sudden movement. He buries his face to my throat but only glides his tongue over my skin. His heart pounds against mine, his hold tightening around my waist.

"I wasn't joking," I murmur.

"Jewel, I—"

"Let me feed you."

Sucking in a small breath, Kingston kisses my neck again before lifting me off my feet. The world spins, and my back gently presses against the cool stone façade of the wall below Austin's balcony.

"Ready?" he whispers against my skin.

"Yeah."

I barely get the word out before Kingston's fangs pierce the sensitive skin on my neck, making me release a soft breath that sounds like a cross between a moan and a plea. He hums his pleasure, his voice vibrating across my skin under his lips as he sucks just long enough to make me crave more of his touch.

"I just want to devour you," he mumbles, pressing his fingers to his bite mark to staunch the bleeding. He doesn't waste a single drop, licking the tips of his fingers after, much more a clean biter than I'm sure I'll ever be. I shudder even to think that Diego let me walk from the bathroom in the condition I was in.

"Later," I whisper. "It's Austin's turn to eat. I'm sure he's hungry, too."

"God, I sometimes hate sharing," Kingston says, strolling me back toward where Diego, Austin, and Samantha stand together, chatting with their backs toward us like this is all normal. And I know it is despite rarely feeding my guys straight from my body and in front of others.

I cup Kingston's face in my hands and kiss him once more. "Well, I appreciate that you do."

Kingston sets me down on my feet and nudges me toward Austin. "Not too much."

I roll my eyes and lace my fingers through Austin's and tug him away, wiggling my fingers at Kingston and Diego as they watch me go. Samantha doesn't even look in our direction, keeping her gaze trained on the sprawling garden in front of us.

Austin strolls next to me, smiling when I swing our arms together as I guide him deeper into the garden to the small bench under the lush oak tree. Yellow, orange, and white koi fish dart under the lily pads of the pond in front of us. I dangle my legs over Austin's and sit close to him.

"You don't have to do this," he says, resting his hands on my knees.

I lean closer and kiss him. "I know."

He pulls away before I can even attempt to deepen our

kiss. "We could go back to our room, and I can get my kit. Have the staff bring you something more to eat. You barely touched your dinner. Not to mention all your blood loss tonight."

"I feel fine," I say, extending my arm up to his mouth. "Let me take care of you for once."

"You care for me all the time," he says, smiling. "In all the best ways."

"Austin," I say, giggling.

He laughs again and touches the warmth blossoming in my cheeks with his cool finger. "I love you, you know. I am sorry I didn't help you with the Brayla thing."

"It was fine. I get it."

"I know."

"But I don't want to talk about that anymore. I want to feed you."

I raise my arm to his mouth, hovering it in front of his lips until he gives in and extends his fangs. He laces his fingers around my wrist and elbow and kisses the length of my arm between. I squirm a bit under his touch, the idea of his bite sending my body buzzing.

"You ready?" he asks, keeping his eyes trained on me.

I nod. "The anticipation is driving me crazy."

He smiles and bites down, piercing my skin so quickly that it only pinches a little. His lips take over, and he sucks harder, his stomach rippling against my other arm as he swallows. Austin closes his eyes, and I watch him drink, his pleasure clear on his face and right under my ass as he adjusts me on him to feel the extent of his arousal at my closeness.

He licks a few stray drops and kisses his bite mark, making sure it doesn't continue to bleed. I smile at him and rest my head to his shoulder, just enjoying the sound of our hearts beating and the trickling of the pond.

"Jewel?" he asks. "You okay? Can you sit up for a second so I can look at you?"

I blink a few times and lift my head only to lose focus. "Whoa. I think I need to eat."

"Here, drink some of my blood," he says, biting into his own arm.

"Mr. Divine," a familiar female voice calls, coming from somewhere I can't see. "I must request you do not proceed. The board requires Jewel's attention, and you must bring her inside immediately."

"It is my right to assure my Blood Match's health," Austin says.

"And how often do you give Jewel your blood?" Viorica appears in front of us, crossing her arms over her chest.

Samantha stands by her side, frowning at the both of us.

Austin scowls. "That's none of your business."

"Tonight, it is," she says.

My head lolls, and I rest it on Austin's shoulder. "Leave us alone," I whisper. "Why don't you just go home?"

"My apologies, Jewel. But something has come to the board's attention tonight that confirmed something I suspected. We need to discuss your Blood Matches."

"What do you mean?" I ask.

Viorica steps closer, her heels click-clacking on the cement walkway. "It's quite possible your testing had been tampered with."

"Kingston would never," I mumble.

Austin shifts me away, and Diego and Kingston appear in front of us, blocking my view of Viorica. The two of them silently dare her to try to get past them to face me. My head pounds with my racing heart, and Austin brings his arm up to my lips.

"I'm going to ask you again not to do that," Viorica says.

Austin doesn't listen and helps me drink the blood from his arm. Hands lock around the both of us, and Austin launches to his feet, still embracing me. All of Viorica's daughters surround us, blocking us in. Kingston, Diego, and Austin sandwich me between them without backing down.

"Do you really want to break our alliance?" Kingston asks.

"My sons, please back down." Mitchell appears next to Viorica, meeting my gaze from over Kingston's shoulder. "Jewel isn't in any danger, and I will not allow you to threaten the Vaduvas."

"What does the board want with her?" Diego asks.

Mitchell sighs. "It seems they still doubt the results of your Blood Matches to her. It has come to our attention that her mind might've been tampered with before her testing."

My stomach clenches at his words, and I grip onto Austin, hiding my face against him. "What?"

"Austin, I'm sorry," Samantha says. "You heard the Ortegas. I just knew something had to have gone wrong. But don't worry. I'm sure you're still Jewel's Blood Match. But I think I am too. It makes better sense than them." She points at Diego and Kingston. "The board agrees."

I gasp in a few deep breaths, panic stealing my ability to breathe. This can't be happening. It can't.

"So what do you expect us to do?" Kingston asks. "Jewel is my Blood Match. Just because you don't believe it, doesn't make it any less true."

"He's right," Diego says. "We're perfect for each other."

"All of us," Austin adds.

Viorica glances at Mitchell. "If it's true, then you will all have your chance to prove it. Because of these unforeseen circumstances, we're requiring Jewel to reapply."

"Reapply?" I ask. "What?"

"You can't do this," all three of my guys say in unison.

Mitchell clears his throat. "I'm sorry, boys, but the board can. Don't worry, though. You have nothing to worry about. I'm sure Jewel is still your perfect match."

I bob my head. "He's right. We'll show them."

"That means no more blood, Mr. Divines," Viorica says.

Mitchell steps closer and faces my guys. "It also means Jewel must come with me."

WORST NIGHTMARE

"NO." I THRASH MY HEAD back and forth and latch onto Austin as tightly as I can. "Please. You're wrong. Don't make me do this."

"Stay calm, Jewel," Austin whispers.

"Calm! Stay calm? How can I stay calm? Look what they're trying to do to us!" My high-pitch voice rings through the air so loudly I'm sure the whole estate can hear me. "Please, don't make me go."

"Ms. Jordan, don't make me pry you away and restrain you," Viorica says.

"Don't call me that!" My chest clenches, stealing my breath. I grip Austin with all my strength and bury my face in his neck. "You can't let them take me. You guys promised me forever. Please."

"Mr. Divines, release Ms. Jordan into Mitchell's care now. If you resist, you will be disqualified from matching."

"What? No." Tears burn my eyes. "No. No. No."

"Just give us a few minutes," Diego says, touching my shoulder. I don't even have to look at him to know it's him. I'm so in tune with his body that I can sense his presence. "Can't you see she's upset?"

"I don't even see why these dramatics are necessary," Kingston says, keeping his voice even. "You've already accepted her application to a Blood Vow, which pulls her from the program upon completion."

"Her application was approved based on her Blood Matching to a Divine. Now that your matching status is in question, her application will need to be re-visited."

"And if the three of us decide not to proceed and instead hire Jewel's services and family's entrance into Haven Springs?" Kingston asks.

"She does not qualify for a staff position with the Jordan blood debt. If she does not agree to a re-test, she will be turned over to Mr. Ortega. Her heirs will return to Dark Terrace Ranch," a masculine voice says. I can't put a face to his voice, but I know he's on the board.

Mitchell closes the space, and I stare at his shiny dress shoes from Austin's arms. "Boys, please just do as you're asked. There is no need to argue. This is purely for the record. By tomorrow night, you can return to your normal lives."

"Unless the accusation proves to be legitimate," Viorica says. "In that case, Jewel will have a fulfilling life in the Vaduva household."

"I'd rather accept my family's blood debt than match with a Vaduva," I say, spinning to meet Viorica's smug expression.

"Does that mean you're withdrawing your application?" Merrick slides up beside her mother and rests her arm on her shoulder.

I blink a few times.

"You realize you can't back out after the initial questionnaire, right?" the redheaded Vaduva sister asks. I think I recall her name being Heidi.

"I can breach my contract," I say.

"And risk your heirs' lives?" Gabriella asks.

Shit balls.

Kingston leans his face down to mine to meet my watery eyes. "Don't worry, babe. We'll arrange work contracts for them. They're old enough to take on apprenticeships."

"I think we'll have to change the contract agreement to prevent such an occurrence," Viorica says.

I tense and glower, hot anger washing through me. "Are you kidding me?"

"Agreed," several voices say. A few mention something about my final donation, sending fear through me.

Footsteps sound out, and my guys release low growls.

"It's time to release Ms. Jordan into Mitchell's care. We

have a new contract to arrange and testing to prepare for," Viorica says.

"Come along, Jewel," Mitchell says.

They're going to have to pry me away if they think for one second that I'm willingly going to go with anyone besides my guys.

"Just give us a minute alone with her, please," Diego asks again.

"One minute," Viorica says.

The vampires surrounding us disperse, but I still don't detach myself from Austin. Kingston and Diego engulf us both in a hug, trying to smother the sobs wracking from my chest in the grossest, snottiest way possible. Austin doesn't shift me away, and for once, Kingston doesn't complain.

"You think running away is a bad idea now, Austin?" Kingston asks, keeping his voice so low that I barely catch the words with my super hearing.

"We're going to be fine," he assures, rubbing his hand carefully across my back, avoiding my knife scratch.

"And we have a day to plan if we're not," Diego says.

I heave a few gasps against Austin's shoulder. "What if they're right about Orlando? What if he got into my head and made this possible? He is a Blood Rebel."

"You can't start doubting our Blood Matches, Jewel," Austin says.

"But what if I'm not? I mean, what were the chances that I'd equally match with all of you? What if this was all just a twisted game? What if your real perfect matches are still ou—"

Austin cuts me off with a kiss, stealing the rest of my words from my mouth. But silencing them doesn't stop me from thinking them. And I can't help it. I love Kingston, Diego, and Austin, but what if we're just pieces to a game to be played with between whatever blood feud Orlando has against the Divines? I know my dad somehow had prior ties to Orlando, but I don't know how or why. The more I think about it, the more things don't add up. And I'm frustrated that I can't even ask my dad. Why a blood debt? Why pass me a life sentence with no benefits to try to keep me from Blood Matching? Why leave at all?

"I hate to say this, but thanks for shutting her mouth," Kingston says. "And babe, do I need to remind you why you should never question our body match? I mean, a minute isn't exactly a proper amount of time."

I release a ragged laugh, his words lightening the tense situation. "Kingston."

"That's better. You need to have a clear head for the re-test."

"I still don't get how this is going to accomplish anything," I say. "My answers aren't even going to be the same anymore."

"That's the point," Kingston says. "It shouldn't matter."

My lip quivers. "I don't think I'm going to survive this."

Austin rests his head on my shoulder. "We'll make certain of it."

"Time's up," Viorica says from behind me.

"No," I whisper.

Mitchell strolls up beside us and nudges Kingston and Diego back. "Come along, Jewel. I promise you'll be safe and taken care of."

I hook my fingers together around Austin's neck. "Just let them take me back to Dark Terrace Ranch."

"I'm afraid that's not possible," he says. "Austin, please let her go."

Austin drops his arms from me, but I hold on tighter.

"Ms. Jordan," Viorica snaps. "Don't make me drag you away. I cannot promise you will not come out uninjured."

Diego and Kingston step between her and me. "That's not necessary."

Austin leans away to look into my eyes. "Jewel, I know you're scared, but we will be nearby. We're not going to abandon you."

"Please," I whisper again. "Don't make me."

But Austin doesn't get a say. Mitchell latches his fingers to my sides and rips me away from Austin. I scream out and thrash, fighting against his strong grip on me. Fear kicks my limbs into action, and I swing my arms, attempting to get away from Mitchell, but all he does is toss me over his shoulder, squishing my arms against his chest.

And then the world blurs.

Mitchell drags me away from my guys without giving me a chance to say goodbye. What if it's the last time I ever see them? What if the results change?

I'm not so sure how I'll survive.

"Wait, what? They can do that?" Fallon asks, her mouth gaping open at the horrible news.

"I didn't know, either." It takes everything in me not to cry.

Dana bares her teeth in anger. "That's bullshit."

I don't have it in me to correct her language and only nod my agreement. Because it is bullshit. Everything Mitchell and the board involve themselves in is bullshit.

"Time to hang up with your heirs," Mitchell says from his spot on the lounge chair across the room.

I glare at him. "But I always get as much time as I want to talk to them."

"It wasn't intended to be a social call. You've passed along the news, now you need to hang up. They will be informed of the results after your Blood Match tonight."

Dana and Fallon both glare at Mitchell, but he doesn't react. Instead, he leans back on the chair and closes his eyes, looking way too content. I should take comfort in his confidence that everything will be as it should, but I don't trust the man who would slaughter dozens of humans to prove a point no matter if he was supposedly the savior of humanity with the rise of Donor Life Corp.

I take a breath and turn my attention back to my cousins. "I'll call you two later, okay? I love you."

Tears rim their matching blue eyes, but for once they don't argue. "Okay. Love you," they say in unison. "Good luck, Jewel. But you won't need it. They're your perfect matches. I know it," Fallon adds.

I disconnect the line and get to my feet to pace. There's no way I'm going to attempt to sleep, especially with Mitchell so close. I'm pretty sure I couldn't, even if I tried. I haven't ever slept alone. Before my guys, I always shared my sleeping space with Ramona and my cousins, and after, I've been snuggling with one of my guys every night since arriving.

"You should get some rest, so you have a clear head come nightfall," Mitchell says, opening his eyes again.

I shake my head. "Can't. I'm in too much pain." It's only half truthful, but I don't want to get into it with Mitchell.

Mitchell sits up straighter and slides his legs over the edge of the lounge. "I can have someone on staff bring something to help."

A knock bangs on the door at his words, and Austin's muffled voice sounds through the thick wood. My heart nearly bursts at the familiarity, but I can't even react. I'm not supposed to be able to hear him. My super hearing has never been more frustrating since I have to be ultra-aware of things around so many vampires.

Mitchell beats me to the door and swings it all the way open. Austin's eyes dart to mine immediately, and I catch sight of Diego and Kingston behind him. I frown, seeing they're not alone. Beside Kingston, Merrick and Samantha stretch to look at me from over Austin's shoulder. On Diego's side, Gabriella and Layla stand, looking less invested in my state of being.

"We brought a few things for Jewel," Austin says, holding up a bag for me to see. "The board approved our visit."

"As long as the Vaduvas were granted permission by Jewel to visit her as well," Kingston adds, answering my silent question as to why my guys are hanging out with the enemies.

"May we come in?" Diego asks, peering past his dad to me.

Mitchell swivels to look at me, and I realize I'm the one that must grant them permission to enter. With my current un-matched status, apparently all my freedoms as a donor have been returned to me. I should be able to stay in this top floor suite of the Blood Match Center alone, but I'm pretty sure the board doesn't trust any of us not to do anything rash. There was no way I was allowing Viorica to hang out with me, and despite my negative feelings toward Mitchell, he's the lesser threat.

"I guess," I say, trying to keep my face expressionless. There's no way I'm not going to agree. I'll deal with shadow dwellers if it means I can see Kingston, Diego, and Austin.

"We brought you something, too," Samantha says, following behind Austin to enter.

I frown. "Why?"

"As an apology," she responds. "The last thing I want is to have my possible Blood Match hate me."

"It'll take more than a gift to make that possible," I mutter. "You're why I'm in this position."

"I'm sorry, I just—"

"Stop," I say. "I don't want to hear it."

"I did the right thing. I know we haven't had the chance to get to know each other, but I fully believe that your mind was tampered with to skew the results. I know you like the Divines, but you could like us too, you know. How would you feel if you were me? I was certain we'd match, Jewel. Wouldn't you feel cheated?"

I try to keep my face expressionless and fail miserably. "Are you kidding me? You want *me* to empathize with *you?*"

Merrick scowls. "You should be thankful that we found out now so that you can be with your true match. The program was intended to be fulfilling for both participants. What we have to offer is just as good, if not better, than the Divines. We don't care about your blood like they do. We have plenty of our own blood sources."

Her comment weirds me out. "Then why apply? I'm supposed to be an exclusive donor."

"And offer companionship. How you interpret that is between matches," Layla says, speaking up for the first time.

"You applied solely for my companionship?"

"Mother wanted to grow our family," Samantha says. "It's not unheard of."

Gabriella smirks at me. "But I do like you and wouldn't mind your blood. You smell fabulous. Like..." Her words trail off, and she doesn't finish her sentence.

"Um, thanks." I raise my eyebrows, turning my attention to my guys. I knew they were also looking for something more than a blood donor, but it's still been a huge part of our relationship, and something I never knew I'd actually enjoy. Because feeding them is how I take care of them.

"Which is why none of you matched with my babe," Kingston mutters.

"We saw her last night. She looks like she could happily spend the rest of her life without feeding any of you," Merrick says.

"I entered the program with intentions to only be a blood source." I can't help defending parts of my relationship they have no clue about.

"Why would you do that?" Samantha asks. "People enter the program for hopes of a better life."

Wow. I can't even find my voice to answer her. The Vaduva's are delusional. No one enters the program for a better life. Everyone to have applied from The Boxes has done so out of desperation.

Reading my expression, Diego closes the space to me first and slides his arm over my shoulders. I sink against him, inhaling a small breath of his sweet, sugary scent. I don't know if it's because it's been hours since we were this close, but I can't stop myself from burying my face into his shirt, wanting nothing more than to drown myself in the scent that leaves my skin buzzing. And hungry for syrupy waffles. Shit balls. That's weird.

"Jewel applied because she couldn't support her heirs with her blood alone," he says, pouting his bottom lip at me.

"Yeah, she didn't even have the complete brochure," Austin adds.

"You should've seen her face when she realized—" Kingston snaps his mouth shut. "This is pointless. You're wasting all our times. That body of hers is mine. Her heart too."

Kingston laces his fingers through mine and spins me into his arms, kissing me so softly on the lips that for once he doesn't steal my breath but helps me breathe. I nod my head to Austin to join us, and he completes our circle that obviously annoys the Vaduva sisters, because Merrick has the nerve to tap Kingston on the shoulder.

Her brown eyes narrow. "I'd like a moment with Jewel as well. You can't hog her."

"Are you friggin' kidding me?" I ask, giving the sultry vampire a once-over.

"It's only fair."

Mitchell returns to the chaise lounge to recline on it and catches my eyes. He subtly nods his head in confirmation. Looks like I don't get a choice in the matter. Knots twist in my stomach at the memory of what life was like before my guys and how little say I had in what happened to me. Kingston, Diego, and Austin gave me the freedom I never had, and now the thought that I could possibly lose it scares the shit out of me.

"You realize that forcing Jewel to do stuff she clearly doesn't want any part of will do nothing to increase your odds of outmatching us," Diego says. "What we have with Jewel came naturally."

"Don't help them," Kingston mutters.

"I'm trying to help our girl."

Merrick purses her lips and ignores my guys. Gingerly grabbing my shoulder, she risks tugging me a foot away from them. Austin relents and releases me, but he remains ultra-close that if I take one step backward, I'd fall into his arms.

Samantha, Gabriella, and Layla close the space, creating their own circle. Each of them studies me with the same vampire intensity my guys carry, except I have no idea what they're thinking. I tighten my jaw in an attempt to keep my expression even. My first instinct is to turn away, but something about the sudden softness in these vampires' eyes makes me hesitate.

And then Merrick lifts her arms and wraps them around me in what I can only describe as the universe's most awkward hug. I stand frozen, listening to her soft breathing turn into a quicker pant, and she sniffs me.

"She's hot," Merrick says to her sisters.

I clear my throat. "Thanks, I guess."

Kingston chuckles from behind me.

"This must be why they're always touching her," she adds.

I realize she's referring to my temperature. I have never

thought much about the way I feel to my guys. They run colder than me except when I get them worked up like they borrow some of my body heat. It's kind of weird for me to think about now.

"Let me try," Gabriella says, nudging Merrick away from me.

I don't even get the chance to brace myself before she envelops me in a much more relaxed hug than the awkward embrace of Merrick. She doesn't sniff me either. Pulling back slightly, Gabriella meets my gaze with eyes as dark as Kingston's. I hold my breath at her closeness, afraid she might attempt to get into my head without my permission.

"I thought hugging you would be better than this," she says, tilting her head. "The Divines have much lower standards, I suppose."

"I thought hugging her was nice," Samantha chimes in.

I peel myself away and cross my arms over my chest again to hopefully combat any more Vaduva hugs. The sisters look at each other and shrug, and then Samantha holds up a bag to me. I nearly forgot that they had mentioned they brought some things for me, which also draws my attention back to Austin, who carries a bag on his shoulder.

"Here," Samantha says. "We hope you like everything."

Peering into the bag, I try to keep my face from giving away my surprise. I don't know what I was expecting, but it wasn't the collection of candy, different makeup products, and a rather large velvet box that must contain a piece of jewelry inside it. And I hate that I like everything.

"Open the box," Layla says. "Samantha picked it out."

I pull out the navy blue box and set the gift bag at my feet to open it. A locket rests in an inlaid compartment, shining with diamonds and sapphires. Samantha steps closer and pulls it out for me, using her nail to pry the locket open.

I gasp, staring at the two pictures inside—one of me with Ramona, Dana, and Fallon and the other of our entire family. "Where did you get these?" My cousins have the original copies in Haven Springs. "If I find out you went to—"

Merrick groans. "She hates it, Samantha. I told you—"

"No, she doesn't," Samantha snaps. Turning to me, she adds, "And Donor Life Corp had these available in your file. I know how important family is, so I thought you might like them." She glances from me to Austin, and they both share an indecipherable look.

I don't know how I should respond. I mean, hell. The Vaduvas put a lot of thought into giving me something, and I'm taken aback by their sudden kindness. I was set on hating them, especially after our first encounter, but I still don't trust them.

"Would you like to wear it?" Samantha asks, filling in the silence I drag out.

My head nods without my permission, because I want to hate her so badly, but my mind is having second thoughts. Slowly turning around, I lift my hair for her. Kingston, Diego, and Austin stare at me with worry pinching their faces. My lip quivers at the sadness stealing away their usually light-hearted, smiling faces, and I can't help wonder if accepting the necklace might be a form of betrayal.

And then the sudden release of my vow necklace cements the idea. The rose pendant I never take off drops from my neck and to the floor with a thud. The tiny vial of my guys' blood shatters, splattering their promises to me across the pristine white tiles.

Samantha hooks the necklace in place and drops the heavy locket where my vows used to be, sending pain exploding through my chest. I stand in shock, staring at my guys and then to the floor, but I don't get a chance to respond.

A few different chimes ring through the air, and everyone vanishes at a vampire's speed without even a single goodbye. I touch my fingers to the pictures of my family and bring my gaze up to meet Mitchell's again.

Without reacting, he pulls out his phone from his suit pocket and looks it over. "It's time to get ready, Jewel."

I blink, trying to clear my eyes and quickly bend down to swipe my vow necklace off the floor. "Okay."

"Can you help me with this?" I ask him, my voice quivering.

He shakes his head. "Not now. We have to wait for your results and to find out if you're meant to be a true Divine."

RE-MATCH

"YOU HAVE TO TELL ME something, Austin," I whisper, watching him, instead of the phlebotomist, who merely waits for the vials, extract blood from my arm.

My second attempt at the Blood Match questionnaire was a breeze, considering I didn't have to put too much thought into my answers. I knew what to expect and also didn't have Kingston's presence distracting me.

I inhale a deep breath and add, "My answers changed, which means so could who I match with, right?"

He bobs his head slightly but not enough for anyone to pick up on. "You're right, but we don't want you to worry."

"How can I not?" I whisper.

"You will not lose us, I swear."

"Does that mean you're going to fight? Will we run away?"

He quickly removes the needle and presses a cotton ball to my arm before applying synthetic skin. "This will do. Please take the vials to the tasting room," he says to the technician.

I stare in shock, counting the five smaller than usual vials. Five vials means five people, and last time all the Vaduva sisters didn't make it past the questionnaire phase. Something changed. Because I'm as certain as hell that Master Caruthers and Katherine Duchanne haven't magically resurrected from their eternal damnation I'm sure they're enjoying.

"Five," I say under my breath. "Shit balls."

Austin laces our fingers together and brings my hand to his mouth to kiss my knuckles. He holds me in the intensity of his green eyes and gives in to my trembling body to engulf me in a much-needed hug.

"Don't worry," he repeats.

"But who?"

Pulling away, he shakes his head. "I don't know. The board is taking extra care to keep us all uninvolved. They're monitoring the whole process together. I haven't even seen Diego and Kingston."

I uncontrollably whimper, tears burning my eyes to trickle down my cheeks. Austin swipes them away and leans in to brush his lips to mine, doing his best to get my mouth to stop trembling. He shouldn't kiss me because of the rules, but I think he's beyond caring.

"Austin you shouldn't."

"There's no way I'm not going to console you. You shouldn't—we shouldn't—be in this position. Now don't worry. No one is watching. The phlebotomist won't tell."

"This is bad," I whisper, struggling to grasp the hope he offers. "What if—"

"Don't. You can't doubt our matches now, Jewel."

"I'm not, it's just—"

A buzzer sounds through the room, and Austin kisses me once more, hugging me close until the door swings open. He disappears from my side and slides past Mitchell, who motions for me to come to him.

"Don't look so worried, Jewel. Everything's going to be fine. It's interesting to see how the results vary so far from last time. It might be quite possible that you won't have to decide on who you permanently match with after all."

I jerk my gaze to his. "What?"

He offers me a smile. "Wouldn't that be nice?"

"Um." I shrug, trying not to give my thoughts away.

I was scared before, but now that he mentioned a new possibility, I'm freaking the hell out. I never considered that I could possibly match with only one of my guys. Most donors would probably find relief in that possibility, throwing away the ability to choose to a game of fate. It's what I had prepared to do before I matched with all three of them in the first place, but now the thought of having my choice—the decision I made to be with all three of them forever—ripped away, leaves me sick to my stomach.

I don't even want to imagine how it would play out or the doubt it could cause us. What it would do to my relationships with them, or what it would do with their relationships with each other. Would whoever matches with me allow this to work if they didn't have to? I can only hope so, but I worry.

"I guess we'll have to wait and see. All you have now is the interview portion," he says, guiding me out of the room.

Thank friggin' God. I got to skip the medical exam this time since it wasn't that long ago since I had one, and Austin monitors my stats frequently enough to satiate the information portion about the condition of my body.

"And how does that look?" I don't want to flat out ask him who I'm interviewing with, but I'm desperate to know. Austin's words to stay calm only make my rising panic worse.

His phone beeps from his pocket, and he raises his eyebrows, peering at the screen. "Looks like it will be interesting. You have four possible matches. One more than last time."

"Huh?" Mitchell gives me a look that speaks volumes, and I nearly forgot that my guys wiped the matching process of Master Caruthers so that he wouldn't be on record.

"Come along. It's best I do not discuss the matter with you. Your initial reaction to meeting your potential matches is part of the results," he says.

"Which are skewed now."

"I wouldn't complain, Jewel. It's a rather good thing, don't you think?"

I hate to admit he's right, but I also hate that I'm back in the Blood Match Center again in the first place, wearing another white dress just begging for me to bleed all over it.

Mitchell guides me into the same interview room as the last time. I nearly startle at the sight of my audience through the window. Along with the entire board, I spot all four of the Vaduva sisters. None of my guys are in the room, though. The door behind them opens, and another figure enters, but the light switches off, turning the window into a two-way mirror, preventing me from seeing who else joined the group.

"Please take a seat, and I'll get you hooked up," Mitchell says, glancing at the mirror.

I plop on the chair and let Mitchell sticker the wires to me that sends the machine beeping like crazy. He gently pats my hand and heads to the door at a human's pace. When he opens it, my heart picks up speed at the tall, familiar frame of Diego. He shakes his dad's hand and smiles at me from over Mitchell's shoulder.

"Hey, beautiful," Diego says, gliding across the room to me. We both watch Mitchell close the door, and then Diego lifts me off my feet in a hug that gives me the strength I need to stop myself from freaking out.

If only he didn't deny my need to kiss him.

"Not in here," he whispers. "But there will be plenty of time after."

We take our seats, and Diego rolls his chair close enough that I can rest my knees between his. He touches my cheek, searching my eyes for a moment, just checking for himself to see that I'm still holding up okay.

"I can't wait for this to be over," I say, taking his hands in mine. "I expect a huge apology from the board when they see that you're my perfect personality match."

He grins and bobs his head. "They better, because it's supposed to be my night, and I had amazing plans for us."

"Like what?" I ask, leaning close enough that I rest my hands on his thighs so that he can whisper into my ear.

"We were going to drive to our favorite spot." His low voice sends tingles through me. "The weather was supposed to be perfect for stargazing."

I smile. "And then what?"

He licks his lips, turning just enough to meet my eyes. Heat rises from my chest to warm my neck, and the machine I'm connected to starts beeping rapidly. Diego releases a whisper of a breath near my ear, tickling my skin, and I rest my head on his shoulder, silently filling in his lack of response with my own imagination.

"Let me save it as a surprise. There is still a lot of night left, and I have the same feelings I did on the night we matched."

I swallow, rubbing my lips together. "You do?"

"They're even stronger. I just know that you're the one for me."

The buzzer over the door sounds out, and Diego hugs me once more before standing. His height towers over me, and he touches my shoulder where his previous bite mark is nearly finished healing. I wiggle my fingers at him and watch him head to the door to open it. Diego pats Austin's back as he passes his brother, and Austin closes the space to me, greeting me with a smile that sends my heart racing.

"Should we finish what we had started the last time we were in this room together?" I ask, biting my lip between my teeth at the memory of how Austin saved my life with his blood, but in doing so released a whole shit ton of lust through me with one of the side effects of blood consumption.

Austin chuckles and pats his legs. I automatically slide from my seat to sit on his lap, leaning my face close to his.

"If only we didn't have an audience," I whisper, peering at the two-way mirror from over my shoulder. "The Vaduva sisters are probably memorizing every moment to try to recreate what we have together like that awkward ass hug."

"You saw them?" he asks, keeping his voice so low that I doubt anyone could hear us. With our backs toward the window, it looks as if we're just sitting quietly together.

"The light was on in the viewing room. Makes this feel even more uncomfortable than the last time. I kind of thought all the possible matches were watching, but I was hoping they weren't."

"It was only Kingston last time since he was running your test," Austin says. "If the Vaduvas are in there, it means none of them matched with you."

I grimace. "But Mitchell said there were four interviews."

"He did?"

The buzzer on the door sounds out, drawing our attention away from each other. I'm nearly certain the board has lessened the interview times to hurry up to get to the results. If what Austin says is true, then Viorica probably regrets ever dragging me here.

Austin glances at the two-way mirror and then to the door. Without saying anything, he taps a button on the machine to grab the paper it spits out. He hugs me once more and slides me back into my seat before getting to his feet, following what I'm sure are instructions on how to conduct himself. I imagine the board will look for anything to disqualify my guys, and they're aware of it.

"I'll see you in the lobby, okay?" He crosses the room and looks at me over his shoulder. "Don't worry. You're my perfect match. I just know it."

And I believe him. I blow him a kiss, making him smile, and Austin swings the door open and freezes, stiffening at the sight of whoever stands in the hallway outside.

"What's going on?" Austin asks, peering at the two-way mirror behind me. "What's this about?"

Brayla offers her hand out to Austin, and he automatically shakes it. "Glad to see you've made it this far, Austin, but don't be too sad over the results."

Brayla shoos Austin away, not giving him a chance to find out the answers to the questions clouding his eyes. She shuts the door in his face and spins to face me, beaming me a smile that reminds me exactly of who she was in The Boxes.

"Brayla, what are you doing here?" I ask, getting to my feet.

She flies across the room and flings her arms around me, knocking me off my feet and onto the lounge chair. Propping up on her elbows, she hovers over me, her blond hair veiling the both of us from view.

"I'm here to match with you, Jewel," she says. "I couldn't believe that Donor Life Corp opened up your application again. The fee was friggin' crazy expensive, like triple the usual cost, but I thought you were worth it. Orlando agreed. Now here I am."

I frown. I can't help it. "But why?"

"Because you're my best friend. Forever, remember?"

"But it doesn't mean we're a perfect match," I say, shifting myself to sit up.

She moves off me but stays sharing my seat. "I think we are. I made it this far, haven't I? And I have to say, your blood—"

I bring my hand up and cover her mouth, most definitely not needing her to finish her thought out loud. Just the thought of someone else besides my guys enjoying my blood makes me sick. It was different as a gen. pop. donor because they mix blood, and I never thought much about it, but being exclusive now holds an intimacy I save for Austin, Diego, and Kingston. "Even so, I don't get why you're doing this." My voice cracks, and I lose my resolve, blinking tears from my eyes. "You know I love th-them."

"I just want what is best for you, Jewel. I can offer you a great life. And eternity. A Blood Vow doesn't have to be romantic, you know. If this is about all the hot sex you have with them, then—"

I frown. "Shut. Up." The last thing I want to get into in front of the board is my sex life.

She smiles. "I'm only saying that I understand."

Except she doesn't.

The buzzer on the door rings through the air, and I turn away from her and cover my face with my hands. I know I shouldn't be freaking out, but it's like the board is determined to do anything to see to it that I don't get the same results as last time. And it pisses me off.

Taking a deep breath, I get up and stroll to the two-way mirror. I cup my hands around my eyes and press them against the glass to try and peer at the board, but it's still too dark.

I tap my fingers to the window. "I want Brayla Ortega to be disqualified on the grounds that you're trying to manipulate my results. She was not part of my first testing and shouldn't be allowed to participate now."

"Jewel," Brayla says, coming up from behind me.

I knock my hand to the glass again. "The Ortegas have an unhealthy obsession with my family, and I'm being purposely targeted."

Brayla grabs me by the shoulder and spins me around.

"That's not true."

I yank away and pound my fists to the glass. "Are you listening?"

The buzzer on the door goes off again, but Brayla doesn't move to open it. "Jewel, please calm down."

"Mitchell, are you going to let them walk all over the Divine name like this?" The two-way mirror rattles under my palms. "Don't you see what they're doing? They're trying to destroy everything you have. Your sons love me. They're not going to sit back and accept this. I'm not going to sit back and accept this bullshit either."

"Jewel," Brayla says again, pulling at my shoulder.

Swinging my arm, I use all my strength to knock her away from me. She hisses and hops to her feet, but I turn my back on her and slam my fists into the window. It shatters, sending glass spraying across the room. Pieces slice into the sides of my hands, sending blood drops raining over the floor.

The door to the interview room flies open, and Kingston yells, the noise sounding more like a scary ass roar. My back hits the tiled floor, and pain snaps through me. The edges of my vision shadow as I struggle to focus on the vampire straddling me.

"Kingston, stop. You'll be disqualified," Mitchell yells.

I jerk my head to glance beside me and catch sight of Kingston holding Brayla by the throat, both of them flashing their fangs at each other. Sharp nails dig into my cheeks, forcing me to look away, and I stiffen at the closeness of Viorica.

She could rip my throat out in a matter of seconds, and there would be nothing anyone could do.

"Please, don't hurt me," I beg, grasping her wrists.

She inhales a deep breath, her eyes darting to the blood seeping from my wounds.

Silence draws through the room.

Everyone freezes.

"Shit," I whisper. "Don't bite me. Kingston, help me."

But he can't. Mitchell holds onto him. Diego blocks the others from getting any closer. Brayla returns to Orlando's side.

"Jewel, look at me and no one else," Viorica says, her smooth voice drawing my attention to capture my eyes.

My body slackens under her instructions.

"You will not fight. You will not scream."

No. No. Friggin' no. I couldn't even if I wanted to under her mind manipulation.

Panic rushes through me as she cracks open my mind. Her foreign presence feels just as awful as Mitchell's had the last time. My soul screams under the weight of her stare, burning through me. I try to fight her manipulation. I concentrate on doing something, anything. But without my guys' blood in my system, I can't.

"Tell me why the Ortegas want you so badly," she says, pressing her nails deeper into my cheeks without breaking my skin.

"I don't know." Tears burn my eyes at the pressure. A

dull ache radiates in my mind at her prodding.

She tightens her lips. "Why does your family have a blood debt to Orlando Ortega?"

"I—" Pain bursts in my head, and I scream out, feeling like my brain will explode at any second. It feels worse than the first time I allowed Diego into my mind when he was trying to find out about the blood debt, but with him, he tried his best not to hurt me. I'm certain Viorica doesn't care.

"Stop it!" Kingston shouts. I can't see him, though I can hear him fighting someone. "You're going to hurt her."

Viorica ignores him and leans in closer so that only a few inches of space remains between us. "Tell me, Jewel. Why does your family have a blood debt to Orlando Ortega?"

Agony erupts in my skull, and the room fades out of view as shadows crowd my vision. A wail rips from my mouth, echoing through the room so loudly that Viorica breaks her gaze on me and covers her ears. The pain in my head grows so intense that I'm sure it'll kill me. I nearly scream for someone to put me out of my misery, but I can't even form the words. My body thrashes and convulses, and I roll over and throw up. Someone grabs onto my shoulders and drags me, and I buck on the floor, clawing my temples, trying to do anything to make the pain stop.

Cool arms encircle me and lift me from the cold tiles. "Jewel, Jewel, listen to me."

It's Kingston. I can't see him, but I can hear him. I can feel him as his whole being pleads with me to focus on him.

"Jewel, I know I promised never to get into your head but please—"

I struggle against him, thrashing so much that he shifts me off his lap and sets me on the floor again. His weight presses down on me to hold me in place, and then someone else slides their fingers through mine and pulls my hands away from my head. Another pair of hands locks onto my ankles, gently restraining me.

"Jewel," Kingston says again. "Look at me. Focus on me. I'm going to help you."

My body reacts to the softness of his voice, and I open my eyes and stare into the midnight darkness of his penetrating gaze. He massages his fingers into my temples, putting pressure where the pain radiates, stopping me from fighting under him.

"That's it, beautiful. Listen to Kingston," Diego says.

"We're all here." Austin strokes his fingers over my calves. "No one's going to hurt you anymore."

Kingston leans closer and swallows, his Adam's apple bobbing in his throat. "I love you, okay?" he says to me. "I need you to trust me."

"I always trust you," I whisper.

He smiles, blinking the glassiness from his eyes. "Then sleep."

MEMORIES

"COME ON, JEWEL. WE HAVE to hurry. Keep up." Dad tugs on my hand, pulling me down Starlight Row. Bright sunshine reflects on the tall glass buildings, sparkling a dozen sunbeams across the cracked concrete in a lit path I stroll along.

"Where are we going?" I ask, jogging to keep up with Dad's fast pace. *"I'm supposed to meet Brayla."*

"Not today." He pulls me to a stop at the end of the block.

A shadow from a skyscraper cuts across the street like an invisible wall to block our way. Lurking against the concrete wall, a man leans his back on the building, watching us. He doesn't move, standing frozen like the headless statue of a long *ago human from before The Divide we passed by a few blocks from here. I blink, and the man disappears, only to materialize in the middle of the street, protected in the shade.*

I screech and stumble back, yanking away from my dad.

Dad rushes to my side and lifts me back to my feet. "Honey, it's okay."

"You always told me to stay away from the shadows. Do you not see him?" Fear squeezes my chest, making it hard to breathe.

Tightening his fingers through mine, Dad drags me closer to the man. "Of course I see him. He's waiting for us. Now, come along. I need you to be brave today."

I try to pull away from my dad, but he only squeezes my fingers tighter. "What's going on? Please, you're hurting me. I don't want to go."

"I'm sorry, honey. Sometimes we have to do things we don't want to, but I hope it's not like this for you forever. And that's why we're here. But don't worry. I'll keep you safe. This vampire only wants to talk for a second."

Thrashing, I break away from my dad and fall back, hitting the ground hard. Dad rushes me, and I scramble away, scraping my hands on the rough asphalt. I don't get far. Dad hoists me up and tosses me on his shoulder, carrying me toward the shadow cutting across the street.

"Dad, stop! Please! What are you doing?" I ask, my voice shrieking through the air.

He covers my mouth with his hand. "Shhh! You'll draw

more attention."

Tears burn my eyes. My chest heaves as I sob into my dad's hand, so afraid of what's about to happen. He's spent all my life warning me about shadow dwellers and Donor Life Corp. He's scolded me and Ramona for coming home too close to sunset. And now, something's come over him, and he's acting like confronting this vampire is no big deal.

"My precious Jewel. How good it is to see you." A smooth, melodic voice breaks over the sound of my crying. "Let me get a look at you."

Dad shifts me off his shoulder and holds me out in front of him. I wince and try to recoil back, but two cool hands cup my cheeks.

"No need to be afraid. Just open your eyes. One peek. It's all I ask," the vampire says.

"Be brave, honey," Dad whispers.

Sucking in a deep breath, I snap my eyes open and meet the piercing blue gaze of the vampire.

"Remember me, precious Jewel," he whispers, capturing me in his gaze. It's a command, not a question.

Suddenly, his features turn familiar, and I stop fighting against my dad's hold. Orlando tilts his head, offering me a smile that speeds up my heartbeat. We stare at one another for a silent minute as he lets me take in his handsome features.

"She's stunning, Noah," Orlando says without taking his gaze from mine. "I'd like to change the terms of our agreement."

"No. We have a deal already," Dad says. "Now hurry up. The sun will set soon, and Helena's waiting for our return."

The mention of my mom's name stirs sadness in me, but I can't figure out why.

"Very well. Maybe another time," Orlando says.

Scooping me into his arms, he cradles me like a small child. I don't even scream as he flashes his fangs, offering me a smile that prods at something in my mind, trying to bring forth a memory that refuses to unlock itself. Orlando bites onto his arm, sending blood running across his skin.

"Do you remember what to do, Jewel?" he asks, holding his arm up to my lips.

"Of course," I say, licking my lips. "I look forward to this every year."

Warmth coats my tongue as I suck on Orlando's arm, and he watches me drink from him. A rush of emotions cascades through me, tingling from my torso and to the rest of me, and I hum under my breath. But it's not desire. It's satisfaction. Like I've been anticipating this moment forever.

"My precious Jewel," he whispers. "It's always my pleasure to see to it you get what you need."

Gently tugging his arm away, he strokes his fingers across my cheek before brushing his lips to the cool spot he left behind. He sets me back down and pushes my hair behind my ear, giving me another once-over.

"You sure that was enough?" Dad asks Orlando. "She's shot up the last few months."

"You must trust that I know what I'm doing, Noah."

Dad scowls. "I don't trust any vampire."

Chuckling, Orlando turns his attention back to me. "Hopefully you won't feel the same, Jewel. You grow ever so ravishing in your maturity. Perhaps the next time I see you your father will let you pay your own dues."

"Not happening," Dad says. "Now hurry up."

Orlando tugs me closer. Capturing my eyes again, he strokes his fingers across my cheeks. "Turn around and forget me, my precious Jewel. And remember, try to stay away from the shadows on your journey home. Tell your mother your father will be late."

I turn my back on Orlando and step into the sun.

"Now for our agreement, Noah."

"Just be quick."

I swivel to turn back at the strangled noise that comes from my dad, but Kingston stands before me in the middle of the road. He opens his arms, remaining expressionless. I don't go to him.

"Jewel, come back to me," he says, motioning me forward.

I shake my head and point at the ground. "But the shadow."

"Jewel, please."

My feet take a few automatic steps away from him. "I can't."

"Jewel." Kingston toes the edge of the shadow, frowning

at the space I create between us. "Don't leave me."

"Just go away."

"I won't," he says. "I'll never leave you."

I wring my hands together. "But you won't have a choice."

"Jewel, come back to me. Please, babe. Come on. You can do it." Kingston's voice resonates around me though he doesn't move his mouth."

Tingles blossom on my hand as a cool, invisible touch engulfs my fingers. "Beautiful, I know this is hard on you, but you have to try. Go to Kingston."

"I can't. I have to go home and tell my mom my dad will be late," I say.

"Jewel, please. Don't leave us," Austin says.

"I just need to go home."

"And I'll take you, but you have to come to me." King-ston waves at me to come closer.

I shake my head.

"Damn it, babe," he says. He disappears from my view. "I'm losing her. She's closing herself off."

"Beautiful, please," Diego begs. "Listen to my voice."

"I have to get home before sunset. I can't be out here."

"Babe." Kingston materializes in front of me, the bright sunshine overhead sending streaks of dark chocolate through his black hair. He flashes his fangs at me, and I shriek and jump back. But he doesn't let me get far. "I'm not letting you go. Ever. I made a promise to you."

"Kingston, please." Tears burn my eyes. "You're hurting me."

He squeezes his eyes shut. "This isn't real."

"I have to go home."

"Jewel, wake up." He cups my cheeks, peering into my eyes. "Please, wake up."

Pain burns through my core under the weight of his gaze, and I whimper, trembling in his touch. "What are you talking about?"

"Wake up, Jewel," he repeats.

"Kingston, please."

"Wake up!"

A scream rips through the air, and I jolt upright. I gasp and scramble to grab onto something, anything, as the world spins around me. Strong arms embrace me, and soft lips brush over my cheeks as everything comes back into focus. My stomach heaves, but Kingston doesn't let go of me. Neither does Diego nor Austin. They crowd me within their circle on the floor, blocking my view of everything around me.

"You're okay. You're safe," Austin says, resting his chin on my shoulder from behind. "You were dreaming."

"It wasn't real," Diego says, combing my hair from my sweaty forehead.

"It felt real," I whisper. "My mom—"

"I'm sorry, babe." Kingston shifts me closer to him to rest his forehead against mine. "I wish they were still alive, but it was a dream. Viorica broke into your mind and pulled something free."

"A memory," I whisper.

"Not necessarily. It's hard to interpret what your mind creates," he says.

"It felt real. It still feels real."

"Care to share what you've witnessed, son?" Mitchell's deep voice draws my attention away from my guys, and I force myself to look in his direction. He and Viorica stand alone, glancing from one another to me. We're still in the interview room, but the glass has been swept up. I realize my wounds have been cleaned and closed with synthetic skin as well.

"Jewel was only dreaming about a moment with her family," he says, leaning back to meet his dad's gaze straight on. "It's why I had trouble getting through to her. Whatever Viorica did made her not want to leave." He doesn't mention Orlando or the fact that I drank his blood in the memory. Maybe he doesn't know.

All three of my guys glare at the redhead.

She remains expressionless. "It was in my right to evaluate her as an applicant."

"Without warning?" Kingston snaps.

She crosses her arms. "Not being prepared makes a donor's minds malleable. You know this. I was following Jewel's request to investigate the Ortegas to see if there were grounds for disqualification."

I tense at the reminder. "And?" My voice comes out raspy from screaming.

"Unless Kingston found something I can use, I do not see any reason to disqualify Ms. Ortega." She looks at Kingston with a pointed look.

Kingston glances at his brothers, keeping his face just as expressionless. "I'm afraid I didn't discover anything useful."

"That's a shame, considering the risk. Donor Life Corp would hate to lose you as a future heir to the Divines and an ally to the Vaduva Region."

I open my mouth to mention the appearance of Orlando in my dream, but Kingston closes the space between us and kisses the words from me before they can escape my lips.

"We won't lose her. And I assure you, babe. You're my perfect match. We won't have to deal with the Ortegas for much longer," he says.

Diego stands and offers his hand out to me and Kingston, helping us both to our feet. "And we'll get you home."

Austin hugs me from behind. "And feed and cuddle you."

"Help you forget this ever happened," Kingston adds.

Diego looks at Viorica. "While savoring the apology from the board."

Mitchell steps forward and trains his eyes on me, motioning for me to leave my guys' sides. It takes everything in me to get my legs to work, and Kingston nudges me forward toward his dad, though I can see it's the last thing he wants to do.

"We shall see, my sons. But first, the results."

I swallow my nerves and hook my fingers around Mitchell's muscular arm. "I don't see why we bother. Your sons are my perfect matches. My mind, body, and blood."

Mitchell's lips slide into a small smile. "Don't forget, Jewel. It can only be one."

I glance at Diego, Austin, and Kingston strolling behind me. They each hold me with their beautiful gazes, sending my heart speeding. Because Mitchell's wrong. It'll never be just one of them.

"But perhaps, you won't have to choose," Viorica says.

"Perhaps," I reply. Even if the results of my new Blood Match change, I refuse to have my life any other way. So she's right. I won't choose. Not now, not ever.

The quiet ride down to the lobby leaves me on edge. There are a thousand things I need to say to my guys before we find out the results, but the second the elevator door opens, all the vampires in the lobby turn their attention to me.

"Jewel!" Brayla races across the lobby to my side, causing Diego to growl. He spins me out of her reach, and steps in front of me to stop her in her tracks.

"Chill out," she says, blocking our way. "I was only checking on my best friend."

"She's fine, no thanks to you." Austin slides his fingers through mine and inspects the cuts on my hands from shattering the glass.

"Your strength is pretty impressive, Jewel," Brayla says. "Orlando promised to help me continue to teach you like your boy toys so that we can do all the cool things. God, I can't wait to take you home. It'll be better than before. No curfew. No restrictions. All the fun."

I can't stop myself from gazing past her to search for Orlando. He remains seated in the lobby with the Vaduva sisters, though they only talk among themselves, excluding him from their conversation. The rest of the board remains standing, looking more bored than anything.

"I will not be going home with you," I say, keeping my gaze locked on Orlando.

He smiles at me, flashing his fangs. Something in his gaze triggers the memory of my dream, and goosebumps prickle over my skin. I shiver, and Austin shrugs from his jacket to put it around my shoulders.

"You okay?" he whispers.

Pain burns in my stomach, and it growls so incredibly loud that everyone looks toward me. I hug one arm around myself, trying to suppress the nausea twisting my stomach. Orlando raises his eyebrows at me, his blue eyes trailing over the length of my body.

"Here, eat this." Brayla holds out a cookie to me with a smile.

I hadn't even seen her move.

"See, like old times," she says, motioning to the coffee table positioned among the plush seating with the food I couldn't bring myself to eat earlier while my re-evaluation was being prepared. "It's probably as stale as anything we used to find in my cupboard, too."

My stupid face picks now to smile at the memory she

stirred in me. The last few weeks before I Blood Matched were so hard that Brayla would sneak me food she wasn't supposed to. Every family was to supply for themselves.

"Come along, Ms. Jordan," Viorica says. "We don't have all night."

Her voice pulls my attention away from Brayla, and thankfully, I get my face to fall expressionless again. Kingston catches my gaze and pouts, offering his hand to me. I stroll between him and Austin as they guide me to the counter with the giant glowing screen behind it.

Diego hooks his fingers to my waist, and I manage to inhale a few calming breaths in the space they don't allow anyone to share with me. Brayla rolls her eyes and leans her elbows on the counter, trying to get a look at the computer Ms. Sybil taps away at.

"Good evening, Ms. Jordan. Mr. Divines," she says without looking up. "It's nice to see you again, Ms. Ortega. I'm happy to see that the program worked out for you."

"I just hope it works in my favor again," she says.

"Doubt it," Kingston mutters under his breath. "Now, please. If you could hurry up—"

The screen on the wall lights up and flashes my picture for everyone to see. All of my stats appear next, and I wobble on my feet, my nerves getting the best of me.

The screen flashes again, and Brayla releases a high-pitched squeal, draining all the warmth away from me. She pushes Kingston back and pulls me to her, engulfing me in a hug. I stand frozen in shock, staring at the results on the screen behind her.

"Congratulations, Ms. Jordan. You're a ninety-nine percent match to Brayla Ortega of the Shadow Crest Villa."

"No," I whisper.

"Best friends forever," Brayla says, rocking me back and forth.

One second I'm in her arms, and in the next, Kingston lifts me off my feet and spins me away. Diego and Austin surround Brayla, and everyone in the room flashes their fangs. Orlando materializes behind Austin and grips him by the shoulders. Mitchell tugs Orlando back.

"Hold on tight, babe," Kingston whispers in my hair.

I cling onto him, preparing for him to run with me, but a beep rings through the air. Kingston releases a breath, and everyone falls silent. Swiveling my torso, I peer in the direction he gazes, his own picture now blinking on the screen beside mine.

"Damn straight," he whispers. "I knew I was still your Blood Match. Fucking delayed results."

"But not for body." I blink a few times, staring at his picture next to Brayla's. Her results mirror Kingston's. If this were the kind of test that you could cheat on, I'd accuse her of doing so, but while the results mirror one another, the breakdowns are slightly different.

He releases a low growl. "The hell I'm not."

Another beep sounds through the air, and Austin chuckles. I draw my gaze from his picture on the screen to him, and he smiles at me. "One hundred percent body match," he says, closing the space to us. "That was unexpected."

"There's no way," Kingston mutters. "Babe, don't look at the results."

I squeeze his hand. "Aw, come on, Kingston. Being my personality match is just as good."

He groans. "I'll never laugh at your lame jokes."

Flicking his gaze to mine, he holds my stare. And then we both laugh.

The computer beeps again, and Diego's picture flashes on the screen next, and he takes an audible breath. He swipes his hand across his forehead and closes the space to pull me away from Kingston.

"Guess Austin can no longer be your Hungry Eyes," Diego teases, referring to Austin by the first nickname I ever gave him.

I hug Diego and stand up on my tiptoes. "Makes sense...because I still think you're friggin' delicious."

He laughs into my hair and spins me off my feet to meet me for a kiss that leaves me breathless. The second Diego puts me down, Austin envelops me into what I'm sure is the best hug he's ever given me. He pets my long hair, rubbing soothing circles on my back until my racing heart calms. Then he kisses me, making it speed up all over again.

"Come on, now," Brayla says. "I want my moment to celebrate my personality match with my best friend."

Austin turns me away, and all three of my guys step in front of her.

"Jewel's canceling your contract," Kingston says. "It's her right to do so at any time."

Brayla huffs. "Does this mean she's finally ready to pick one of you?"

I stiffen.

"That seems to be the case," Orlando says. "I'd think the board would want the program to be fair, and not even allowing you one night with Jewel would look bad. I'd hate to spread the word that the Divines manipulated the results to get Jewel as a permanent match."

Viorica clears her voice. "Mr. Ortega makes a valid point."

"What?" I say.

"You can either decide on your permanent Blood Match now in front of the board, or we can re-start your trial period to include Ms. Ortega in the rotation."

"But Jewel's applying for a Blood Vow as a Divine," Kingston says.

"I'm applying for a Blood Vow on her behalf as an Ortega, too," Brayla says.

My head spins as arguing breaks out. It takes the ever-silent Vaduvas to step in the middle to assure no one starts throwing punches.

"Perhaps you can save us all the headache and save my sons from future heartache if you'd just pick, Jewel," Mitchell says, draping his arm over my shoulder.

Kingston, Diego, and Austin all turn away from Brayla to face me.

"I have to agree, babe," Kingston says.

Austin rubs his lips together. "We will be fine if you do."

"Promise, beautiful." Diego steps closer and takes my hand. "It's better than the alternative."

My heart clenches in my chest, and Mitchell tightens his hold on me, preventing me from spilling to the floor. Brayla steps up beside my guys and gives me a once over, smiling her familiar smile that reminds me of the friendship we had before all of this started.

"You mean the alternative is better for you," she says to Diego. "Not for Jewel."

"Ms. Jordan," Viorica says from her place beside her fellow board members.

They all stare at me without saying anything.

"Your answer?"

I take a deep breath, meeting each of my guys' eyes. "I'm sorry. I can't choose."

"Babe."

I stiffen at his annoyance. "Kingston..." I let my voice trail off. How am I supposed to tell them that the idea of even pretending to choose one of them freaks me the eff out? I can't put that kind of strain on our relationships, and would rather risk a night with Brayla than have to fake my way through choosing. I know the consequences if I do so.

Kingston, Diego, and Austin look from each other and back to me.

Austin subtly nods. "Okay, Jewel. We'll discuss it later."

Instead of arguing, all I do is drop my gaze to the floor.

"Then it's set. You'll complete the already given time before your Blood Vow with the addition of Ms. Ortega to your rotation," Viorica says. "Mr. Divines, you are responsible for dropping Jewel off at sunset in Ombre Noire and Ms. Ortega, you must return Jewel by sunrise. She still gets the days to herself to do as she sees fit."

"Can I have the first rotation?" Brayla asks.

"No," my guys say in unison.

"You can't—"

Mitchell sighs. "Sons, leave it up to that back-world game of chance you seem to favor."

"Deal."

EXTRA BITEY

KINGSTON STANDS IN THE DOORWAY, crossing his arms over his chest. "You should spend the rest of the night practicing on our girl's fighting techniques."

"No, we already had plans, and I tend to stick to them. She needs a break," Diego says.

Kingston glowers. "We don't have much time to prepare her for her night away from us. Even if we give her our blood right before we drop her off, it might not last all night. She needs to be ready for anything."

I blink at his words. "You don't think..." My voice trails off.

Swinging his arm out, Kingston punches the wall next to the door, creating a small crater. "Fuck yeah, I do. There's nothing against a match getting into your head. They don't need permission. Why do you think Ramona always got crazy with calling you brainwashed?"

"Oh, shit. I'm doomed." Obviously, Kingston thinks so too or else he wouldn't be freaking the hell out.

"Kingston, knock it off. You're scaring her." Austin pushes past Kingston and enters the room. He stops in front of me and waits for me to open my arms for him first. Gazing into my eyes, he says, "You're going to be fine. Just because we can't be with you doesn't mean you still can't protect your mind by drinking our blood."

"I'm sure they already thought about that and will search her belongings," Kingston snaps.

"Well, then it's up to me and you to think of something else." Austin turns to Diego. "You guys have fun. Enjoy your new nutrients match, Jewel."

I laugh. I can't help it. "You know I already do. Can't wait for my day with my new body match," I tease, sliding my hand down his chest.

Kingston groans. "Not cool, babe. Just because the test said—"

Turning to Kingston, I motion for him to come to me, and I hug him. "Don't worry, Kingston. One percent doesn't make a difference. I look forward to my next time with you too."

He sighs. "I still can't believe we lost to Brayla. All I want to do is make sure you never forget who your first was...I mean, your first body match."

Diego grumbles. "You won't let the rest of us forget either."

Kingston ignores him. "Now I'm afraid I won't get the chance. What if—"

"Kingston, seriously," Austin says.

He fists his hands. "We can run away."

Austin steps in front of Kingston, grabbing his shoulders to shake. "You know the consequences that will happen to Dana and Fallon if we don't drop Jewel off on time."

"Yeah, bro. Trust our girl. She's badass." Diego slides his hand through mine, tugging me away from Kingston before I can sink back into his arms. "She'll bite back."

"I swear if they even get their fangs near her, I'll destroy the world."

His words send my heart racing. Not because of his threat to destroy the world. He threatens that so often that I'm used to it. It's the mention of anyone other than them biting me. But that's what I signed up for with the Blood Match Program. I have to provide blood to Brayla now that she's my match too.

"I doubt Brayla's going to bite Jewel," Diego says, squeezing my hand.

Kingston throws his hands up. "But Orlando—"

"Can't."

"He's right, Kingston. And we all know none of this is about Jewel's blood anyway," Austin says. "So try to stay calm for our girl's sake. It's going to be fine." He hands Diego a thermos of their blood and kisses my cheek. "Now, you two get out of here and let us handle the prep. Health keeper's orders."

I hug him and Kingston, and then let Diego tug me along like this is any of our other nights together. It's easy to ignore the fact that come sundown, I'll be forced into a night with Brayla in Ombre Noire. The only thing that keeps me from freaking out more than Kingston is that this is my chance to see Ramona, no matter how awkward that may be.

We stop in the hallway outside the elevator, and Diego leans in for a sweet kiss, brushing his lips to mine. "How are you holding up, beautiful?" he asks, trailing his fingers across my cheek.

I shrug. "I honestly don't know. I want to believe that my best friend has some semblance of her humanity left and won't mess with me like Kingston thinks."

"I don't know her well, but I don't think she will."

"Then there's also everything else." I can't stop the words from coming from me. I used to manage to pass off my emotions as being fine until I met my guys. "I'm so confused. I want answers. I know you guys thought that Orlando was trying to use me to get to you, but the dream I had about my parents... I just—it was weird. It still lingers with me. It felt so real. Like a memory. Do you think that maybe? Ugh, that's crazy, right?"

The elevator dings, drawing our attention away from each

other, stopping me from spilling my heart out completely. Diego always manages to open me up without even having to pry. I hadn't realized how much tonight bothered me until I said those words out loud.

He guides me onto the elevator. "Maybe not." Hugging me, he pulls me close and nestles his face into my throat without saying anything more because we're outside the privacy of our living quarters. He worries about listening ears as we walk through the house. And honestly, I do too. I don't trust anyone anymore. Only my guys.

It takes us getting into the car and driving off before Diego turns to me again, programming the car into autopilot. "Kingston doesn't think it was a dream either," he says, tightening his lips. "We think that Viorica might have broken through one of the walls Orlando put in place in your mind."

"So if it was a memory..." I groan, rubbing my palms over my face. "Ah hell. My dad made some kind of deal with Orlando. Beyond a blood debt. I just—I wish I could remember."

Diego falls silent and gently rubs his fingers in a circle across my knee. Taking over the car again, he navigates down the dark stretch of pavement and speeds until the forest turns into a small meadow surrounded by tall trees. He parks the car right in the middle of the road and turns to me.

Clasping my hands in his, he says, "I can try to help you if you'd let me. You haven't drunk any of our blood yet. I can access your mind."

I suck my bottom lip between my teeth, trying hard to suppress the pain that Viorica put me through when she broke into my mind without my permission. "I'm afraid," I finally admit.

He bobs his head, drooping his shoulders. "I understand and don't blame you. I still remember the one and only time I experienced mind manipulation as a human. It was awful having someone else in my mind, even if Mitchell was only trying to help."

"Trying to help?"

"My human life was traumatic after The Divide, at least that's what I remember. Mitchell eased all of the pain for me. That's why things are kind of a blur still."

"It was worse than awful having Mitchell and Viorica in my head," I say. "But you? No. I'm more afraid of—ugh, why do I even care about my dad? He put me in an unforgivable situation. I should hate him. I want to hate him. But a part of me can't. Because what he did brought me to you."

I slouch in the seat and glare at my hands. The cuts from breaking the glass of the two-way mirror at the Blood Match Center bug me enough that I pick at the edge of the synthetic skin, causing the wound to bleed.

Diego inhales a small breath and pulls my hands apart only to press his cool finger down to staunch the seeping blood. "What he did was unfair to you and your family, Jewel, but he raised you. It's hard to separate the good times you had with him from the aftermath of whatever he did."

"I think he was doing what he thought was right for us," I whisper. "But what if he wasn't? That's what freaks me out. The truth could devastate me. My dad's dead and gone, and I can't change that, but I can hold onto the good I have left of him the best I can. But then again, I'll never know the truth. And I want to know why. Why do this? Why take me to Orlando? It doesn't help that I was only afraid of Orlando because I forgot I knew him. And when I remembered? I'm messed up. My head—I want to understand, but I'm terrified of how I'll be if I do. What my dad did was wrong. The position he put us in, what did he gain? What was worth it? Obviously not me."

Diego pulls me from my seat and into his lap. Talking about my dad was the last thing I wanted to happen tonight after everything, but now that my thoughts are out there, I don't think I'm going to be able to think about anything else. And the stupid dream/memory/whatever the hell it was keeps swirling through my head, taunting me.

"Whatever you decide to do or not, I'm here for you, beautiful. Forever. No matter what," he says, nuzzling his nose to the crook of my neck. "If you want me to try to help, I'll be careful. If it's too much, I can stop it."

I bring my lips to his and kiss him. "Thank you, Diego. I just—can we go for a walk? I think I need some air. Some distraction."

He shuts off the car and flings the door open. "You got it. How about something to eat too?" Reaching into the backseat, he pulls up a basket. "A little of everything you like."

I smile. "Maybe I can give you a little something you like as well."

He chuckles. "Then what are we waiting for? I've been dying to celebrate our new match."

Diego carries me from the car with him and sets me on my feet to grab another bag from the backseat. We stroll hand-in-hand down a narrow trail until we reach the small valley. I help him spread out the blanket and plop down on the fluffy pillows he brought along. Standing over me, he grins as I hold up my arms to him to pull him down beside me.

"This was exactly how I wanted to finish our night off," I say, cuddling against him. "You and me, under the stars, and...whatever is in that basket. I'm so hungry. My insides burn."

"It's a good thing I brought extras since you barely ate anything in the last day."

"I was too nervous. What about you? Did you eat?" Because I only gave blood for the tasting portion of the Blood Match test. I was pretty surprised even Kingston didn't complain about being starved on the way home, but we were all in shock that Brayla beat them at Rock-Paper-Scissors and won the next whole night with me. It wasn't until we entered the gates of The Divinity Estate that any of us started to relax.

"Don't worry about me, beautiful."

I crinkle my nose. "But I do. A lot."

He doesn't respond and holds the most delicious smelling

sandwich roll to my lips. The distraction is enough to immediately stop me from voicing my concern over the fact that he had better not have foregone eating a la Kingston fashion because of the board's dumb decision to re-evaluate our matching.

I can't resist the offer of food and take a bite of the sandwich, savoring the robust flavor of the spiced bread. "So good," I murmur, hiding my mouth while I chew. "But it's not going to work to deflect me away from your needs...and feelings about all of this."

Because Kingston made it clear that he'll destroy the world if something happened to me in Brayla's care, and Austin keeps reassuring me that everything will be fine. Diego's been quiet about it all.

"So talk to me instead of watching me shove this whole thing in my mouth. It's only fair that you pour your heart out to me since I basically drowned you with my feelings," I add.

He smirks and tries to feed me again. "We're here to take your mind off all the bullshit, not add to it. And spilling your heart out to me brings you relief. Spilling mine? No, beautiful. Not tonight. Maybe when you get back. Now eat. You're hungry. I'm pretty sure Austin's going to show up at any second if we don't get that growling stomach of yours under control."

Stealing the sandwich from his hand, I set it down on the napkin and look him straight in the eyes. "Diego. Not going to work."

He sighs and stretches out his long legs in front of him, tilting his head back to look at the sky. "Okay, you know I can't deny you. I'll tell you what's going on with me, but then you have to promise to just be with me. I need it."

The softness of his voice cuts into me as he finally opens himself up. It reminds me of my first and only trip to Haven Springs and how he refused to admit how hurt he was. Even though he's now matched more with my blood than my mind, we can still read each other, and I knew something was up.

"Whatever you want," I say, making him smile. It's usually he who tells me that.

He motions for me to lie beside him, and I use the crook of his arm to rest my head. "I thought I was going to lose you today, and it was one of the worst moments of my life. Worse than when you were taken or when we found you with Katherine. Worse than losing my whole family after the divisions when Mitchell found me." He keeps his eyes trained on the sky, and I don't say anything as he continues. "Because when everyone matched before me, I thought something went wrong, and I was eliminated. And the fact that I doubted it for a second kills me. I hate this. I hate how I feel so out of control and how there's nothing we can do. If I didn't match with you..." He shakes his head and sighs. "I did, and that's what matters. So don't worry about me, anymore. I'm fine."

I shift over and touch his face to get him to look at me. "Diego, I know how much faith you put into the results, but it's just a test. It can't compare to everything we have together now. And if that had happened, I hope you wouldn't have given up on us. You will always match with my heart."

"Which is better than anything else." He leans over and kisses me. "And you have no idea how glad I am to hear you say that. I just know that things haven't always been easy, and you were thrown into our life—"

"I jumped in head first," I say. "And I wouldn't change anything...except maybe gaining more enemies."

"That makes two of us," he says, chuckling.

I roll my eyes. "At least I haven't called anyone a beast recently."

Curling his arm around me, he rolls me on top of him, so I meet his eyes straight on. "I just know that while the Blood Match does significantly raise the chances of building a solid connection between a donor and a recipient, it doesn't replace what time and being together actually brings. What it can change too."

"Well, I don't want you to ever worry too much about change, okay? It's always been for the better. At least for me."

Diego smiles and kisses me, sliding his hands around my waist. I frame his head with my arms, deepening our kiss, needing to be as close as possible to him.

In this moment, our world might be on the brink of another huge change, but it doesn't feel life-altering as long as Diego continues to hold me and let me taste the sweetness of his lips, the softness of his tongue sliding over mine, the strength of his embrace promising never to let me go.

"I've been thinking about you since the party," he whispers, playing with the hem of my dress to slide his fingers over my butt. He tightens his hold, pulling me harder into him to feel his body awakening with the lust I elicit from him with a single kiss.

I suck his bottom lip into my mouth and graze my teeth over it. "That was the only fun part besides the dancing. Too bad it was cut short."

"Like I said then, I wanted our first time to be better than that."

"What about now?" I ask, grinning at him. "Seems pretty perfect." As the words come out of my mouth, my stomach growls again, sending hunger pains shooting through me.

Diego freezes mid-kiss and pulls away. "Maybe not. You're still hungry."

I giggle through my embarrassment. "Starved, but I need you first."

Pressing my weight into him, I silence his oncoming argument with another kiss, drawing my hands under his shirt to explore the muscles of his stomach and chest. He sits up enough that I can tug it off him. I break away from his mouth and kiss down his jaw to his throat, his skin tasting as sweet as I remember his blood being.

Diego strokes his fingers under my dress and over my bare hips, dragging his hands up my body to undress me. I straddle him, feeling the length of his excitement through his pants, sending my own desire wild. I've thought about this moment a dozen times, and what it would be like to be with Diego on a new level. How amazing I'm sure it'll be.

He settles back, trailing his eyes over my body bathed in only the soft light radiating through the trees from the headlights of the car. Heat warms my chest, and I slowly reach behind me to ungracefully mess with the hook on my bra. He watches me in anticipation, shifting under me, massaging his fingers into my legs. The clasp releases on my bra, and Diego inhales a soft breath, his heart thudding faster than mine. Linking my fingers through his, I bring his hands up to my chest and silently give him permission to graze his fingers over my breasts.

"I'm ready to finish what we started at the party now," I say, my soft voice whispering through the air. "If you want to."

He licks his lips, his fangs peeking at me. "Are you sure you do?"

I nod. "So much. I love you. You mean a lot to me. I can't stand the thought of another few days passing by. I mean, what if—"

He leans up, so we face each other, my legs resting over his hips as I sit between his legs close enough to still feel his body through his pants. "I don't want you to think you need to do this because you're worried something will happen, and we won't get the chance."

"It's not entirely that. Just look at you," I say, hooking my fingers around his neck. "Friggin' delicious."

My stupid stomach picks now to growl like an angry vampire, and Diego raises his eyebrows. He laughs, beaming his brilliant smile at me—the smile that gets me every time, picking up my heartbeat.

"And I thought you made me hungry," he teases, closing the space to kiss me again. "If that's the case, you can bite me however much you like. We don't even have to—"

My teeth automatically snap down on his lip, breaking the skin. His sweet, syrupy tasting blood trickles into my mouth, and I gasp, pulling away. I cover my mouth with my hand, my eyes bulging at my own shock. What the hell just happened?

Diego touches his lips, surprise lighting his eyes for a second. "Shit," he whispers so quietly I wouldn't have heard it if I wasn't inches from his face, watching a drop of blood dribble onto his chin.

"I'm so sorry. I didn't mean—"

He silences me with a kiss, smearing his blood over my lips again, and my whole body hums with the desire his blood summons from me. "No apologizing," he murmurs. "I was only surprised. It was hot."

Without giving me the chance to study his face to see if he's only saying that to make me feel better about my savagery, Diego gently eases me back on the blanket to lie on top of me. He pulls the blanket around us and kisses the goosebumps from my skin, smiling into my mouth when my fingers work over his pants until I unfasten them to slide my fingers into his boxers.

He's quick to reciprocate my gesture, and I release a loud ass moan against his mouth at the tingles building from his touch. Moving his mouth from mine, he kisses my jaw and works his way to my throat, leaving behind a buzzing trail across my skin. I pant and shift, unable to stay still to allow him to explore me.

I surprise him by guiding him to roll back over, the blanket twisting around us. He moans deep in his throat, grazing his lips across my clavicle and down to my breasts where he gently sucks and flicks his tongue in a way that leaves me gasping and kissing his shoulder, tasting the sweetness of his skin. It's all I can think about.

And it suddenly freaks me out. I've only really bitten him before either by accident or because he asked me, but right now, it's all I want to do.

I flip myself off him, and my stomach releases another growl, one so friggin' embarrassing loud that neither of us can ignore it. Diego shifts up and studies my face, but I can't look at him.

"You know what? We have the rest of the night, beautiful. Why don't we eat? I'm hungry too."

I cover my face with my hands. "I'm fine, really. I just—it's your blood. I haven't drunk what Austin gave me yet, and I think—God I want you."

He grins and kisses me again.

"To devour you," I add.

"Whatever you want."

"No, I mean it. I can't stop thinking about it."

Diego shifts off me, noticing the tremble in my voice. "That's fine. I told you."

I shake my head. "No, something's different. It's weird."

He frowns. "What do you mean?"

"I'm hungry. Starving. But not for food."

"I'm not sure I understand, beautiful."

Feeling around the blanket, I attempt to find the thermos Austin had given to Diego. The urge has me nearly panicked as a dozen thoughts cross through my mind. I've never felt this way before, and now I'm freaking the hell out.

"What are you looking for?" Diego asks, grabbing my hand.

"My thermos," I say.

"I left it in the car."

I comb my fingers through my hair. "Get it. I need it."

"Need it? Why?"

"I think I'm craving blood."

"What?" he asks, cupping my face to get me to look him in the eyes.

"Please. Get it. You have to get it."

My stomach growls again, burning with a fire so intense that I flop back and clutch my arms around myself. Diego startles at the cry I release and gathers me in his arms to pull me against him.

"Austin!" Diego yells, his voice echoing through the air.

But we're too far from the estate unless he's somewhere nearby. Shifting me in his arms, Diego feels around the blanket until he finds his phone with our clothes. "Austin, come here. Now," he says into the line.

The edges of my vision darken, and I bury my face into the crook of Diego's neck. "I think I'm transforming or something," I say, my breath gasping. "The hunger. I just want it to stop."

The click of Diego's fangs sends tingles through me, and I inhale a breath, watching him bite into his arm. His eyes lock onto mine, and my chest heaves at the sight of his blood. I don't even give him the chance to offer me his arm before I pull it to my lips and suck.

"Not too much, beautiful," Diego whispers.

"Jewel?" Austin's voice cuts through the air.

Diego wraps the blanket around us, holding me while getting to his feet. "Over here."

"Whoa, fuck. Seriously?" Kingston asks.

"Shut up," Diego says. "Something's wrong. She thinks she's transforming."

Austin comes up in front of me, drawing my attention away from Diego. "Jewel, can you stop for a second and let me look at you?"

I slowly ease my mouth from Diego's arm and wipe my hand across my lips.

"Can you open your mouth for me?" Austin asks, closing the space.

I open my mouth.

"Do you see anything, Austin?" Kingston asks, coming closer.

Austin carefully rubs his fingers over my teeth. "No, she looks fine still, but I'd have to—"

My mouth snaps down on his finger, shocking the hell out of everyone. I release his hand just as fast and cover my mouth. "Holy shit balls, Austin, I'm sorry."

He blinks a few times, shaking out his hand.

"Something's wrong," I repeat. "All I want to do is drink."

AWAKENING

"YOU'RE A SAVAGE."

"I'm a savage."

Kingston and I both look at each other as we say the words at the same time. He laughs. I don't. Then he engulfs me in a hug and sighs, combing his fingers through my long hair. "Would it be inconsiderate if I begged you to control yourself and not to bite me?"

I groan and nuzzle my face into the crook of his neck. "Definitely," I murmur. "It was an accident. I couldn't control—" Inhaling a sharp breath, I press my lips into his skin, and he stiffens, bracing himself. I suck his neck just hard enough to make him purr deep in his throat.

"You're bad," he whispers.

I kiss his flushing skin and laugh. "You totally thought I was going to bite you."

"And he was going to let you," Diego says from behind me.

"Because I knew our girl would let me bite her back," Kingston says, snapping his teeth at me. "I might do it anyway. You better step away, babe. You're not the only one feeling bitey right now."

I raise my eyebrows at him, trying to hold my face straight. But it's impossible with the way he looks at me, making me feel less like a savage and more like the best thing he's ever seen.

"Come on, Kingston. Let her have at you. Be brave," Diego says. "What if this is our life now? You're not going to deny Jewel something she craves, will you?"

OhmyeffingG. "Diego."

Kingston glares at him. "Waiting for her vampire fangs, thanks. Less aggressive."

I place my hands on my hips. "Guys."

"Except she's not transforming." Cool hands wrap around me and pull me away from Kingston. Austin cups my cheeks in his hands and holds my attention. "I don't see anything different in your blood test."

"So, what? She just has a new biting fetish?" Kingston asks.

I groan. "Kingston."

"Don't let him bother you, Jewel. It could have been a lot of things. Maybe it was your body trying to protect itself after the trauma Viorica inflicted with her mind manipulation. It could've been your hunger and desire mixing and confusing you. It could even be a side effect from Katherine's bite and what keeps you in this half-state. I don't know. This has been the longest you've gone without our blood in your system since then. What's important is that you feel okay now, right?"

"I think so," I say, thinking about all his theories. All of them sound believable enough. "I just wish I knew for sure."

Diego risks touching his fingers to my mouth. "Maybe we can test you again later."

Kingston groans. "Remind me to be busy."

"You'd be the perfect subject, though, bro," Austin says. "Jewel knows you're a chicken, so she'll have better restraint."

"She still needs a lot of work," Kingston murmurs. "But I hate practicing that."

I smirk at him.

Turning to me, Austin continues his exam and presses his fingers into my stomach. "No more pain, Jewel?" he asks, gauging my reaction to see if I'll try to hide something from him.

But there's nothing to hide. "No. I'm good. I feel normal. The food helped."

Kingston steps closer and nudges my shoulder with his knuckles. "I don't think I've ever seen anyone eat like that. That back-world mouth of yours—"

My smirk turns into a glare.

Austin ignores Kingston's comment. "What about your supposed blood craving?"

I blush. "That's gone. It was weird and—"

"Hot," Diego teases. "I felt like a donor."

Kingston laughs. "So Jewel likes to role pla—"

"Dude," I snap. "Enough."

Diego chuckles next. "No shame in discovering what you like, beautiful."

"Diego."

Austin covers his mouth to hide his smile. They are way too amused over this mortifying situation.

"I didn't necessarily like what I was feeling," I continue. "I mean, yeah when I—shit balls. I don't want to get into this. You guys are looking at me like this is totally okay."

"Because it is," Diego says.

I groan. "But I felt weird."

"It's possible for you, even as a human, to experience bloodlust during sexual situations because of the side effects of Diego's blood. While it's not addictive, your body would remember the pleasant feelings brought on—"

I cover my ears. "Austin, I'm done discussing this. I liked your other theories better."

"Really?" Kingston asks. "Come on, babe. Having a sex fetish is way better than—"

Austin punches his brother. "Stop it, Kingston. You're embarrassing her."

Fuck me.

Kingston growls. "You brought it up."

"He's just trying to be an informative health keeper," Diego says, getting between the two of them. Looking at me, he adds, "It's important. I know it feels awkward—"

I purse my lips together. "It's just—I don't want to partake in this group discussion. What happened to the rule about not discussing details?"

"I'm on our girl's side. As long as she's okay, I'd like to pass on hearing you guys discuss her sexual awakening when it doesn't involve me."

"Kingston!"

He chuckles. "I'll save it for the next time we're alone."

I cover my eyes with my hands and sigh.

"Jewel," Austin says, prying my hands from my face. "I know you're freaked out, but I want to assure you there's nothing wrong. You're not transforming into a vampire yet. I can prove it."

"How?"

He reaches behind him and grabs something from off the table. Pressing his lips together, he tightens his jaw to stop what suspiciously looks like an oncoming smirk. Two hands cover my eyes from behind, and Diego chuckles near my ear. Kingston snorts from somewhere to my right.

I shift on my feet. "What are you guys doing?"

"Testing you, babe," Kingston says.

"For what?"

Something warm drips on my bottom lip. Kingston clears his throat, trying not to laugh. "Bloodlust. The supposed craving you thought you had. It's easy enough to trigger if you're a vampire."

I grimace, trying my best not to lick my lips. "This better not be what I think it is on my bottom lip. If it is, I'm going to—"

Soft lips mold against mine, kissing the threat from my mouth. Diego uncovers my eyes, and Austin rubs his lips together, licking away the evidence that makes me want to throw up. He quickly runs a napkin over my mouth for me, keeping his face expressionless. But Kingston cracks up, flashing his fangs at me in the process.

"Shit balls, you did," I say, swiping at my mouth again. "What the actual hell? Gross."

"Sorry, Jewel," Austin says. "And you're fine. No fangs. No pain in your stomach or the need to bite. A seriously unpleasant reaction."

"Well, yeah. How did you expect me to react to gen. pop. blood? Nasty."

"It was, wasn't it? I can't stand the stuff," Kingston says, coming up beside me. "We're going to have to suffer through it together after our vows, babe. Because that's your future."

When he puts it like that...ugh.

"We're her future, and you're a picky little bastard," Diego says.

Austin nods his head. "It's a miracle he's survived all these years."

It's my turn to laugh. "Well, I'm glad he did." I turn to Kingston. "And you're probably right about having to suffer together, especially if it doesn't taste as good as the three of you."

"Uh-oh," Kingston says. "She has that bitey look. Please say it's me you crave now."

I lick my lips. "Come here and find out."

Before Kingston gets a chance to move, Austin blocks his way and bites into his arm, startling me. I freeze, narrowing my attention on the two circular wounds bleeding his dark blood across his wrist.

"Austin, really?" Kingston asks. "I volunteered."

Diego touches my chin, guiding my face to look away from Austin. "Fuck, I want her to look at me like that."

Austin holds his arm up while Diego expertly restrains me without making me feel like he's doing so. "Sorry to have startled you. Just the last test. How do you feel? Any more pain?"

I blink a few times, trying not to look back at Austin. "No. I'm fine." Which is true. I don't feel the burning in my stomach. I don't have the urge to bite him.

"You sure?" Austin asks.

I shrug. "I think so."

"Damn it, Diego. You gave our girl a biting fetish," Kingston mutters.

Diego flashes his fangs in a beaming smile. "It's a good thing you're her new personality match."

Austin ignores them and staunches the bleeding on his arm. "I'll run a few more tests when you return from Ombre Noire, Jewel. But right now, I think it's best that you just rest."

"And feed me," Kingston adds.

I run my finger along Kingston's chest. "Only if you promise to cuddle with me after."

"You bet."

Wiggling my fingers, I motion for Austin and Diego to follow behind me. "All three of you."

Kingston groans. "Really?"

"Yes, really. I want to spend time together with all of you before...just in case."

"Not just in case," Austin says, taking my other hand. "You want to be with us just because."

I smile. "Just because," I repeat.

"Everything will be fine," he adds.

I can only hope.

"Be brave, honey," Dad says, nudging me forward. "He won't harm you."

The vampire stands in the shadow of the building, smiling at me with his fangs, his blue eyes flashing silver the closer I shuffle forward. He extends his hand to me, motioning me to hurry up and close the space between us.

I freeze in my tracks. "Dad, I can't. Please. You said to stay away from the shadows."

"Just this once," Dad says, pushing me hard enough to send me stumbling.

I scream and skid forward, scraping my palms on the rough asphalt. Two cool hands latch onto my wrists, yanking me to my feet. Flailing, I try to fight against the vampire's grip on me, but all he does is gather me closer, sliding his arm around my waist.

I stiffen at his tickling breath near my neck. "Don't bite me."

"My precious Jewel, let me get a look at you," he whispers. "Just one peek."

"Do as he asks, Jewel. We don't have time to waste. You can't miss your first appointment," Dad says.

"Still not up for renegotiations, Noah?" the vampire asks.

"I told you, we already had a deal," Dad snaps.

"But things have changed. Your sweet Helena—"

"Don't say her name."

"You have all those girls to look after, and now forcing Jewel to join the donor population? She deserves a better life. You know I can provide it." His words freak me the eff out.

Tears burn my eyes at the mention of my mom's name, and I sniffle. "Dad?" I beg. "Please, help me. Don't let him take me. I don't care about donating. I told you I didn't."

I open my eyes to meet my dad's silence, fear slicing through me, thinking he abandoned me. He remains in the sunshine, shading his eyes, his face scrunched as he loses himself in his thoughts. He refuses to even look at me.

"It's barely a sustainable life at best, Noah," the vampire says. "Not to mention your dues if you'd like our agreement to continue."

I struggle in the vampire's arms. "What is he talking about, Dad? If you're that worried about our way of life, then we can look into the Blood Match Program. I saw the flyer. They have contracts. Guarantees."

"No, Jewel," Dad finally says. "Never that."

"I can provide safe travel and a transfer out. Stipends. Visitations, if you'd like."

"The Orchards?" Dad asks.

"Anywhere. Think about it."

"Dad!" I yell, pushing my hands into the vampire's chest. "No! You can't do this. Please!"

The vampire grabs my chin and pulls me to look at him, capturing me in the blue depths of his startling eyes.

"Stop fighting and remember me, Jewel," he says, staring at me so intently it's like he can see the blood flowing through my veins.

My body slackens as recognition settles in. "Oh, Orlando. It's nice to see you," I say, offering him a smile.

"And it's always a pleasure to see you, my precious Jewel. If only your father didn't insist on you forgetting me, you wouldn't be so scared of me every time."

"Why is that?" I ask without taking my eyes away from his.

"You'll have to ask your father. Unless he changes our

agreement." Orlando spins me around, pressing his chest into my back so we can both look at Dad. "What do you say? Jewel will come with me, and I will care for her needs. She'll be rather happy. I promise."

Dad sucks in a few deep breaths and glares at Orlando. "No. Jewel was right. Together, we can handle it. Now, hurry up, Orlando. If you purposely make Jewel miss her first donation, I'll—"

"Always a fighter, that father of yours. I can see he passed that down to you," Orlando whispers, turning me back around to lean even closer. "Now, Jewel. Do you remember what to do?"

I nod my head and lace my fingers through his to pull his arm up to my lips.

He flashes his fangs and bites down on his arm, our faces so close that our breaths mingle. Blood coats my lips, and I suck on his skin while he watches, my body tingling.

"I look forward to the day when you must pay your own dues," he whispers too softly for Dad to hear. "You'll beg me to bite you."

"I think she's had enough," Dad says, locking his fingers to my shoulder.

Orlando growls and grips me tighter. "Look at me, my precious Jewel."

I hold his stare, continuing to suck on his arm.

"You'll forget me now, but I vow to you that one day things will change. Go along to your appointment. Your fa-

ther will meet you there. And don't forget. Stay out of the shadows."

I gasp and flail my arms, looking for anything to grab on to. Kingston grunts from beside me, and hands slide under me to tug me into an embrace that stops my body from thrashing.

"Beautiful, it's okay. You're okay," Diego whispers into my hair. "Open your eyes."

I do as he says and meet Austin's green gaze as he lies in front of me. Kingston sits on the edge of the bed behind him and massages the red spot on his cheek.

I bare my bottom teeth. "I'm sorry, Kingston. Come here. Let me see."

Kingston climbs over Austin and shoves himself between us, making Austin sit up. Diego lets me go so that I prop myself up to properly meet Kingston. I cup Kingston's face and lean in to brush my lips over the spot, making him chuckle at my affection.

"You know, I'm pretty sure you kicked me in the—"

Austin punches him hard enough to send him toppling off the bed. "Don't even, Kingston."

I link my fingers through Austin's. "He was just playing with me."

Kingston hops to his feet and plops back down. "Stop trying to prove our personality match right, babe. I was serious."

I throw a pillow at him, and he lets it hit him in the face. "And I thought you were afraid of the possibility of me biting."

Austin and Diego laugh as my words wipe the smirk off Kingston's face. He flares his nostrils at me and shakes his head. "That's low."

Bringing my hand to his mouth, Austin kisses my knuckles, getting me to look at him instead. "It's a risk I'm willing to take...again."

I swat him with the back of my hand. "Austin."

"Perfect body match," he adds, keeping his expression serious. And then he smiles and winks.

"Shit," I murmur, my whole body buzzing at his teasing.

"You're a dick, Austin," Kingston grumbles. "I'd expect this fuckery from Diego, but—"

Reaching out, I cover Kingston's mouth with my hand. He licks my palm, but I don't give in and yank my hand away, which only makes him test my resolve even more as he grazes his fangs along my skin.

"Can we please not do this now?" I ask him and Austin. "We have, like what? Only a few more hours until we have to leave?"

"Two at the most, beautiful," Diego says, resting his chin on my shoulder. "We agreed you needed to sleep in."

"Even though it seems it was pointless with the way you were thrashing," Kingston says.

I glance at the sun lowering in the sky through the tinted window. He's right. It feels like I just barely fell asleep. Maybe I did. All three of my guys clonked out before me, and I spent an embarrassing amount of time just creepily watching them during our first official slumber party all together. But I couldn't help it. I'm scared. I don't know how I'll be without them for a whole night. This is just as bad as my first day at the Divinity Estate and experiencing life without my family. And now I'm going to have to experience life without my guys. It sucks, even if temporary.

"The nightmare must have been awful. You were all fight. Didn't even give up one sexy ass moan either," he adds.

Diego nudges my shirt off my shoulder and kisses my skin. "Want to talk about it? Your heart's still racing."

I sigh and rub the heels of my hands into my eyes. "It was like a repeat of the memory with my dad."

All three of them inhale sharp breaths at once.

"Slightly different. My mom was already dead. I can't tell if it was a real memory or not, because I remember my first blood draw with my dad, and he..." My voice trails off.

"He what?" Austin asks.

"It was just different than I recall. I remember leaving the apartment with him that day. Ramona walked with us down the block and then Dad told her she couldn't go all the way. She was mad. I remember my dad and I watching her walk all the way back, but then I also remember him meeting me at the lab. I can't remember why."

Diego shifts to meet my eyes. "So, what happened in your dream that was different?"

"We walked together, and he took me to Orlando on the

way," I say. "That's what's weird. The dream makes sense and explains the fogginess of that day I pushed out because of my first blood draw. I didn't even think anything of it until now."

Kingston swears and rakes his fingers through his black hair, pushing it from his forehead. "He's been manipulating you for who knows how long."

"And giving me his blood," I whisper. "At least I think."

"But why?" Austin asks. "That doesn't make sense."

"Yeah, it does. Jewel's dad was a Blood Rebel," Diego says. "Orlando must have been his source."

Kingston releases a strangled sounding groan while rubbing his cheeks. "It would explain the block on our girl's mind."

"But I think it was my dad who insisted Orlando made me forget him," I say. "He made me forget like how Mitchell had tried when he gave me his blood."

"What?" all three of them ask me in unison.

I shrug. "It was part of their deal, but not the blood debt. This was something different. I just—I don't know. It's fuzzy."

"What else can you tell us?" Kingston asks, pouting his kissable mouth at me.

"I..." I drop my gaze to the bed, remembering Orlando giving me his blood, how he asked Dad if he could arrange to take me away to keep me, and how Dad considered it.

Something dark snaps inside me, and I punch my hand into the headboard. But unlike with Kingston and his strength to break through walls, my fist hits the solid wood, sending pain radiating through my hand and up my arm without leaving a dent. I cry out and shake my hand before cradling it in the other.

"I can't believe this shit," I say, blinking through my angry tears. "How could he?"

Austin tugs my hurt hand away from my chest and inspects it, checking the damage I inflicted to my now bleeding knuckles.

"Gotta be more specific, babe," Kingston says. "I might be your personality match, but I can't read your mind."

I heave a breath, my thoughts swirling through my head. "Yes, you can. And maybe you can confirm it."

Diego kneads his fingers into my back. "Confirm what exactly, beautiful?"

"That the deal was regarding me. Orlando was feeding me his blood for some reason. He told my dad that he—" I pause and swallow, dreading saying the words out loud. "He wanted to take me from my dad. He offered him a way out of Dark Terrace Ranch. My dad said no...but I think he might've eventually said yes. That's why he left us. He was supposed to get the transfer out. Dad was trading me to save our family."

"Why do that when you could've Blood Matched and had the guarantees?" Austin asks. "Look how well it turned out for all of us."

But I'm certain Dad didn't think it would. "My dad hated Donor Life Corp. I don't think he even trusted Orlando, but he needed him for me," I say.

Kingston tightens his jaw. "It still doesn't make sense."

I turn to him. "Then make it make sense. Read my mind. Pull it out of me."

He raises his eyebrows. "No fucking way. That's all Diego. I promised you I wouldn't and the fact that I already broke that promise once kills me."

Leaning forward, I rest my hand on his leg. "But you're my personality match. I want you to do it this time."

Resting his hand on mine, he squeezes my fingers. "What if I hurt you?"

"You won't."

"Are you sure about this. Diego can—"

Diego shakes his head. "No, not me. She asked you."

I scoot closer and wrap my arms around Kingston, staring into his dark eyes. "Please. For me."

He bobs his head, sucking his bottom lip into his mouth. "Okay."

"Yeah?" I ask with a smile.

Brushing his lips to mine, he sinks against me, pushing me back on the bed to prop himself over me. "You know I'd do anything for you."

SO MUCH FOR FOREVER

KINGSTON RESTS HIS BACK ON the pillows he piled against the headboard. I crawl closer, and he pulls me into his lap to face him, adjusting my legs around his waist so that we can sit with only a few inches between us.

He slides his hands down my back and tugs me even closer, making me laugh. "Have to be able to concentrate solely on you," he muses, arching his back slightly to lock me in his gaze.

"You mean you don't always?" I tease, squeezing his sides with my thighs.

"Not like this." He swallows, his Adam's apple popping in his throat.

"I'm sure you can handle it."

He nods. "I just need you to relax, babe. And don't get all bitey on me."

I shift and inhale a deep breath. "Got it. I'll do my best."

"And no squirming."

I laugh. "Well that's no fun."

"And no creating fantasies," Diego adds.

I stick my tongue out at him. "You don't have to worry about that. I'm not going to sleep."

Kingston raises his eyebrows and hums. "Actually, maybe you should."

I laugh and slap his chest. "Next time."

"Hurry up already," Austin says, taking a seat on the edge of the bed. "I don't want to leave Jewel's mind unprotected longer than we have to."

Kingston cups my face, ignoring him. "Ready, babe?"

I shrug and purse my lips. "I guess so."

The second he locks his eyes on mine, I inhale a deep breath and shake out my nerves. He releases my face without looking away and moves his hands back to my back, slowly rubbing up and down to knead away the tension of my muscles.

"You can tell me to stop at any time," he says, "and you don't have to answer something you don't want to."

"Okay."

Kingston leans close and kisses me for a second. "Now relax. I'm going to start by asking you a few simple questions."

My muscles slacken, and I don't respond, losing myself in

his eyes. My trembling body gives into Kingston's touch, and I study the depths of his eyes as they hold onto mine.

"Tell me, babe. What do you like most about me?"

Austin swats Kingston's arm.

"That you're imperfect," I automatically say.

"Not my body?" he asks.

"It's a close second," I respond.

Diego stands up, and I'm pretty sure he's about to rip me away from Kingston. "You can't ask her stuff like that."

Kingston waves his hand, motioning for Diego to stay back. "I told her she didn't have to answer anything she didn't want to. You got that, right, babe?"

"Yeah."

Kingston looks smug as hell. "What do you want to do with each of us the most?"

Austin and Diego groan. "I hope she says bite," Diego mutters.

"Live forever," I respond.

If I could imprint the looks the three of them give me in my mind forever, I would.

"Fuck, babe. You know how much I love you, right?"

"I do."

Kingston bends forward and rests his head against mine. I expect him to kiss me, but he doesn't. "I think I love you ten times more than that now."

"Shit, me too," Diego says. "Ask her if she knows that."

Sighing, Kingston says, "Do you know that Diego loves

you too?"

I smile. "Yes. And Austin."

"What else do you know?" Kingston prods, his soft smile turning serious.

"That we might not get forever." My chest tightens at my words.

Kingston pouts, and I wish with everything in me that I could throw myself at him. I also wish I could take the words back, but I can't. "Why do you think that?"

"Because my dad ruined my chance."

"Why?"

"He hated vampires."

Kingston releases a breath. "I mean, how? How did he ruin your chance?"

"With a vaccine," I say.

"Are you certain you were vaccinated?"

I nod. "I didn't transform when Katherine bit me."

"That doesn't mean anything," he says.

"I didn't transform when I triggered your venom."

"You didn't—"

"Yes, I did. I know it. It hurt. I got sick."

"But the bite healed quickly."

"Doesn't matter. I can't turn. Dad assured it. Orlando helped him."

Kingston stares at me with wide eyes, and Diego and Austin inch closer to all peer at me directly, though I can't break my eyes away from Kingston's. "Orlando? What does he have to do with it?"

"I don't know," I reply.

"Come on, Jewel. Think. You said it. It's in your mind. Remember," Kingston says, leaning closer.

Pain pinches behind my eyes. "I can't. He won't let me."

"Then remember your dad. How many times did he take you to see Orlando?" Kingston asks.

"Um..." My eyes water. *Once a year. Every three months after I turned sixteen.* "I don't know." *Every month after my eighteenth birthday.*

"Think, Jewel," Kingston says. "I know you can remember."

"I—" I wince as more pressure builds in my head.

Kingston cups my cheeks, closing the space completely, touching our foreheads together. "Tell me, Jewel. For how long did Noah take you to see Orlando?"

"All my life!"

My voice screeches through the air, startling Kingston. He bumps his head into mine, sending stars bursting in my vision. Our eye contact breaks, and he releases his hold on my mind. I flail back and land on the bed, my chest heaving, dizziness washing over me. Austin hovers over me, touching his cool hand to my forehead. I blink, trying to push the shadows away.

"All my life?" I whisper, gripping the blankets in my hands. "Kingston?"

"Babe, I'm sorry. Are you okay?" he scrambles next to me.

I reach up and pull him to me, searching his eyes again. "Ask me why."

His lips twist in a frown. "No, I can't. That was enough. You're bleeding. I hurt you."

"I'm fine," I say, touching my fingers to the knot forming on my forehead. "It was an accident. Just try again. I need to know why."

He growls deep in his throat, his eyes flashing silver. A look of agony crosses his face, but he locks me in his gaze anyway. "Jewel, don't look away from me."

I slacken beneath him.

"Kingston, careful," Diego whispers. "Not too hard."

"Jewel, why did Noah take you to Orlando?"

My head pounds as my mind and mouth fight for control. I grind my teeth together, the answer sticking to my tongue, causing me so much pain as Kingston tries to extract it out of me.

"I don't know," my mouth finally says.

"Jewel, tell me why," Kingston says again.

I arch into him, digging my fingers into his shoulders. "I don't know."

His eyes flash silver, and he leans into me, touching his nose to mine. "Jewel."

I groan at the pressure expanding in my skull.

"Kingston, stop," Diego says.

"Jewel, answer my question. Why did Noah take you to Orlando?"

I scream out, clawing my nails down his chest, thrashing as the information breaks free in my mind, nearly crushing me with the truth. Kingston jerks away, covering his eyes with his hands. Austin scoops me up in his arms, massaging his fingers into my back until my scream turns into a sob.

"Babe, I'm sorry," Kingston says. "I'm so sorry. Don't ever ask me to do that again. Never again."

I heave a few breaths, my body shaking through another round of trembles. I scramble away from Austin and crawl to Kingston, slumping against him, my head still pounding as my thrashing heartbeat rings in my ears.

"I'm okay, Kingston," I whisper, my throat hoarse. "I'm fine."

"I didn't even get an answer. All I did was hurt you."

I lick my lips and wrap my arms around him. "You did, though. I know why."

He rests his head on my shoulder, his own chest rising and falling with his deep breaths. "Please don't tell me you're betrothed or something."

"It's worse."

I motion for Diego and Austin to join me and Kingston. Reaching out, I grab each of their hands while Kingston still holds onto me. The three of them wait with anticipation, all leaning closer, begging me with their eyes to hurry up and spit the words out. But I'm afraid. I'm afraid once they're out there, they will really be true. That the life I thought I knew as Jewel Jordan in Dark Terrace Ranch was built on mind manipulation and lies. Of secrets.

I clear my throat.

"Come on, babe. You're killing me," Kingston says.

"Just give her a moment," Austin says.

Diego runs his knuckles across my forehead. "Yeah, Kingston. She probably has a terrible headache."

"But I need to know. Right now. Spit it out, Jewel."

I bob my head and take a deep breath. "My dad took me to Orlando all my life, because if he didn't, I'd—I'd die."

"I don't have time to run tests," Austin says, facing Kingston.

Kingston fists his hands at his sides. "We can't just drop her off without all the answers."

Austin combs his blond hair from his forehead. "We don't have a choice."

The two of them have been arguing since Kingston opened my mind. Kingston's freaking out for me over the entire situation, allowing me just to stand numbly, trying to process the impossible.

"We'll go to Haven Springs," Kingston says. "We can make it." He's been trying to figure out how not to take me to Brayla's, including picking up my cousins to assure their safety.

"And then what? You know how dangerous it would be. The community won't just let us take them. Not to mention we can't bring them back here." Austin makes a good point. The last thing I want is to scare the community, giving them a reason to think vampires are suddenly going to charge in and steal people.

Kingston fists his hands. "Then we won't come back."

"We'll be disqualified." How Austin manages to stay so cool is beyond me.

"I don't fucking care! She's our girl. We gave her our vows." Kingston turns his attention to me. "If you'd pick one of us as an official Blood Match, we wouldn't have to do this."

I stiffen. "Kingston, I—"

"Don't you dare put Jewel in that position," Austin says. "She already told you she was terrified it would change things between us."

"Things are already changing," Kingston says.

Austin places his hands on Kingston's shoulders. "Just calm down and take a breath."

Diego slides up behind me and trails his fingers along my stomach, hugging me from behind. "Come on, beautiful. You have to finish getting dressed."

"They're going to start throwing punches if I turn my back," I say.

"You bet I will," Kingston mutters to me. I knew I was the only reason he was holding back apart from the fact that we all know that Austin is better at fighting. But Kingston doesn't care. He'll do it anyway.

I sigh and stroll across the room to Austin and Kingston, tugging Diego along with me because he doesn't let go of my hips. Kingston straightens his shoulders and meets my gaze, his eyes flashing silver like crazy. He flares his nostrils, all tense and broody, and I'm not even sure I could do anything to make him relax.

"Beautiful, it's a bad idea to step between them with Kingston on the verge of a nervous breakdown," Diego says.

"How can I not be!" Kingston shouts. His fangs peek out from his lips as his nature grabs hold of him. "You two are pissing me off. We're supposed to stand together. We are the Divines. We can't just let someone think they can steal Jewel from us. She's ours."

Whoa. My eyebrows shoot up on my forehead. "Reel it in, dude. You're making me feel like a possession."

One second I'm standing next to Diego and in the next, my back presses into the wall. Kingston breathes deep breaths into my hair, tightening his fingers around my back. Diego and Austin come up on each side of us, grabbing onto his shoulders, but I motion for them to step away. They'll just make it worse, and I know Kingston won't hurt me.

"Kingston," I whisper, near his ear, brushing my lips to his cheek in the process. "Look at me please."

He shakes his head, burying his face deeper into my neck.

I rub my fingers up and down the back of his neck. "Pretty please."

"Nu-uh. If I look at you, you'll try to convince me that everything will be okay, and it's not." His voice trembles, and he clears his throat. At least with me, he doesn't yell.

"I know it's not okay," I say. "This situation sucks. My

dad—"

"I'd rip his throat out if he were still alive," he mutters.

I sigh. "He wasn't a bad man, Kingston. He did the best he could."

"You're defending him? He was going to trade you," he snaps.

Sliding my fingers through his hair, I tug on the strands until he gives in and pulls from my shoulder to meet my eyes. "We don't know for certain, but what I do know is you need to understand something. Where I come from, I was raised with two very specific ideals. My mom used to tell me that there was more to life than what my vein could offer. And my dad? He always told me that sometimes you have to do things you don't necessarily want to. I doubt he ever thought he'd find himself in the position of having to make the decision for my future. But that's how our life was. I'm a—I was a donor."

"I still hate him, babe. I want to make sure you never have to do something you don't want to," he says, resting his forehead to mine. "Especially go to the Ortegas. And it infuriates me that no one else cares." He huffs a breath against my lips.

"The hell we don't care," Diego says. "You think we're jeopardizing Jewel, but what you want will—"

I hold my hand up to cut Diego off so that I can focus on my pouty, distraught new personality match. "It's just a night, Kingston."

"It could be your last," he says. "I'm not willing to risk it.

You're too damn important to me. I'll die without you."

I release a breathless laugh. I can't help it. "You wouldn't if you'd just drink the gen. pop. blood."

"That's not what I mean," he murmurs.

"Well, I'm asking you now to try hard not to if something ever did happen. That's not what I want, okay? Who would your brothers fight with then?"

"Each other," all three of them say.

I puff out a breath. "You guys. It's going to be fine." Maybe if I say it enough, I can will the universe to let it be true. "I'm pretty sure they don't want me dead."

Kingston rubs his lips together. "You're right. They want you caged. They want you never to see us again."

I pout my lip, staring into his glassy eyes. "Kingston, you won't let that happen. Like you said, you're the Divines."

"You mean w*e're* the Divines, babe," he says, breaking his serious stare to smirk.

I smile and kiss him. "So let me show you how badass I am. You're probably overreacting anyway. I bet Brayla will just want to spend the night catching up. Who knows, maybe she will give me some answers to all this. Maybe I can just confront Orlando."

"Hell to the no," Kingston says, going full-on back-world on me. "He can't know you know or that we're breaking his grip on your mind. He'll do something crazier. This is the only advantage we have."

"But—"

He releases a guttural noise from his throat, the tiny smirk he gave me turning serious. "Damn it, babe. That's it."

The world spins, and wind whips through my hair, startling me. Bright sunshine stings my eyes, hazing my vision. The scent of oranges tickles my nose. I take an automatic breath of the fresh air, nearly gasping at the speed of the world blurring around me.

"Kingston, get back here!" Austin calls.

"We don't have time for your bullshit," Diego adds.

The world finally stops, and Kingston holds me against him, leaning his back on a tall, wide tree. He shields his eyes from the sunshine beaming through the forest around us by ducking his face into my neck.

"What the actual hell, dude?" I ask, wiggling in his arms until he loosens his hold enough for me to shrug from the oversized sweatshirt I stole of Diego's. I pull it over Kingston's head, managing to squeeze the both of us inside it, so he has to look at me.

"We're running away," he says, meeting my eyes in the darkness created by the thick fabric.

"We are not," I say. "Just take me back."

"No, if you won't run away with me, then I'm babe-napping you. Your curiosity is going to put you in danger. Confronting Orlando? That's just asking for trouble. So, fuck that. You're coming with me. I don't give a shit what anyone says."

"Kingston—"

He silences my argument with a kiss, tightening his hold on me. "No more talking. They'll hear you," he whispers against my mouth.

"But—"

He molds his lips to mine once more, sliding his tongue into my mouth to caress it over mine, stealing my breath away. I give in and let him continue to kiss me while his hands roam down my back, pressing into the tight fabric of our makeshift shield from the sunlight around us with only the tree shade keeping Kingston from getting more burned than his pink skin already is.

"Please, babe," he whispers. "Let me take care of you. My brothers will listen to you if you tell them this is what you want."

"I can't ask them to do this. I mean, where would we go? And my cousins—"

"We'll figure it out."

I shake my head. "Kingston, no. I'm sorry. I can't take this chance. I know you're freaked, and I am too, but this isn't the answer."

"Babe, please."

He holds my gaze, pleading with his eyes to consider what he wants, to trust him when it comes to the decision about our future. But it's not him I don't trust. It's the rest of the world. We can't just run away.

I suck in a small breath, hearing the crunch of someone moving through the brush nearby. Kingston tightens his hold on my waist and kisses me again, practically devouring my mouth as he silently tries to convince me to go along with his plan.

And it sucks, because I can't. "I'm sorry," I repeat. "No."

Kingston's face falls, his dark eyes glassing over for a second before he blinks. He tightens his jaw, searching my face once more, and then he sets me on my feet and tugs the sweatshirt off our heads.

I can see in this moment my words broke his heart. *I* broke his heart, and I don't think there's anything I can do to change it. I can't run away. I can't. Not at the risk of my cousins' expenses. Of my guys'.

"Kingston," I whisper, reaching out to touch him.

But he disappears, abandoning me in the forest of trees, braving the streaks of sunbeams to get away. A sob wracks my chest, my heart ramming so hard against my ribs, I nearly beg for it to break through already because I can't stand this moment. I can't stand what Donor Life Corp allowed to happen or what Orlando and Brayla are putting us through. Or that my dad assured this fate for me. A life of uncertainty. A life where I might never get to be free, no matter how hard my guys try.

Cool arms wrap around me, and Austin pulls me against him, ducking us into the shade of the tree. "You okay, Jewel?" he asks through his full-faced beanie.

Tears spill on my cheeks. "No. Kingston, he—I—fuck!" I scream.

He lifts his hat up and squints, meeting my gaze. "You're doing the right thing. He's just scared."

"I'm pretty friggin' sure I broke his heart."

"It's not you."

"But it is," I say, drooping my shoulders and tilting my head back to look at the starbursts of light peppering through the trees.

Diego appears beside us and wraps his arms around both me and Austin. "Come on, we have to get packed."

"But Kingston—"

"He's not..." Diego scratches his neck under his beanie. "Beautiful, Kingston's not going to go with us."

I shudder a breath. "What? Kingston!" I yell, turning away from Diego. "Don't do this. I need you."

Kingston doesn't respond.

Austin lifts me off my feet and holds me against him. "I'm sorry, Jewel. We have to go."

Diego squeezes my shoulder. "Don't worry, beautiful. We're here for you, okay? Kingston will come around."

"But I want him here for me now. I need him. I need all of you," I say, swiping tears from my cheeks.

"Not as much as we need you," Austin says. "So, let's go. I'm not willing to risk getting disqualified from our matching."

ENEMY TERRITORY

"JUST ONE MORE MINUTE," I say, standing outside the running car. "He won't let me leave without saying goodbye."

"Jewel, we're going to have to practically fly to get you there before sundown," Diego says from behind the protection of the tinted glass window.

I fold my arms over my chest and stare at the looming front door to the estate. "I don't care. I can't leave like this."

"Come on, Jewel. Please, get in," Austin says from the backseat.

I sigh and open the door, relenting to his pleas. Because they're right. We don't have much time, and I don't want to risk the consequences that I'm sure Orlando will insist Brayla ask the board to implement for breaking my part of the contract.

I slump into the seat and rest my head on Austin's shoulder. "This sucks."

"Totally sucks. And not in the good way." Kingston plops in the seat beside me and slams the door.

Diego hits the throttle, not even giving any of us a chance to get buckled.

"Kingston!" I throw my arms around him and snuggle into his neck for a second before pulling away and smacking my palms to his chest. "You are so lucky I don't push you out into the sun right now. I thought I wasn't going to get to say bye and—"

He cuts off my words with a kiss. "I'm sorry, babe. I can't help myself sometimes."

I bob my head, kissing him again. My lips can't help it. All I want is our mouths together even after the crap he pulled. "It's okay. I'm just glad you're here."

Kingston pulls back. "I'm not going to lie to you. I don't want to be. It kills me to be."

I pout.

"Then maybe you should stay behind," Austin says. "Diego, stop the car."

Kingston glowers at Austin and tries to reach for him, but I block his hand and twine our fingers together.

"I don't trust you not to do something crazy when we get there," Austin adds. "I mean, you ran out in the sunlight and jeopardized all of us. How do we know—"

I hold my hand up at him, suddenly scared to be in the middle. Austin's getting as riled up as Kingston. They're both livid as hell at each other. I can nearly feel the heat of their anger sinking into me, warming me in a bad way.

Diego puts the car in autopilot and swivels in the seat in an attempt to grab me to pull me into the front, but Kingston hooks his arm across my stomach, not letting him. All three of them flash their fangs at each other, making me nervous as all get-out. I know they wouldn't intentionally hurt me, but everyone's on edge.

"Stop it!" I yell, swiping my now sweaty face on my sleeve. "You guys chill the eff out right now or I'm driving myself to Ombre Noire."

"How am I supposed to chill, babe? My brothers obviously don't see how crazy this shit is and are okay with just dropping you off and hoping for the best."

"Because it's crazier to run away, Kingston," Diego snaps.

Austin flares his nostrils. "Jewel could get hurt."

Kingston punches the front seat, knocking off the headrest only to have Diego catch it to stop it from smashing through the windshield. "She *will* get hurt going to the Ortegas. Or worse, what if she decides she likes it better and stays? Have you thought of that? Brayla has history with her, and apparently so does Orlando."

"History doesn't mean it's all good." I squeeze his hand, trying to calm him down. "And I love you guys. I won't ever choose anyone else over you three."

Kingston slumps forward, resting his elbows on his knees. "What if you don't have a choice?"

"I'll fight for one. But not tonight. I won't put my cousins' lives in danger, Kingston."

"You should have faith in me, Jewel. I'm capable of taking care of this. Of you." His low voice cuts me deeply, opening up pain inside me that's hard to ignore.

I swallow the burning in my throat. "I do have faith in you, but..." I let my words trail off for a moment as I gather my thoughts. "I'm not going to let you jeopardize your lives either. I can't let you give up everything for me."

"But we're willing to," they all say in unison.

"I mean, what if my memory is right about needing Orlando to live? What if I am truly vaccinated and can't transform? I—I'm not worth it, not if you have eternity and I don't."

Austin slides his fingers through mine. "Don't say that. You are worth more than anything the Divine name brings us."

Diego touches my knee. "He's right, beautiful. And we're going to figure things out."

"I promised you forever, and I intend to keep that vow," Kingston adds.

I bob my head and turn to each of them, meeting their gazes. It only takes my own self-doubt to get them all on the same page. "See, this is what I needed right now. I know you can't always agree and you drive each other crazy—"

"And you crazy," Diego quips.

I release a breathless laugh, touching his cheek. "That too. In a good way."

"Damn straight," Kingston says.

"Sometimes not," I add playfully.

He rubs his cheek to my hand. "You just had to ruin it."

"She's only keeping you in check," Austin says, sliding his arm around me. "All of us, really."

"Because it's our balance that makes this work. It's knowing that we all want the same thing," I say. "And that we will fight for it no matter what. I'll do anything to see this through, even if it means dealing with an asshole stalker vampire, who I'm pretty certain is obsessed with me."

"Can't blame him there, though I do want to rip his fucking head off," Kingston mutters.

"And I plan to let you," I muse. "Just not tonight. Tonight is going to be my chance to show the board that they can try all they want to see that this doesn't work out but they can't do anything to break us. Tonight will be my chance to get answers too."

"Carefully," Austin adds.

"Through Brayla only," Kingston says. "I mean it. You call us if Orlando tries anything."

Diego punches his palm, drawing my gaze to him. "And give that asshole a hard punch or kick in the—"

The navigation system dings, drawing our attention to it. Diego swivels in the seat and turns the car off autopilot to take over the wheel. A few human guards stand outside a looming gate in the distance even more intimidating than the one at the Divinity Estate.

"Okay, Jewel. It's time to drink." Austin pulls out my thermos from his bag and hands it to me.

"What about later?" I ask.

"There's a thermos in your bag too. Expect them to take it. Make a big deal about it," Austin says.

I frown.

He tugs a vial from his pocket and hands it to me. "Hide this one on you. Somewhere obvious."

Taking it from his hands, I roll it between my fingers for a moment and shove it in the front of my jeans pocket.

Kingston steals Austin's bag and pulls out two plastic pouches filled with blood. "I came up with this idea, so I get the honor of helping you hide them."

I raise my eyebrows.

"Blood bags for your fun bags of course." Kingston flashes his fangs at me, enjoying his idea way too much. Hovering his hand over my chest, he adds, "May I?"

"I think I can handle it."

He pouts.

I poke his shoulder. "But okay. If it'll make you that happy."

"Just be lucky Austin threw out my other hiding place ideas."

I grimace and smack his shoulder with the back of my

hand. "Dude."

He chuckles. "Desperate times, babe."

Kingston takes his time adjusting the blood bags into my bra while I watch him and chug the thermos of blood. Diego and Austin both laugh when Kingston slides his fingers under my boobs to give them a good bounce to show they still look natural.

"Drink one earlier than usual. Maybe midnight. Save the other one just in case," Austin says.

"In case what?" I ask.

"Brayla's responsible for returning you to the Divinity Estate. Shit happens, beautiful. And if it does, hit the button on your bracelet. Stick to the sunlight if you get stuck away." Diego hands me a bag from the front seat beside him and shows me the few weapons. "Do what you have to if you have to."

"Everything's going to be fine," I say, taking the bag anyway.

"And one more thing." Reaching into his pocket, Kingston pulls out my vow necklace and holds out his hand to show me. "I fixed it."

I rub the small teardrop vial of blood hanging under the rose pendants between my fingers. "Are you sure I should wear this?"

"Only if you want to," he says, holding his face expressionless.

I nod. "I do."

Fastening it around my neck, Kingston adds it to the

locket the Vaduva sisters gave me with the pictures of my family. Kingston kisses the skin below my ear before I drop my hair back down. Diego brakes outside the gate but keeps the windows rolled up because the sun still hovers in the sky. Two human guards approach the vehicle and tap on the window.

"Ms. Jordan, we're to escort you to the estate," a man says, adjusting his big ass gun on his shoulder. "Ms. Ortega insists you come alone considering the possible hostility of the situation."

"You've got to be fucking kidding me!" Kingston yells.

"You're out of your mind if you think we're going to entrust Jewel's care into your hands," Austin says.

Diego revs the engine. "Open the gate and allow us through. It is in our contract that we personally deliver Jewel to Brayla."

"I'm sorry, Mr. Divines, but—"

Diego stomps the throttle, jolting us forward. The car rams through the gate, and it flies off and lands in a twisted pile of metal on the dirt. Shouts sound out from behind us, but none of the humans follow. None of them fire their weapons either.

Austin and Kingston both hold onto me as the car bumps and jumps over the uneven gravel of a road in serious need of maintenance. Bushes of yellow wildflowers grow in huge bunches, adding bright color to the dirt. I shift in my seat to get a better look at my surroundings and gape at the green landscape sprawling endlessly. The road takes us down an incline before wrapping around to give me a view of a rundown small city, unlike anything I've seen before. Nestled against the cliff and next to a river, a portion of the old city still remains in the shadows despite the setting sun. My guys were right. This place seems to have been made for vampires.

Except it's now abandoned. Not a single human or vampire walks the broken streets with remnants of a time before the Blood Hunger Plague. The ghost town sends goosebumps prickling over my skin, and I snuggle between Kingston and Austin, shoving my arms behind each of them so that I can pull them closer to me.

And then I see her.

Brayla stands in the shade outside a wrought iron gate, wearing a pair of dark tinted sunglasses. She waves both her hands over her head and beams me a brilliant smile. Behind her, a huge brown and yellow mansion looms. Tall palm trees decorate the vibrant grass, and perfectly manicured hedges wind through a rose garden and around a huge fountain to lead to the stairs of the porch.

Light trickles from the crystal and wood front doors, and I shiver, spotting a figure standing just behind the glass. I know it's Orlando without having to clearly see him. His presence always brings nothing short of uneasiness despite the sudden unbidden joy Brayla's excitement releases inside me before I even leave the car.

She tugs on the backdoor a few times until Austin relents and unlocks it. "Jewel!" she squeals, reaching over Austin to lock her hands to mine to pull me out. All three of my guys growl, and she releases me to step back. "Sheesh, sorry. I can't help that I'm excited."

"Excited over messing up Jewel's life? Some friend you are," Kingston snaps.

She frowns. "I'm her best friend."

"Keep telling yourself that—"

I reach over and squeeze Kingston's hand. "Relax. You're going to get yourself worked up."

"Oh, I'm already worked up. The Ortegas are lucky that—"

Using his technique against him, I silence his threat with my mouth, kissing him so passionately that there's no way he'll try to break away. His hands slide around my waist, pulling me onto his lap, teasing me with his suddenly bulging excitement.

I try to pull back, but he begs me with a whisper not to just yet and caresses his tongue to mine, allowing me to taste the sweetness of his soft, pouty lips.

"Just say the words, and we'll get out of here," he says against my lips.

I cup his face. "I'll be fine. I promise."

"I promise too," Brayla says, speaking up. "She'll be better than fine. It's going to be the best night. She might even ask to stay longer."

Kingston glowers at her, and it takes me pressing my hands to his chest and kissing him one more time to get him to finally let me go. Austin helps me out of the car and engulfs me into a hug that stops my body from trembling with nerves. He meets my lips next, kissing me a dozen times every time I try to peel myself away.

I nuzzle my nose to his and kiss him softly once more. "Save all this affection for me later, okay?"

He bobs his head. "Call us if you need anything."

"She won't," Brayla says, crossing her arms. "We've taken care of each other all our lives. That won't change."

Ignoring her, Austin releases me to Diego, and he lifts me off my feet so that I curl my legs around him. I kiss the nape of his neck while I hug him and work my way up to meet his lips. We caress our mouths together, enjoying each other's touch until Brayla sighs and taps me on the shoulder.

"I know you have a lot of fun with your boy toys, but you'll see them in the morning...that is unless you decide you want to spend the day with me too. The contract says it's your choice," Brayla says.

"I'd prefer to sleep in my own bed," I say.

"You mean one of theirs," she quips.

"I share them, so technically mine."

She smirks at me. "Well, you get your own here. Or we can share like old times. Orlando doesn't mind taking a guest room. I know how much you hate to sleep alone."

Kingston groans.

I try to stay expressionless at the suggestion. "Probably not this time."

She shrugs and looks at my guys. "We'll play it by ear. If plans change, I'll call you."

"No, Jewel will call," Diego says.

She sighs. "Whatever. You'll be notified."

Her words make me uneasy. If it wasn't for the tracker hidden in my bracelet, I'd freak out that she'd try to tell my guys I chose to stay when I don't want to. They obviously suspect the same thing with their insistence that it be me who communicates.

Linking her fingers through mine before I can say anything, Brayla tugs me a few feet away and toward the house. Kingston, Diego, and Austin rush to cut us off, and Brayla halts in her tracks.

Austin holds out my bag to her. "You almost forgot your bag, Jewel."

Brayla shakes her head and pulls me around them. "We have everything she needs here. See you later, Divines. Don't hang around too long or I'll have the guards escort you from the premises."

I grimace. "Is that really necessary?"

She nods. "Totally. Look how possessive they are. It's a wonder how they can even share you with each other."

Glancing over my shoulder, I meet my guys' gazes, each one of them watching us with such intensity. I half expect them to intervene and steal me away at any second. But none of them moves. Not even when the front door swings open. I inhale a shuddering breath, nerves twisting my stomach. I clench my teeth to stop myself from crying as I wave to my guys before I turn toward the house.

Orlando smiles at me from the doorway and extends his arm to welcome me inside. "Precious Jewel, how lovely it is to have you home. How was your trip?"

I don't respond to him. I can't.

All I can do is turn back to Kingston, Diego, and Austin as they stand in the shade by the car. Brayla slams the door, cutting off my view of them, and swings me around to pull me into a hug that leaves me shaking.

I close my eyes and listen for the car doors to shut outside.

Then I whisper my goodbyes.

UNFORGIVABLE

"SO THIS IS YOUR ROOM," Brayla says, swinging the door open to a small bedroom a quarter of the size of the rooms I share with my guys. "I know it's not much, but I didn't have a lot of time to prepare."

"It's not like I'm sleeping here, so I don't even think this is necessary," I say, leaning on the door frame.

She purses her lips. "Hopefully you'll be comfortable enough to do so some other time. Can I show you around? This place is kind of crazy. The human who built it thought she was cursed with ghosts and kept adding onto the house as a way to confuse them."

I blink a few times. I thought it was strange that we had to basically circle through a few rooms to avoid a random drop onto another level. I assumed they were just renovating the shit show Master Caruthers called home. I'm pretty sure I saw his box bedroom down the hall too.

"You sure it was a human? Sounds like a way for a vampire to confuse humans."

"Oh, it served that purpose as well. Also, you should know that parts of the house remain unfinished and decaying, messed up by earthquakes. Watch out for low ceilings and some sudden low rise staircases. Stay off any of the windows in the middle of the floor. They drop three stories down if broken."

I grimace. "So, you live in a walking death trap for me. Awesome."

She laughs. "You'll get used to it and will be able to navigate it yourself soon enough. After my tour, we can head to the weird ass kitchen with an open ceiling to the second floor and eat," she says. "It'll be like old times."

We. We as in the both of us. Old times? Yeah, right. Brayla didn't drink blood before.

I don't know why it bothers me so much, but the thought of providing my blood to Brayla as sustenance skeeves me out. She was my best friend as a human, and it shouldn't be so weird. But because I've been in the mindset of only feeding my guys, it's hard to include her. I just hope Diego was right and she won't bite me.

"I also thought that after dinner I could show you how happy our new staff members are," she adds. "The ones I saved for you from the game."

Man, finders keepers seems like so long ago. I nearly forgot that Brayla spent the game catching people to prove to me that she was on my side—that she was still the same person I knew back in Dark Terrace Ranch despite her being a vampire.

I hope with everything in me that she is, and that whatever Orlando's insisting she do to get to me backfires on him, and she gives up this game of who gets to keep me in their possession. It's been weeks since I've felt like a piece of property, but I feel like it more than ever.

"What about Ramona?" I can't stop the question from flying from my mouth. "I'd like to see her too."

She presses her lips together. "You'll have to ask Orlando."

"What?" I ask.

"He's her keeper."

"But when you invited me over, you said that I could see her."

She sighs and turns to face me. "I'm sorry. I shouldn't have offered that before consulting with Orlando. I don't mean to disappoint you, but he's a little annoyed by how rude you're being to him. You didn't even greet him."

Anger rolls through me, and I huff a few breaths. That friggin' asshole. "Seriously? You expect me to play nice with him after everything? He came in and tried to collect on a blood debt my father owed him. He took Ramona from Haven Springs. He—he—" I ball my fingers into fists and punch the wall, sending plaster crumbling to the floor. "He turned you into a vampire!" I scream.

"Jewel, calm down," she says.

But I can't. I'm furious. "Then you had the nerve to apply to Blood Match with me. How could you? You know I'm in love with the Divines."

"They don't deserve you," she says.

"And you do?"

Brayla flashes her fangs at me. One second I'm standing beside her, and in the next my back rams into the wall, knocking the breath from my chest. Tears flood my eyes as she snaps her teeth in my face, sending a wave of fear over me. I squeeze my eyes shut, gasping for breath that doesn't come. I can't even beg her not to bite me.

"Of course I don't deserve you. No one deserves you, Jewel," she says, her voice deepening with her own rage in my ear.

"My guys do," I manage to spit out.

"They don't! You're just a means to show off the Blood Match Program. To get more donors to apply. Make the selection better so that Donor Life Corp can charge more."

"And what's wrong with that? It gets people out of the city. Saves families," I say. "I'd be dead if it wasn't for the Blood Match Program. So would Ramona. Dana and Fallon. What about your family? About Dougie?"

"You love the guys who helped do this to us. We

should've never been put in this position in the first place," she snaps.

I grip onto the front of her dress, trying to push her back. "You mean the position where my dad was trading my freedom to Orlando to save the rest of my family?"

She stiffens at my words. I know I shouldn't have said them. Orlando shouldn't know that I know, but I can't help myself. I want Orlando to know I'm onto his games and that he can't get away with this.

"Or how about the position *you* put me in by murdering my dad," I say, glowering.

"I was just—" She bites her bottom lip between her teeth, accidentally drawing blood with her fangs.

I push her back. "You were just what?"

"Trying to save you from the Divines." Her soft voice barely comes out a whisper, but the words still get to me. How dare she think she had the right.

Throwing my hands up, I say, "I didn't—I still don't—need to be saved."

"But you do. You can't give them what they want. When the board—"

Orlando appears behind Brayla and covers her mouth with his hand. His blue eyes flash silver, and her tense muscles relax under his touch. They turn toward each other and lean in closely, ignoring the fact that I'm standing right here.

"Now's not the time for revelations, lover," Orlando whispers, trailing his finger across her cheek to collect the hair that had fallen in her face.

"Then when?" I ask. "Because I'm pretty friggin' tired of the bullshit—"Ah, hell.

Brayla and Orlando turn to me, capturing me in their startled eyes. I let my anger control me and gave myself away that I can hear them at a pitch I shouldn't have been able to.

Squeezing my eyes shut, I try to think of a million things to say to respond to their heavy silence that threatens to suffocate me. I scrub my hands up and down my face, praying that when I do decide to drop them that both vampires will be gone, and I'll wake up from another freaky ass nightmare.

"You don't know what my guys want or what they're capable of," I whisper, refusing to look.

"*Your* guys," Brayla says. "They're not yours. They claim you and not the other way around."

My deflection works. Neither she nor Orlando calls me out about hearing Orlando whisper. At least not yet.

"They are *my* guys. They all proposed a Blood Vow. I love them. They love me."

"And how long do you think you'll be able to keep this all up, Jewel? I've read the contract. I know what happens if you decide not to pick. If you don't pick me, you'll have to pick one of them. Can you survive that? They all act nice now, but you know they'll fight over you."

I don't answer. She's playing on my obvious insecurities since I refused to pick during the re-match.

"Do you think you can get away with not picking?" she

asks, reading my expression.

Again, I don't answer.

"What do you think will happen? That you can all live this weird happily ever after life? Do you even know what happens if you don't pick?"

"I breach my contract, and my family loses their benefits," I whisper into my hands.

"And?"

"And nothing. That's what happens."

Cool fingers lace around my wrists and pry them from my face. "Jewel, look at me," Brayla asks.

I finally get the nerve to open my eyes.

"Is that what they told you?"

I nod.

She shares a look with Orlando, and it drives me crazy that they still manage to have a conversation that I can't be a part of. They now know each other well enough that they don't have to use their words. And I can't help but wonder if they don't because of my mess up.

"What else did they tell you? That your family will be okay? That they'll figure it out?" she asks.

I rub my lips together, keeping my face expressionless.

"They did," she says, glancing back to Orlando. "You were right, lover."

"What are you talking about?" I ask despite my fear. I turn my gaze to Orlando. "I'm tired of these games. If you have something to say, just say it. You've ripped apart my life enough. I want answers."

Orlando materializes in front of me, flashing his fangs. I screech and stumble back, startled by his movements. Brayla catches me in her arms, sliding her arm over my chest. She locks me in place, stopping me from moving.

"I'm sorry, Jewel. I wanted to build your trust first. This wasn't how everything was supposed to happen," she says, breathing into my hair. "But I'm afraid we've run out of time."

"Please, just let me go," I whisper.

Orlando steps in front of me, sandwiching me between him and Brayla. I close my eyes, refusing to let him try to capture me in his gaze. Fear pours through me, breaking sweat out on my forehead. My whole body trembles.

"My precious Jewel, please look at me," Orlando says, running his finger across my cheek.

I thrash my head, shoving myself into Brayla. She huffs, hitting her back on the wall.

"You're scaring her," Brayla says. "Just let me tell her."

Orlando growls low in his voice. "Not now. We have a plan."

I whimper in Brayla's arms, sensing Orlando's closeness again. "No, please."

"It's going to be okay, Jewel," Brayla says. "It'll be over soon. I'm going to breach your contract and not give the board a choice but to release you from the Blood Match Program and the Divines. You'll go to Haven Springs without anyone getting a say. You'll be free of your matches and can come back to me."

"What?" I say. "You can't do that."

"It's the only way," Brayla says. "Now, please. Open your eyes for Orlando."

"No!" I scream. "I won't let you do this!"

"Please, Jewel. Open your eyes. Don't make me pry them open. If you just look at Orlando, you'll understand."

Tears burn my cheeks. "Understand what? Just tell me."

"If I do, will you open your eyes?" she asks.

I nod.

Gentle fingers run under my eyes, smearing my tears. "Go on, lover," Orlando says. "As long as she opens her eyes first."

"Come on, Jewel. Do as we ask," she says. "And then I'll tell you."

I flutter my eyes, turning my gaze straight to the ceiling. "Tell me first and then I'll look completely."

Brayla hugs me tighter to her. "The Divines are using you, Jewel."

"They're not," I argue. "They love me."

"Then they wouldn't give you such hope. They promised that they'd guarantee you didn't have to choose, right? They promised to take care of everything even if it meant that you breached their contracts."

"So what?"

"They begged you not to choose, didn't they?"

I blink my eyes, clearing my tears. "Because we make it work."

"And you think they'll give up the Divine name for you? That they'll go against Mitchell? All for you?"

"I accepted their Blood Vows. We make this work," I repeat.

"Not you. You don't make it work. They do. They wanted you to be unable to pick between them. It's why they demanded that the board allow it. You honestly think that the board or the Divines would put the fate of their future into a donor's hands? Do you really think this will turn out well?"

"Yes," I say. "I do. We'll do it together."

"But that's the thing, Jewel. If you decide not to choose them, you breach your contract, and your family loses their benefits, but there's a penalty. If you don't pick someone, your contract passes on to Mitchell because of the time and finances you wasted. You'll be his property and blood source."

"What?" I ask, shifting my gaze to Orlando. My stomach tightens with knots. This revelation reminds me of what the board had planned to instate for Haven Springs and how instead of matches getting sent to Haven Springs if something were to happen to their vampire that they'd end up getting passed to the next in the household, which for me meant Mitchell. But Kingston assured me it never went through. Why wouldn't my guys warn me of this now? "You're full of shit. I saw the contract."

"The new one?"

I furrow my brows. "What do you mean?"

"When the board insisted you re-match, it opened you up to renegotiations. The Divines took advantage of it," Brayla says.

Orlando holds my gaze. "They know how special you are, Jewel."

"They love me," I say.

He runs his fingers over my cheeks. "They know you're different."

"But I'm not."

"You are, Jewel. You might not realize it yet, but I assured it," Orlando says. "Now look at me and don't look away."

I slacken my body just like I've been trained any time a vampire tries to get in my head. I do what he says and hold his stare, allowing him to lock me in his eyes.

"Jewel, remember me," Orlando says, staring at me with all his hot intensity.

I blink a few times, trying to think of something to say.

Orlando's serious face falters, and he frowns, realization settling in his gaze. I jerk my leg up to knee him in the groin, but he expects my move and jumps back. Brayla's hold on me loosens, and I take the chance to ram my head back, hitting her in the nose. Stars pepper my vision, but the surprise of my fight throws her off, and I manage to break free of her. But Orlando already grips my hand and spins me into him.

His hand runs over my body, digging into the pockets of my sweatshirt and then he tugs the small vial of blood from my jeans. Sighing, he chucks the vial at the wall. My guys' blood sprays across the light paint and cascades across the floor.

"Vampire blood consumption," he says over my shoulder to Brayla. He turns his eyes back to mine. "How often, Jewel?"

I don't respond.

"I swore they only did it just to increase her good time," Brayla says.

"It's worse than I thought." He trails his finger down my face and to my neck to slide his fingers into the long tresses of my hair. Tilting his head, he studies me. "They're not manipulating her mind like we had assumed."

"But Ramona said—"

Orlando rubs his lips together and doesn't take his eyes off mine. "It's only what she believed, lover. She can't accept anything else otherwise."

"Of course they're not. They'd never," I say, smacking his chest in an attempt to put space between us. He's close. Too close. All he'd have to do was lean in, and he could kiss me. And the way he stares at my mouth sends a weird mixture of emotion through me. Because I can nearly imagine what it would be like. I've dreamed of it. "You don't do that to people you love," I add, pursing my lips and glaring.

His jaw twitches. "They're more powerful than I thought. This is Jewel's truth. She believes them completely. They didn't just get into her head. They got into her heart."

"So what now? Can't you do something?" Brayla asks. "We can't give her back."

"You have to," I say.

Orlando flares his nostrils, the look he gives me igniting fear in my chest. "We can't just let the blood leave her system and try to fix the damage. They'll know. Mind manipulation can't be used to get her to pick us."

Brayla rubs her hands over her face. "But she needs us. We can't send her back. If they find out what you did, who knows what they'll do with her. This might be our only chance to save her. This was the plan. I promised—"

Orlando drops me and covers Brayla's mouth with his hand. He stares at her for a long moment, waiting to make sure she doesn't say anything else. I take their distraction to inch my way toward the door. There is no friggin' way I'm waiting around to see how this plays out. If I can get outside, I can run into the sun. They won't be able to follow me for another ten minutes. It'll give me a tiny fighting chance.

"Pack a bag for both of you," Orlando says. "We can't stay here and play by their rules. I will not risk losing my investment. I've grown too fond. I'll not let Donor Life Corp mess up the arrangement."

Shit. Shit. Shit. Spinning around, I rush toward the door. Neither Orlando nor Brayla tries to come after me. They continue to talk about a plan I want no part of.

I run down the narrow hallway that turns into another until I reach a set of stairs. Except the stairs go up and not down. And they're short and wide. Brayla wasn't kidding about the weird floor plan.

I open a hallway door on the left and freeze. It leads straight outside with a two-story drop. Friggin' deathtrap house. I consider jumping for all of a second but decide against it because of all the hard ass concrete to break my fall. Voices sound out from behind me, and I glance at the stairs. I step up a couple of them and realize that at the top of the landing, they split with regular stairs heading back down.

I take them as fast as I can, not even touching the rickety banister. The stairs lead to a short door that I have to bend down to even walk through. I enter into a strange, octagonal room with etched crystal windows that obscure my view of outside. A glass door on the left side leads to what looks like a balcony that disappears around the side of the house.

I take my chance and run to it, thrusting the door open. From here, I can see the vast property and the enormity of the house. From the front, it doesn't look all that big, but the size seems comparable to the Divinity Estate now that I can see all the additions.

The balcony narrows as I walk the length of it, passing by several stained-glass windows that I don't bother trying to look into. When I reach the end, I'm left with either breaking the narrow window to go into a room with one of the floor windows Brayla talked about or to turn around.

I pull my sleeve around my hand and break the window.
Big mistake.

Glass shatters and cascades across the wood floors, the noise loud enough to alert Brayla and Orlando of my location. I'm actually rather surprised neither of them has caught me yet, and I'm starting to think that they're waiting for me to get completely lost or to wear myself out so that I don't put up a fight.

I enter the small room and slide around the window and enter into another room with a beam from the ceiling strewn on the floor. The walls crumble around me, and dirt covers the floor, untouched by footprints. It looks like people haven't been in here in a long time despite the narrow unmade bed under a window now boarded up.

I heave a breath and sit on the edge of the bed. Concentrating on my surroundings, I listen for voices or footsteps. Hearing neither, I take my chance to pry off one of the sapphires on my bracelet with the com device my guys insisted I wear. I'm not supposed to use it unless it's an emergency, and I'm pretty friggin' sure this qualifies.

I press the button and a tiny light flicks on and glows on the wall in front of me.

Diego's face fills up the video screen immediately. He searches my face, already looking for signs of me being injured.

"You have to come back and get me right now," I say.

"Are you hurt?"

Tears burn my eyes. "They're going to take me away. This was never about the Blood Match. Brayla only applied so she could breach her own contract to pull me from the program."

"Stay calm, beautiful. We're not far. We were never planning to go home. Get to a window and call out for Kingston. He took to the trees while Austin and I drove into town."

I rush back toward the balcony and crunch over the shattered glass from the window. "Kingston," I whisper-hiss, terrified that if I yell out, Brayla or Orlando will materialize out of nowhere.

"Yell louder, beautiful. Austin already alerted Kingston. He'll get to you first. Don't worry," Diego says.

Clearing my throat, I yell, "Kingston!"

He appears below the balcony and holds out his arms to me. "I knew I was right."

"And I'm sure you won't let us hear the end of it," Austin says through the line.

"I'll take his bullshit as long as our girl is safe," Diego adds. "And I would've stayed if you hadn't demanded to, bro. You knew we couldn't all—"

"It doesn't matter," I say. "I just—catch me, Kingston."

Climbing over the balcony, I latch my fingers onto the banister and peer back over my shoulder to make sure Kingston's there. He motions for me to hurry, and I squeeze my eyes shut and release a small scream for the drop.

Kingston catches me and runs, blurring the world around us. I snuggle into his neck, kissing him a dozen times. I don't care that it hasn't been more than twenty minutes since I said goodbye. I missed him. I miss all of my guys.

"Jewel!" Brayla yells. "If you let him take you, I'll call the board and tell them that they breached the agreement."

Kingston growls in my ear. "Fuck off! You're not taking my girl."

A figure darts from the trees, and Kingston spins, swiveling me out of Brayla's reach as she tries to snatch me away from him. Orlando appears on our other side, and the two of them surround us.

"Jewel, listen to me," Brayla says. "If you let him take you, I can't help you."

I cling to Kingston as he tries to look for a way around them without putting my safety in jeopardy. "I don't need help."

"You do. You have no idea what truly goes on in our world. The Divines are using you," she says. "They know you're special."

"Of course I know she's fucking special. She's the best," Kingston says. "But I'm not using her. I love her."

"He loves only your blood," Brayla says. "He can't help it. But you need Orlando."

"I don't," I snap.

"Damn straight," Kingston says.

"I'll prove it," Orlando says.

"How?" I ask.

"Let the vampire blood run its course," he says.

"So you can continue to manipulate her mind?" Kingston

asks. "No fucking way."

Brayla and Orlando both stroll closer, making Kingston flash his fangs. He adjusts his grip on me, shifting me over his shoulders so that he can have his arms free. I wrap my legs around him to grip on as tightly as I can.

"Come on, brothers," Kingston mutters.

Diego and Austin don't respond through the line, but I think it's for a reason.

"Jewel, this is your last opportunity to do things peacefully," Orlando says. "If you don't, I will kill the Divine. I'll send my staff after his brothers."

My heart races at the threat. "You won't."

Brayla grabs at the back of my sweatshirt, making Kingston spin. The sudden jerk of his movements loosens my grip, and I fly off his back and skid across the ground, rolling a few times until the world stops.

Three figures blur around me as the vampires fight at a speed I can't follow. Kingston slams into the ground next to me only to have Orlando drag him back to his feet to hold him by his neck. Kingston's face turns red as he squeezes, and Brayla comes up behind him and presses her hand against Kingston's back.

"Stop!" I yell. "Please! I'll go!"

Kingston thrashes. "Babe, run! I'll catch up."

I hesitate.

"Run!" he yells again.

My legs kick into action the second Kingston breaks his

arm free and clocks Orlando in the face, sending him back. I rush away, gasping for air that isn't quick to come into my lungs. Brayla yells out, and I can't stop myself from looking back to see Kingston flip her over onto her back.

I collide into a hard chest, and Orlando picks me up off my feet, making me scream.

Kingston jerks his attention toward me, giving Brayla an opening. She jerks her hand up and into his chest, and Kingston hollers, his whole body flailing. She flashes her fangs, her eyes blinking silver, showing exactly what kind of person Orlando turned her into—a monster, just like he is.

"Brayla, don't! I'll never forgive you!" I scream.

Orlando slaps his hand over my mouth and cuts off my words.

Brayla thrusts Kingston back, sliding her bloody hand from his chest. She gets to her feet and kicks him onto his side.

The last thing I see is Kingston lying in the dirt. He doesn't move. He doesn't get up. He doesn't do anything as Orlando and Brayla take me.

BREACH IN CONTRACT

"RELAX, JEWEL. AS SOON AS the vampire blood is out of your system, you'll feel a lot better. Promise," Brayla says.

I mess with the door handle, trying everything I can think of to pry the thing open. If I get it open, they might slow down enough for me to jump. Even if they don't, I'll still jump. I'm stronger than ever. It'll hurt like hell, but I think I'll survive...at least I hope.

"I'll only feel better because you'll mess with my head," I snap.

Orlando swivels in the front seat to look at me. "I've only ever done so by request or out of necessity."

"Fuck you! When have vampires ever taken orders from humans?" I ask. "Because I highly doubt that was the reason you went along with my dad's request."

He tightens his jaw. "So you remember something. Then you must know I don't enjoy you being afraid of me. I much prefer the opposite."

"Yeah, right. You messed with me and purposely scared me. You threatened to drain me dry. You promised Katherine Duchanne that she could bite me."

He twists his lips. "All necessary to make this work. And if I recall, I saved you from her. Held her while you ravaged her like the fighter I enjoy seeing. Think, Jewel. If you remember—"

"I don't know what the hell I remember or what is real. It seems that people have been messing with my head so much that I can't tell anymore. The only time things are clear are with my matches—not including you." I glare at Brayla. "We are done, so you know."

Brayla frowns. "Jewel, please. I know you're scared, but you have to trust me. We were friends before you met the Divines. You're just going to throw away everything we have? For what? Good sex and money? That shit doesn't last forever."

"You murdered my dad!" I scream.

"Jewel."

"Don't fucking *Jewel* me, Brayla. I don't care if you think you're saving me or whatever. I don't need to be saved. I don't want to be saved. I don't want anything to do with you or that fucking stalker asshole. Just stop the car and let me out. If you don't, I can't stop my guys from coming after you." I yank on the door handle again before giving up and leaning back to kick at the glass. It doesn't shatter. It doesn't even flex under the pressure of my force.

"No," Orlando says. "This was the deal, and I already messed up by underestimating your desirability to the program. I would've done more to prevent you from ever reaching the center. Noah didn't want you to ever Blood Match in the first place, but you couldn't wait."

"Couldn't wait?" I shriek, fury igniting inside me. His words get to me so much that I can't even process everything he says about my dad. "We were going to get kicked out of our apartment and onto Starlight Row. My dad left us! I don't give a flying fuck what he would've wanted. I don't care whatever deal you two had, but he's dead, so it's over. Leave me the hell out of it and let me go."

I give up on trying to break out through the window and do the only thing I can think of. Flying forward, I shove my arm against Orlando's neck to brace against him and grab the wheel, jerking it as hard as I can. The car squeals off the road, and my whole world bounces as Orlando tries to regain control of the vehicle. Slamming the brakes, Orlando sends me sprawling into the dashboard. I smack my head on the windshield, sending pain and stars bursting through my vision.

"Damn it, Jewel," Brayla says, yanking me onto her lap. She looks down at me, combing her fingers through my messy hair covering my face. Blood coats her hands, and she flares her nostrils, grimacing.

"Brayla, control yourself," Orlando says.

She flashes her fangs at me.

"Brayla!" he yells.

Shadows crowd my vision, and everything goes dark.

"Why can't I go with you?" Ramona asks, standing in front of the door with her hands on her hips.

"Sweetie, you have school," Mom says, holding out a small bag to my sister.

Ramona huffs. "But I can help."

"Don't worry, honey. Jewel's going to be fine. Dad and I are taking her to the Human Health Center. They'll take good care of her."

I shift on the couch, clutching my stomach. "Maybe I'll still make it to school after."

Mom embraces Ramona. "She's probably right, Ramona-babona. A little medicine will do the trick. And if she's not there to walk home with you, I'll have Dad pick you up."

Ramona sighs. "No thanks. I'll walk with Brayla."

"Okay, sweetie. Just remember to stay—"

"Stay out of the shadows. Yeah, I got it." Ramona shrugs her bag over her shoulder. "And if I can't, at least Dana and Fallon are slower than me."

"Ramona!" Mom snaps.

Ramona rolls her eyes. "It's a fucking joke. Jeez."

Mom swats her on the shoulder. "Language. And jokes

are intended to be funny.”

“Yeah, whatever.” Ramona turns her attention to me. “Feel better, Jewel-babewel.”

Ramona leaves from the apartment, and Mom returns to my side and helps me to my feet. Pain gnaws at my insides, twisting my stomach. She touches her warm fingers to my cool face and purses her lips.

“Can you walk okay?” she asks, worry lining her eyes.

I shuffle forward and bend over, grabbing my knees. “Sh-h-h-h-it,” I groan.

“Noah!” Mom yells. “Hurry.”

Dad rushes from my parents’ bedroom, and he clicks a few buttons on the phone to hang up with whoever he was talking to. He takes one look at me and hooks his arm under my legs to lift me into his arms. Tears blur my vision as pain swells through me. Both my parents whisper to me that I’ll be okay soon enough and to just hold on.

Dad nearly flies down all five floors worth of stairs with Mom right behind us. I think I black out from pain near the bottom because when I open my eyes, we’re outside and a few blocks away from our tower complex.

“Stay in the sunlight, Helena,” Dad tells Mom. “I’ll take her to him.”

“Be careful, love,” Mom says, stopping short. “And Jewel, be brave, honey.”

My stomach clenches again, and I writhe in Dad’s arms, desperately needing to change my position. Dad adjusts me, facing me outward. I blink through my hazy vision at the looming shadow in front of us. We're nowhere near the Human Health Center. And there's a man in the shadow. A vampire.

"Dad, watch out," I say, struggling in his tightening grip. "Don't you see him?"

"It's going to be okay, Jewel," Dad says.

"Give her to me, Noah." A smooth, melodic voice sounds through the air, drawing even more panic from my insides to combat the pain clenching my stomach.

"No!" I yell. "Dad, please. No."

Dad covers my mouth with his hand, silencing my screams. My eyes widen at the fangs protruding from beneath the vampire's lips, and he smiles at me with silver flashing in his eyes. He motions Dad forward, holding open his arms. Panic engulfs me, and I buck so hard that Dad drops me to the ground.

"Jewel, sweetie. Stop fighting. You're going to hurt yourself," Mom calls.

"You know, Noah. Your over-protectiveness will only do Jewel harm," the vampire says. "What is it you're afraid of? We have a deal. You can trust me."

"I trust no vampire," Dad snaps, yanking me back to my feet.

The man hums under his breath and steps as close as he can without crossing into the sunlight. "You can't honestly continue this way of life forever. You know the terms. Jewel *will eventually—"*

"Shut up and help her. That's the deal." Dad's low voice ignites as much fear inside me as the vampire.

"Dad," I whimper. "Please, don't. I'm in pain. You're hurting me."

He ignores me and shoves me at the vampire. I scream out only for a split second before the vampire places his cool hand over my mouth and lifts me off my feet to cradle me against him. I pant a few breaths, torn between my pain and fear. I close my eyes and brace myself for what is surely to come.

"Precious Jewel, open your eyes," the vampire whispers. "Let me get a good look at you."

My whole body trembles. "Don't bite me."

"Do you see how scared she is?" the vampire asks. "You're raising her improperly."

Dad huffs. "I'm raising her with good sense. Isolation not immersion. We cannot risk it. Not yet."

"Then allow her to remember only me."

"Not the deal. She needs to fear for her survival."

"Noah, maybe he's right," Mom says. "Jewel, honey. It's okay. You're safe. We're right here. Please look at Orlando."

"Helena, no. Don't," Dad says.

A warm hand brushes the tears off my cheeks. "Sweetie, I'm here. Open your eyes."

Fluttering my eyes open, I peer at Mom watching me over the vampire's shoulder as she stands behind him. She smiles at me, not even moving away when the vampire shifts so that he holds me between us, turning his back on Dad.

"Now, look at Orlando," Mom says. "Be brave for me, will you. This is a good thing. You'll get better real quick."

I slowly turn my attention to the vampire. He captures me in his blue gaze, beaming a brilliant smile at me, displaying his fangs. The only thing stopping me from panicking is that Mom doesn't flinch or run away.

"Jewel," he says, stroking his fingers across my damp cheek. "Remember me."

I blink a few times as his familiarity sets in. "Oh, Orlando. It's nice to see you again."

"It's always a pleasure to see you, precious Jewel." He bends forward and brushes his lips to my forehead. "How are you feeling?"

I pout my lip. "Like death. My stomach is killing me."

"Blame your father. I warned him that he was keeping you away for too long," Orlando says.

"Don't tell her that bullshit. You know it was a test to see how long she could manage," Dad says, practically spitting.

"It'll only get worse with maturity, Noah. She's nearly a woman now. An enchanting one at that," Orlando purrs.

"Just get on with it," Dad says. "We don't have all day."

"Very well." Orlando brings his arm up to his mouth and bites down.

"Jewel? Jewel, can you hear me? You need to open your eyes," Brayla says.

"I'm so happy to take care of you," Orlando says, capturing my eyes while I drink from him.

"I think that's enough," Dad says.

Someone shakes my shoulders. "Jewel, please."

Orlando pulls his arm away. "Forget me, Jewel. If anyone asks, you went to the Human Health Center for medicine. You feel much better now."

"I do," I say.

"Now, Noah. It's time to pay her dues."

"Jewel!"

Cool hands grip my cheeks and nails bite into my skin. I snap my eyes open only to close them again. Dizziness washes over me, and my stomach heaves and convulses. A splitting headache consumes me, making it impossible to focus on anything besides my body rebelling against me.

"Shit, she's really hurt, Orlando," Brayla says. "Pull over."

"Not here," he says. "Just give her to me."

Brayla shifts me from her lap and into Orlando's. My shoulder presses into the wheel, sending more pain through me. He looks down at me, his blue eyes searching over my face.

"Jewel, I need you to open your mouth," he says.

I clench my teeth and shake my head.

He sticks his finger into the corner of my lips. "You know, I enjoy how much fight you have, but I need you to let me do this."

I lock my hand around his wrist and jerk his hand away.

"No. Not your blood."

"I'll do it," Brayla says.

"No!"

I thrash in Orlando's arms, managing to flip myself toward the steering wheel. Neither he nor Brayla get the chance to stop me as I hit a few buttons on the dash, disengaging the autopilot. Orlando has no choice but to grip the wheel. I fight him for it, jerking it in the opposite direction he tries to navigate. He stomps the brakes at the same time Brayla grabs onto me to stop me from jostling around.

Something hits the windshield, cracking it.

"Don't let her go," Orlando tells Brayla. "I'll take care of this."

A growl sounds through the car, coming in from outside. Then another and another.

I shimmy to sit upright, relief washing over me.

But then an unfamiliar vampire bangs on the window, stealing my hope away. It wasn't my guys like I had thought. This is a shadow dweller.

And there are a ton of them.

SHADOW DWELLERS

A BLOODY BODY LANDS ON the windshield, crushing it. "Holy shit balls!"

The strange vampire flips over and rams his fist through the fissured glass to rip away the shards. His blood splashes across my face, and I swipe it off as fast as I can. Brayla grabs his hand and twists his arm, snapping the bone. The vampire howls and punches his other hand through, locking it into my hair.

Neither of us has time to react as another figure comes up behind the vampire and rips him off the hood of the car. The world blurs around me as the asshole drags me away with him, ripping the sleeves of my sweatshirt on the way out.

I hit my back on the hood and slide off it to the pavement. Another figure materializes next to me and punches the guy only to grab me by the front of the shirt. The new vampire man flashes his fangs and holds me up. I ram my hand into his throat, struggling to keep his snapping teeth from my neck.

Brayla clutches the vampire by the shoulders, yanking us both away from the car. "Just let him bite her, Brayla. It's what we need. You can take care of him then."

Eff that. I do my best to claw at the man as Brayla struggles over the idea of letting him bite me.

"I don't think I could stop him after," she calls to Orlando.

"I will. Just don't let him get away."

Brayla flares her nostrils. "I'm sorry, Jewel. It's the only way. We can use this to break your contract. But don't worry. I won't let him kill you."

The vampire manages to lace his hands around my wrists and yanks them down to trap my arms against him. He's a disaster. Seven tattooed lines mark his forehead, the sign he's been cast out of a city according to my guys like the shadow dwellers we saw on our holiday. A layer of mud or blood or something disgusting lines him in filth. His eyes remain glowing silver, and some of his teeth between his fangs are broken or missing. I was completely wrong all the times I thought a vampire looked starved. This guy looks batshit, out-of-his-mind friggin' famished.

I thrash, flailing as hard as I can to get him to let me go.

Fear consumes me as I meet his silver eyes.

"Stop fighting," he whispers, trying to capture me in his gaze.

"Fuck no!" I surprise him and ram my head into his.

The world turns dark as I black out for a few seconds—long enough to find myself on the ground, but still out of the vampire's grip. Jerking my leg up, I kick him in the groin, making him yell. Brayla loses her hold on him, and he turns around and shoves into her. The two of them disappear as they fight.

I roll to my knees and push myself up. My head throbs, blood seeping from a gash to spill across the pavement. Everything hurts. I can barely see through my hazy vision, but I know if I don't get my ass in gear, someone here will bite me. Or continue to try to kidnap me. Most likely both. All things I want no part of.

I crawl forward and under the car to try to shield myself. Something crashes into the metal next to me, and a vampire hits the ground, meeting my eyes. She glowers and bares her teeth while reaching her dirty, bloody nails toward me. Someone stomps on her arm, stopping her from grabbing me, and then she flies off her feet and disappears.

My strength gives out on me, and I lie on my stomach under the middle of the car. My head throbs too much to focus. Pain radiates through my whole body. I always thought that my life would end by the hands of vampires, but I never in my craziest nightmares thought it would end like this, alone and scared, completely betrayed by Brayla. A senseless death at that. I imagined I'd die doing something for my family or my guys. Not because I found myself in the middle of a blood feud.

Another body drops to the ground, and sharp nails dig into my jeans. I swear and kick my foot, trying to get the guy off me. He drags me closer, scraping my body on the rough asphalt, but he doesn't pull me all the way out. It's then that I realize he's not going to. He doesn't need to. He's not trying to steal me away like the others. He just wants to—

"Fucking shit!" I scream as pain radiates in my ankle. The vampire bites onto my leg, piercing me so deeply with his fangs that I'm certain he might have reached my bone. And it hurts like hell.

The exploding pain pushes my body to react, and I kick him so hard in the face that I smash his nose in. Blood sprays across my pants, and he releases a guttural wail that reverberates through me. I scramble away on my stomach to get out from under the car. I can't stay here.

I shimmy to the cracked sidewalk and manage to push to my feet, using a rusty metal bench of an old bus stop to get up. Bodies fly around me at a speed I can't follow. Sucking in a breath, I hobble away, practically dragging my aching foot with me. I reach the corner of the old red brick building and clutch it for a moment, trying to pull myself together, but it's so friggin' hard. Worse than having to hike up the Divinity Estate hillside.

I push myself to walk another few feet, but my legs give out on me. I just can't. I can't do it.

I slump on the ground and roll to the side of the old, weathered sign of something I can't read. From my spot, I take in a view of the gross, decrepit city, a place I've never been to. It looks worse than even Midnight Valley, and that place was a wreck. I spot the glow of a window on a building only a few dozen feet away. I have no idea what's inside, but it can't be any worse than what's out here. If I could just get a minute to breathe or to find a phone, I can call my guys for help since Orlando stole my bracelet.

I take a few heaving breaths and drag myself along the wall of the building. Icy fingers lock onto my wrist and yank me up, startling me. Another vampire dangles me in front of him, inspecting my face. He runs his sharp nail across the front of my sweatshirt, ripping the fabric down to my chest to expose my clavicle.

I kick out my legs, struggling against his grip. "Put me down!"

He flashes his fangs at me. "You're Divine property."

"And you're gonna be dead." I swing my body and lock my legs around him to take my weight off my wrists in the most awkward body hug of my life. My sudden movement throws the guy off balance, and he spins with me, hitting my back to the wall. I release a gasp and wince.

"You're funny," he says, leaning forward to sniff my throat. "I like that."

Ugh. "You won't be laughing when the Divines show up."

"You're right. I'll be gone by then. It'll be satisfying enough just to take a taste," he murmurs, grossing me the hell out with how he licks his lips.

I tremble, attempting to press harder into the wall, hoping maybe the building will collapse on us or something. "Please, don't. If you don't, I can promise you a reward."

He raises his eyebrows at me. "I'm listening."

"I've been kidnapped, and my misters are searching for me. Return me to them, and they'll pay you." Kingston once told me that people can be bought, and I realize that the same goes for vampires. At least shadow vampires. "You will be accepted as a permanent guest at the Divinity Estate."

His nostrils flare as he contemplates my offer. "You will have a deal if you let me bite you just once."

I grimace. "Seriously?"

He flashes his fangs. "Do we have a deal?"

Everything in me screams of course we don't have a friggin' deal, and I'm not going to continue to straddle this guy and let him bite me. But then a figure materializes behind him, rushing so quickly toward us that all I can do is brace myself. The vampire doesn't get caught off guard though. He spins us both out of the way and sets me on my feet in an alcove before disappearing to fight the other shadow dweller. Their figures blur through the air, and I jiggle the doorknob to the entrance of the building. Swiveling, I catch sight of a human guard, positioning his gun to prepare to fire at me.

"I'm human!" I yell, regretting the high-pitch of my voice immediately. "Please! Let me in."

The man frowns at me and shakes his head. Reaching for his radio, he hits the button. "Sorry, kid. Closed for curfew." His voice sounds through a speaker on the wall.

Tears burn my eyes. "Please, I'm the Blood Match to the Divines."

He presses his lips together. "Still can't let you in. I see the fight. What you can do is take the alley to the left. Down the block there's the entrance to an old cellar. You can hide out there until sunrise."

I rest my forehead to the glass. I'm pretty friggin' certain I'm not going to make it. I'm also damn sure my foot is going to fall off. But what does that matter? I'm going to be devoured any minute.

"Please," I beg. "Please."

"Sorry. The best I can do is notify your next of kin," he says.

A flicker of hope lights inside me. "Yes, that! Do that! They're the Jordans in Haven Springs. Tell them exactly where this place is. Tell them to contact the Divines. They'll know how."

Hands grab the back of my sweatshirt and yank me from the door, making me scream. I meet the flat brown eyes of the vampire who was fighting against the one who was going to take me up on the reward. Damn it. If he's here, that means the other dude must be dead or gone.

"Hello, Jewel," the vampire says. "Don't scream. Don't fight. Your master asked that I bite you just a bit."

I swing out my hand and slap him so hard across the face that his head snaps to the side. "No!"

He drops me to the ground, not expecting to be unable to manipulate my mind. My whole body wails in pain from the force of my fall. Fog edges my vision, and I curl in on myself. The fight drains from me with my energy. Everything hurts. My body, my mind, my blood. My soul.

The vampire kneels over me and grips my hair, exposing my neck to him. He lunges forward and bites down, piercing my skin. I scream out, clawing at him, pushing him back. He only shoves his hand against my face and bites again, sinking his teeth into the fabric of my bra because I buck and shimmy higher in an attempt to break free.

He pops the blood bag Kingston had expertly stuffed in my bra, sending blood pouring from my chest. The burst of blood shocks him for a moment, and he freezes. He recoils, swiping his hand over his disgustingly bloody mouth. I've never seen a vampire apart from Chomper Jonas from Starlight Row look so messy in my life.

"What the fuck," he says, spitting blood in my face.

I do the only thing I can think of. I grip his wrist, yanking the hand that covers my mouth sideways, and bite down as hard as I can on his fingers. The second his blood touches my tongue, something dark breaks inside me derived from my fear and desperation. From my sheer will to survive this asshole.

He yowls and tries to rip away from me but ends up dragging me with him. I fall on top of him and bite him again, burying my teeth so hard into his flesh that Diego would be so proud and Kingston would probably beg me to keep my mouth far from his.

The vampire shoves me back, making me accidentally bite a chunk from him. I gag and hock his flesh from my mouth. He stands up, his glower flashing silver with murder in his eyes. He's so intent on inflicting the same damage on me that he doesn't see the figure blur behind him.

The vampire silently screams as the other shadow dweller slices through his neck with a silver dagger, sending his head rolling to the ground. Blood cascades over me, and I lie in shock, licking my lips accidentally. And I can't stop. I'm so injured that my body begs me to consume his blood.

The weird hunger and pain I had after not drinking blood from my guys during the re-match ignites in me, leaving me freaking the hell out. And now I'm too shocked by my actions. I'm not the only one, either. The other vampire stares at me in surprise for a moment, and we both watch the man's body fall.

"Please, get me out of here. You can bite me. I don't care. I just—"

Orlando and Brayla materialize behind the vampire, and I reach up to point behind him. He doesn't get the chance to move before Orlando punches his hand right through his chest, sending the guys friggin' heart onto the pavement next to me. His eyes widen, and his body twitches. Orlando pushes him toward the wall, not allowing him to get near me.

Brayla reaches me first and drags me off the ground. "Shit, Jewel. I'm sorry. That guy wasn't supposed to—"

Headlights beam over us and Orlando doesn't have time to move before a car collides into him. He hits the hood and catapults onto the roof before the car crashes into the brick wall. The world blurs as Brayla makes a run for it, but she doesn't get far.

"You're dead, Brayla!" Kingston yells.

Strong hands rip me from her, and I sob, my body giving out the second Austin's arms wrap around me. "Hold on, Jewel. We're getting you out of here."

"Jewel!" Brayla screams. "Jewel, help me!"

Austin slides his fingers through my hair, pulling me closer to stop me from turning in her direction. Her scream rips through the air, and both Kingston and Diego release some scary ass growls that sink deep into my bones.

"Austin," I whisper, sniffling.

"They'll never stop," he says. "We can't just—"

Someone rams into us, and Austin flips through the air, taking the brunt of our fall onto him. He skids across the concrete and thunks into a wall. Just as quickly, we're back off the ground and facing Orlando. He snaps his teeth at Austin, trying to grab at me at the same time.

"Give her to me, Mr. Divine," Orlando says.

"Fuck off," Austin says, twisting to shield me with his body.

Orlando steps closer. "You know I can take her from you. Alone, you're powerless against me."

"Touch her, and we'll sever Brayla's head," Kingston says, his deep voice igniting a blip of fear inside me. I've never heard him so menacing. It sets off my fear response, my body reminding me of the predator he is.

Orlando jerks his head to glance behind him. I follow his line of sight and release an uncontrollable sob seeing Brayla crying in Diego's arms.

Tears burn down her cheeks in pink rivulets, reminding me of who she was before. I can't take it.

"Jewel, are you going to allow such a monstrosity?" Orlando asks me.

I heave a breath. I can't think. I want so badly not to care. Brayla brought this on herself. She teamed up with Orlando to ruin my life.

"It would be a shame for something to happen to Ramona," Orlando adds. "Possibly to your blossoming cousins."

"I'll kill you if you try!" I scream.

"We'll get to them before anything happens," Austin says, hugging me tighter.

"You won't!" Brayla screams, her fear turning into anger.

Austin pets my arm and meets my blurry gaze with pleading eyes. "Don't listen to her."

"Babe, I know you have a past with Brayla, but she's not the same. She murdered your dad. You said it yourself that she wanted to breach your contract to take you away from us. We can't let her go. The only way to stop it is if you let us handle this." Kingston's chest heaves as he says the words. "It kills me to put you in this position, but we'll get through it. I promise. Forever, remember?"

I close my eyes, my head swimming with a thousand thoughts. "I—"

"Jewel," two familiar voices say in unison. "Jewel, is that you? We can't see you."

My muscles tense, and I nearly scream at the sound of my cousins' voices erupting through the air.

"Orlando, looks like we have a bad connection," Mr. Diggs says. "Is everything all right?"

"I'm afraid not," Orlando says to Brayla's dad. "Looks like we have a small problem. It seems the Divines want to intercept in Brayla's match to Jewel."

"I see," he says.

My blood cools at his words. He sounds strange, different than I've ever heard him. Something's wrong. Oh-so-terribly wrong that I can feel the agony swelling in my soul to scream at me to do something. Because if I don't, I'm afraid my life will fall apart.

"I want you to wait on standby for my call back. If I don't, you know what to do," Orlando says.

Ah, hell. "Are you kidding me? Mr. Diggs. Please, don't

do this. They're in your head."

"Sometimes we must do things we don't want to, Jewel," he replies. "Your father taught me that."

"Mr. Diggs. What are you doing?" Fallon asks, her voice squeaking.

"What's wrong with him?" Dana's voice sends my whole body trembling.

My heart nearly explodes at the sudden terror rising in my cousins' voices.

"Jewel!" Fallon screams.

I flail away from Austin, and he stumbles at my shift in weight as I throw myself at Orlando. "Don't you dare touch them!" I scream.

Orlando clicks off the phone and steps away from me, crossing his arms over his chest. Austin stops me from hobbling at him, my mind going against my body like I'm even capable of hurting the vampire.

"You have two choices," Orlando says to me. "Have the Divines release Brayla, and everything will continue as it should or allow them to be the monsters they truly are and see exactly what kind of damage they leave in their wake."

Kingston and Diego release Brayla before I even have a chance to say anything. "Get out of here before we change our minds," Diego says. "We're taking Jewel home. Come near us again and you'll see exactly what the Divine name is capable of."

Deep growls sound out around us, making Orlando grin.

"Whoever stands against the Divines and survives will be heavily rewarded and welcomed as permanent guests at the Shadow Crest Villa in Ombre Noire."

The shadows shift and move around us.

Austin eases back, his body tensing. I can't see how many shadow dwellers remain, but it's enough to send panic rising in my chest.

Orlando smiles and wags his eyebrows, stepping closer to me. I don't even have time to react before I realize what's happening. I make the mistake of letting him lock his gaze to mine, and my body relaxes without my permission. He doesn't even have to say a single world.

Diego and Kingston fly up behind him as he taunts me with a smile. "Jewel, don't go. Come to me."

Something snaps inside me as my body reacts. This is like Mitchell all over again. I'm too hurt and exhausted, and it's been too long since I drank enough blood to counteract someone as powerful as Orlando's mind manipulation.

The second I break free of Austin, Orlando hooks his arms around me, yanking me away. The world blurs, spinning my head like crazy. Yells and sounds of fighting echo through the air over my labored breathing.

I scratch and smack Orlando, fighting against my body's desire just to give in and let him hold me. Because I'm so tired. I'm in pain. And something familiar about his embrace nudges at my mind. But it scares me.

"Relax, Jewel. You're safe with me," he whispers into my

ear. "They'll never have you."

His words bite me so hard that I scream into his face, just the thought of never being with my guys again tearing me into a thousand pieces to scatter amongst the trash littering the ground. Fury consumes me. I want nothing more than to hurt him the way he hurt me, the way he tormented me.

"Always a fighter." He runs his hand over my cheek to get me to look at him. "My beautiful fighter."

"Shut up! I'm not yours. I'll never be yours. You don't own me."

My back hits a wall, and Orlando smiles at me, trying to capture me in his gaze again. I don't let him. I can't let him. If I do, I know I'm lost. I can feel my soul begging me to comply just to let all this be over. But my heart tells my soul to shut the hell up and hang the fuck on like my guys need me to.

Swinging my arm, I clock Orlando in the jaw, but my body can't keep up with the fight my mind possesses. And then I heave and slump against him. This is it. I've lost. If he steals me away, it's my own damn fault.

"Jewel, look at me. Just one peek," he whispers, sliding his hand up my neck and into my hair.

I can't resist him, my body placid from the overexertion. Meeting his eyes, I blink a few times. "Let me go."

He leans closer. "I can't. This was part of the deal."

"There is no deal."

"There is, Jewel. Now, hold my gaze. Allow me into your mind. The blood should be running its course, but you have to open up and allow me in," he says.

I shake my head. "No."

"Please, Jewel," he whispers. "Don't make this harder than it has to be. I will help you."

"No!" I scream. "You can't! No!"

Orlando's eyes flash silver as he attempts to lock me in his gaze again.

Still, I resist.

Orlando jerks his attention behind him and snarls. Kingston, Diego, and Austin fly toward us. The only reason I can see them at all is because they speed like bullets directly on course at me.

Shaking my shoulders, Orlando knocks my head into the wall out of desperation in an attempt to get me to focus and comply. Stars burst in my vision. It takes everything in me to hold onto my consciousness.

"Jewel, open your mind to me," he says, his voice raspy and scary as all get-out. "I command you to look at me. Do it now or your cousins are dead!"

My hair blows out of my face, and tears burn my eyes. My body automatically slackens. Pressure builds in my mind, making me wince.

I'm too hurt to resist him, to do anything. My head lolls forward, and I rest it on Orlando's shoulder, managing to break our stare. Something bangs in front of me, and Brayla screeches.

Orlando spins again, using me as a shield. I hear the familiar clicks of his fangs extending, preparing to sink into my skin, but the sting doesn't come. He doesn't run or threaten me, either. He just holds me against him, massaging his fingers along my back.

"Careful, Divines," he says, his voice humming against my shoulder as he shifts me again to look in my eyes. "You don't want to accidentally hurt Jewel even more. Her life's in a fragile state. Just listen to her heart. It's slowing. She can barely stay awake."

I close my eyes, trying to focus on my super hearing, but my ears ring. "Austin," I whisper. "What's wrong with me?"

"Just rest, Jewel. The Divines won't let you die," Orlando says. "They'll see that I can help you and give you what you need. Just rest."

I try to open my eyes back up, but my lids refuse to budge. My lips seal shut, preventing me from calling for help.

"Give her to me," Austin says, his voice breaking. "Please. She has head trauma and her posterior tibial artery looks damaged. I need to help her."

Orlando continues to rub circles on my back. "You think you know what's best for her, but you know nothing. You're too blinded to care for her properly. She will get taken from you. If not by me, then Mitchell."

"Fuck it," Diego says. Something crashes into the wall behind us.

My body shifts again, my hair flying around my head. Wind freezes the tears on my cheeks. I think I lose consciousness until cool fingers pinch my chin.

"If you want her to survive, you'll allow me to have her," Orlando says. The world sounds different. The unsettling noises of the shadow dwellers gone. My eyelids turn red for a moment. Headlights.

"If you love Jewel, you'd do the right thing." Brayla's voice trickles to my ears, but I can't tell where she is. "Tell them, girls."

"Austin." Dana's voice stabs at my heart.

"Kingston, Diego. Please," Fallon adds.

Kingston roars, yanking me from the dark recesses of my mind I nearly lose myself to completely. Glass shatters. Something thuds nearby. The world doesn't stop spinning as Orlando jostles me around in a game of keep away.

"Kingston, stop. The movement is making her lose more blood," Austin says. "She has a concussion too."

Orlando nuzzles his chin into the crook of my neck. "Let me take her, and I'll see to it she has an amazing life. Tell him, Jewel."

My mouth opens and closes at his command. "Kingston, I can't stay here."

"Let go of her mind!" Kingston yells.

Orlando clicks his tongue. "Rest, Jewel."

Silence presses in on me, and the world goes still. Ice seeps through my body though I can feel my sweat dripping down my neck. Maybe it's blood.

"He's going to let her die if we don't," Austin says, his

soft voice wrapping around me to tug at my consciousness again. "We'll get her back."

"I'd rather die trying," Kingston mutters. "I don't trust him not to anyway."

"He'll make her forget us," Diego says. "Austin, we can't."

"But look at her," Austin says. "She has minutes if that."

"Babe! Babe! Look at me!" Kingston yells. "Damn it, Jewel, come on. I know you can hear me. Pull that hot ass of yours together."

Orlando shifts me in his arms, cradling me against his chest. My body refuses to react. Anger and grief wash through me. All I want to do is open my eyes. To scream. To do something, but the pain inside me becomes all-consuming.

"Last chance, Divines. Let us go, and I'll assure she lives. You want to live, right, Jewel?"

"Yes," I murmur.

"Babe!" Kingston shouts again. "I fucking love you. I love you, okay?"

"Stay back," Orlando warns.

"We all love you, beautiful. Now don't be scared. Be brave." Diego releases a low groan.

"Just hang on, Jewel," Austin says. "Fight for us. Break his hold. Don't make us let him take you."

Fight. Fight. Fight.

The words swirl through my mind over and over again. Fight. Be brave. It's what my parents have told me all my life.

It's what I promised my guys. I vowed I would never let them down. I promised to fight for us.

Orlando jostles me, molding me around him to hold me tighter. My face presses into the nape of his neck, and something prods at me.

The sweet scent of his skin sends goosebumps over my body, and a deep hunger burns through me, awakening my senses. It's the exact pain I felt the night before and earlier. The craving. The need. And it's suddenly set off by Orlando. By the pain and exhaustion consuming me. By my guys' pleas.

Orlando doesn't have time to react as I sink my teeth into his flesh, biting down hard enough to break his skin, obliterating his hold on my mind and body. Blood pools into my mouth, tingling over my tongue in a wave of warmth that leaves my whole body buzzing.

Flailing back, Orlando crashes into the wall in surprise, and I lock my fingers to his head and ram it back. He drops me, and I slam into the ground. Pain erupts in my knees, radiating through me.

"Jewel," he whispers, touching his hand to his neck. "Your eyes."

Brayla materializes next to Orlando and takes his hand. "This is our only chance. We have to go. We'll get her back. The plan will still work."

They disappear the same time as hands hook around my waist, yanking me off the ground. Austin, Diego, and Kingston hover over me before Kingston and Diego disappear.

Austin runs his hands along my body, taking me in inch-by-inch, touching his cool fingers to every scrape and bruise and bite mark.

Bringing his wrist to his mouth, he bites down and draws blood. He sits me up and lets me drink until my body stops burning and aching, and my chest stops heaving. The fog in my head clears as his blood revitalizes me enough to compose myself.

"I'm so sorry," he says, hugging me close. "This should've never happened."

I swallow, licking my dry lips. "It's not your fault."

He clenches his jaw, taking a deep breath. "Come on, let me get you out of here. There are a lot of vampires lurking around."

"We lost them," Kingston says, appearing next to Austin. "I should've killed them when I had the chance."

"Dude," I whisper, reaching out for him. "You're okay."

Kingston shows me his torn, bloody shirt. "A few broken ribs. Still got my heart."

I groan.

Taking me from Austin, he touches his fingers to my chest. "Right here. This one's the only one that matters to me."

I slump against him and break, unable to hold back my tears any longer.

All three of them hug me between them, taking turns to brush my tears away and kiss my quivering lips. Diego scoops me into his arms and hugs me to him. He bites his arm and offers it to my lips to drink.

"You need more," he murmurs.

"Looks like you put up one hell of a fight, babe," Kingston adds, biting his arm next.

"Come on. We have to go," Austin says. "I need to fix her up so she can heal properly."

The world blurs, and I clutch onto Diego, snuggling against his neck. Austin sits in the back of the car with me, despite Kingston's protests.

I expect him to slide in on my other side, but he takes the front, giving me room to lie down.

"Where to now? I don't think it's safe to take her back to the Divinity Estate," Diego says.

"Not Dark Terrace Ranch, either," Kingston says. "I don't want her anywhere near the board after this shit show they pulled. Purposely breaching Jewel's contract? Fuck the bastard."

"The board is smart enough to realize the games they're playing," Austin says.

"We'll petition to revoke and disqualify Brayla immediately," Kingston says. "You know we're going to have to send someone in to retrieve the Diggs."

I blink a few times, panic rising in my chest. "My cousins!"

"Already got it covered, beautiful," Diego says from behind the wheel. "The Haven Springs' council was notified, and Dana and Fallon were removed from the Diggs' home."

"I need to talk to them," I say.

Austin pulls my leg onto his lap. "In a minute. Let me take care of you. You can rest now."

I lean back and groan. "I'm pretty sure I'll never rest again," I say. "Orlando—he—shit. He's never going to give up. The things he said..." I let my words trail off.

"What?" Kingston asks.

I shake my head. "It's not important. I know he was trying to get to me."

Diego reaches behind the seat to take my hand. "You know you can tell us anything, beautiful."

Inhaling a deep breath, I summon the nerve. "He was trying to make me think that what we have isn't real. That you don't want me to choose because—" I snap my mouth shut. I can't say it. I can't even think it.

"We don't want you to choose because we're all crazy, insanely, sometimes infuriatingly in love with you," Austin says.

I bob my head. "And I love you too."

"So let's not worry about any of this shit anymore tonight," Kingston says.

Diego shifts in the seat. "I'm taking us somewhere safe."

Austin leans down to wrap his arms around me. "And we'll take care of you. So no more worrying."

"No more worrying," I repeat.

If only I could stop. If only I didn't think there was still a reason I had to.

Kingston touches my cheek. "Damn straight. This will all be over soon."

Except a part of me knows that this might only be the beginning.

DOUBT

A SOFT HAND TOUCHES MY cheek, stirring me awake. "Jewel, I know you're tired, but I need you to wake up for a bit."

I groan and stretch my arms over my head, wincing at the dull ache radiating through me. Austin plops down beside me and helps me sit up. Reaching up, he brushes my messy, sleep-knotted hair from my face before kissing me.

"Where are Kingston and Diego?" I ask, pulling back to glance around the small yet lavish bedroom.

If I hadn't been so exhausted after my guys intercepted me from the batshit craziness of Orlando and Brayla, I would have protested the second Samantha pulled up in a sleek, white car to pick us up from the outskirts of the Duchanne

Region because the car couldn't make it all the way to Midnight Valley.

"They had to head into Dark Terrace Ranch to take care of some things, but I don't want you to worry, okay?" he says, meeting me with a soft smile.

I raise my eyebrows, looking at him like he's ridiculous if he thinks I'm capable of anything else.

He sighs. "And now you're worried. I'm sorry, Jewel."

"Well, duh. You guys haven't told me anything."

He runs his tongue over his lip before sucking it into his mouth. "Kingston doesn't want you to stress out, and I have to agree. You were injured. You need time to heal."

"A day is plenty. I'm already feeling better," I say.

He smirks. "It's been two."

"Two days? What the hell? I've been watching the clock. It's only been six hours since I fell asleep and—"

He wraps his arms around me and snuggles his face into my shoulder. "Don't get mad but we've been reprogramming the clock because you wouldn't stop checking it. You've been asleep for sixteen hours this time. The medicine I gave you—"

Standing up, I take a step toward the door only to have my foot scream at me to sit the hell down. Austin catches me before I face plant on the carpet. He scoops me up and sets me back on the bed to inspect my leg.

"Does this hurt?" Austin asks, lifting my leg up and bending my knee.

I flop back onto the pillow. "Not too bad. I just feel out

of walking practice. Let me get back up."

He slides his arm under my back to pull me against him. "Nope. You're on bed rest for another few hours. I didn't want to scare you, but you could have lost your foot, Jewel. The vampire who bit you damaged an artery."

"What?"

He frowns. "You're fine now. Due for some more blood though. It'll ease the tenderness."

The second he says it, my stomach clenches and growls in the most embarrassing way I've ever heard. It startles Austin enough that he shifts away and brings his hand to my belly, nudging me to lie down so he can gently press his hands into my skin.

"Any pain?"

"Just suddenly starving."

He tilts his head, staring at me for an incredibly long moment as a dozen thoughts swirl through his mind. It takes me grabbing his cheeks and leaning in close to get him to stop staring off into space to meet my gaze.

"What's up?" I ask. "You're being weird."

Shaking his head, he doesn't respond. Instead, he reaches over to the night table and picks up a tray I hadn't noticed. Austin unscrews the lid of the thermos and pours the familiar dark ruby liquid of my guys' blood in a glass. He keeps his eyes trained on me the whole time, burning me with his intensity.

He slowly holds the glass out to me. "Don't drink it too

fast."

"But I'm starving," I say.

Austin lifts a brow at my words. "For blood?"

I crinkle my nose and laugh. "No, for that friggin' amazing looking bowl of fruit you have on your lap...possibly for what's beneath it after."

Blush blossoms on his cheeks, and he smiles at me. "Jewel." My name sounds breathlessly on his lips, sending tingles through me.

I giggle. Full-on giggle. I can't help it. I love the reaction he gives me, because I'm pretty sure that was the last thing he expected for me to say. But all I want is to see him lighten up a bit. All three of my guys are brooding messes, and it makes me extra anxious to tease the gloom out of them.

"It's been a long few days, you know. I've missed your smile," I say, brushing my fingers over his lips.

He sinks into me, shifting the tray off his lap and back onto the night table. "And I've missed your affection. Our alone time."

I tip the glass of blood back and swallow the whole thing, making him chuckle. Handing it back to him, I lick my lips and smile, feeling warmth blossom in my stomach in a good way. He twines our fingers together and tugs me onto him, kissing the skin below my ear. His mouth travels along my jaw in tender, whispered brushes until he meets my lips.

A deep-seated need erupts inside me, and I frantically deepen our kiss, twisting my body to straddle him just to feel as close as possible. He releases a low moan, sucking my tongue into his mouth to caress his over mine. I hook my hands under his shirt, tugging it off of him so I can touch the coolness of his body and rub my fingers along the taut skin of his stomach and up to his chest.

I trail them back down, following the line of his muscles until I glide over his navel. "Is this okay?" I ask him, twisting the strings of his pajama pants in my fingers.

Austin holds my stare, a longing in his eyes I haven't seen in days past the worry he's carried. "Are you sure you feel okay?"

"I promise I'd tell you if I wasn't."

He presses his lips together and finally nods, his chest rising and falling as quickly as his heartbeat. Shifting his hips up, he allows me to undress him without rushing to bring our lips together or our bodies closer. He doesn't react with the furious passion I can see begging to break through his self-control. Instead, he leans back on his elbows with the sexiest amused expression, half-curled smile, lifted brow, obviously enjoying every second that I take checking him out. Because damn. Austin sends my heart banging around my chest, prickling goosebumps across my skin.

I trail my gaze from his deep green eyes and down the rest of him, drinking him in, familiarizing myself with his body. He doesn't move or hurry to undress me, but a dozen emotions light up his face in anticipation that matches his flexing muscles. Desire pours through me the longer he waits for me to make the next move, allowing me to decide what happens next.

I don't know if it's the fact that I almost died today or nearly got taken and might have never seen Austin again or maybe because I don't want to think about the uncertain state my life is in. But something inside me shifts, and I can't help wanting to forget that the world still goes on and shit could explode and ruin everything at any second. I'd much prefer to be with Austin and to lose myself in his love. Something I didn't know how much I might have regretted if I never got to experience this with him. I'm also pretty sure expressing my love to him physically might now be the only thing that'll make me feel better. He looks so ready for this too, like he's been waiting forever for me, and he kind of has though I'd never guess.

Summoning my nerve, I say, "I want you to make love to me." The second the words come out of my mouth, I realize just how badly I want to do this. I've thought about it a million times. I know my guys all have their ideas of the perfect moment, but now feels perfect with Austin.

He's the one waiting for me to decide. He's been like that since our first official date, relying on me to guide the direction of our matching and the relationship we've built. And I just know after everything, I'm ready for this. I love Austin. I love everything about him, and I want nothing more than to show him exactly what our new body match entails.

"I mean, if you want to," I add, because he's not quick to

answer.

He blinks away his thoughts, his heart racing, beating louder than mine, and he leans closer and gently twists the hem of my shirt between his fingers. "So much."

Ever so slowly, he undresses me and kisses my exposed skin as he does so. His lips map down my clavicle to my breasts, and he glides his tongue over my curves at a pace that has me panting and squirming, making him smile the whole time.

"You're stunning," he whispers against my skin. "I just want to take my time to enjoy you."

His fingers slip into my pajama pants, and I shove myself back and grab a pillow in an attempt to suffocate every and all embarrassing noises that manage to escape my mouth. Tugging my pants off, he eases my legs open and kisses each of my knees and whispers for me to relax. He draws circles over me with his finger, and I gasp at the gentle pressure he creates, leaving my body buzzing and tingling. I blindly reach down, on the verge of exploding, and comb my fingers through his hair. He moans softly against the skin of my thighs and works his way back up until he tugs the pillow from my face.

"Was that okay?" he asks, studying my eyes.

I reply by reaching down to stroke my hand up his muscular bare thigh until I wrap my fingers around his erection. He shifts next to me and lets me take control, and I roll back on top of him, kissing him deeper, aligning our bodies to fit perfectly together. I sink down onto him, and he closes his eyes and slides his hands around my waist to guide my movements in a rhythm that leaves us both gasping.

He kisses me over and over again through my veil of hair, whispering how much he loves me against my skin until he's through. Pulling the blankets around us, we snuggle together, our bodies entangled, hot with the passion we shared with each other as we explored and entered another part of our relationship I now can't stop grinning like crazy about.

"You're my everything," he whispers, twining our fingers together. "I promise you, Jewel. I won't ever let anything like what happened to you happen again. I can't stand that it ever happened at all or that I didn't try harder."

I trace my finger across his chest. "You did everything you could. Please don't blame yourself."

"But I feel responsible. I should've listened to King—"

I interrupt him with a kiss, pressing my hands into him to stop him from spilling his heart out. "We can't change what happened, but we can focus on how we act now. You did the right thing no matter how wrong it felt or how badly it ended."

"I just want to be good enough for you. You're so incredible and brave."

I shake my head, pelting him with my hair. "I'm not. I'm scared of every little shadow. But you know what?"

"Hmm?"

"Never with you. That's how I know you're good enough for me. I feel like a brave friggin' badass...with my back up."

He chuckles and kisses me, enveloping me in his arms to hold me close. "You're my back up, too. I feel safer with you than even my brothers. My hero."

It's my turn to laugh. "I'm telling them that."

"Good."

Austin's phone chimes from the nightstand, and he groans and reaches for it. "I hate that I have to answer, but it's Kingston." Holding it close to his face, he turns to me once and holds his index finger to his lips, making me laugh. He accepts the call, shifting slightly to obscure Kingston's view.

"How's our girl?" Kingston asks, his voice deep and sullen. I bet if I could get a good look at him, he'd be pouty as hell.

"Still sleeping," Austin says, keeping his voice even.

I swat his arm, but he doesn't even flinch. Without having to ask, I know exactly what he's doing, trying to prolong our private moment to assure his brothers don't figure it out and react.

Kingston sighs. "Can I see her? Just for a moment."

"Kingston, don't be a creep," Diego says, his voice sounding through the line. "Austin's got it under control."

"I just—" Kingston huffs.

I snatch the phone from Austin, unable to stand another second of how sad Kingston sounds. "Miss me?" I ask, smiling at how quickly his face morphs from annoyance to happiness, his eyes lighting up.

"Fuck yeah," he says. "God, I wish I was there to see you

wake up. Sleeping Beauty with all the medical attention bull-shit. I'm so—"

"Happy that you're smiling," Diego says, cutting Kingston off. He nearly presses his cheek to Kingston's to beam me the grin that I love.

"Austin's taking great care of me," I say, eyeing him with a smile.

He runs his fingers over my leg under the blanket, making me release a weird ass cross between a moan and squee because I'm still tingling all over.

Kingston sucks in a sharp breath. "Babe, you're supposed to be resting."

I narrow my eyes. "I am resting."

"Are not. I know what that cute, sexy-ass noise is, and I also know that Austin can't tell you no if you—"

"Shut it, Kingston," Austin says, taking the phone back from me. "Tell me what's going on."

"Why am I not there? Babe, I hope you still have energy for when—"

Kingston oomphs and swears under his breath before disappearing from view altogether. Diego takes up the whole frame, his eyes darting away from Austin's to glance at me. I mouth, "love you," to him, and his face softens.

"We called because Orlando did exactly as we expected."

The warmth Austin aroused in me disappears the second the asshole's name comes from Diego's mouth.

He notices my reaction immediately and shakes his head.

"But don't worry, beautiful. It's being handled."

"Handled how?"

"Mitchell and Viorica know exactly what happened. There is no way they're going to allow him to get away with this shit."

My frown deepens, and I sink lower under the blankets. "Like I can trust them. They're why I was in that position."

"Not completely. The whole board was responsible. Not everyone is a Divine ally. Choices get made all the time to ease territory tension." Diego presses his lips together, and I can tell there's a lot more going on than I realize.

"Babe, I don't want to freak you out, but the only reason the board has left us alone so far is because of who we are. If it were any other coven, even the Vaduvas, you wouldn't have had a say. Your match would most likely have been given to the highest bidder."

I grimace. "Shit."

"You know how important the Blood Match Program is. The profits assure peace among the surrounding regions. Your Blood Matching to the three of us makes everyone nervous. Not many humans would want to be you, and we rely on it being a free choice. If people stopped applying, even for the benefits, the program could turn into a requirement to keep the pool plentiful."

Austin takes the phone from me. "That's enough. You're scaring her for no reason. Get to the point of what's going on with our situation."

Kingston releases a low growl. "You have to bring Jewel here."

"What?" Austin and I say in unison.

I lean closer to Austin, pressing my cheek to his. "You can't be friggin' serious."

Kingston puffs out his bottom lip. "Super serious. The board wants your recount of the situation..."

I stiffen, numbness traveling over me.

"Under the influence of mind manipulation," he adds.

Why did I expect something more? Of course Donor Life Corp would insist on the most invasive way to rip the truth out of me even though I would be honest.

Tears burn my eyes, and I slump down and flip over, pulling the blankets over my head. Austin says a few things to Kingston and Diego, but I can't hear them over the pounding in my head. My body decides to pick now to shut down on me, suppressing everything magical it had just experienced with Austin.

"I shouldn't have answered it," Austin says, draping his arm over my side to snuggle his chest to my back. He brushes his lips across my shoulder, nudging my hair off my neck so he can kiss my throat. "I'm sorry, Jewel. I didn't—" He pauses and inhales a deep breath. "I'm sorry if this was ruined for you."

I shift over to face his brooding face, steeled from reflecting my emotions back to me. Drawing my finger back and forth between our chests, I say, "This between us wasn't ruined." It's just hard to be as excited as I was. I don't tell him that, though. His eyes relight with the same emotions he had before the call. "Promise. I just wish we didn't have to leave."

Leaning forward, I rest my forehead to his without meeting our lips together, just feeling his closeness. Austin lasts all of a minute at keeping the space I tease him with before he digs his fingers into my hips to pull me to him again.

"We have a few hours," he whispers.

I smirk. "What are you suggesting?"

"That you let me assure this is perfect. No more interruptions. No more worries. Just you and me together."

I smile against his mouth, relishing how easy it is to push the bad in our lives away while in each other's arms. "I'd love that," I whisper. "But maybe feed me first?"

He chuckles. "You know how much I like that."

I glare at the side of Samantha's face from my spot on Austin's lap in the backseat of the car. Next to her, Merrick watches me in the visor mirror, not even attempting to hide the fact that she's gawking at me. Gabriella and Layla sit next to us, looking bored as hell, reminding me of Viorica. At least she's not here. She and the last Widow-sister, Heidi, are already in Dark Terrace Ranch with Kingston and Diego.

I'll admit it. I was a total baby about having to carpool with the Vaduva Coven to the city. I had expected at least Diego to come back to escort me with Austin, but apparently, now that the sisters saw they didn't match twice, they've sort of accepted that I'm destined to be a Divine. Still doesn't mean I like them. It doesn't help that I freaked out, and Austin had to embarrassingly carry me to the car because they set off my human fear instincts just walking behind me. Total confident predators. It makes me question how the hell I'll ever cut it.

It's one thing to drink blood from my guys and attempt—and fail—to act all steely and unfazed in front of vampires, but it's a whole other lifestyle to drink human blood. To turn from donor to receiver. To be the source of another being's fear. Shit balls. I think being around Brayla might have messed with my head.

"Is she always so intense, Austin?" Merrick whispers without turning around. "She looks ready to kill Sammy."

Friggin' great. It's hard enough to be alone in the car with them, but now I'm going to have to pretend I can't hear them talk behind my back.

And she might be a little right about the urge to strangle Samantha. She's partly responsible for this disaster. I don't care if she was certain that someone messed with my first matching process. She could've left everything the hell alone. I mean, come on. If she was so set on wanting me to choose Austin, she wouldn't have tried to match me out from under him.

Austin nestles his face in the crook of my neck, trying to get me to relax and keep my rebel mouth from acting out against us. "No." He doesn't offer anything else in an attempt to stop the conversation from continuing.

"Give Jewel a break, Mer. She's been traumatized by someone she trusted," Samantha says.

"Or maybe because you put our matching in jeopardy," Austin mutters.

"Austin, I truly am sorry," Samantha says.

"It's not me you have to apologize to. I'd also appreciate it if you all would stop whispering in front of Jewel. She knows you're talking about her." Austin speaks up in a pitch I'd be able to hear if I didn't have super hearing.

Merrick twists in her seat. "How?"

I narrow my eyes at her without saying anything.

"She's perceptive. My brothers and I only managed to get away with it for a few days in the beginning."

"Get away with what?" I ask, glancing at him.

We share a look, and he presses his lips together to keep a straight face. "The whispering."

"Oh, yeah. So rude," I quip, flicking my gaze back to Merrick. "And annoying."

"You forgot necessary," Layla says from on the other side of Gabriella. It's the first time she's spoken since...I can't remember. "You'll understand with your Blood Vow."

My heart betrays my resolve and picks now to start thrashing about, and not in a good way. Everyone turns to look at me, setting my cheeks on fire. Sweat prickles along my hairline. Austin stiffens under me at my intense reaction. And then my stomach starts to twist and turn, the air suddenly heavy around me.

"Or maybe not," Merrick says, raising her eyebrows. "Jeez, Austin. I don't think I've ever seen a donor with such an adverse reaction...except Blood Rebels." Her voice comes out low, her tone more smug than concerned.

The fact that she mentions Blood Rebels in relation to me cools my blood like ice formed in my veins, my heart now working even harder. Her words make things a helluva lot worse, and I squirm on Austin's lap, banging my hands on the door panel in an attempt to open the window.

"Can you open the window?" I finally ask, getting the nerve to speak. "I'm getting car sick. You drive like Austin, Samantha."

"Not here, Jewel. We just entered the city," she says.

Ugh. I press my nose into the glass, watching the lights streak by at her speed. I want nothing more than to escape the car right this instant. I don't know if it's because I'm annoyed or because my fear instincts are alarming me like crazy again, but I feel like I'm going to lose my shit if I can't get out soon.

"Hand me my bag," Austin instructs Gabriella.

I blink, and suddenly a glass of water hovers in front of my mouth. Austin combs my hair back and whispers for me to take a few slow drinks before taking a deep breath until I can't suck in anymore air. He rubs his fingers in circles on my wrist, trying to get me to relax.

But I can't.

And the second Samantha pulls up in front of the Blood

Match Center, and I hear the doors unlock, I practically throw myself from the car. Austin yells out, but I don't get a chance to prepare myself before strong arms wrap around me and stop me from eating shit on the pristine pavement. Several low growls echo around me, doing nothing for my panic.

"Let her go," Austin says from in front of me.

"If you insist." Orlando's sultry voice tickles my ear.

I stiffen at the sensation of a soft breath on my neck. I feel stupid as hell for leaving the car before the others, but I couldn't breathe. I needed out. But now? Holy shit balls. I might not even survive getting inside the Blood Match Center.

One second Orlando hugs me, petting my back, and in the next, I'm flying through the air like a friggin' discarded body after being drained. I scream out Austin's name as the world spins. Tensing, I brace myself to smash into the ground. Or get devoured and ripped apart by the shadow dwellers making all sorts of freaky ass noises around me.

I hit a solid body with an oomph, the air knocking from my lungs to send my vision shadowing. My head spins, dizziness twisting through me so much that my stomach clenches. And then I throw up.

"Damn it, babe," Kingston says, flipping me around to face out. "I just showered."

I heave again, trying to catch my breath. "I'm s-sorry."

"Now I have to shower again," he murmurs. "Preferably with you."

I breathlessly laugh, my body finally relaxing as it realizes I'm not in any danger. Kingston turns me back around to face him and offers me a fake pout that immediately turns into a smile. His dark eyes reflect the city lights around us, and he playfully snaps his teeth at me.

"Are you okay, Jewel?" Austin says, coming up behind Kingston to look at me from over his shoulder.

I rub my lips together and nod. "I think so."

"What the fuck happened anyway, Austin? I should kick your ass for letting that asshole even touch our girl," he says.

"It was an accident." Austin's eyes flash silver. "Jewel got—"

"I don't give a flying fuck. She could've been—"

I press my lips to Kingston, startling him, and he jerks back and grimaces. "Enough."

"Gross, babe," Kingston says, holding me out. "Banned from cuddles until we get cleaned up."

"Then give her here." Diego wraps his hands around my waist and tugs me from Kingston.

The world blurs as he runs me inside and out of the view of the gathering shadow dwellers becoming invested in us the longer we stand outside the Blood Match Center. The second we enter the lobby, someone calls my name, and I inhale a sharp breath at Brayla's familiar voice.

"Keep her away," Diego says.

"I just want to make sure she's okay," Brayla says. "I'm so sorry about what happened."

"Did you not hear my brother?" Kingston snaps. "Keep her the fuck back."

"Settle down, Kingston," Mitchell says from behind me.

I squeeze my eyes shut instead of twisting around to spot him. My heart crashes around, my whole body trembling all over again. I can't stop the flood of emotions consuming me in a bad way. I don't want to be here. I don't want to be around any of these people.

"Diego, take her upstairs," Austin says. "She's panicking."

"Jewel, I'm sorry," Brayla calls. "I never meant for you to be in this position. It was an accident. You have to believe me."

OhmyeffingG. She's acting. And way better than I ever could. Her remorse is all for show.

"If the Divines didn't wreck our car, I could have kept you safe," she says, yanking my attention away from my beating heart and to her as she stands between Viorica and Orlando, facing the familiar vampires on the board. "Can't you see they're conspiring against us?" she asks them.

Anger swells through me, and if Diego didn't tighten his grip on me, I'd lunge.

"Don't say anything, beautiful. I'm begging you," he whispers.

I groan. "I can't be here. I can't do this. Look at her. She'd have never done this as a human."

Diego adjusts me in his arms to meet my gaze. "You're brave and badass. The best person I know. We're going to get through tonight, and everything will settle. I promise. Trust me."

Tears burn my eyes as a horrifying thought consumes me. That maybe my dad was right all along and how if he really did vaccinate me against turning into a vampire, then maybe I'll somehow manage a good life still. Because I don't know if I could live with myself if I changed like Brayla. If I started to care so little about the people I love. My family. The people I consider family.

I swallow the burning in my throat. "I do. I just—" My throat locks up tight, my body trying everything it can to stop my mind from speaking out.

Diego's eyes search mine for a long moment, realization sinking in. He knows me so well. He doesn't need to hear the words to see the doubt clouding my vision, to know that my sudden panic isn't truly about what's happening right now.

"Beautiful," he whispers. "You are nothing like her."

"But I am."

A hand touches my shoulder as Austin leans in close. "Let's get her upstairs. We can't do this here."

"Do what? What's going on? Are you okay, babe?" Kingston asks.

Diego nods at him. "She's going to be."

He steps next to us. "I was asking our girl."

I don't meet his gaze. I don't meet anyone's. "I don't know," I whisper to him. "I just don't know."

CHANGED

KINGSTON LACES HIS FINGERS BEHIND his head and stares out the window at the lit city below. "I knew someone was going to ruin this for us. We should've run away."

"Stop it, Kingston," Austin says. "Jewel feels bad enough as it is. She needs time to process everything."

"Time will make it worse. I know it. I saw her face. She's going to despise us. If that happens—"

Two big hands cover my ears, muffling Kingston's increasingly, louder-by-the-second voice.

Diego guides me away from the spot near the door and to the shower running in the bathroom. He offers me a small smile and closes the door, turning the volume up on the stereo.

"No listening to Kingston when he's upset. He might say something that will hurt your feelings by accident," Diego says, resting his hands on my shoulders.

"I deserve it," I whisper.

Diego frowns. "No, you don't. Especially after everything you've been through."

"I just—I'm scared, Diego. I love you, and I love our life and the idea of our futures together, but...I'm afraid that I'll change. Are you sure you could handle me like...*that.*" I don't have to explain for him to know that I'm talking about Brayla's batshit craziness.

"Of course I can. And if I struggle, I have backup," he says, eyeing the door. "Who might come barging in any second, so...can I?" he asks, trailing his finger over my sleeve.

I slowly nod my head. "You sure you want to risk it? I heard the board saying that if someone tries to give me blood before the interrogation that they'll be automatically disqualified."

He gives me a longing once-over. "It'll be tough, but I can manage a foot of space. Maybe."

"Stupid space," I murmur, puffing out my bottom lip.

Reaching up, he caresses his finger over my mouth before cupping my cheek. "I hate it too. I've missed you."

I sink into Diego's arms for a hug I didn't realize how much I desperately needed. He kneads his fingers into the tight muscles of my back, gently tugging at the zipper of my dress in the process.

It drops to the floor, and he steps back a little to gaze down at me, his eyes flashing silver as he drinks me in.

Gently, he glides his fingers over my bra strap to knock it from my shoulder. "You know, as much as I want you to be like us, I'll understand if you can't. I know it's hard."

"I kinda hate myself for thinking this way," I say, staying utterly still as he completely undresses me without initiating anything between us. "Because I want forever with you guys."

"Just maybe not like this," he whispers, his brows puckering.

"I just—"

The door to the bathroom swings open, and Kingston and Austin stroll in, stopping short to give me a once-over as I stand bare in front of Diego. I don't move to hide myself, even under the friggin' hot intensity the three of them warm me with under their gazes. A mixture of emotions crosses through all of their expressions, and I shift on my feet.

"Fuck," Kingston breathes.

Austin's Adam's apple pops in his throat. "Sorry, Jewel, we didn't mean to—"

I suck my bottom lip between my teeth. "It's fine. Come in and shut the door. I should talk to you all anyway."

"Talk? I don't want to talk now," Kingston says. "I want to join you."

I smirk. "I bet."

Austin elbows him. "We have to stay focused."

"There's no way I'm focusing on anything other than—"

Kingston appears right in front of me so quickly that I startle before laughing and patting his chest. Diego mutters that he better watch himself under his breath, but Kingston ignores him and opens his arms, pleading with his eyes for me to step closer.

I give in to his friggin' pouty as hell face and slide my arms under his, pressing my boobs into his chest. "Five seconds to enjoy this, and then I'm getting in the shower."

He reaches down and squeezes my ass, purring deep in his throat. "Need more time than that."

I laugh and step back, wagging my finger at him. "I don't think so."

"Seriously," Diego says, hooking his fingers to my hips.

I spin in his arms and hug him too. "Five seconds for you too."

"Damn it," he murmurs. "Kingston was right. Need more time."

Heat rushes over me as he plays with the loose strands of my hair to get a better look at my body. "Maybe later," I tease. Turning to Austin, I motion him closer. "Don't think I forgot about you."

He hesitates, drinking me in. "You're deflecting your emotions with affection, you know."

I place my hands on my hips. "And?"

"Yeah, and?" both Kingston and Diego say. They laugh and knock their fists together.

"She's finally relaxing some. Let her," Diego says. "She

needs it before another shit show."

Austin finally closes the space to me and opens his arms. "You're right." He keeps his hands firmly in place on my lower back. "We'll talk more about the Blood Vows after. What's important is making sure you're okay through this whole ordeal, especially after—"

All three of my guys' phones chime at once. Only Kingston pulls his from his pocket and looks at the screen. Glancing from me and back to his phone, he slumps his shoulders and glares at the floor.

"We have twenty minutes," he says. "And I have to meet Viorica. Something's come up."

My eyes widen. "What?"

"Don't worry, babe. We're going to get this fixed, and then we're going to talk about our forever, okay?"

I nod. "If I make it."

"You will," all three of them say.

Kingston kisses me softly and heads to the door. "It's the only thing I can really promise."

"This is bullshit. I don't see why we have to," Kingston says, his voice echoing through the sturdy door from the hallway. "Our word should be enough. You saw her condition. You know Brayla is lying."

"I'll see what I can do," Viorica says. "Your father is meeting with them now. Don't worry too much. He's rather attached to the idea of Jewel being a true Divine."

"Don't worry? Don't worry! You're fucking putting my match in danger by allowing this shit to go on," he says, not even attempting to keep his voice even. "She doesn't deserve this kind of treatment. It was one thing to have her sit in front of the board, but now you expect her to have to face the Ortegas? No. I won't allow it."

"It's protocol. You know this better than anyone," she says. "They have the right to counter your accusations."

"Fuck that!" Something crashes outside the door. "Jewel nearly died. The Ortegas were kidnapping her. They purposely breached their contract so that we'd lose her with a damn loophole you allowed."

She hums under her breath. "I know it's what you think, but how can you be so sure? Were you with Jewel? Did you hear them say that? The board wants solid proof. The Ortegas said they were merely on an excursion, and it's Ms. Ortegas' right to travel with her match."

"Are you kidding me? You know as well as I do that this is a power play. I told you that Brayla purposefully attempted to break her contract to release Jewel from the program so that Orlando can collect her for the blood debt."

"You know it has to be Jewel or her heirs to be the ones to file. Extensive proof is needed. And as far as I'm concerned, Jewel is in acceptable condition. No permanent damage," she says with a sigh. "It's under control. After the interrogation, I'll insist on disqualifying Brayla. The board will follow suit. So relax."

"Not until it's over."

"I guess I shouldn't expect anything less from you, Kingston. Please, try to keep your cool the best you can and bring Jewel to the meeting room. I'll wait for you there. Assure her that we know what we're doing."

Like that makes me feel any better.

I glance away from the door and meet Austin and Diego's eyes as they both study me, gauging me for a reaction. Austin pulls me from my spot. I'm sure if I had allowed it, one of them would have covered my ears to stop me from hearing Kingston's conversation with Viorica. But now that I have, I'm in shock. I'm pissed.

Kingston enters the room and clicks the door behind him. He leans his back to it and doesn't meet my gaze.

"Are you effin' kidding me?" I ask, my voice squeaking. "They're letting them sit in and not even going to immediately disqualify Brayla?"

Kingston tightens his jaw. "I'm sorry, babe. The board is full of a bunch of assholes."

"They have to see that this was all a setup." My breathing comes in quick pants, and it takes everything in me not to yell my frustration. "I can't just sit here and hope for the best. My cousins, they'll—"

"They're safe and fine. Orlando and Brayla can't use them against us to file the breach." He swallows, his Adam's apple bobbing with the motion. "We're going to be okay. You have to believe it. This is basically a pissing match."

I grimace. "Ugh."

"I'm going to insist that it be Viorica to do the mind manipulation, okay?" he says. "She'll make sure all the right questions are asked."

Tears burn my eyes. "You sure she's not messing with us? I'd rather have Mitchell over her. That's how much I hate this." Because I can feel something so utterly wrong deep in my bones. It nags at me, clawing its way into my chest to dig at my heart, threatening to implode it.

"I'm sorry," Kingston says again. His cracking voice does nothing for my nerves either. "Just think. If you were a vampire—"

Austin flies across the room and lifts Kingston off his feet, shoving him hard into the wall.

They flash their fangs at each other, and Diego leaves my side to intervene, pulling Austin back before he can punch Kingston in the face.

"You're not using Jewel's fear to convince her to do something she has doubts about!" Austin shouts, his whole face turning red with anger.

"Why the fuck not? Don't you want her to agree?"

Diego grabs Kingston by the shirt and tosses him a few feet away. "Knock it off. You know Austin's dying inside over this. He feels responsible."

Jumping to my feet, I cross the room, suppressing my good senses that scream for me to sit the hell back down and shield myself from possible flying and biting vampires.

Kingston and Austin freeze, realizing that I've moved from the bed. Diego swivels on his feet to face me.

Then they all friggin' pout, looking like they could use a bigger hug than me.

I hold open my arms. "Come here. All of you. I want to smother you for a minute. Maybe grope you. Whatever gets you to stop fighting."

They all chuckle and close in on me, sandwiching me between them just the way I like.

"We're sorry, beautiful. It's just—"

"Friggin' tense?" I ask. "Awful? Damn annoying? Hella lame?"

"Fuck yeah," Kingston says, nuzzling his face in my neck. "So please keep talking back-world to me."

"Later," I whisper. "Gotta give you something to look forward to, dude."

He groans. "Then let's get this over with."

It's my turn to groan. "Let's just run away."

Diego and Austin hook both their arms around Kingston, stopping him from taking off with me. Because we all know he'll try.

"I was kidding," I murmur.

Kingston play-growls at me. "Tease."

"You like it."

"Do not."

"He's right. That's me," Diego says, taking my hand. "Now, come on. We're not leaving your side. We'll make sure everything goes smoothly."

"And if not, we'll go with my plan," Kingston says, looking at his brothers. "So be ready. And keep up."

BLOOD DEBT

MY HANDS TREMBLE IN MY lap, and sweat drips down the back of my neck. I remain seated alone in the corner of the boardroom, silently watching the ultra-quiet group of vampires look over the towering pile of documents Kingston laid before the board members to read over.

"And why were you on the Ortega property, Mr. Divine?" a vampire with silver hair asks Kingston. I wish I had taken the time to remember the rest of the board members' names, but they're neutral in regards to who they are to the Divines. Only the Vaduvas permanently side with the Divines. Basically, if they're not allies, they're possible enemies. And we have a lot.

"Because I didn't trust Ms. Ortega to properly care for

my match," he says.

He leans on his elbows. "So, are you saying that she did breach her contract to Ms. Jordan?"

"Yes and no."

"Please, clarify."

"The only reason Ms. Ortega applied to Blood Match was to breach Jewel's contract in the program, releasing her to Haven Springs where Mr. Ortega could request to nullify her exemption and collect on the Jordan blood debt."

"That seems like a stretch considering we granted Mr. Ortega his petition to collect the debt on Ms. Jordan's next of kin," the only other female vampire besides Viorica says.

Austin growls. "It's not about the blood debt. It's about Jewel."

"Why's that? What is so special about Ms. Jordan?" another man with dark hair says. "Tell us why anyone, including yourselves, insists on going through so much trouble for a donor, one who poses a risk to the foundation of the Blood Match Program at that."

I blink a few times, thinking about his question, wondering exactly how my guys will respond to that. Kingston's eyes dart over to me, and without him having to say so, he's apologizing in advance for whatever's about to come out of his mouth.

"She's exquisite," Diego says, speaking up first. "The perfect match."

Austin smirks at me. "Receptive to our needs. Protective

over our daylight household. She's an amazing companion. Unlike anyone I've ever known."

"And fucking delicious," Kingston adds.

Both Diego and Austin glare at him.

"What? It's true." Kingston turns his attention to me. "Not sorry, babe," he mouths without anyone seeing.

The man leans back, satisfied enough by their answers that he doesn't continue to question them. I kind of wish he did, because I love hearing my guys talk about me like I'm the best thing in the world, like I'm worth all the hassle and trouble. Because sometimes, I can't help but think I'm not. Especially now with the rising doubt over the vows.

Viorica stands up. "Everyone satisfied thus far? I'd like to proceed with Jewel's interrogation to confirm their story. If her story aligns with theirs, then I motion to disqualify Ms. Ortega and penalize her with a lifetime stipend due to one of Ms. Jordan's heirs."

"Agree," everyone says.

I release a breath, feeling slightly better about her words. I never dreamed I'd like Viorica, but if she helps us, I'll surely learn to.

She materializes in front of me, startling me, and I throw myself back into my chair. She tilts her head and smiles at me, and my sudden urge to like the woman disappears with her amusement over messing with me. We stare at each other for a few seconds before Kingston, Diego, and Austin surround me to offer their support. Austin and Diego each hold one of my hands while Kingston rests his on my shoulders, leaning over the back of the chair to get as close as possible.

"Ms. Divine," Viorica says instead of using my Jordan last name. Hearing her say my name as such helps ease some of my nerves. "I assume your matches have informed you of what will take place, correct?"

I nod. "I'll do whatever to get you all to believe me. I just want to go home to the Divinity Estate."

"I'm sure it's what everyone wants," she muses.

But from one look over at the board, I can tell that none of them cares what happens to me. They don't put worth on a donor like my guys do. Even like Viorica. They look bitter they have to be here in the first place.

Viorica touches my cheeks. "Now, if you could please look at me and not look away."

I inhale a deep breath, squeeze Diego and Austin's hands, and do as she says. My muscles relax under her mind manipulation as she prods into my head. For the first time with someone outside my guys, I'm not scared. I don't feel taken advantage of or wronged. I feel like this is a good thing despite having to leave myself vulnerable.

Viorica leans closer until I can't focus on anything but her. "Jewel, I'm going to ask you a few simple questions."

My body relaxes even more, tingles rushing through me.

"What is your name?" Viorica asks.

"Jewel Divine," my mouth automatically responds without conversing with my mind.

"And how do you feel, Jewel?" Her fingers gently dig into my cheeks, her eyes flashing silver.

"Pissed off."

She flares her nostrils. "Why?"

"Because Donor Life Corp shows so little respect to humans that this kind of bullshit happens."

"Do you mean we let you get matched to multiple vampires?" she asks, shifting slightly away from me to hold her finger up to the murmuring board.

My guys suck in their breaths and hold them.

"No." They are so hearing about this once I get my freewill back. But in the best way. Because I get it. I still sometimes can't believe how lucky I am to be loved and wanted by them for more than what my blood offers. I'll make it a point to remind them that I've never been happier in my life than being with them together.

"Please explain what you meant by bullshit," she commands.

"Donor Life Corp allowed more applicants in to match with me. It shouldn't have happened," I say.

"It was a business decision," a masculine voice says, but I can't put a face to him.

"A business decision?" Kingston asks. "Are you fucking kidding me?"

"She is going to be a Divine heir," Austin says.

Diego squeezes my hand. "She's more."

"More like an inconvenience," another man says.

My guys growl.

Viorica raises her hand at them, silencing the room. "Jewel, we apologize for the unfortunate circumstances you experienced. Will you state exactly what happened?"

"The Ortegas don't think the Divines deserve me. They thought my mind was being manipulated and when they discovered that my love for Austin, Kingston, and Diego was real, they decided not to continue with the rotation and instead to kidnap me to breach my contract. Orlando believes I belong to him."

"Because of the blood debt?" she asks.

"No."

"Then why?"

Pain erupts in my skull, and my eyes water. I don't respond. Without an answer, I have nothing to give.

Viorica digs her fingers into my cheeks, searching my eyes. "Jewel, answer my question."

Again, I don't respond.

"Jewel."

Diego covers my eyes with his large hand, breaking Viorica's hold on my mind. All the vampires begin to argue in quick, hushed voices I can't follow. My head pounds, pain poking behind my eyes. I release a whimper and sink back, trying to catch my breath.

"She told you what you needed to know. The lock on her mind against the Ortega Coven should only be more proof," Diego says, keeping his voice even.

"If Viorica can't break it, then give me a try at her," the silver-haired vampire says.

Panic ignites in my very soul.

"Absolutely not," Austin says. "As her health keeper, I will not allow it. You could permanently cause damage."

"It's a risk—"

Diego and Austin abandon me to fly across the room at the board member. Kingston picks me up from under my arms and snatches me away to protectively block me from anyone who dares try to get near. Mitchell lets his sons get in a few punches until the silver-haired vampire lands on his back, his chest heaving, before he interjects and steps between them.

"Respect my heirs, Pierce," Mitchell says calmly. "They've been nothing but cooperative to this entire preposterous situation.

"Your heirs jeopardize the foundation of—"

Kingston spins around and covers my ears, yanking me to his chest to assure I don't try to look. A high pitched wail rips through the air, Kingston's hands doing nothing to muffle the guttural shriek from making me wince. Bones crack and a strange ripping sound, like tearing wet fabric soon follows the screams.

Liquid splashes on my head, and I wiggle in Kingston's arms to tip my head to look up. Huge friggin' mistake. Blood and guts drop from the ceiling and pelt over my face. I screech and hide my face against Kingston, but it's too late for my resolve. I heave a breath at the sudden pain igniting in my stomach, making all sorts of freaky-ass noises. It clenches and twists, and Kingston swears, but I don't heave or throw up. I disgustingly and most definitely uncontrollably lick my lips.

"Babe, stop, there's—" Kingston swears again, pressing my back into the wall. He grasps my chin and studies my face. "Babe, your eyes," he whispers.

Growls sound through the room, and a few things crash and shatter. Someone hisses. Another yell. More blood splashes on the wall next to me.

Kingston stiffens. "Shit."

I blink a few times, shifting my gaze away from him to watch the rivulets drip across the textured wallpaper to splash on the pristine wood. "Kingston, something's wrong with me," I say so quietly, I'm not even sure he heard me.

"Fuck yeah, there is," he says. "But it's not a bad thing...to me. Don't freak out, but I think you're transitioning. For reals."

"What?" I ask, my heart picking up pace.

"Your eyes flashed silver," he murmurs, studying my face. "I've never seen them do that. Show me your teeth."

I don't get the chance. An arm drops on the ground next to me, and I startle and scream. Kingston hoists me up against him, cocooning me in his suit jacket, shielding me the best he can as the crazy ass vampire fighting stops.

"Time to leave, Kingston," Diego says. "Beautiful, please don't look."

To make sure I don't, Kingston covers my eyes with his

hand. I don't complain though. The blood dripping on the wall and the body part on the floor freaks me the hell out enough as it is. The last thing I was expecting was for a board member to get slaughtered on my behalf by Mitchell. I know it was he who did it because the gaudy watch on the severed arm isn't something he'd wear. And that man is powerful.

My hair sweeps away from me as Kingston turns and strolls the perimeter of the room, cautiously carrying me toward the door.

"Hurry the hell up," I whisper against his collarbone.

He strokes his hand up and down my back. "No sudden movements when everyone's on edge."

"They want to murder me, don't they?"

"Only half."

"Shit balls."

Kingston chuckles. "Don't worry. We won't let anything happen to—fucking hell."

I pull my face away from Kingston's chest to attempt to see what has him suddenly stopping. "What is it?" I ask quietly when he shifts his hand up to the back of my head.

"Your sister."

I don't even get the chance to wiggle free from Kingston before he gently sets me on my feet and spins me around to see for myself. And I kind of wish I hadn't looked, because the first thing my eyes turn to is the torso of the silver-haired vampire and the board, covered in his blood. Even Diego and Austin have blood splattered across their faces.

"Oh, my God, Jewel." Ramona's voice trickles through the air, drawing my attention toward the door where my sister stands in front of Brayla and Orlando. Only she looks at me while Orlando and Brayla take in the bloody sight of the boardroom.

Ramona surprises me by bravely entering, and she rushes to stand in front of me, giving me a once-over, her mouth quivering, her eyes shining. She looks young, just like the girl I left in our apartment on the day of my Blood Matching.

Turning her attention to Kingston, she tightens her jaw and says, "May I hug my sister or will I end up in a pile of guts like that dude over there?"

Austin and Diego materialize on both Ramona's sides, startling her. She automatically bows her head to look at the floor, keeping her hands twined together, waiting for someone to respond. But my guys don't. They wouldn't. I'm not their property. The decision to whether or not I hug Ramona is solely up to me.

A dozen memories flash through my mind from Ramona at Haven Springs. How she murdered Laurel and nearly staked me. How she planned to exchange my freedom for our dad's and was determined to ruin my Blood Match. But the girl standing before me doesn't look like that girl. The girl in front of me is my sister, and I love her and missed her so much.

But I don't open my arms to hug her. Instead, I say, "What are you doing here?"

Ramona shifts her gaze from the floor to look at me. "I've come to help you."

I frown, furrowing my brows. "Help me? I don't understand."

"Brayla told me what happened. She told me how badly you were injured and how the board denied the petition to cancel your Blood Match contract," she says.

I swivel and turn to Kingston, raising my eyebrows.

"Because Jewel doesn't want to cancel our contract," Kingston says for me. "So you're wasting your time."

Ramona shifts on her feet and steps away from the middle of Diego and Austin to face the board all quietly engrossed in what's unfolding between us. Even Mitchell tilts his head curiously, listening to every word my sister says. "It's my right as an heir to file the petition for Jewel. I fully believe that the only reason she doesn't want to is because the Divines are in her head."

"That's bullshit," Diego says. "It's Orlando who's in her head. You all saw it for yourselves."

Orlando steps into the boardroom from the hallway with Brayla behind him. I wonder if shit went down if he'd protect her. I can't help wondering what their relationship is based on and how real it is. If he's just using her.

"The only manipulation I've ever done on Ms. Jordan was to make her forget me. If I were going to mess with her head, don't you think I'd have insisted she liked me?"

The remaining board members look at each other. My

heart sinks into my stomach at their subtle nods. Effin' A. They're agreeing with him. It doesn't help that his words make sense. I friggin' hate the guy. I want nothing more than to see his blood spill. Ugh. I shake my head, pushing the thought away. I don't care if he didn't manipulate me to like him. It doesn't mean anything. He's still a monster.

Austin steps forward next, looking at the board. "That proves nothing. Jewel recounted Ms. Ortega's plan to purposely breach her contract to send her to Haven Springs so Orlando could collect her for the Jordan blood debt."

"And of course Ramona would be willing to file the petition. It gets her out of it," Kingston says. "You do realize if you allow this bullshit to happen, you're opening up Haven Springs to another possible Blood Rebel infiltration."

Ramona clenches her hands at her side. "This is my right as an heir! My sister nearly lost her life. If you don't cancel her contract, then word will spread. I promise you that."

Mitchell reacts to my sister's threats by slamming his hands on the table, shaking it. He flashes his fangs, but Ramona doesn't even step back. "You will not threaten Donor Life Corp. Don't think I won't come over there and assure your final donation. Be thankful that the only reason I'm refraining is because I respect my future heir."

Ice floods over me, stealing every ounce of warmth from my body.

Ramona places her hands on her hips. "I'm not afraid of you. If I die here right now, it won't stop this from getting out."

A man stands up from the table. "You have a lot of nerve to make such threats."

"They're not threats. They're promises," Ramona says.

"Control your debtor, Mr. Ortega," Viorica says, getting to her feet. "Donor Life Corp will not stand this."

Orlando materializes in front of Ramona and nudges her to walk back to where Brayla quietly waits. Her intense gaze burns on the side of my face, but I refuse to look at her. I'm livid. Beyond pissed.

"Is one donor really worth the trouble?" Orlando says, smirking at the board.

"Babe," Kingston whispers. "Come here. We're not staying around to see this unfold."

Austin and Diego must have the same thought as Kingston, because they return to my side. The three of them share a silent look and nod to one another. Something about their rigid postures makes me nervous. For the first time in weeks, they look a bit scared. I haven't seen them look like this since Laurel kidnapped me during daylight hours and they couldn't reach me in the sun. "Diego, you lead. I'll take the back."

"No, I think we've allowed these games to go on for far too long," the other woman vampire says. "I vote to give Mr. Ortega what he wants and allow the Jordan heir to file the petition."

"Without proof?" the guy sitting beside Viorica says. "That opens us up to more petitions."

"But I have proof," Ramona says, interrupting.

Diego and Austin get into position, readying themselves to get me out of here. Kingston lifts me in his arms, and I hook my legs around his waist and rest my head on his shoulder. It would be easier for him to carry me on his back, but he's as afraid as I am that someone might attempt to grab me, especially with the way the board's conversation heads.

"Ten seconds," Diego says.

"I have a video of the attack," Ramona says. "It's clear that Orlando and Brayla didn't set Jewel up and that the breach was real."

Brayla plays with her phone, and my whole body tenses as a video projects on the wall. It looks like a video taken from the dash of the car. I watch myself ram my arm into Orlando's neck while grabbing control of the wheel.

"Shit, she's really hurt, Orlando," Brayla says on the video. "Pull over."

"Not here," he says. "Just give her to me."

I cringe at the sight of blood dripping from the gash on my head and how Orlando tries to offer me his blood.

Panic tightens my chest as the board silently watches the video conveniently started at a spot to look like Brayla did her best to protect me but failed and breached her contract. Kingston's chest heaves, pressing against mine. He holds me tighter and gets ready to run.

"Now," Diego says.

The world blurs for all of a second before two board

members block our exit. Diego throws a few punches, his form blurring as he fights the two guys away. When another comes, Austin shoves them back. Kingston adjusts me in his grip and shifts on his feet for an opening.

"If you leave, you will be disqualified from the program!" one of the vampires Diego was fighting says from the floor. "Mitchell, control your heirs."

Mitchell clears his throat. "Boys, please release Jewel. You will not be going anywhere just yet. It seems the video evidence is quite compelling."

"What!" I screech, wriggling free of Kingston's hold. "It was cut. You can't possibly believe them."

"Even so, I agree with Zara. One donor isn't worth the effort. Her matching to all three Divines already shook the foundation of our program." I can't believe the board is doing this.

"I will not allow it," Mitchell says.

"What are you going to do, Mitchell?" the other female vampire, Zara, says. "Slaughter us all? Pierce's region will surely retaliate. I can't imagine you'll want to deal with a war."

Mitchell's jaw twitches as he considers what to do. My worst nightmare comes to life right in front of me. I always thought if it came down to it, Mitchell would do what the board asked to maintain peace. Because who am I to him? I don't even like the guy. He's only nice to keep his sons' loyalty. We both know I changed them.

"Dad, don't do this," Austin says. "You can't let her end

up with him."

Mitchell closes the space between us and reaches out to squeeze my shoulder. "I'm sorry sons. It's not something I can risk, but I assure you, I won't allow Jewel to be responsible for the Jordan blood debt."

"Dad," Kingston says. "Please."

Diego frowns. "You can't."

"I motion to grant the Jordan heir her request to cancel Jewel Jordan's Blood Match contract," Zara says from the table.

The three vampire guys nod their heads. "Agreed. Viorica? Mitchell? It's already a majority."

Mitchell and Viorica don't say anything.

"Okay, Ms. Jordan. You have been granted exemption and will join your heirs in Haven Springs. Ms. Ortega, you must pay the lifetime stipends to satisfy your breach in contract and cover the costs of the re-matching applications for the Divines. Understand?"

Brayla grins at Orlando, and Ramona releases a deep breath.

I stand frozen in shock, my heart pounding louder than anyone's in the room. The edges of my vision darken, and pain rolls through my body as my life with my guys shatters before me. Anger suppresses my grief, and I snap. Running at Orlando, I crash into him before anyone can react, and he lets me. We skid across the floor for all of a second before Diego yanks me off him and hugs me in his arms.

"They can't do this!" I scream. "You can't let them do this."

Kingston and Austin surround me, sandwiching me between them. "We won't," they whisper.

"Jewel, I know you have doubts about transitioning," Austin says, leaning close to me.

"Bite me," I whisper. "I can't lose you guys. I can't end up with that asshole."

Orlando clears his throat, drawing our attention to him. "While I'm here, I'd like to go ahead and file to transfer the Jordan blood debt from Ms. Ramona to Ms. Jewel Jordan."

"Granted," the four vampires say while Viorica and Mitchell say, "Denied."

The board all looks at each other, and Zara says, "Majority agrees."

"Overruled," Mitchell says. "I'm granting Jewel amnesty from the Jordan blood debt. She will no longer carry the name and will be considered a Divine."

"Seconded," Viorica says. "Ms. Ramona Jordan will remain as the debtor to the Jordan name. Jewel, you've been absolved from the blood debt and your Blood Match contracts. We will arrange transportation, and you're now officially an exempt member of Haven Springs."

"What!" Ramona yells.

Viorica turns to Orlando. "Mr. Ortega, I suggest you leave immediately. Stop by the front counter on the way out and pay Ms. Ortega's dues."

"Very well," he says. Turning to me, he holds my gaze for a second. "And congratulations, Ms. Divine. Feel free to reach out to me any time."

I stand in shock in my guys' arms. I can't believe this just happened. Mitchell and Viorica stood up for me. But why? This can't be from the goodness of their hearts, because I'm pretty friggin' sure neither of their hearts has an ounce of goodness in them.

"Babe," Kingston whispers. "Please don't leave us. We want forever with you."

I swallow and turn my attention away from the board. "It's what I want too," I whisper.

"Mr. Divines, please step away from Ms. Divine," Viorica says. "I'll assure you she gets to Haven Springs safely."

We all ignore her.

"I'm ready. Do it now," I whisper.

"Brace yourself, Jewel. This is going to hurt," Austin says, linking his fingers with mine to pull my arm up to his mouth.

Diego hugs me from behind and positions his lips at my neck. "But don't worry. We're here. We'll make sure you're okay."

"We promise you won't be like Brayla," Kingston says, tugging my other arm up to his lips. "I swear."

I nod. "I trust you. Do it."

The board doesn't have a chance to react as all three of my guys bite me and release their venom. Fire burns over my skin from their bite marks, sending tears welling into my eyes.

I muffle my cry against Austin's chest, and he lifts me off my feet. Shadows edge my vision, threatening to steal my consciousness.

Muffled voices grow louder, yelling over my heartbeat pounding in my ears. My body convulses, agony stealing my breath. But I'm not scared. I'll gladly face the pain if it means no one can force me away from my guys.

"I love you. All of you. Forever," I whisper, unable to keep my eyes open through the pain consuming me.

"Always," they say in unison.

"You're our girl," Diego says.

Austin brushes his lips to mine. "Us against the universe."

Kingston snuggles against me. "And we're going to kick its ass."

EPILOGUE

EXEMPTION

"JEWEL, CAN YOU HEAR ME?" Austin's voice whispers into my ear, attempting to tug me from the dark recesses of my mind.

I can't move. I can't talk. I can't even feel anything. Everything's numb.

"Why won't she wake up?" Kingston asks. "She should have transitioned by now. I'm pretty fucking sure she had started before we even bit her. Her eyes changed."

"What do the blood results say?" Diego asks.

Austin sighs. "There was only a slight change in her genetic markers, but she's still human. I'm afraid Mrs. Diggs was right about the vaccine. This proves it. She's resistant to vampire venom."

"Fuck." A gentle hand touches my cheek. "Please, babe. You have to transform. We can't lose you."

"What are we going to tell the board?" Diego asks. "We can't tell them she's permanently stuck in a transitional state. They'll know about her regenerative blood."

"We have to tell them it was a power play to keep her from Haven Springs and that we didn't release our venom," Austin says.

"No," Kingston says. "We can't. They'll force us to send her there."

"What else can we do?" Diego's voice deepens in desperation. "She won't pass as a vampire."

Kingston groans. "I'll hide her in my room, or we can run away."

"Like this?" Austin asks.

"Fuck. I don't know!" Kingston yells. A chime rings through the air, piercing my eardrums. "And it just got worse. The board asked to see us. They want an update."

A knock sounds on the door. "No change?" Mitchell asks from somewhere to the right.

Austin groans. "No, she's human."

"Then I'm sorry, sons. There's nothing I can do. I hope you can forgive me. Please say your goodbyes."

My breathing quickens at his words. Goodbyes? But where will I go? What's going on? Holy shit balls. Stupid body. I can't even ask.

"Beautiful." Hands shake my shoulders, but I still can't

move or respond. Cool fingers touch my eyes, and light burns my vision. Three blurry forms hover over me, sending my heart racing. "Did you hear her body react?" Diego asks.

"Jewel, I'm sorry," Kingston says. "Please, you have to fight. Be my badass."

I wish with everything in me that I could respond. That I could open my arms and ask them to smother me with their love and hugs.

Austin touches my cheek. "Listen to Kingston. He knows what he's talking about for once."

Diego's tall form closes in on me, blocking out the light. His gray eyes clear, turning into the only thing I see. "Listen to me, beautiful. Whatever happens, I want you to be brave. Trust that we haven't abandoned you."

"It's just—" Austin's soft voice hitches. "We don't know what to do."

"We'll come for you, okay?" Kingston says. "Promise."

"And I swear on my life I'll fix this. You're our forever," Austin says.

If only I had forever.

I slip back into darkness.

Shadows dance through the room, twisting and moving around me, drawing me closer. The long dining table stretches out forever with crystal goblets set in neat rows in front of dozens of seats. The world blurs, and I fall on my stomach.

The shadows crowd around me, flipping me onto my

back. Sharp nails rip at my dress and leave me exposed on the table. A figure materializes next to me, white fangs and silver eyes flashing. My body reacts, arching up toward the figure, going against the swirling thoughts flitting through my mind.

"My precious Jewel," a familiar voice says. Orlando bends over me and bites his fangs into his bottom lip, splashing his blood across my face. "So nice to have you home."

Three figures blur through the air, ripping Orlando away from me. I cry out, struggling to pull myself from the table, but the shadows restrain me. "Let me go!" I yell, fighting the best I can.

Blood rains down from the ceiling, coating over my body, making me slip and slide on the wood until the shadows finally release me. I land hard on my knees but don't stay on the ground long. Cool hands lift me from my feet, and familiar dark eyes capture mine.

Kingston flashes his fangs at me. "How could you, Jewel?"

Tears burn my eyes. "What are you talking about?"

"You should've told us," Austin says.

"Told you what?" My chest heaves at the disappointment in Austin's voice.

Diego materializes in front of me, growling. "That you belonged to him. You were our girl."

"I am your girl."

"You're not," Kingston says.

"We can't have forever with you," Austin says.

Diego shakes his head. "You broke our promise."

Another figure materializes beside them, and I tense at Mitchell sliding his arms around all of his sons' shoulders. "Don't be so upset, my sons. At least you can enjoy her now."

The sound of a scream startles me awake, and a warm hand slaps over my mouth, stifling the noise. I buck, swinging my arm out, trying to orient myself to what's going on. Someone else's body weight presses me into the bed, and I manage to free my hand and punch my attacker in the side of the head.

"Fuck. Grab her," a familiar masculine voice says. "Hurry up. We only have a couple of minutes until dawn."

Hands lock around my waist and yank me from my bed. "Calm the hell down, Jewel. Don't think we won't snatch your cousins."

My cousins? What the actual fuck?

I stop fighting as a guy slings me over his shoulder, dangling me upside down. I peer around the dark, strange room, trying to figure out where the hell I am. The last thing I remember were my guys talking to me.

The guy carries me toward a window where another figure waits. A dozen thoughts swirl through my mind as I replay everything I can remember over and over again in my head. The board freeing me of my contract and denying Orlando. My guys biting me and releasing their venom. How Diego told me to be brave...

Holy shit balls.

Recognition settles through me the second the guy shifts me in his arms, and I get a view of the endless identical houses that go on for as far as I can see. I've only been to Haven Springs once, but it's a trip I'd never forget. But how did I end up here now? And why?

"What's going on? Where are you taking me?" I ask, finding my good senses to fight again.

The man grunts and flips me off him. The world flies around me for a few seconds, and I land on my back in the softest grass I've ever felt.

"Stay with the cousins. Don't want them calling out if they realize Jewel's gone," the familiar masculine voice says.

A thump sounds next to me, and I shift and glance up. "Oh, hell no," I say, scrambling to get to my feet.

Hayden doesn't let me get far. Grabbing me by my hair, he yanks me off my feet and holds me against his chest. The fucker is ridiculously strong, gripping me tightly and walking unfazed as I buck to break free.

"Relax, Jewel," he says. "You'll realize you're fighting for nothing soon enough."

"What am I doing here?" I ask. "Where are we going?"
"You'll see."

Hayden carries me to the line of trees on the outskirts of the unfamiliar property. I flail once again and finally manage to knock him off balance. We both fall to the ground, and I roll away from him and scoop my hands into the rough, woody dirt and chuck a handful at his eyes.

He yells out, and I hop up and run away from him, wishing that I wasn't in a T-shirt and socks. I have nothing but my sheer will to survive to get me out of this.

"Jewel, get back here!" Hayden yells.

I push myself to move faster. "Fuck you!"

My heart pounds as I dash deeper into the grove of trees, scented with the zesty freshness of lemons. I have no idea where I am or where I'm going, but all I know is that I can't stop. I need to get to the wall that surrounds the community. If I can climb over it, I can...I don't even know. It's still dark, and I don't have a car. I can't leave and risk coming across a vampire. Shit balls.

A figure darts through the trees in front of me, and I stumble. Cool hands lace around my waist, lifting me off my feet. I scream out and try to fight, but my back hits the hard trunk of a tree. I tense, meeting Orlando's vivid blue eyes.

"Just leave me alone," I say, swinging my hand out to smack him.

He catches my wrist and brings my hand to his mouth to kiss the back. "Lovely to see you too, my precious Jewel."

"I'm not yours," I say, wriggling in his hold. "Let me down."

"Always the fighter," he whispers, adjusting his grip on me. "I've always loved that about you."

"Fuck off."

He chuckles. "Come on. Don't be so difficult. Just look at me. One peek."

Thrashing again, I struggle in his hold. "No!"

I hear the familiar click of his fangs extending, sending panic through me. Orlando brushes my stray hair from my face, just holding me up against the tree. All I can do is keep my eyes squeezed closed and continue to fight until he either kills me, kidnaps me, or disappears with the sun.

Something wet drips across my lips, and I freeze as a drop dribbles onto my chin. My nostrils flare at the crazy good scent, like sugar and something spicier. Hunger burns through my stomach, threatening to send me curling in on myself.

"Just open your eyes," Orlando whispers.

I relent and do as he says. I can't help it. Something's wrong with me.

Blood drips on his arm in red streams, splashing onto the front of my shirt. He doesn't give me a chance to freak the hell out or argue. Instead, he presses his arm to my lips, coating my mouth with his blood.

Leaning in close, he looks me deep in the eyes and whispers, "Precious Jewel, remember me."

To be continued...

To stay up-to-date on new and future releases, including *Blood Feud, The Divine Vampire Heirs,* Book 4, sign up for Ginna Moran's newsletter, join her Facebook Group called Paranormal Center for Matches and Mates, or follow her on Amazon and BookBub.

OTHER SERIES BY GINNA MORAN

REVERSE HAREM

The Divine Vampire Heirs Series
The Royale Vampire Heirs Series
Academy of Vampire Heirs Series
The Pack Mates of Lunar Crest Series

YA PARANORMAL

Call of the Ocean Series
Demon Watcher Series
Demon Within Series
Destined for Dreams Series
Finding Nate Series
Going Ghostly Series
Spark of Life Series
The Merman's Spark Series
When Souls Collide Series

YA CONTEMPORARY

Falling into Fame Series
Life After Lila

ACKNOWLEDGMENTS

THIS BOOK WOULDN'T BE WHAT it is without the incredible support and help from my team. Katie and Sarah, as always, you two are invaluable, and I'm so happy to have you on board through my writing and publishing journey.

Thank you to the ladies of Write Bitches—Yvonne, Jade, Em, Heather, Frances—I'm so grateful for your encouragement, knowledge, and support. It means the world to me.

And lastly, thanks to the readers who have shown great enthusiasm for Jewel and the Divine brothers. You're the bomb! It makes it so much more fun having you around. ♥

GINNA MORAN IS a writer from sunny Southern California. She started writing poetry as a teenager in a spiral notebook that she still has tucked away on her desk today. Her love of writing grew after she graduated high school, and she completed her first unpublished manuscript at age eighteen.

When she realized her love of writing was her life's passion, she studied literature at Mira Costa College in Northern San Diego. Besides writing novels, she was senior editor, content manager, and image coordinator for Crescent House Publishing Inc. for four years.

Aside from Ginna's professional life, she enjoys binge watching television shows, playing pretend with her daughter, and cuddling with her dogs. Some of her favorite things include chocolate, anything that glitters, cheesy jokes, and organizing her bookshelf.

Ginna Moran loves to hear from her readers so visit her online at www.GinnaMoran.com. You can also find her on Facebook, Twitter, Instagram, and Snapchat. To stay up-to-date on new releases, sign up to her newsletter. You'll not only get exclusive access to extra stories, but you'll be able to participate in monthly giveaways!